Praise for Veronica Chadwick's
Rude Awakening

"With realistic emotions and sensuous love scenes, this long awaited novel definitely is a winner. Veronica Chadwick's RUDE AWAKENING is intense, powerful and mesmerizes the reader into craving more from this talented author. Don't miss this satisfying and amazing read – I highly recommend RUDE AWAKENING. It will leave you breathless!"

   ~ *Romance Junkies*

"Rude Awakening is a must buy. I loved how Ms. Chadwick hooks her readers with vivid characters and keeps them with action and scorching love scenes. I cannot wait to see what she will come up with next."

   ~ *Fallen Angels Reviews*

"Rude Awakening is a long awaited novel from Veronica Chadwick. I wasn't disappointed in fact I found this book scintillating, provocative and exciting. Well-balanced and three-dimensional characterization adds to an exciting plot with some very interesting twists. ...Veronica may not have had a book out for several years but she's more than made up for it with this one."

   ~ *The Romance Studio*

Rude Awakening

Veronica Chadwick

A SAMHAIN PUBLISHING, LTD. publication.

Samhain Publishing, Ltd.
577 Mulberry Street, Suite 1520
Macon, GA 31201
www.samhainpublishing.com

Rude Awakening
Copyright © 2010 by Veronica Chadwick
Print ISBN: 978-1-60504-605-1
Digital ISBN: 978-1-60504-595-5

Editing by Tera Kleinfelter
Cover by Natalie Winters

First Samhain Publishing, Ltd. electronic publication: June 2009
First Samhain Publishing, Ltd. print publication: April 2010

Dedication

To all of you who never gave up on me,
To all the lovely ladies of the forum,
And to Nat, Jen, Janine and Annmarie: *the* best Posse in the world,
I dedicate this book.
All my love.

Acknowledgements

Many thanks to:
Capt. Steven Floyd of the SPD (retired after 30 years of service)
for his wonderful suggestions and willingness to read and re-read.
To Monica Floyd for her invaluable input and for being the go between.
And to
Marcia Sanderson LPN, for her expert advice and humor.

Chapter One

Sweat trickled between Jaimee's shoulder blades to pool at the small of her back. Wisps of damp hair had escaped her haphazard ponytail to cling to her neck and face. Her triceps burned, her calves and thighs burned, but it was a good burn. Careful to breathe out with each squat she glanced over at the tan Herculean stud who stood at the Nautilus machine, doing pull downs.

Normally, she could leave school, be at the gym by three thirty and be finished no later than five, thereby avoiding the health club when most of the guys showed up after work. The parent/teacher orientation ran late tonight, which meant she had to deal with the oppressive fog of testosterone or miss working out, and she hated to miss her workout.

She lifted the weight and tried to focus on her biceps. Constantly bracing for the occasional sneer from an egotistical jock or disparaging snicker from a passing supermodel wanna-be made for an uncomfortable workout at times. Her plump five-foot-five frame was conspicuous when surrounded by sweaty, muscle-bound guys and tall willowy females.

Usually they were friendly, mostly courteous, always eager to give her advice on diet. Low carbs, low fat, eat only the foods compatible with her blood type, go organic only, don't eat at all. *Ugh!* And she really hated the people who told her not to use weights. Those who insisted she focus on aerobic exercise and would be better off just walking the track until she slimmed down some. But she didn't like walking the track. She liked working with weights. And what was it to 'em anyway?

The stud working on his upper body was watching her. A slow smile curved his well-shaped lips when he caught her looking. Gorgeous. Her heart skipped several beats before she reminded herself that he probably thought she looked ridiculous. She wasn't ugly, and even though she was still full-figured, she didn't consider herself obese anymore. More the scholarly type, she never thought of herself as attractive, especially not sexually so. Still, as if she were a train wreck, he just couldn't seem to help but gawk.

Anxiety had her chest tightening and she fought the urge to cut and run. In a flash her curious interest turned to irritation. And still he stared, meeting her gaze. She gripped the five-pound weights tighter, imagining they were his neck. She leveled her best *don't mess with me* glare and refused to look away in hopes that he would just go on with whatever it was he was here to do and quit staring at her. Instead of respectfully turning away and minding his own business, he arched a dark brow and tilted his head. Evidently she was an oddity he needed to study, which only served to piss her off all the more, in spite of the rush of arousal whipping through her body.

His face was all hard planes and angles, with high cheekbones and a slightly over-large, regal nose. His long black hair was pulled back into a sleek ponytail. Muscles rippled with each rep as sweat ran in rivulets down his smooth chest. A gold ring glinted in each nipple. Now see, one should never trust a man without chest hair, and since when did she find nipple rings so appealing? What was he, seven feet tall? Why was he looking at her that way?

Dark eyes traveled her body like she was a tasty treat. That thought made her tingly all over and, at the same time, want to laugh out loud at the absurdity of it all. In spite of the fact that he was big, sexy, intensely sensual, absolutely beautiful and so not the picture of a typical male, he was looking at her with unguarded, unmistakable lust. Her mind filled with erotic images of that amazing body rising over her, pressing hard against hers, his mouth, his hands on her. She looked away to try and shake the flare of raw desire becoming more and more intense.

In all fairness, she was noticeable, just not in a good way. She didn't look at all like most of the female members with their sporty, tummy-baring, spandex sport tops and short shorts with the waistbands rolled down until they barely covered their asses. Then there were some who did bare them in leotards that were just short of being thongs. What was the point of those anyway? These were the kind of women who had no cellulite and looked naturally beautiful and ethereal without makeup.

Jaimee had bought a leotard, however it completely covered her wide ass. The idea of a constant wedgie while she worked out was less than appealing. Anyone who wore those things couldn't be at the gym to seriously benefit from a workout anyway. The plain, deep purple leotard she'd chosen wasn't unattractive. Not that she had the nerve to wear it alone, but having it on under baggy gray sweats helped remind her to hold her belly in. She'd even rolled down the waistband of her baggy sweats since she'd lost a few inches; but no way was she going to be seen in just the leotard.

She probably did look pretty ridiculous clumsily going through her workout with her stringy wet wisps of hair clinging to her red face and covered head to toe in fleece wear. It didn't matter what she looked like. Her reasoning for coming to the health club had nothing to do with anyone else. The time she spent here helped her work out more than just her body and she was feeling better physically and emotionally. Brent had always been a safe haven for her, a quiet undemanding love that she could hide away in and not have to face the world or herself for that matter.

Now it didn't seem such a healthy thing, but Brent had been her best friend, her anchor. When he died she thought she'd lost her whole world, such as it was. The truth was, she would still be lying around feeling sorry for herself if her friend Maxine hadn't been so freakin' pushy. A membership to the posh, upscale, spa-style health club had been Max's idea. Of course, Jaimee had resisted, but Max nagged and nagged until she finally gave in. Making herself go hadn't been hard, considering the big chunk it took from her budget. And as usual, Max had been right, it turned out to be just what she needed.

Eight months since the accident and she still missed Brent. Every single day she missed him. Theirs hadn't been the perfect relationship but she had loved and needed him, maybe too much—no, definitely too much. Working out at the gym gave her something to do besides sit and think of all that was wrong in her life, all she had lost, all she had let slip by. It helped her begin to let go and she was stronger all the way around even if Mr. Muscle and his obvious amusement at her expense was just a tad hurtful. Shame wasn't far behind, reminding her of her naughty little fantasy earlier.

But she couldn't escape the fact that there was lust in his eyes. No doubt about it. Just because she hadn't seen it in a few years didn't mean she didn't know what it looked like. What about that? The reminder only triggered more images. Naked, hot, sweaty images of sex with an incredibly sexy stranger had her body heating, tingling with sensations. She nearly whimpered in response. Her mother was right; she was just like her dad. Cursed with an overactive libido from puberty on. How ironic was it that the only man she ever loved was never all that interested in sex.

You're just making it harder on yourself, Jaimee, she silently admonished herself.

She refused to buy in to the self-pity and instead fought to turn her attention to her workout. She replaced the weights, picked up her water bottle and moved to the leg machine. Even though it was dry, she wiped down the bench, just to be sure. The last thing she needed was the flu or a cold or some other nasty disease. She lay down on her stomach, changed the weight from sixty pounds to twenty, hooked her heels on the padded bars, gripped the handles and turned her face to the side.

She drew her heels toward her backside and began the first set of ten reps. The pull, the burn, let her know she was being productive. At the same time she struggled to ignore an altogether different sort of pull. She closed her eyes, clenched her teeth against the disturbing sensation and concentrated on her breathing. When she opened her eyes she found herself looking at two very muscular, powerful legs and she forgot to breathe.

Her thought processes went from surprise to embarrassment to annoyance when her natural assumption was that his presence meant exactly the same as the other muscle-bound male patrons of the gym. Personal trainers in training that saw her as their next project. Dammit. That was it. She'd had it. Anger, bitter and cold, drove away the heat of her lust. Good, she needed to use her common sense, for God's sake. She'd be damned if she'd lay there and let him humiliate her like the others had. Hell no, he had no right. None. She dropped the weight with a crash and rolled up to sitting position then stood as tall as she could.

"Okay, go ahead and get it out of your system so I can go back to my workout." She tried for cool anger as she scowled up at him, hoping he didn't notice the thread of pain in her voice. Damn, he was pretty. In spite of her fury and mortification, her fingers itched to reach out and touch him.

"Whoa! Calm down." His voice was so deep and dark. It rumbled through her and gave her goose bumps.

"Calm down?" Her eyes narrowed.

He frowned back at her. "Look, your technique is excellent. I just came over here to ask who was training you and..."

The indignity made her grit her teeth in frustration. "No, you look. I don't have a trainer. I don't want a trainer. I just want to work out without some moosehead coming over to tell the fat girl what she's doing wrong."

There went that slow smile again. He arched a brow, folded his big sinewy arms over his bare chest and silently stared down at her—with condescension, no doubt.

"What is it with you guys anyway? You big muscle-bound oafs think you're all God's gift to women." She couldn't seem to stop herself as she pointed up at him now, barely resisting the urge to poke him in his well-defined, rock-hard, pierced-nippled chest. "You think every woman, especially us full-figured ladies, are just praying you'll come give us a pathetic second of your precious time to instruct us on how we can be more appealing to you. Well let me tell you something, mister. I didn't ask for your attention, nor do I want it. You don't buy my club membership, my meals, or anything else for that matter, so I don't see how my workout choices or the size of my ass are any of your damn business."

He just stood there with that arrogant smile on his face, watching her, as if she were an amusing puppy.

"Why are you just standing there smiling at me like that? Why don't you scurry back to your rat hole and leave me alone?"

"I'm smiling because I find it humorous that you're all hot and bothered over your preconceived notions that I think a certain way about you based on your outward appearance. When all the while you've judged and sentenced me on the basis of my own."

She stared at him for a moment and bit her lip. She *had* gotten carried away and it irritated her that he was right, and worse, he knew she knew he was right. She could see it in his rich brown gaze that was once again traveling over her body. Much to her surprise he reached out and gripped the bottom of her baggy sweatshirt and yanked it over her head in one smooth move. There she stood, with her mouth hanging open, in her sweaty purple leotard that clung to her body. Her full breasts were flattened to her chest and spilling over the low neckline, her hard nipples obvious against the damp cotton/spandex material, baggy sweatpants rolled down over her wide hips, revealing her pooch stomach and her round hips. Heat crawled up her neck and she balled her hands into fists, then quickly crossed her arms over her breasts.

"Much better." His murmur was almost a moan. His smile spread into a toothy grin then he winked at her, turned and walked away with her shirt and disappeared into the men's locker room.

Nearly everyone had paused or stopped what they were doing to watch. The two Barbie-like blondes on the stepping machines whispered to each other and giggled. Her first instinct was to hightail it out of there but she refused to give in to it. There was no way in hell she was going to let that man, the Barbies or anyone else screw with her newfound confidence or her workout. With steely determination she took a deep breath, lifted her chin and went back to working on her upper thighs.

An hour later she was pulling on her jeans and baggy blue Tigger T-shirt. She blow-dried her hair and pulled the unruly mass up into a banana clip. Guilt pricked her at the way she let the stud have it. He had certainly put her in her place, which for some reason she found thrilling. That wasn't setting well with her either, and she just wanted to forget about it.

The whole weekend stretched out ahead of her and she had a lot to get accomplished before it was over. Lesson plans, however, would wait until Sunday night. Tonight she wanted to get home, have dinner and crawl into bed with a good book. Which in a way was sad, considering it was only five something on a Friday night. Times like this were when she really missed Brent, even though were he still alive they would probably just watch a movie on TV. She missed the companionship, the comfort of having someone else in the house. Tennis shoes tied, sweaty workout clothes stuffed in the duffle, she headed out of the locker room with a heavy sigh.

The beat of the workout music thumped through the building and the gym was crowded. Thankfully, she was on her way out. Lana, the bouncy aerobics instructor smiled and waved as she walked by the wide window and Jaimee waved back. Her smile was still in place as she pushed open the glass door and walked out into the warm night.

"Nice smile." There he was, the stud, propped up against a column, exuding virility like he was posing for a centerfold. He'd changed into light blue jeans that hugged his narrow hips and clung to the healthy bulge behind the fly as if he were poured into them. The jewel tone blue shirt worked beautifully with his bronze skin, especially with the sleeves rolled up and the two top buttons left open to reveal his throat. He was hot, and that voice of his had a way of reaching out and touching her in all her private areas.

"Where's my shirt?" she asked quietly, not quite achieving the coolness she was going for as her smile faded from her lips.

"I tossed it in the trash." He pushed away from the column and stepped toward her.

"Unbelievable. You owe me a shirt." She stared at him in disbelief. "You had no right to do that." She turned to walk away, then paused and spun around to face him again. "Why did you do that?" Her voice was a bit higher than she had intended it to be but she'd never been so angry.

His brows arched and he leveled her with his piercing gaze. "You were hiding."

For a moment she just stared at him with her mouth open, incredulous at the man's audacity. She couldn't believe her ears. The unmitigated gall!

He took a cautious step toward her. "The sweatshirt was unnecessary. Your face was beet red, you were too hot." His lips curved slightly as he placed one long finger against her chin, closed her mouth, then let it fall away. "And, you were hiding," he repeated softly.

Oh man, that one insignificant touch left her quivering inside. More would probably kill her. What a way to die. Argh! What was she thinking? *Focus, Jaimee,* she admonished herself.

"So what if I was, and that's a big 'what if', it's none of your business. I don't know you." In order to gather some degree of calm, she took another deep breath. "What did you get out of embarrassing me?"

He stilled, frowning, his brows pulled together over dark eyes. "Embarrassing you wasn't my intention. I..."

"What if I wasn't wearing anything under it?"

For a moment he looked as though he was questioning himself and his actions. "You were wearing something under it."

"But what if I wasn't?"

"You were."

With a disgusted sigh she shook her head and spun away from him, eager to get to her car.

"Wait." One very tan, very large hand reached out and snagged her wrist, forcing her to halt in her retreat. His fingers circling her wrist were warm and strong, but gentle, as he turned her to face him. His touch was charged with sexual energy. Her entire body reacted and she struggled not to step closer. Instead, she stiffened and focused on his arrogance. "I'm sorry I embarrassed you." He let her go before she could jerk away.

She raised her eyes to meet his gaze but kept her scowl firmly in place.

"I'll replace the shirt." He looked sincere as he offered his hand. "Let me start over. I'm Lucas."

After a long pause, she took it. He had such sexy hands; very warm, long strong fingers. Images of what wondrous delights those hands could be capable of producing flashed through her mind—and

13

body—again.

She cleared her throat. "Jaimee."

He held her hand firmly as she tried to pull away. His palm was warm against hers and his fingers just calloused enough to elicit more imaginative ideas. Her gaze traveled down, pausing to watch the intriguing way his throat worked as he swallowed before gaping at the span of skin exposed by the V of his open collar. The flush to her cheeks was rapid and mortifyingly obvious.

Jaimee licked her lips as she looked up at him. The mischievous smile that curved his mouth and the sparkle in his dark eyes told her just how obvious she'd been.

"Actually I believe I've seen you before, up the street from me. I just moved here from California. I bought a house in Wood Crest, 512 Meridian." He reluctantly freed her hand. Damn, his voice was so deep, and it seemed rougher than before.

He was right; hers was only a few houses up from him, in 507. How did she miss seeing him? Did he take a step closer? He certainly seemed closer. "Oh, well, welcome to the neighborhood."

"Have you had dinner?" he asked slowly, watching her mouth. Had she licked her lips again?

Okay what was he up to? Men like him didn't ask out women like her. It simply wasn't done. "Why?"

Without question, those gorgeous eyes of his darkened even more. One brow lifted and his smile turned just a tad wolfish. "Well, I'm hungry, and from the looks of it, you are too."

"Excuse me?" She narrowed her eyes in disapproval. He chuckled and his eyes took on a predatory gleam that sent hot shivers dancing up and down her body. It was hard not to wiggle and shake them off.

"Have dinner with me."

"No, I don't think so."

If he expected her to just go all fluttery because he showed her attention he was sorely mistaken. Okay, so she was all fluttery, and overheated and dammit...wet and tingly. But she wasn't going to give him the satisfaction.

"Are you married or dating someone? I didn't see a ring but I guess that doesn't necessarily mean anything anymore. I should have asked earlier."

"Widowed," she interrupted.

"I'm sorry."

"It's okay." And it was. Maybe it shouldn't be, but it was.

He tilted his head and watched her. "But you won't have dinner with me?"

"No."

"May I ask why not?"

She met his gaze and wondered at the flames that seemed to flicker in his eyes. Intrigued? Maybe. Tempted? Definitely. Still, she didn't know him or trust him and didn't understand at all why he seemed to be attracted to her. It only added to her frustration that her traitorous body was vibrating with lust from merely looking at him and briefly holding his hand.

"No, you may not," she answered with as much cool indifference as she could muster. She quickly whirled around and walked away before she gave in to her ridiculous little fantasies and hurled herself at him. Though it was very, very difficult, she didn't look back, and oh did she want to. She could practically feel his gaze on her butt. Oh God. Was he looking at her butt? She cringed at the slick, sensual rub of the swollen flesh nestled between her thighs, sensations spiraling through her with each purposeful step away from him.

No, she couldn't have dinner with him, and she couldn't tell him the reason why was that she didn't trust herself. As she reached her car she gave in and glanced back at him. He hadn't moved. He was still standing there, smiling as he watched her walk away. Despite her resolve to remain coolly detached, she returned his smile. Before she could change her mind she got into the car and headed home, wondering if she would see him again.

Chapter Two

Lucas pushed the windows open but left the lights off. He had taken off his shirt and the evening breeze was cool against his overheated skin. Before he sat down to the rubbery, tasteless meal he had just pulled out of the microwave, he put on his headphones and adjusted the settings on the equipment. It was sweet torture listening to the soft sounds of Jaimee moving through her room preparing for bed.

It wasn't that late but he didn't expect her to get any calls. Her house had been bugged for several weeks and he'd been scanning them. In that time she hadn't had all that many and most of those were from her mother. A couple had been from a woman by the name of Maxine Pruitt, whom he gathered was a very close friend.

Evidently, Ms. Maxine was a hellcat, and from the conversations he'd heard thus far she was more than adventurous, especially sexually. There was something about the way Jaimee's voice got breathy with incredulity that caused Lucas to arch a brow. That throaty laugh and those longing sighs had elevated his heart rate, pumping all his blood southward to elevate other valued organs. More than once he imagined what it would be like to initiate Jaimee's lush body to the pleasures Maxine had detailed for her...and even more.

Lucas hadn't originally been pleased with this new assignment. This kind of mundane undercover and surveillance work required someone who liked to sit around and wait for something to happen. Lucas preferred to be in the middle of the action as much as possible. Which was why he chose to take on the more risky assignments. Two months ago he had been briefed and handed Jaimee's file. From the moment he'd seen her photo he knew he wouldn't have to pretend to be attracted. The laid-back, easy assignment of watching out for a pretty little innocent schoolteacher would be refreshing after the last few he'd dealt with. If for no other reason than the slower pace and the enticing scenery, he'd accepted the assignment immediately.

He shoveled a forkful of bland fettuccini alfredo into his mouth and chewed unenthusiastically as he flipped open the file and looked over the photos of Jaimee once again. She looked like innocence personified. Wide baby blue eyes stared back at him from a lovely heart-shaped face completely unaware of the photographer. Her full pink lips were slightly parted and she had the most adorable little freckled nose. Her thick sable hair was shot with gold and hung in wild, loose waves just past her shoulders.

At the health club it had taken Herculean self-control to keep from groping her. Remembering the way her sumptuous ass flexed as she worked out had his body reacting on its own...again. He'd been right; underneath all that fleece she was magnificently crafted. All soft, lush curves. He couldn't help but think about the way she moved around the house singing along with Joan Jett. She had a nice voice, great tone quality. He was growing fond of just listening to her talk. But damn he wished they had installed surveillance cameras too.

Behind that sweet exterior hid a wild cat that didn't know how to break free. Recalling the conversation they'd had only hours ago and the way Jaimee's eyes had blazed like blue flame brought a smile to his lips. She was by no means the fragile flower she appeared to be. But underneath all that bravado he saw the raw pain she harbored, and though it wasn't at all a rational notion, he wanted more than anything to change that, to replace that deep-seated sadness with pleasure, passion...

Lucas shifted uncomfortably and forced his train of thought onto a more rational track. Mrs. Jaimee Turner was the widow of Brent Matthew Turner. Brent had ties with one cell of an organized crime ring called The Collective. The FBI had been working on busting them for two years. Evidently Mr. Turner either underestimated the men he worked for or he overestimated his own abilities. Either way, embezzling funds from a bunch of modern-day gangsters was stupid. There was a Swiss bank account worth several million in his wife's name, though they had soon discovered Jaimee knew nothing about the account, her husband's connections or his murder.

She believed, like many, that he'd been driving along the mountainous and curvy back roads of eastern Kentucky when a heart attack sent him careening off the road into a ravine. His vehicle had exploded on impact, leaving very little for investigators to work with. Lucas shook his head as he dropped the empty microwave tray in the trash. It had to be hard to lose someone you loved the way Jaimee had lost her husband. No wonder she was so sad.

In the very beginning Mrs. Turner was a suspect, though she was quickly cleared. It became evident that leaving her in the dark could help them garner valuable evidence against the criminals her hubby worked with. Ronald Marshall, of the higher echelon, had dropped by once or twice but Jaimee hadn't been home. His wife, Sandy, had called her recently to invite her to yet another dinner party. Mrs. Marshall didn't sound all that disheartened when Jaimee had politely declined, again. They wanted their money back and eventually they would go to extreme lengths to get it. So for now, Jaimee's not knowing would allow him to keep her safe. Hopefully it wouldn't be much longer before they had most of the key players in custody.

The FBI wanted the same information The Collective wanted, therefore it was time to acclimate himself to Jaimee, get past her defenses. Though he had hoped she would take him up on his offer tonight, he hadn't really expected her to after her indignant tirade. Her pale blue eyes turning icy with anger was intriguing. How would they look filled with fiery passion? Would they darken, dilate with desire or glaze over with calculating and frigid ice? Frigid...ha! Cold and calculating maybe, but no way was she frigid. He shifted in the chair, adjusting his erection.

The sound of the shower being turned on triggered his imagination. Lucas closed his eyes and envisioned her curvy body stepping out of her sweatpants and peeling off the bright body suit, her nipples tightening, her full breasts swaying gently as she raised her arms to let her hair down. Her nipples were round and plump, like berries, when they hardened. Earlier in the gym he'd wanted to free the ripe globes and take a nipple between his teeth, lave it with his tongue.

He could imagine her now, water cascading over those juicy nipples, hips, thighs. Her hands moving over her soapy body, her breasts, her stomach, her mound...were there soft golden brown curls there or did she shave—or wax maybe. His hands tingled as he imagined touching her, his fingers sliding through the slick swollen folds of her pussy. Shit. This assignment was proving to be quite enjoyable and could only get better...as long as he didn't let things get out of hand.

The phone ringing, followed by Jaimee's soft curse interrupted Lucas's fantasy and he pulled his headphones off as he grabbed the set that allowed him to scan her phone conversations. "Fuck!" With all the technology and high tech shit the government had, couldn't they eliminate this fucking headphone shit? He adjusted the headphones, sat forward and listened in as Jaimee picked up the receiver.

"Hello," she said breathlessly. Damn she had a sexy voice. Lucas scowled at the way his body, his already engorged cock, reacted to that sound.

"Jaimee?" the masculine voice asked. "How ya doin' babe?"

"I'm sorry, who is this?"

"It's Ron, I called a couple of weeks ago but you didn't return my call." His voice took on a slight edge.

"Oh, hello. I'm sorry, you didn't leave your number." Jaimee sounded a bit confused and more than a little uncomfortable.

"Come on, Jaimee, you have my number. I know Brent had it. In that black leather day planner thing he carried around."

"Day planner?" Jaimee asked. Day planner? Hmmm.

"Yeah, you know, Brent kept all his appointments in there. Phone numbers and stuff like that."

"I don't remember any day planner. I didn't see one among the things they brought me from his office." She paused. Lucas heard her shift, switching ears he imagined. "Maybe they overlooked it and they still have it at his office. I'll call Alice and ask her. If anyone would know about it she would." She paused again. "Anyway, what can I do for you, Ron?"

"Huh? Oh, Sandy told me you couldn't make it to the party. I was hoping I could change your mind." His voice lowered and Lucas's eyes narrowed.

"No, thank you, Ron. Please tell Sandy thanks again for thinking of me, but no." Lucas could hear the tension in her voice.

"You know, it wouldn't hurt you to get out, Jaimee, circulate again. I'll take you to dinner, get you out of the house for a while."

"I don't think that's a good idea."

"I could invite a friend of mine along. He's Italian, he likes his women fleshy."

"Fucking asshole," Lucas grumbled as he shook his head.

Sighing impatiently she waited before she answered tightly. "I'm not interested."

"Aw come on, Jaimee, it's been several months since Brent died."

"Eight months. Don't be crass, Ron..."

"Look," he cut her off. "You have to be horny as hell by now. Unless you really are frigid?"

"What the hell is that supposed to mean? Never mind. I don't care. Goodbye, Ronald," Jaimee said harshly and slammed down the receiver.

Lucas winced at the sharp sound and scowled as he pulled off the headphones and put on the others as he adjusted the volume on the bugs. Silence. After a few minutes he checked the connection. The sound of Jaimee opening a drawer then closing it again had him sighing with relief—until he heard the whisper of the towel falling from her body.

Jaimee was still steaming as she grabbed the bottle of lotion and walked back into the bedroom. She sat the bottle on the nightstand, snatched her panties off her bed and pulled them on.

She smoothed lotion over her legs as she remembered the day she went to his office to pick up his things. His secretary, Alice Sinclair, had been shocked and brokenhearted at Brent's death and had retired. She'd been more like a mother to him than his secretary. Keeping him organized and on track had been her job, and he'd even joked about how if she ever got fed up and quit on him he'd be lost. It was weird; Jaimee couldn't imagine him with a day planner. But that didn't mean he didn't have one.

Jaimee finished rubbing the lotion into her arms and hands then glanced at the clock. It was only eight forty. If there had been a black day planner Alice would know about it. She pulled on her nightshirt then quickly found Alice's phone number in her address book.

After five rings the answering machine picked up. "I am unable to accept your call at this time. Please leave a message. Thank you."

"Alice, this is Jaimee. When you have a moment please give me a call. The number is the same. Thanks." She returned the phone to the cradle. Monday she would call the office and see if perhaps they had overlooked it.

With a sigh, she climbed into bed and after getting comfortable she picked up her book. Intriguing as it was, her mind just couldn't focus on the Scottish laird and his attempt to seduce the Sassenach wench who had traveled into his world from another time. Too much was occupying her thoughts. Ron's annoying call had her curiosity up.

What was Ron up to anyway, the jerk? She'd been to a couple of parties Brent's friends had thrown. Most of the wives or girlfriends were always standoffish and the men just smirked at her, whispered comments to Brent and elbowed him in the ribs. He wouldn't even look at her when they did that. She spent most of her time sitting by herself, watching everyone have a good time while she politely sipped the diet Coke they made a point of supplying just for her. But Brent enjoyed the parties so she went. Why had she done that? Why had he insisted she go, knowing how uncomfortable she was?

Jaimee suspected things weren't as they seemed with that group. More than once Brent had accused her of being paranoid. "Just because I'm paranoid, doesn't mean they're not after me," she'd say half in jest, half seriously. Brent merely smiled, gave her a quick kiss, declared his exhaustion and went to bed.

The book just couldn't hold her attention. She gave up and laid it aside. She stared at the ceiling in lonely silence, trying to ignore the ache in her heart. Not once had she doubted his love for her, and she wasn't going to start doubting him now that he was gone. The memory of Brent's tender lovemaking, his slow and gentle touch had her closing her eyes against the pain.

Sex had never been the best part of their marriage. It was never something Brent needed a lot of, mainly because he occasionally had erectile issues. When that happened it left them both frustrated. Even when everything went well she was often left aching for something. Something she couldn't name, something more. Those memories never failed to leave her feeling ashamed and selfish. *There's more to marriage than sex and no man is perfect,* she had told herself so many times. It was so wrong of her to even entertain such thoughts. Brent was her best friend and he loved her above all else. Didn't he?

Her thoughts went to "the stud" from the gym. Lucas. Her body flushed with heat and her nipples tightened. Against her better judgment she briefly entertained the fantasy of him—his body heavy on hers, his sensual lips pressed firmly to her own, his wide palms massaging her breasts, his long fingers trailing down her body, touching, probing...

With a groan she turned onto her side and hugged a pillow tightly against her breasts, trying desperately to push the erotic scene from her mind. What would have happened had she gone to dinner with him? And why had he asked her in the first place? Almost on cue, her stomach rumbled, reminding her that she never did get around to eating dinner. And yes, she was hungry for much more than food could satiate. It was a wrenching hunger, a clawing beast, gripping her soul, demanding gratification.

The longer she acknowledged her need the more painful it would become and the harder it would be to accept reality. She knew that all too well. Fantasy only led to disappointment, and self-pity was counterproductive. With a sigh of resignation, Jaimee closed her eyes and willed her body to go numb and relax as she slowly drifted off to sleep.

Chapter Three

Uneventful and tranquil were not words that would describe a day spent with a bunch of hormone-laden, puberty-driven eighth graders. Jaimee took her time walking to the mailbox to retrieve the mail. Several of her students were going to make this year tough, to say the least. Of course she'd do the obligatory calls home but there was a pretty good chance the parents would just placate her and do nothing to encourage their trouble-making children to improve their behavior.

Then there were the reoccurring dreams keeping her nights restless and frustrating. Disturbing erotic dreams of Lucas deep inside her, taking her, making her scream and driving her mad with pleasure. They'd all been so real and when she woke up, her body on the edge of orgasm, in order to go back to sleep she'd touched herself, moaning into her pillow as the unsatisfactory climax washed over her. Even so, when sleep returned so would the dreams.

Tired and frustrated, Jaimee had just opened the mailbox when a black SUV pulled up right behind her. She knew who it was before the tinted window slid down.

"Hi, Jaimee." His sexy voice seemed to flow over her. It was as if she had psychically beckoned him somehow. She couldn't stop the groan that came from deep inside her.

How in the hell did he get so close so fast without running over her? His spicy scent mingled with leather interior teased her. Jaimee could definitely appreciate a nice car, especially with rich leather interior. The fact that this one had an extremely hot guy behind the wheel with wonderful lips that had done amazing, unspeakable things to her in her dreams only made it worse. Those sexy lips curved into a knowing smile and made her weak in the knees. Damn. Jaimee squared her shoulders and met the onslaught of erotic heat she found in his eyes with defiance.

"Hi, Lucas."

He smiled. "This is for you."

She looked at the blue gift bag then met his gaze. "For what?"

"I owe you a new shirt, remember?"

Oh yeah, she'd forgotten. She shrugged, feeling oddly self-conscious. "I didn't actually expect..."

His smile faltered. "You should have, I told you I'd replace the one I threw in the trash. Go on, take it."

"Fine." She sighed and took the bag from him. "Thank you."

"My pleasure. I'm looking forward to seeing you in it." He watched her so closely it made her want to run away—or take a step closer.

In an attempt to change the subject, she tilted her head to the side and tried for cold indifference. "Nice wheels. I'm surprised it's not a Hummer, but it's nice."

His smile slowly spread into a toothy grin. "Yes, I have to agree. Hummers are very, very nice." His voice had dropped even lower, lids lowering slightly as he captured her gaze, eyes lit with mischief.

Jaimee blinked in confusion. Obviously he had something entirely different from big, overpriced automobiles on his mind. When understanding dawned that his thoughts obviously went straight to his groin she blushed furiously. She could feel her cheeks practically glowing. The idea of taking his cock into her mouth only increased her embarrassment. And worse, the image of his mouth on her, humming against her throbbing sex had need drumming a slow cadence through her. Her body instantly responded to him, just as it had Friday at the health club, just as it had every night this week. Clenching her teeth, she resisted the urge to squeeze her thighs together.

She wanted to grab his ears and kiss him madly while dragging him into her house to rape him. Instead, she crossed her arms over her aching breasts as she feigned ignorance, as if he couldn't see that she knew exactly what was on his mind.

"Oh no, huh uh. You can't call a Hummer nice. That's like calling a lion a cute little kitty. A Hummer is a badass vehicle. At least the military-issued vehicle is. It's big, rugged, tough, a force to be reckoned with. It's not nice." She sounded so snippy she almost grimaced. But she didn't, it was his fault anyway.

One brow lifted and without saying a word, the intent was clear in his eyes and she couldn't look away. "Big, tough and forceful appeal to you? More so than nice, I mean."

Oh yeah, big, hard, fast... As he watched her, desire bloomed brighter and hotter, sending her heart into overdrive, her blood searing through her until she found it hard to breathe. Finally, she cleared her throat, narrowed her eyes at him and took a step back, jerking a thumb toward the door. "I have to go," she mumbled and turned to go.

"Jaimee." It wasn't a plea, or a shout. It was a low rumble that held confidence, power and authority. Though it grated against her, she stopped in her tracks and turned slightly, giving him the meanest look she could. An arrogant smile slowly curved his lips, much to her distress. "You appeal to me."

Oh wow. More than the actual words it was the look in his eyes that made her heart leap. Damn if she didn't feel like a giddy teenager ready to melt at his feet. Instead, she stiffened her spine, refusing to give in to the butterflies.

"I hate that for you," she said with as much of a smirk as she could muster under the circumstances. Somehow she doubted her attempt at cool disinterest was convincing. His chuckle confirmed it for her.

She narrowed her eyes and spun around, walked across the lawn, desperate for escape. The sound of the SUV's smooth idle tempted her to turn around to see if he was watching her, but she refused to give in as she stepped into the house and slammed the door.

She took a detour through the kitchen to grab a bottle of water from the fridge to try and cool down. Unbelievable. She leaned back against the counter and gulped the cold water. Her heart was pounding, her body shaking as she fought to make sense of the all-consuming arousal flooding her system. Had she ever desired anyone this strongly before? Surely she had, she had to have, but not Brent. No, her relationship with Brent had been based on stronger stuff. That was reality, love, and far more meaningful than butterflies and heart palpitations. Lust had never been a part of what she and Brent had. For that reason, her marriage, her life with the man she loved, was more stable and rock solid than any sexually charged involvement based on nothing more than lust.

Which was why it irked her to no end that she could be so shallow that the first incredibly sexy man who showed any carnal interest reduced her to a quivering mass of wanton lust. Maybe it wasn't just that he was sex walking, she reasoned with herself. There was an immediate attraction that went beyond his body. In his eyes there was strength, wisdom, and she liked that he looked her in the eye. Even though it was annoying as hell, she had to admit she liked that he kept her on her toes and didn't back down when she got a bit snippy with him. It might be nice to spend time with him, get to know the man, have a conversation. If she weren't so afraid she'd end up begging him to fuck her brains out. She rolled her eyes; surely she wasn't that stupid or weak.

With a deep sigh she opened the gift bag and looked inside. She wasn't sure what she expected to find. Underneath all the tissue paper she found a very nice navy, light blue and white Nike tank top with a built-in bra and racer back for support. She didn't even know they made Nike sportswear in plus sizes. The best part was that it would cover her tummy and it looked like it might fit loose enough that she wouldn't look like a sausage. There were also yoga pants that matched the top. Both were size eighteen. The prices had been cut off the tags but she knew the outfit wasn't cheap, and he'd gotten it in her size. Yikes, he knew her size. How did he know her size? She blinked, trying to process the revelation as it hit her. This man, this very sexy man, who could have any woman he wanted, was completely aware of her size and found her appealing.

The modestly decorated little house was situated a block down the street from Jaimee's home. It was a far cry from the upscale apartment in California Lucas had lived in on his last assignment. Not that he really paid much attention to things like décor. It was all just part of the job and at the heart of it Lucas was, for the most part, just an actor playing a very dangerous role. But in this play, breaking character would cost lives. With his growing attraction to Jaimee it would do him good to keep that in mind.

She wasn't making it easy on him. The sound of his name escaping her lips on an urgent moan was torture. When she awoke only to give herself some semblance of release it was all he could do to keep from going to her aid. The night she'd cried herself back to sleep though, that had been hell. She hadn't just softly cried into her pillow. It had been a gut-wrenching, soul-deep sob that nearly drove him to break his cover and go to her. Not good. Not good at all.

He took off his jacket, hung it on the hook by the door and walked into the kitchen to put on a pot of coffee. While waiting for it to brew he leaned back against the counter. Jaimee was sexy, smart, strong; she had a lot of admirable traits going for her. She deserved to be desired and loved. That he had to deceive her nagged at him. That was new. Lucas Grayson was known for his ability to coldly bed a woman only long enough to get her compliance and the information he needed to bust her criminal ass.

It was his job to find out all that Jaimee knew, as well as what those around her knew, and of course, keep her safe in the process. It wasn't like he'd never had a case like this before. He had. However, when it was all over other agents moved in and he moved on. No muss no fuss. The women he fucked never cared any more for him than he did them. Frowning, he sighed, poured a cup of coffee and crossed the short hallway to the tiny bedroom he'd converted into an office. He sat down at the L-shaped desk filled with computer and surveillance equipment and leaned back in his chair.

Sex wasn't the plan in this case. Mrs. Jaimee Turner had only been intimate with her late husband. She had a strong moral code and wouldn't be easily seduced. The course of action had been to woo her, flatter her, make her feel special until they could retrieve pertinent intel, and keep an eye on her. Simple. Yeah right. He genuinely liked Jaimee; she was lovely, intelligent, adorably spunky. But she heated his blood, made him want something he couldn't even name. He cared what happened to her, hated deceiving her, even if it was his job and ultimately, for her own good.

The scanner picked up a call and was recording. Lucas mentally shook his troubling thoughts before pulling his hair back and putting on the blasted headphones.

"Oh my God, no you didn't!" Maxine said with incredulity.

"Yep, I did. Then he soundly put me in my place and yanked my shirt off. Thankfully, I had a leotard on underneath."

"No, he didn't!"

"Yes, he did. He said something about me being too hot and hiding."

"Damn!" Max said in awe. "What did you do?"

"Nothing, he walked away then. But he was waiting for me when I left." Jaimee kicked off her shoes and curled her legs under her in the big overstuffed leather chair. "He asked me to have dinner with him but I told him no."

"What? Why not?"

"Well, I don't know who he is. He could have been a serial killer for all I knew. He could have been eyeing me thinking I would make a nice jacket." Ah, that was bull. He didn't fit the profile for a serial killer, if there really was a specific profile. It was true that she was afraid of him. A man could do worse; he could take something more valuable and painful to lose than your life. He could destroy your heart and soul.

"He probably just wanted to get to know you."

"Yeah right." Jaimee snorted. "That's what he said. That man is not my type. Oh he's pretty to look at and all, but he's not real. Max, he can't be real."

"You're crazy."

"And worse, he lives on my street. He just about scared me to death a while ago. He pulled up behind me while I was getting the mail. And...he replaced the shirt he threw away...with interest." She fingered the soft material.

"For real?"

"Yeah. A very cool Nike outfit."

"Wow! That rocks. What color?"

"Navy, light blue and white."

"To match your eyes. He's good."

Jaimee snorted sarcastically. "He's male. Don't all males like blue?"

"No, not all. Man you really don't know guys, do you?"

"That's an understatement." Jaimee chuckled. She'd only dated a couple of guys before Brent and she had never gotten very close to them. "Brent liked blue."

"I choose to believe he picked blue to match your eyes."

"Anyway, get this...it fits! Can you believe that? I can't believe they actually had them in my size. Well, my new size. Who would have guessed Nike makes plus sizes? Still, I can't believe I can wear this. I guess I really have lost some weight."

"I told you!"

"But I haven't been trying."

"Yep, because you let yourself have a life again. You're no longer trying to be Brent's little woman."

Maxine was never one to keep her opinion to herself and though often correct, it still hurt. No, not so much hurt as it made her feel guilty that it was true. Brent was a passive man and being that she wanted so desperately to make him happy and at the same time encourage him to assert himself, she had tried to be softer, more passive, about everything, something she wasn't inherently born to be.

"You should have invited the hunky stud in."

"For cryin' out loud, Max. I said I don't really know him."

"Well hell, get to know him! Invite him over for dinner or something."

For a moment she considered it. She could march right over to his house and invite him to dinner. But it was the "or something" she was interested in. If he really wanted her she might give in and have sex with him. She needed it, wanted it more than anything else right now.

But what if her body turned him off? Could she handle that rejection? She'd always believed sex outside of marriage wasn't right, would only hurt her in the long run. Besides, she didn't know the man! There was too much at stake, too dangerous.

"You're not listening," Jaimee sighed. "I said he's not my type. He said he just moved here from California."

"What's that mean...not your type? He has a cock and he seems interested in putting it to use."

"Max." Shaking her head, Jaimee folded her new clothes and put them away. The outrageous things Max said didn't shock her anymore. Her disapproving school marm voice came naturally. "He's not the relationship type and even if he is, I'm not ready for a relationship, it's only been..."

"He's dead, Jaimee, dead. You're alive. So live already."

Can't argue with that. She pushed away the guilt for not grieving like she ought to be. She did miss him, and at times that made her sad. Shouldn't she be broken-hearted, devastated, really truly grieving? She shifted on the sofa, stretched her legs out and lay back, closing her eyes.

"How artfully put." Maxine sugarcoated nothing.

"Besides, who said anything about a relationship?"

"I did. I don't think I want to be a 'just for kicks' kinda girl, Max, even if I could be. You know that..."

"Hey! I got an idea," Maxine interrupted, ignoring Jaimee's argument altogether. "I'll come over and we'll go for a walk around the block and see if we can get a peek at him. Then you can flirt with him. I'll be right there to save you if he tries anything."

"No!" Laughing in spite of herself, Jaimee rubbed at the headache budding behind her forehead.

"Seriously, James, give him a chance. What are you gonna lose by getting to know him. He may be a really great guy."

"I don't know. He looks like he just walked off a glossy fashion mag. Oh! You know what? He could be one of those impossibly sexy romance cover models. You know one of those hunky bodice rippers with his hair flowing in the breeze, a busty redhead swooning in his arms. Hell, he could be a Playgirl model."

"Damn, now that's an issue I'd buy."

Jaimee snorted, "Me too." She stared at the ceiling, trying to imagine Lucas naked.

"See you think he's sexy. You want him, just admit it."

Hell yeah, she wanted him. She wanted him so bad it hurt. But she had learned long ago that she didn't have to have what she wanted. "You act like you have a vested interest in my going out with some guy I don't even know just 'cause he's hot."

Jaimee could almost hear the grin in Maxine's voice. "And he is hot, too, isn't he?"

"God, you are so shallow." Jaimee couldn't suppress the feral smile that curved her lips. "Yeah, he is. You know, you would really like him. He has nipple rings, of all things."

"Mmm, nipple rings...yeah that's hot. You sure you don't want him? 'Cause maybe he's got a thing for chocolate." Jaimee couldn't help but chuckle at that. Maxine was an exotic beauty; her skin was like warm milk chocolate, smooth and creamy. Mischievous humor lit her feline eyes. They tilted slightly and were so dark they were almost black. At five feet nine inches tall with an hourglass figure she looked like an Amazonian goddess. With her sharp wit and no nonsense attitude, Maxine Pruitt was a force to be reckoned with.

"Hey, babe, go for it." Jaimee laughed. "I'd be willing to bet he's at the health club every day."

"Cool. Let's go Saturday then, you can wear your new gear."

"Saturday?" Jaimee asked warily, nibbling her lower lip.

"Yeah. It has to be this Saturday. I'm leaving Monday for another business trip. I'll probably be gone two weeks this time. I can't wait that long."

"Oh no, no way," Jaimee said sternly. "Saturdays are way too crowded, besides you have no guarantee he'll be there."

"So if he's not there we'll still get a good workout. We haven't gone to the gym together in a while. Hey! Let's get a massage."

Max had that determined tone that said arguing was futile. Jaimee weighed whether getting out of going was worth the fight she'd have to put up. There was a good chance Lucas wouldn't be there. Even so, the gym would still be crowded. But it would be fun to go with Max, and the pool and the sauna would feel really good. However, she drew a line at the massage. Max just had to deal with it.

Long after Max and Jaimee had ended their call, Lucas listened to Jaimee talk with the parents of her wayward students. Though faint, there was determination in her voice when the parents tried to give her the brush off. The woman was tenacious and wasn't easily dismissed. He liked that about her. He liked it a lot.

He couldn't help smiling at her description of him. No use denying that women found him desirable. It was funny, he wouldn't have chosen the nipple rings, they were part of another assignment, but women did seem to like them so he left them in. Plus, they had proven to add a little extra pain/pleasure during sex.

It was odd to him sometimes how women were so drawn to him. He'd been blessed with good genes. Hell, he wasn't complaining; he loved women, everything about them. There was no shame in the fact that he enjoyed sex and very rarely turned down an offer. Although there had never been any particular woman who interested him for more than just a few hours of mutually satisfying sex.

However this woman was not interested in him for merely a quick fuck. And damn if that didn't intrigue him even more. Okay, maybe that made him a shallow prick but he didn't care. Nope, this assignment wasn't boring in the least. He leaned back and plotted out his Saturday.

Chapter Four

Lucas slowed his jog to walk purposefully toward Jaimee. He watched intently as she wiped the sweat off her forehead, sat on the steps of her porch and toed off her sneakers. Her cherry-stained lips sliding up and down a drippy popsicle was the most erotic thing he'd ever seen, and God help him he'd seen a lot.

"Need any help?"

Jaimee lifted her head to look up at him with wide baby blue innocence at the same time her cheeks hollowed as she sucked on the frozen treat. Holy shit, where his restraint came from he didn't know. She pulled it from her mouth with a pop and licked her lips. Lucas tensed, fighting the urge to grimace as his cock tented the flowing material of his shorts.

"With what?" she asked, frowning in confusion.

With all that bottled-up repressed desire and need? "With the lawn. I didn't see you when I left for my run or I would have offered sooner."

Luscious, there was no other way to describe her. Even in her baggy T-shirt and long denim shorts. Stray locks of wavy hair had escaped her hair clip and clung to her sweat-dampened face. She had sexy knees, well-shaped calves that tapered gracefully to elegant ankles and pretty bare feet.

Her brows lifted and she shook her head slightly. "No, just finished. Front and back. I was just cooling off before I put the mower away. I know, the yard's not that big, but it's really hot today. But then, I suppose you're used to the heat. It's still pretty hot in California in September isn't it?"

"Not so much up north. Close to the same as it is here."

She nodded as the popsicle disappeared between her sensuous lips again then withdrew. Lucas bit back a groan. "I guess I just assumed you'd lived closer to the desert."

That's when she noticed his obvious arousal. It was hard to miss. He was hard as a rock, but hell, it was her fault. Nearly choking, her body went rigid, her eyes widening in surprise or shock or disgust. He couldn't tell for sure. Quickly, she looked away but couldn't seem to look back up at him. Her reaction would have been laughable had he not wanted more than anything else at that moment to take her hand, lead her into the house and fuck her blind on the hallway floor.

He tried not to smile as he cleared his throat and acted as if he didn't notice her reaction. "Nope, closer to Sacramento. You got another one of those?" He needed cooling off in a way that had nothing to do with the southern heat or his jog around the neighborhood. Though, he doubted very seriously a popsicle would be of any help, but it would give him a little more time with her.

Without looking at him she nodded again. "Grape, orange or cherry?"

Lucas shrugged. "Doesn't matter."

"Okay, be right back." Turning she went back into the house.

He pushed her mower into the garage and quickly scanned the interior. Nothing much was there. Not even a toolbox. There were hedge clippers, a weed eater in the corner, cans of motor oil and a bottle of windshield cleaner on a small shelf. Didn't have time to look through her car before she came back. He was just coming around the corner when she hopped down the steps, her breasts bouncing lightly. Sucking in a deep breath he reined in what was left of his self-control. "I put your mower away."

"Oh...thanks. Um..." She rolled her lips inward. "I only had orange and grape left, is orange okay?" Evidently she'd thrown her own popsicle away. Damn, he would have liked to watch her finish it off.

"Sure. Thanks," he said softly, taking the popsicle as he took a step closer and caught her gaze. With his other hand he brushed a damp curl from her face, tucking it behind her ear. She flinched as his fingers lightly stroked over the rapid pulse at her throat, but she didn't back away or scowl up at him. It was crazy how much that pleased him. Her lips parted slightly on a soft gasp as his thumb brushed over her lush bottom lip before he let his arm fall to his side. He just couldn't resist touching her; he had to, and it wasn't enough. But then, he didn't expect it to be.

He tore the paper away from the popsicle he really didn't want and took a bite. He smiled at her as he chewed, enjoying the view. He liked watching the changing emotions play across her face.

"Thank you for the outfit." Her voice was unsteady. She cleared her throat and stood straighter. "It's gorgeous, perfect actually." He couldn't help but smile as she swallowed and lifted her eyes to his before continuing. The fire in her gaze was banked but still sparkled at him, tempting him. "I was totally blown away. You really went overboard. You only owed me a cheap sweatshirt."

He shook his head slightly, ridiculously pleased that she was happy with his gift. "I didn't go overboard at all. I embarrassed you and I honestly didn't mean to do that."

She blinked up at him. "Thank you."

"You're welcome, I'm glad you like it."

The short silence that followed wasn't exactly comfortable but Lucas enjoyed watching her gaze darken with the erotic heat swirling between them.

"So, what brought you to Tennessee?" Lucas found it endearing that she was trying to defuse the sexual tension between them with an attempt at innocuous conversation. But she wasn't running away, and that was encouraging.

"Work." He licked his dripping popsicle and finished off the last bite. There was a longing in her gaze as she watched him that did nothing to help curb his current aroused state. "I'm a construction safety engineer. I'm working on a new project downtown."

"Ah, hard work." She shifted from one foot to the other.

"Can be, yeah." He smiled at her. She was so damn cute. "I like hard work. Anything worth having is worth working hard for."

Her brows lifted and she smiled back at him. "True," she murmured, crossing her arms over her chest. A little late. He'd long ago noticed her nipples hardening in spite of her sensible bra and blousy T-shirt. "I'm a teacher." She stumbled through her explanation. "Eighth grade. English. As a matter of fact I have a huge stack of homework to grade. I really should go."

Lucas nodded, but noticed she made no move to leave. "Hard work."

"Can be." With a little shrug she smiled. "Do you miss California?"

He held her gaze. "No, not at all."

"It has to be a lot different from Tennessee. Especially Nashville."

"Yes, it is and I like that about it."

Jaimee smiled up at him. An easy curve of her lips that made him think of sweet juicy peaches. "It's nice here. Kinda laid back, not too big, not too small."

"I never really liked California. Tennessee has better scenery." He purposely let his gaze travel slowly over her body, his head tilting slightly as he appreciated her long legs, her curvy hips, her ample breasts. "Real, earthy, lush." He finally met her gaze once again and inhaled deeply. Even hot and sweaty she smelled great, like summer rain. She was flustered, her cheeks were rosy, and her eyes had turned darker and silvery, broadcasting her desire.

She cleared her throat again and spoke a little too fast. "Yes, that's true. Tennessee is a beautiful state. It has a lot to offer."

Lucas didn't even try and suppress his grin. "I have no doubt about that. I do have one question though."

"What's that?" Her voice was a little high pitched.

He lifted a brow, quirked his lips and let her off the hook. "What's the deal with Old Hickory Boulevard?"

A relieved smile curved her lips then she laughed. It was music to his ears. "Yeah. Old Hickory Boulevard always seems to throw off the newcomers. It circles the county but with the construction of interstates and lakes it's been chopped up."

"Ah, I was so confused when I first got here." He had been, too. It was irritating as hell to try and decipher directions.

"I can imagine. Three interstates go through Nashville and Old Hickory Boulevard intersects all three, twice." Her eyes actually sparkled like crystal pools.

"Maybe you can give me a tour sometime, keep me from getting hopelessly lost again."

"Maybe. But tonight, work calls." She grinned, a mischievous look in her gorgeous eyes as she gestured toward the door. "I better get to it. Thanks for putting the mower away for me." She turned to go in.

"Listen," he said, effectively stopping her. "If you ever need..." he emphasized the word, then paused, "...help with anything at all..."

Her emotion was so clear in her expression that it was a struggle not to follow her into the house. Every cell in his body demanded he quell the aching need she harbored. But then her expression changed.

"I appreciate the offer but I'm capable of taking care of myself."

The corner of his mouth lifted as he tilted his head and silently waited.

She frowned and paused for a moment. "I mean I'm not a helpless female."

"I know you're not."

"So, I'm fine."

Lucas nodded again. "Yes, you are. I'm glad I met you, Jaimee. Thank you for the popsicle." With a wink he turned and forced himself to walk away. As realization slowly permeated his mind, his smile faded. His interest in Jaimee had turned from intrigued and horny to something much, much more. It hadn't been an act, not one word of their conversation, not one response from him. Shit, things were about to become a lot more complicated.

Chapter Five

With a frustrated sigh Jaimee dropped her red pen on top of the stack of graded papers, unfolded herself from the chair and stretched. The conversation with Lucas had been interesting and pleasant even if it was way too sexually charged to be comfortable. The sound of his voice, the way he stood there...obviously aroused...looking at her the way he had was still playing through her mind. All that stimuli made it damn hard to concentrate on the task at hand.

She tingled all over at the memory of his tongue gliding over the tip of the popsicle. Dammit. Lucas seemed to cause her body to have some kind of hormonal combustion that left her wet and throbbing every time he crossed her path...or mind. Granted, he was outrageously sexy but he also had a really nice smile and the most incredible eyes she'd ever seen. They actually changed colors, darkening some during their conversation.

The sharp peal of the doorbell broke her train of thought. Having no idea who it could be other than her mother, she was hesitant to open the door and for a moment she considered not answering it at all. The night had started off so nice. The long overdue and inevitable confrontation with her mother would seriously wreck it. Oh well, no need trying to evade the inevitable. She rose, her frown firmly in place, and strode through the hallway. She braced herself as she swung open the door, her defensive wall firmly in place, just in case.

"I have a proposition to make."

That was the last thing she ever expected to come out of the incredibly sexy mouth of a man like Lucas. What sort of proposition did he intend to make? Her normally chaste and irreproachable thoughts nose-dived straight into the gutter. Images of this superior specimen of manhood naked and ready to give her pleasure, his hair loose and trailing over her hot, quivering body played fast and feverishly with her imagination. Every prudent and sensible thought melted, leaving her an overheated nymphomaniac.

"You have a what?" she stuttered as she stifled a shiver.

The slow curve of his lips, the intensity of his gaze, clued her in that Lucas knew exactly where her mind had detoured.

"I offer my help with all that homework you have to grade if you'll share dinner with me, which..." he hefted the large bags he held in either arm, "I brought, just in case you say yes. I don't want to have dinner alone...again."

Yeah right, he didn't have to eat alone. Plenty of women would be thrilled to spend some time with him. He wouldn't even have to buy them dinner. But she was suspicious of the way those smoldering eyes of his held a promise of something not even remotely wholesome, while his expression was that of vulnerable supplication. Did he think she was a dingbat? Evidently her skepticism showed.

"Aw come on, Jaimee. I brought a great meal and I'm pretty sure I can handle eighth-grade English."

Okay, he'd won. There was no way in hell she could resist that affected sulk regardless of his motives. And females were always the ones accused of pouting to get what they wanted. Sheesh. Who was she kidding? She did enjoy talking to Lucas, very much, and what's more, she was sick and tired of eating dinner alone too.

Narrowing her eyes, she propped on hand on her hip and played it as cool as she possibly could. Teasingly, she inquired in her most authoritative tone, "Well, I don't know. Do you know the difference between comparative and superlative degrees in irregular adjectives and adverbs?"

"Yes, ma'am, good would be positive, better is comparative..." one brow slowly arched, "...and best is superlative. Would you like another example?" Was that a twinkle in his eye?

"That's fine, moving on..." Jaimee answered hesitantly. Eyeing him closely, she continued. "Have you read *The Pearl* by John Steinbeck?"

"Uh...yeah, I have. When I was about fourteen, but yeah."

Nodding, then lifting her chin, she attempted to look down her nose at him, which was no easy task being that he towered over her. "Can you remember enough to discuss the meaning behind the symbolism found therein?"

The corner of Lucas's sexy mouth tilted. "Yes, ma'am. Are we discussing the symbolism of the scorpion, the doctor, the priest...?" He shifted the bags he was carrying as he searched his memory for the answer. He was so damn sexy. "...the baby—Coyotito, the pearl itself, or... Hell, Jaimee, the whole damn book is symbolism."

Jaimee snickered and held up her hand. "Okay, okay, so you qualify." She sighed and paused for a moment in a last ditch effort to try and think of a reason not to accept his offer.

"Woman, quit being so stubborn. You'll get done faster if you have help." The mouth-watering scent of whatever he had in those bags had her traitorous stomach grumbling loudly. Damn bad timing. Lucas cocked a brow. "And you're hungry."

He was right. She had only had a small bag of Doritos for lunch and she hadn't taken time to eat dinner yet. Why was she pushing him away anyway? She was a grown woman and surely she wasn't so weak that she would lose control and attack him. Was she? Nah. She stepped back with a tilt of her head and motioned for him to come in. "Okay fine, dinner wins."

"Great." He grinned, kissing her on the nose as he brushed past. The casual, good-natured show of affection caught her off guard and it took a few seconds to shake off the strange rush of emotion and longing before following him into the kitchen.

"I'll plate up the food, the dining room is through there." She motioned around the corner. "Make yourself comfortable."

For a moment he didn't move. Was he just going to stand there and watch her? "All right. Will do."

"Iced tea okay with you?" She took the plates and glasses down from the cabinet.

"Perfect."

"It's sweet," she warned. He was, after all, from Northern California. She knew from experience that sweet tea was a Southern thing.

"I like sweet."

Now why did the way he said those three little words make her toes curl? Damn, she was either deprived or depraved...or both. He had brought the restaurant, it seemed, and the man evidently liked meat. Grilled chicken breasts smothered in ham, bacon and Monterey Jack cheese. But she had to give him credit for the salads, steamed veggies and baked potatoes. Although there were several containers of potato toppings that he had ordered on the side. That was considerate. He'd also brought hot yeast rolls and a couple of huge, decadent slices of cheesecake for dessert. Man, she was going to have to double up on her workouts.

When she brought out the plates he was standing in her living room holding her photo album and she nearly dropped the food.

"Wow, Jaimee, this picture of you is amazing."

Huh? She was much heavier in every single picture in that album. Ah, that's it. He was probably referring to how much weight she had lost. "Yeah, I guess I have lost some weight."

"What?" He looked up and frowned as she set the plates on the table. "No, no, come here."

She crossed the open space to glance at the picture he was pointing to. It was a picture of her in college, a while after she'd started dating Brent. She and a group of her friends had been goofing off at the lake and Sarah, her best friend, had snapped that picture of her. Her hair was blowing in the breeze off the lake and she genuinely looked happy. She was larger then. She blamed that on late-night cram sessions with friends and a whole lot of munchies. Even so, there was something incredibly attractive about her that she'd never noticed before.

"There's so much in your eyes here, in your expression. You look as though you believe you can rule the world... Jaimee, you're breathtaking." His voice was soft but deep and sincere.

He was right. Not that breathtaking was a word she would have used to describe herself, but she was pretty, and back then she *did* feel like she could do anything she wanted. When did she give up that strength, that drive, that raw, in-your-face self-confidence? When had she stopped being herself, and when had she started again? The answer bloomed in her mind like a dark cloud and quickly she pushed it away. Maybe the weight loss was the result of her "waking up" again, rather than the other way around.

"I guess it is a good picture. Not sure I'd use that word..."

"Oh yeah, use that word. Breathtaking." Lucas lifted his eyes and met her gaze.

"Well, thank you."

As adolescent as it may be, Jaimee was giddy, ridiculously pleased that he described her as "breathtaking" then. She was even larger in that picture than she was now. Did he find her "breathtaking" now? Didn't he say he found her appealing? Lucas was watching her as though he knew what she was thinking. Quickly, she turned away, hoping he didn't notice the heat crawling up her neck to flush her cheeks or the goofy smile she couldn't seem to suppress. A little too cheerfully she announced that the food was getting cold. Thank God he didn't push it. He slid the photo album back into the space on the shelf and followed her to the table.

"Nice house," he said appreciatively, scanning the long space that made up the living room and dining room as he sat down across from her.

"It's small." Jaimee shrugged. "But I don't need a lot of space."

"It's cozy, I love your furniture."

She chuckled and nodded. "Me too." The overstuffed, butter-soft leather sofa and the matching wide chair had been an extravagant purchase, but there was nothing like curling up in her little living room with a hot cup of coffee and a good book on a rainy day. It had been worth every penny she'd spent. "The set was a self-indulgence I couldn't resist."

All through dinner Jaimee had a hard time not watching his mouth. Small talk with Lucas didn't seem that small at all. Jaimee found herself smiling, leaning forward, even laughing occasionally. Conversation was surprisingly comfortable and enjoyable in spite of the naughty thoughts that kept materializing in her mind.

His white button-up shirt was open at the throat and she had the irrational urge to taste him there, breathe in his scent. Her fingertips tingled, she wanted so much just to reach out and touch his bare forearm. Just to see if the tanned skin was as warm and smooth as it looked, the muscle underneath as hard. Clearing her throat, she sat up and pushed away from the table, picking up the plates as she stood. "Time to get to work."

"Yes, ma'am," he chuckled.

The deep rumble sent tingles running over her. And, oh man, when he smiled... Heat spread through her and her heartbeat kicked up a notch. God, she was pathetic.

She shook her head and gave him a crooked smile. "Make yourself comfortable. I'll just get this cleaned up real quick and be right there."

She put the food she didn't finish in a plastic container and put it in the fridge for dinner tomorrow night and scraped the plates. She stacked the dishes in the dishwasher as she tried fervently to replace the warm arousal from her mind and body with cool.

"Mmm, now that's a damn nice view."

Jaimee stood so quickly she nearly lost her balance. Lucas grinned at her, a big toothy grin as he dumped the melting ice from their glasses into the sink and leaned across her to set the glasses on the top rack of the dishwasher.

"I thought you were going to the living room." It was difficult to keep a clear head while he was making flirty comments. He was so close she could feel the heat from his body. Everything in her wanted to lean into him.

"And leave you with all the work? Nah." His voice was low, softer, his eyes seemed darker.

"You brought dinner, no problem...really." He wasn't backing up at all. Though it seemed like every cell in her body screamed in protest, she chose to back off. She had to do something. Stepping aside, she moved away before she did something stupid like beg him to do her right there on the kitchen floor.

"My pleasure." His lips tilted into a knowing smile. "And now everything's put up and cleaned up. Let's go tackle that work."

How about you tackle me? Nuh uh. She didn't really think that did she? Good Lord. She'd become a completely wanton hussy.

"Well all right then." She put her hands on her hips. "Let's get at it."

By nine there were only a few papers left to grade. Lucas had been a huge help and Jaimee found herself genuinely enjoying his company. Thankfully, the sensual tension had lessened to a more comfortable level as they settled into the task at hand and chatted as they scanned the papers. Lucas made occasional comments that had Jaimee laughing more than once.

"Uh...by any chance are Corbin and Seth buds?"

"Huh?" Jaimee looked up from the paper she was scanning. "Oh, yeah they are. Partners in crime more like."

Lucas grinned and nodded. "Looks like they've been doing their homework together, too."

Jaimee growled. "Let me see." She didn't bother to hide her exasperated sigh as she reached for the papers. The boys had done a half-assed job of trying to hide the fact that they both copied the same work. Work that was obviously not theirs in the first place. Lucas's low chuckle caused her to scowl. "This is not funny. These two are the bane of my existence. You have no idea."

"Oh I have a pretty good idea. No doubt they're troublemakers. It wasn't them, I just thought your reaction was cute."

She narrowed her eyes at him. "I am not cute."

"You are." It was a stone solid statement that dared opposition.

She lifted her chin as she paper-clipped the papers together and set them aside. Before she could say a word Lucas continued in that same quiet but hard "don't challenge me" tone.

"Jaimee, I told you I'm attracted to you. I think I've made it clear that I'm interested in more than just a casual friendship. Yet you seem hell bent on keeping me at arm's length and that's okay...for now. But if I tell you I think you're cute, or beautiful, or sexy as hell, don't piss me off by contradicting me."

Torn between being shocked, irritated and a little bit turned on by his arrogance, Jaimee blinked at him like a dimwit. Licking her lips, she took a deep breath and tried to choose her words carefully. "Look, if you don't wish your opinions of me, or anything else for that matter to be contradicted, maybe you should keep them to yourself."

His sly smiled had her breaking out in warm goose bumps, her tummy doing flips.

"Just to clarify, I have no problem with your calling my opinions about anything other than you into question." Lucas took another paper from those left to grade. "And...I could keep my thoughts about you to myself. But then I suppose I'd have to be more...demonstrative."

Again she narrowed her eyes at him. "Look, Lucas, I don't know why someone like you would be attracted to someone like me but...whatever." She waved her hand in frustration. "The thing is, I lost my husband just eight months ago and I'm not ready to get involved with anyone." A reasonable explanation, so why did it feel like a lie?

"You mean not with me," he said, holding her gaze.

"Not with you," she agreed reluctantly. He scared the hell out of her but she wasn't going to admit that. There was so much in his dark eyes. That was just it; he was too much for her, much more than she could handle. But then she could and did handle Brent, quite easily in fact. Hadn't she hated that very thing about their relationship?

His lips curved into an easy, sexy smile as if he could read her mind. "Whatever you say."

Why did she feel like that statement of surrender was anything but? Instead it held a promise...or a threat. Either way, it sent a sensation of eager anticipation sizzling along her spine.

Chapter Six

He'd listened to her toss and turn in bed, sigh in frustration until finally she'd fallen asleep. Lucas found himself wishing she would masturbate just so he could hear her moan and sigh with pleasure. Like Jaimee, Lucas had taken a shower as well, but he imagined his had been much cooler than hers. Not that a cold shower helped redirect his blood flow northward any.

Spending time with Jaimee had been nice, really nice. It was wicked of him, but he really liked it when he caught her off guard and annoyed her. The way her cheeks went all rosy and the glitter in those incredible eyes of hers heated his blood. He got lost in her wide, blue, unguarded gaze as she became engrossed in whatever it was they talked about. And God, watching her mouth move... Nearly everything about her aroused him.

It was when she looked as though her heart was caught in a vise that he wanted to pull her into his arms and melt the pain away. Give her something to feel good about, something solid she could hold on to. When her expression was stricken, her eyes bleak pools of fathomless blue, she made him feel something other than searing lust. That's what scared him.

He had just begun to doze in his desk chair when Jaimee's phone rang. The chair nearly flipped over then he scrambled to switch headphones, pulling his hair in the process. "Damn it to hell," he swore, adjusting them.

"...hard and fast. Sweaty, bone-melting sex."

Lucas could tell from the caller's sultry voice it was Maxine. Already she had his undivided attention.

"Shut up, Max." Jaimee sighed. "Is this why you woke me up in the middle of the night? To tell me you've decided I need sex?"

"Well you do. You know you do." Lucas could hear the smile in Max's voice. "Sorry I woke you up."

"S'okay," Jaimee murmured, her voice soft and husky from sleep. Lucas heard her shift in bed and he squeezed his eyes shut in hopes of ridding himself of the images that flashed through his brain. "You're home early. Did you have a good night?"

"Yeah, oh man, I have to tell you what happened." Max was wide-awake evidently.

"What?"

"Nick showed up with one of those little butterflies," Max said. "You know the clit stimulators."

"You mean like a toy? As in vibrator?" Lucas heard Jaimee shift in her bed, her voice rose slightly in surprise.

"Yeah, and it was remote controlled." Max laughed. "He told me to go put it on before we left and he kept the remote so he could make me come whenever he wanted."

Lucas lifted a brow. Not a bad idea, not bad at all.

"Oh my God. Did you do it?" Jaimee gasped.

"Hell yeah I did it. Then we went to dinner. I got off at least three times at the restaurant."

"In public," Jaimee squeaked.

"Uh huh."

There was a pause. "How'd you keep from making noise?"

Every cell of Lucas's body was at attention.

"That was the hard part. I bit down on the napkin one time." Max laughed.

"Wow. Three times?"

"Yeah at the restaurant. Then when we got back here. Girl, I lost count. Mmm the man has a magic tongue."

"Oh my gosh. Seriously? You know I've heard of that happening but I didn't know you could really do that."

"Do what?"

"Have multiples."

"Orgasms? Oh yeah, sure you can have multiple orgasms."

"Wow. Well, I'm just a one shot kinda girl I guess." Jaimee sighed, the longing evident in her voice. Damn. No woman was a "one shot kinda girl" if her man knew what he was doing.

"But I don't think I'd want him to waste time licking around down there anyway." She laughed and Lucas forgot to breathe. Licking around...? Was the man totally inept?

"Well maybe Brent didn't know how to do it right," Max said.

Silence. Or...did he go down on her at all?

"Uh, Brent did go down on you right?" Lucas stilled, waited for Jaimee's answer.

Silence.

"Jaimee?"

Jaimee drew a deep breath. "No, Brent didn't like oral sex."

Oh hell no! How many times since he'd been on this case had he thought of tasting Jaimee's sweet dew, imagined feeling her throbbing flesh hot on his tongue... Lucas grimaced and shifted in his chair in an attempt to relieve the discomfort of his restricted swelling erection.

"Shut up! Are you serious?" Max asked.

"Uh huh, but it was okay. It is kinda messy. Well for him anyway, know what I mean? No big deal, I didn't miss it," Jaimee said softly.

Yeah he knew what she meant and it made him nuts thinking about her wet and ready. And the truth, Lucas feared, was that Jaimee missed a whole hell of a lot more than oral sex.

"So, did you do Brent?"

Yeah, did the bastard make you suck him? Lucas ignored the irrationality of his anger. He recalled the image of her sucking on the little popsicle that afternoon and had to unzip for relief. Did she ever dream about sucking him?

"No. I wanted to. I mean, I offered several times. He thought oral sex was gross...uh, unnatural," Jaimee replied softly.

Lucas nearly fell out of his chair. "It's official. The man was a moron," he mumbled.

"...but you know what? I've been having these dreams of my new neighbor, you know..."

"Lucas?"

"Uh huh."

"Hot sex dreams?"

"Uh huh."

She was killing him. His cock was so hard it ached. The thought of her dreaming about him drove him wild. He could just imagine tasting her honey, the sweet softness of her pussy. Holy shit.

"Oooh! Tell!"

"Uh uh!" She chuckled. "Guess what? Max, you're gonna flip. He brought me dinner tonight and helped me grade papers."

"Yeah!? Please, tell me somethin' good! Tell me you did not send that man away without gettin' yourself a taste."

"*Ugh*! No! We just ate dinner and talked and graded papers."

"Are you serious?" Maxine made a sound that was distinctly disappointed. "Damn, girl, I keep telling you you're gonna have to get you some of that!"

Jaimee just laughed. Soon, Lucas vowed, very fucking soon or he was going to go insane.

Max paused for a moment. "Jaimee?"

"Hmm?"

"You have had an orgasm right?"

"Sure, yeah, I have." Jaimee sounded a bit defensive.

"But you've never had multiple orgasms?"

"Well..." Jaimee paused. Lucas held his breath. "There was this one time when Brent and I did it in the afternoon then again later that night. I had two that day. That doesn't count though, does it?"

"No, I mean during one session," Max clarified.

"No, I guess not. But I almost always achieved...orgasm every time we had sex," Jaimee hurriedly explained. "Sometimes just from him sucking my nipples."

Those beautiful breasts with those juicy nipples and so sensitive too, perfect. Lucas groaned out loud.

"Wow," Max said. "You're easy."

"Yeah." Jaimee laughed. "I used to tell Brent that he was lucky I was so easy, he didn't have to work so hard."

And she never had multiple orgasms. The asshole had no idea.

"So when you got off from him sucking your nipples then you climaxed again when he fucked you right?"

"No, Max." Her irritation didn't stop Maxine though.

"Damn. So when he was inside you and rubbing your clit you still couldn't..."

"No, no, no, and he never touched my clit." Jaimee yawned.

Dear God. The man was gay. There was no other explanation; he had to be gay. Lucas shook his head.

"Shut. UP!"

Jaimee sighed. "I didn't want him to anyway, Max, it's really sensitive. Like I said, I could get where I was going without it."

"Yeah, but sometimes you just gotta take the scenic route."

He chuckled at that. True, so very true.

"But seriously, it would kinda hurt. Especially after."

"Nuh uh! It may seem that way but it's a good pain. You're supposed to work with that ultra-sensitive ache, not back off of it."

Lucas nodded in agreement. He could hear Jaimee shift uncomfortably in her bed. Maxine was right, there was a raging passion locked away deep inside Jaimee and she desperately needed release from that bondage.

"Wow, so you've never had multiples, not even when you masturbate?" Maxine kept pushing. It was hard to believe that a tough woman like Jaimee would tolerate lukewarm affection from the man she lived with, loved, for seven years. Shit, seven years. Were there lovers before Turner? If there were, they were just as pathetic as Turner. It was more than clear to Lucas that Jaimee didn't know her own body or her own desires.

"No," Jaimee snapped. "Why are you so interested anyway?"

"I'm sorry. I just never knew things were so..." Max paused, then continued with a sigh. "I'm sorry. I didn't mean to upset you"

"It's okay. Look, I know sex between Brent and I was lackluster, but I did love him. I really did. He was a good man and he loved me, really loved me. Sex is not the most important thing in a marriage, you know."

Lucas grimaced, wishing she didn't have to face the truth of what was to come.

Chapter Seven

Just as she predicted, the health club was packed Saturday with mostly beautiful people posing and preening for attention. Jaimee didn't feel half as frumpy in the new sportswear. The outfit fit perfectly and although she was a little uncomfortable that her big butt wasn't covered by her usual long T-shirt, she looked pretty good.

"Good afternoon, ladies," the bouncy blonde at the desk sang. "I'm Deirdre. Can I page a trainer for you?"

Jaimee resisted the urge to roll her eyes as she signed in after Max. "No thanks."

"So how do we go about scheduling a massage?" Max asked casually.

"That's no problem, there's a couple of openings in an hour. I'll set it up for you," Deirdre said.

"No, no, that's not necessary." Jaimee scowled at Max.

"Oh why not?" Deirdre pouted. "It does wonders for your whole outlook on life."

Jaimee stared at Deirdre for a second then turned on Max. "I told you I wasn't getting a massage."

Max folded her arms over her chest and arched a brow. "Chicken."

Jaimee frowned. "Quit trying to manipulate me."

"Quit being a weenie," Max said matter-of-factly.

"Um...I can assure you that the massage therapists are all professional. Oh here's Blayne now. Blayne!" Deirdre called.

Jaimee and Max turned to see a muscular man move toward them. White jeans hugged his slim hips and the white T-shirt stretched over his massive chest stood out in stark contrast against his bronze skin. He looked as if he'd baked himself in the tanning bed. His thick chestnut mane of hair was streaked with gold and copper and black and it fell just above his shoulders. Too-full lips tilted at the corners and he had wide aquamarine eyes lined in navy eyeliner. Contacts, had to be. No one had eyes that color.

"Blayne, this is Ms. Turner and Ms. Pruitt. They're considering a massage this afternoon but Ms. Turner is undecided," Deirdre said sweetly.

"Oh?" His voice was warm and soothing as he lifted a perfectly plucked brow. He was about the same height as she and moved with grace and style that were at odds with his bulk. Fascinated, Jaimee watched him as he turned the sign-in sheet toward him with one finger. "Jaimee, may I call you Jaimee?"

She nodded, trying not to cross her arms and he moved around her, looking her over as though she were a broodmare he was considering. She almost expected him to check her teeth next.

"You're very uptight, aren't you, sweetie?" Blayne asked, sympathy filling his unnaturally colored eyes.

"Well, n—" Jaimee began.

"Listen to me," he interrupted softly. "I'm a professional, dear. I have the credentials if you would like to see them. And besides that—" he grinned, showing perfectly straight, incredibly white teeth, "—I'm as queer as a football bat. Not that a sensual massage wouldn't be heavenly, but you just don't have the equipment I'm interested in. I can give you a list of books that you could share with your man. Oh and there's a really nice instructional DVD," he purred.

"I don't have a man," Jaimee snapped without thinking. Damn, she was doing a lot of that lately.

Blayne tilted his head with a sigh, his brows furrowed in sympathy. "Tsk. Oh, darling, no wonder you're tense." He took her hand between his two. They were oddly cool and soft. "Let me do this for you," he appealed. "I promise to stop if you feel the slightest bit uncomfortable."

She opened her mouth to speak but he lifted one short finger, placing it over her lips to silence her. "Deep muscle, twenty minutes in the sauna, followed by a cool shower and herbal spritz. You'll feel born again." He sighed dreamily.

Max bit her bottom lip to keep from laughing. Jaimee could see the glint of mischief in her eyes. Okay so maybe it wasn't such a big deal. But, man, it was gonna bite that Max won. She would rub it in too. Oh well.

"All right, fine," Jaimee ceded, wincing at Max's smirk of victory as she turned and headed for the machines.

Maxine's commentary kept her laughing and their twenty minutes

49

on the bikes went by quickly. Max took an aerobics class with the stipulation that Jaimee come drag her ass out if Lucas showed up. A couple of times Jaimee scanned the room for him to no avail. She wasn't sure if she was relieved he wasn't there or disappointed. Oh well, she shrugged it off and tried to focus on her workout. An hour later she was finishing the last of the extra ten reps of leg extensions when Max came over and popped her on the thigh with her towel.

"Time for our massage, let's hit the showers." Max's dark eyes sparkled as she looked down at Jaimee. Damn it if the woman wasn't glowing. Sweat had soaked Jaimee's workout clothes and plastered strands of hair to her reddened face. Max on the other hand stood tall and straight, her face luminous and smooth. She was willing to bet the woman never had a zit in her life. The burgundy sports bra and matching leggings that barely made it to her hips looked amazing on her. The diamond dangling from the gold ring drew the attention of every male in the room to her navel, her flat stomach and the rest of her well-toned figure.

"Fine. I was done anyway." Jaimee stood and took the fresh towel Max offered and wiped the sweat from her face. "Let's go get this over with."

After a quick shower they left the locker room and turned down the hall toward the treatment rooms. These rooms were lavishly decorated with overstuffed seating in earth tones and large, elegant stone pots overflowing with lush plants. The subtle scent of vanilla and the tinkling of a faux waterfall sitting in the corner filled the perfectly conditioned air. Jaimee's left eye began to twitch as the pretty, petite receptionist tilted her head and said "Welcome, ladies. My name is Pam. I'm assuming you are Maxine and Jaimee?"

Without waiting for their answer Pam came around the desk and handed Max a thick white terry cloth robe then scanned Jaimee's body. The sorry little slip of a woman tapped a long manicured nail to her collagen-plumped red lips. Jaimee put her hands on her hips and narrowed her eyes waiting for the remark. "We'll have to see if we have some plus-sized robes. Wait right here, I'll be right back."

"Bitch," Max said, scowling after the receptionist.

Jaimee just shook her head. "Ah, just ignore her. Poor thing's probably hungry."

Max chuckled. "True."

Pam returned with a smug lift to her brow, her glossy red lips pursed. "You're in luck, dear. We had one," she said, handing her the bundle. "Follow me to your dressing rooms." She turned and crooked her finger at them.

Max looked at Jaimee and mouthed "bitch" as she followed her, mocking the exaggerated swing of Pam's bony ass. Jaimee put a hand over her mouth to keep from laughing out loud.

Pam stopped at the door of one opulently decorated dressing room and turned on her heel like a runway model. "Here you are, Jaimee. You can leave your underwear on if you like or you can take them off. It's entirely up to you and your comfort level." She gave her the once-over again, her brow lifting slightly. "When you've undressed, put on the robe. Blayne will come for you shortly." Indicating a door down and across the hall from Jaimee's, Pam lifted her chin. "And your room is right there, Maxine."

"Okay, look." Maxine waited until Pam walked away before laying a hand on Jaimee's shoulder and leveled with her. "It's gonna be a bitch to give you a decent massage around your bra straps. I guess if you just can't stand it you can leave your panties on. Best thing to do is just get naked though."

"Naked?" Shit. Butterflies fluttered in her stomach like crazy.

Maxine grinned as she backed away toward her room. "Come on, James. Do it. I double dog dare ya."

Jaimee snorted. "Completely naked?"

Nodding, Max opened her door and nodded. "Completely naked. Blayne has seen it all and then some, babe, and you might as well do this right."

"Fine," Jaimee groused as she entered her room. Oh well. Maxine was probably right and Blayne did seem very nice. She doubted very seriously he would make comments about her big ass or her thunder thighs. And besides, she told herself silently, the man's gay. He wouldn't care what shape she was in. If anything he would go on and on about how she could go about losing weight and she was very adept at enduring that by now.

Her mother put her on her first diet at seven years old and she'd been off and on one weight loss program after another ever since. About a year before Brent's death she'd given up on diets altogether. It was insanity to keep doing the same thing over and over again expecting different results. Working out at the gym had trimmed her down a bit, but she did that because she enjoyed it. The fact that she'd gone down a couple of sizes was just incidental. Though she wasn't entirely comfortable with her body she didn't let the fact that she wasn't thin and gorgeous depress her anymore. To be strong, healthy and energetic was all that mattered to her now.

The sharp knock on the door had her jumping as she sat her athletic shoes on the bench beside her pile of neatly folded clothing. Blayne stuck his head in. "You ready, babe?"

With a sigh Jaimee pulled the soft robe closer together and folded her arms over her breasts. "I suppose."

Blayne winked at her and waved her to follow. "Come on then."

Very conscious of the fact that she was completely naked under the robe, she padded after him to the small adjoining room, its design in greens, golds and creams obviously meant to calm and relax the soul. In the center stood the thickly padded massage table. Nearby on a counter sat assorted bottles, towels, sheets and a stereo. "Where's Max?" Jaimee asked nervously.

"She's in the other room with Allan." Blayne motioned with his head toward the far wall. "Here's what I want you to do. First, step up here and lie down on the table," he said as he patted the table.

He sighed when she paused. "Do I take off the robe?" she asked finally, a bit snotty.

"No, not yet." His reply was just as snotty. Then, with a sarcastic smile, he patted the table again.

"Fine." Jaimee sighed as she stepped up and lay down on her stomach.

"Super, now," Blayne said as he busily draped the sheet over her body. "Take off the robe and hand it to me. You're covered now, silly woman."

Jaimee tugged and wiggled until finally she got the robe from around her and pulled her arms out of the sleeves. With a twist of his wrist and all the elegance of a bullfighter, Blayne impatiently snatched the robe from underneath the sheet and draped it neatly over the bench. "All right, love, now. Rest your pretty face here." He patted the oval hole at her head.

Surprised at just how comfortable she was, Jaimee settled onto the soft flannel-covered table. She arranged her breasts so that they were more evenly flattened against the thick foam padding as Blayne folded the sheet down just under her shoulders.

"Comfy?"

"Uh huh," Jaimee replied.

"Okay, be right back, don't move."

"I'll be here." She took a deep breath then blew it out again. The experience hadn't been bad so far and Blayne was pretty cool. Already she was feeling more relaxed. Closing her eyes, she moved her arms above her head. Yep, this was pretty nice.

She'd started to drift off when the soft click of the door closing alerted her to Blayne's return. He moved to the counter and went through the CD selection. "Hey, Blayne, don't play any of that New Agey instrumental crap, okay?"

It wasn't really a laugh but she could tell he found humor in what she'd said. Thank goodness, for a moment there she was afraid he might really like New Agey instrumental crap. Instead he put on Tina Turner, the really sexy one she sang with Barry White. Odd. Oh well, she loved Tina Turner and what red-blooded woman didn't love Barry White's voice?

Blayne walked closer to her and folded the sheet down to right above her butt. There was clinking of bottles then he began rubbing his hands together so she closed her eyes and waited.

Warm oil-slicked hands pressed lightly at the small of Jaimee's back on either side of her spine. Firmly they stroked upward to her shoulder blades. She surrendered to the tranquility melting her tense muscles as Blayne's hands curved around her shoulders and smoothed back down her ribs. His fingertips grazed the rounded sides of her breasts and she sucked in a breath. She shook off the uneasy feeling as his hands moved down, circled right above her hips and moved up her back and over her shoulders.

Again his fingers brushed the sides of her breasts and Jaimee cleared her throat. Blayne paused for a moment then continued. Each pass of his hands over her breasts sent warm sensations feathering through her body. Don't be such a prude, Jaimee, she told herself. It was just because she'd been neglecting those needs since Brent died. She hadn't even wanted to touch herself. Well, she'd wanted to, and she had and it only served to remind her of what she didn't have. She'd tried so hard to close off that part of herself, maybe even before she lost Brent, maybe, just a little.

Blayne hadn't said a word since he came back. The pamphlet had said that conversation during the massage should be kept to a minimum to allow for relaxation and concentration. Jaimee took a deep breath and slowly let it out again. Concentrate. Okay she could do that. Anything to take her mind off the fact that this man...this gay man...was making her feel things she wasn't prepared to feel. She wanted to laugh at herself. Stupid to believe that just because the man was gay didn't mean she wouldn't become aroused by his touch.

Liquid heat spread through her with every long firm stroke up, around and back down her body. She squeezed her eyes shut as his

Veronica Chadwick

hands began moving over her body in a circular motion. Steadily, with firm pressure, his hands were very warm, almost hot on her body. They moved up slowly, back down over the slope of her ass, back up. He moved around the table to the other side. Though he lifted his hand from her back to lift the sheet from her legs, fold it and lay it across her butt he kept his hip pressed against hers, never breaking contact.

He poured more oil into his palm and warmed it between his hands. Starting at her ankles he moved up her calves in long firm strokes. Thank God she'd shaved. As his hands moved upward, past the back of her knees, she held her breath. Using the heel of his palm he smoothed his hand up her thigh in long strokes and she held her breath as his hand curved around, his fingers an inch away from her pussy as they smoothed over her inner thigh.

Alarm bells were going off and at the same time her body reacted heatedly, aching for more of his touch. Her nipples ached as they hardened, pressing against the table. Afraid to let Blayne know what was happening to her at his touch, Jaimee bit her lip. She focused on trying to make her body go numb, trying to block out the pleasure that spiraled through her with every stroke.

Up again, his hands were moving up her leg, this time milking her muscles. Jaimee couldn't contain the moan that escaped her lips as strong oil-slicked hands moved over her body, working up her back over her shoulders and arms Desperately she tried to control her breathing. Strong hands kneaded her flesh, long fingers...those weren't Blayne's fingers. Blayne's fingers were short. These fingers were long...

"Flip over for me, Jaimee."

Chapter Eight

It took less than a minute for her to realize to whom the dark sexy voice belonged. She held perfectly still, mortified by the flush of heat that infused her, knowing it was Lucas who touched her.

"Get. Out," she said through clenched teeth. Shaking with anger, her voice was strained as she moved to push herself up from the table.

Possessively, Lucas's hands moved up her body again, gently pushing her back down.

"Relax," he demanded, his voice husky.

"Let me up. Now!" she growled. Who the hell did he think he was? Oh she knew who he thought he was. He thought she should be grateful that he put his hands on her without her permission. Hell, worse than that, he had tricked her. "You son of a bitch!" Again she tried to sit up without success.

Lucas continued to knead her muscles. "Hey, hey, hey. You don't even know my mom."

"I know she didn't raise you with any manners or respect or common courtesy for others," Jaimee snapped.

"Calm down." The humor she detected in his voice only fueled her fury though she still nearly sighed with pleasure as he began to lightly rake his fingertips down her back

Calm down? Damn him! He had no right to do this to her, to make a fool of her in this way. She lay there with nothing but a sheet over her ass while he got his kicks making fun of her. She wanted to cry but she wouldn't let him have the satisfaction.

Oh hell no! She reached down to grab the sheet, felt for the edges and pulled it up around her before pushing herself up with determination. He didn't stop her this time, he just stood behind her watching; probably smirking at her while she fought to cover herself.

"Where's Blayne?" She jumped down from the table and whirled around to glare at him.

"On a long break I guess," he answered quietly. To her surprise there was no humor in his eyes. What she saw there she immediately chose to dismiss as her imagination. No way would she back down or look away. She lifted her chin another notch and narrowed her eyes. His warm brown eyes had gone dark and smoldering as they moved over her body. "Your massage isn't over yet, Jaimee."

"The hell it isn't." She spoke with a little less conviction than she had just moments ago.

"And see, you've gotten yourself all worked up and you've undone all the work I'd done...for the most part." The corner of his mouth tilted in a wry smile as his eyes focused on her breasts. It was the soft rasp of the sheet that had them tightening, she struggled to convince herself, not his lazy, sultry perusal of her body, not the hot tingles still flooding her body from the skilled touch of his hands.

"You had no right." Her voice was softer, more vulnerable than she had meant for it to sound.

"What difference does it make if it was Blayne or me who gave you the massage? Are you and Blayne best buddies? No, I believe you just met him today, did you not? At least I'm a neighbor and friend." The mischievous glint in his eyes only increased her ire. How dare he use logic to discount her outrage and humiliation?

"It makes a difference to me!" Unintentionally, she raised her voice and instantly regretted it as the triumph lit his eyes and the knowing smile curved his sexy lips.

He calmly picked up a towel and began wiping away the oil from his hands, one finger at a time. She held the sheet tighter between her breasts. Delicious sensations speared through her as she crushed them closer to her body with her forearms, her nipples stubbornly refusing to relax. Her mind was filled with the erotic images of all her fantasies. She wanted nothing more at that moment than to fling the sheet aside and wrap herself around him. Instead, she forced herself back into reality, cleared her throat and said with as much dignity as she could muster, "What is it with you anyway? What do you want from me?"

Her breath caught in her throat as he met her gaze. The wicked smile faded from his lips as his jaw tightened. He tossed the towel on the table and purposefully walked around it toward her. She took another step back and found herself against a wall. He stood so close she could feel the heat radiate from his body. She fought against the impulse to grab his shirt and pull him against her body. Silently he waited until she finally got the nerve to lift her head and look up into his eyes.

"I want your eyes." He spoke barely above a whisper—hoarse, deep, hungry. Dark eyes looked through her before lowering to her lips. "I want your mouth." A shiver danced over her as his fingers brushed her cheek. "Your skin, the taste of your desire on my tongue, the sound of your pleasure playing like a song over and over again in my mind."

Instantly self-conscious, she bit her lip. Yes, her body was tighter than it had been but still her breasts were large and heavy, her hips too wide, her stomach too rounded. There wasn't much remarkable about her face either in her opinion. It wasn't that she wasn't attractive; she was, in a very understated kind of way. She just wasn't the kind of woman a man like Lucas typically wanted. And he was the polar opposite of Brent. Everything in her screamed to get a clue, take a chance. But, this couldn't be real, it couldn't be happening. He didn't want her. He couldn't want her. If his interest in her was a cruel joke and he laughed in her face afterward it would be too much to deal with now. No, she was just beginning to heal.

"I can't," she whispered.

"Yes. You can." The way his eyes unabashedly roamed over her was driving her crazy.

She could feel the heat crawl up her neck and knew her cheeks were probably splotchy. He stepped closer, and she grappled for an escape. "I'm...I don't..."

"Don't lie, Jaimee." He groaned as he pulled her close, his mouth descending on hers. Gently at first, just a soft nip. Then his eyes met hers as he tilted his head and kissed her, his tongue teasing her lips, urging them apart. Her heart stopped, her breath caught. Unable to resist the intoxicating taste of him and the raw emotion coursing through her, she leaned in, opening to him. All she cared about at that moment was the feel of his lips firmly moving over hers, demanding, his tongue caressing the tender interior of her mouth.

All she could do was feel. Every ounce of common sense faded as she clutched at his shoulders. His hand moved up along her side to cup the side of her breast, his thumb found her hardened nipple. The whimper that escaped her throat sounded tortured. All that separated her body from his hands was the flimsy sheet. His lips left hers and traveled over her jaw to nip at the sensitive skin beneath her ear. One long muscled thigh pushed between her own, rubbing against her throbbing pussy.

She could feel the rock-hard bulge behind the zipper of his jeans. That had to be real. He couldn't fake that, right? His free hand smoothed over her ass, pulling her tighter against his straining shaft. Oh God, she couldn't resist him. Her thoughts were spinning out of control.

It was just a kiss but so incredibly powerful. His hands molded and kneaded her breasts, and she trembled as his mouth devoured her throat. Biting her lip to keep from crying out, she struggled for breath. It was too intense, too much, she was losing her mind, her will.

One hand smoothed over the sheet, down her stomach, between her thighs to touch her throbbing flesh. "You're burning, Jaimee. So hot. Wet," he rasped against her neck, then bit as he stroked deeper as if the now-soaked sheet wasn't a barrier at all. "Open for me."

His finger, covered with the wet material, grazed over her engorged clit and Jaimee came apart. Her legs went weak and she clung to him as if her life depended on it. Though she tried to keep it down, a groan from deep inside tore from her as she rode his hand. She couldn't breathe and she didn't care. Rapid-fire waves of sensation shot through her, ensnaring her in the power of her orgasm.

Without giving her a chance to regain her sanity, Lucas lifted her and carried her to set her on the massage table. His body was so hot, on fire against hers, his breath rapid as he kissed her hard, sucking her bottom lip between his teeth. With purpose and urgency he moved, his hand fisted in the sheet to pull it away.

It was now or never. She had to stop, had to. "No." The word was barely audible above the roar of her blood pounding through her veins. God, she didn't want him to stop, she wanted him to fuck her, drive into her without mercy. The fact that she wanted the pain frightened her. She'd come so easily at his touch. So easy. With vivid clarity she realized just how easy she was being. If she took him, gave in to what her body so desperately screamed for, would she be able to deal with it when he walked away? No, she couldn't deal with that. Not now, not yet. She pushed at him.

"Please stop."

She tasted like cinnamon and desire. He had only meant for it to be a soft kiss on her lush mouth, just to show her he meant what he said. In the process he was swept away by her spontaneous response, ravenous to taste more of her. That, in combination with having his hands on her supple body just moments ago, was driving him mad. Now her mouth was so warm, so inviting. Her nipples strained against his chest, firm, plump, begging to be sucked and everything in him wanted to oblige them. He wanted to give her pleasure, more pleasure. She needed it. Almost as bad as he needed to be the one to give it to her.

Lucas reluctantly raised his head as he struggled to control his raging need. Jaimee rolled her swollen lips inward as she looked up at him, her desperate eyes dilated with need. She pushed him. He wanted more, wanted to give her more and her body was so open, so supple, wet and ready for him. But the fear in her eyes had him resisting the urge to hold on to her. Dropping his hands, he stepped back. She clutched the sheet against her and hopped down from the massage table. She quickly put distance between them and stood with her back against the door to the adjoining dressing room.

"I'm sorry," she panted, her voice husky. "I can't do this."

"Yes, you can."

Frowning, she lifted that stubborn chin and squared her shoulders. His cock jerked in response. Go ahead, challenge me, baby.

"I won't," she said with the determination of a line backer.

If she knew how much restraint he was exerting she wouldn't be so bold as to dare him like that. Or would she? She was breathtaking standing there looking like a sexy nymph with her cheeks flushed rosy with arousal, her lips swollen from his kisses, her lush body draped in the damp white sheet she clutched above her breasts. It took a moment before he realized his cell phone was ringing. Reality flooded in with a vengeance and he clenched his teeth. Caller ID told him it was the case agent, Michael Butler. Shit. For the first time in his career he wasn't stalwartly focused on his job. All he had on his mind was Jaimee and his all-consuming need for her. He let his gaze travel her body, memorizing the way she looked, and narrowed his eyes.

"You will, Jaimee. We aren't finished. Not by a long shot."

Her eyes widened, only a fraction, but he noticed it before he turned away from her and walked out the door. Attraction was one thing. What he was feeling for Jaimee was a great deal more powerful. Damn, he was in trouble.

Chapter Nine

Still in shock, Jaimee leaned against the door of the dressing room and touched her swollen mouth. Never had she been kissed that way, ever. Memories of Brent flashed through her mind like an angry accuser. She remembered the passionless way Brent had pressed his lips to hers, awkwardly shifting them in a sad parody of a kiss. Finally she'd convinced herself it was okay. She clenched her teeth, stamped down on the rush of pain, frustration and anger and blinked back the tears. It *was* okay. How he kissed shouldn't matter, didn't matter. Their marriage had been based on stronger stuff: solid devotion, admiration and respect. And love, of course love. There were many who had pretty good marriages based on much less.

By the time she was showered and dressed she was a bit less shaky, but she couldn't forget the feel of Lucas's touch, his mouth on hers. Her imagination went wild at the memory of his tongue caressing her lips, her neck. She'd been so wet, his hands gliding over her body sent her senses spiraling out of control. Had she ever had an orgasm that powerful before? If she had she couldn't remember it. Not like that. And he'd only touched her. Even now her body eagerly responded.

Guilt added a whisper of bitterness to the emotions overwhelming her. The last three years of marriage she and Brent barely touched at all, and he had never touched her so unabashedly. Lucas's desire had swept her away, overwhelmed her. What took her breath away more than anything else was the fact that Lucas wanted her so badly. No man, not even Brent, had ever been that passionate for her. Not ever.

Maxine was about to explode with curiosity by the time they got to her car. Thankfully, she didn't see Lucas or Blayne when they left the gym. While Maxine listened intently, beyond intrigued, Jaimee recounted everything that had happened.

"I can't believe you could stop him." Max spoke softly as she tried to concentrate on the road in front of her. "I mean if it was good, James..."

"It's confusing." Jaimee sighed. "It was spontaneous, like a flash fire out of control. It was never like that with Brent. I guess I was afraid," she admitted. "And, Maxine, I don't do that. There was no one before Brent. I can't just have sex because it feels good."

"So now you feel guilty."

"Yes. I do."

"I guess I can understand that."

Completely taken aback, Jaimee stared at Max, her mouth agape. "You do?"

"Well, yeah. I mean I don't think you have anything to feel guilty about. But I understand why you, Jaimee Turner, would feel that way...on several levels," Max answered. Jaimee continued to watch her friend in astonishment. Max kept her eyes on the road ahead and chewed on the inside of her cheek. That was never a good sign; it meant Max was considering, contemplating.

"Okay, what are you thinking?" Jaimee finally asked.

"You need to get out," Max said matter-of-factly as she turned into Jaimee's drive.

"I am getting out. We go out every weekend," Jaimee countered. "And what does that have to do with anything?"

"No, girl, we go out for lunch or dinner, hang out at the book store, go shopping. I mean you need to go *owwt*."

Jaimee's brow knitted together in confusion. "I don't think I follow."

Max shook her head. "Let's go in. I need to see what I have to work with." She sighed with exasperation as she got out of the car.

"Huh?" Max didn't answer, she just went up and stood impatiently, tapping a foot at the front door. Feeling completely out of control of the situation, Jaimee followed, unlocked the door and stepped aside to let Max in. She was obviously a woman on a mission. Without hesitation Max walked down the hall, turned on her heel and took the steps two at a time.

Yep, she was on a mission. "Hmmm, guess I'll just get some coffee," Jaimee said to herself as she turned into the kitchen.

Maxine had been Jaimee's best friend for at least five years and over those five years Jaimee had learned that it was best to just let Maxine run with whatever scheme she had concocted. She'd never really pushed the envelope enough to have Jaimee putting her foot down. Max had to have her hands in everything and if she suspected there might be something wrong in Jaimee's life Max set out to right it...on her own terms.

Normally it didn't bother Jaimee so much. She'd just smile and nod and say "Yeah, you're right, Max," then just do what she wanted to do in the first place. But this time she wasn't sure Max would let her get away with her usual passive aggressiveness.

"Max?" she called out as she reached the top of the steps with two cups of coffee.

"In here," Max answered from Jaimee's bedroom.

She found Max standing in her closet going through her clothes. "Hon, nothing I have is gonna fit you."

"Nothing you have is gonna fit you."

"They fit."

"Yeah, like sacks."

Setting the cups down on the dresser, Jaimee snorted. "I haven't lost that much weight, Max."

"Inches, it's all about the inches. You need some party clothes. As soon as I get back from this damn business trip we're going shopping," Max continued.

That unflinching determination of hers made Jaimee want to cringe. Oh man, she was working a plan this time.

"What are you up to?" she asked with a sigh.

"I'm trying to find something to dress you up in. We're going out."

"Max, I have papers to grade and lesson plans to make..."

Max rolled her eyes and threw her hands up in disgust. "Okay, all right, fine. You don't have anything decent to wear out anyway. As soon as I get back from New York..." She narrowed her eyes. "You better have your work done at school 'cause that excuse won't work twice."

"I'm not the goin'-to-the-club-dancin'-and-partyin' type." Jaimee shrugged. "I don't know why you insist on me going."

Max took a drink of her cooling coffee. "Because, sweetheart, you don't know what you like. Hell, you don't even know what type you are because you don't know who you are."

"Oh please, I'm thirty-two years old. Don't you think it's a little late for me to try and 'find myself'?" Jaimee laughed.

Max's expression remained stoic. "Yeah, I do, but since you haven't as of yet, better late than never."

"Come on. It's silly, ridiculous..." Jaimee paused, trying to find the right words, "...immature and self-absorbed."

Arching a brow, Max pursed her lips. "And what's wrong with that?"

Jaimee opened her mouth to say something but had no idea what.

Max smiled and hugged her tightly. "I'm gonna run. I'll drop the cup off in the kitchen." Without so much as a pause or a look back she walked out the door, wiggling her fingers in farewell. "I'll call you when I get home. Love ya."

The quick conversation with Butler left Lucas tense.

"We intercepted a call from Zachary to Marshall. Turner had incriminating evidence on file. You have to get inside...hack into her PC. You're looking for a disk...probably a CD but don't rule out a floppy or a flash drive..."

Edward Zachary, an exceedingly charismatic man, oozed with power. Men admired and respected him as a brilliant businessman and women from all walks of life desired him. It didn't matter much that he owed his good looks to a talented plastic surgeon or that his rumored virility and incredible stamina came from a little blue pill. He owned way too many people, which allowed him to control the whole organization. There were no lengths he wouldn't go to in order to keep it secure. It would only intensify his fury to know a dumpy little peon like Turner had the power to bring him down.

Absently, Lucas poured a cup of coffee. It bugged him that Zachary would have let his anger get the better of him though. Why did he have Turner killed before he secured the disk unless he didn't know about the disk? That was highly unlikely. Turner was probably fool enough to threaten him with it. Which was why he was dead. The question was, was Zachary fool enough to believe Turner was stupid enough to have the disk with him? Taking his mug, he went into the office and sat down at the desk.

"...You're going to have to turn up the heat, Grayson. Move in, get closer... She's in danger..."

Jaimee was a target now more than ever. It wasn't like it was the first time he had to "get closer" to a woman in order to do his job. However, no woman had ever affected him like Jaimee did. The thought of someone doing anything to hurt her made his chest tighten and his blood boil. It made him crazy when she talked about Turner, about how much she loved him, how much she believed in him and his love for her. She constantly made excuses for him. Yeah, he'd move in and get closer. He wanted her closer in a way that had nothing to do with the job. He wanted her. For his own, possibly, forever.

There was amazing strength in Jaimee that drew him, a question in her incredibly guileless crystal blue eyes that made him want to be the answer. Getting closer to her wouldn't be a problem for him. It was what happened when all this was over and done with that would be the problem. When she learned the truth about her husband it would break her heart, tear her apart, leave her with nothing but seven years of lies. But that wouldn't be all.

After he worked to break down her walls, win her trust, her faith, possibly make her believe she could be loved again, she would think he was no better than Turner. She would believe it was all a lie. When she found out who he was, what he'd been doing, there was no way he'd make her believe it wasn't just his assignment. She would hate him. To her very core she would hate him. Nothing he would say could change that.

It was too late to call in another agent at this point and he wouldn't even if he could. Jaimee had gone from being an assignment to being important to him. She was his responsibility now and he would keep her safe. Yeah and who would save her from him? Slamming the mug down on the desk, he leaned back in his chair, combing his fingers through his hair.

"Goddammit," he groaned. They were both in serious trouble if he couldn't push his emotions out of the way and focus on the task at hand. With a self-deprecating laugh he shook his head. Emotions. Shit. Lucas Grayson, undercover agent known for his heartlessness. His ability to gain a woman's compliance long enough to bust her criminal ass. Lucas Grayson didn't have emotions. Lucas Grayson didn't know love.

Chapter Ten

Jaimee finished brushing out her hair and left it down. Her scalp ached from wearing a damn banana clip all day. Lucas had been on her mind all weekend. She hadn't seen him again, nor had she heard from him. That was a good thing. Well, at least she kept telling herself that. If nothing else maybe the erotic episode at the gym would help her move on. It made her realize how weak and out of control she'd become. And it was ridiculous to shut herself off from everything beyond this little bubble she'd created for herself because she was too apprehensive and unsure.

No doubt, Lucas shook her up, made her want. She thought hard about what Maxine said about not knowing herself. It dawned on her just how long it had been since she went out, laughed, allowed herself to have a good time. The possibility of being free, letting go and having a good time was kind of intriguing. No, it was very intriguing.

What was so wrong with being silly and just a little bit wild? Or even acting immaturely and self centered for just a while? She'd been way too sheltered growing up, left home to marry her one and only love and wrapped herself up in her man. Brent had been her everything and when he was gone she was left floundering without a foothold on anything. This time on her own had been so good for her. She'd learned to stand on her own without anyone to depend on but herself. Who knows, maybe someday she'd meet someone else, fall in love again. Instantly Lucas's face materialized in her mind. Those smoldering brown eyes, dark with desire...for her...

The chirp of her phone startled her and she drew a steadying breath. "Hello," she croaked and winced at her husky tone.

"Hello, sweetheart." The soft voice attempted comfort.

"Oh hi, Momma." Jaimee squeezed her eyes shut and prayed her mother was too tired to talk very long. "How are you?"

"I'm fine, how are things with you?"

Immediately her "encounter" with Lucas came to mind. Good Lord, if her mother knew what she had done, in a public place no less, she'd probably call an exorcist to cleanse her of her demon of wanton lust. Jaimee bit her lip to keep from laughing.

"I'm doing good."

"Are you sure you're all right? Maybe you should spend a couple of weeks with Jason and I. We have the room and I don't think you should be alone so much."

Jaimee rolled her eyes. She wished her mom lived in some other state, country maybe. "No, I'm fine."

"You know, I still think you should take a hiatus from school, Jaimee. Take some time to deal with your grief. You haven't let yourself grieve."

"I seriously doubt that lying around on my butt for weeks on end will help me with my grief." Sometimes it seemed her mother wouldn't be happy unless she was dressed in sackcloth and ashes, wailing in misery.

"Well you could go to one of those nice health spas where they help you lose weight and get fit..."

"I'm a member of a health club."

"No, no, I mean one where you go and they re-teach you how to eat less and that sort of thing."

"I promise I'm fine. Keeping my routine is the best thing for me." Jaimee was beginning to feel the frustration well up.

"Perhaps you're right. Well, I'll come over and spend the night and we can talk more about how you're feeling. I'm sure Jason won't mind."

Anxiety started to gnaw at her insides. "No, Momma. It's a school night and I have some work to do. Really, I'm doing fine." She hated the way her mother spoke, the way she acted, as if she had a corncob up her butt.

"I'll be over in an hour, we'll have some tea."

"No..."

"Jaimee, I want to talk to you about some things. I'm concerned about your future, and I know you get angry when I mention it. However, I can't just stand by and not say anything. You're my baby, you'll always be my baby and you know I worry about you." She paused for effect, softening her voice. Jaimee wanted to throw the phone across the room. "Now you know, you and Brent didn't eat properly. That's why he had a heart attack. And, as his wife, it's partly your responsibility, Jaimee. I told you time and time again that you should make out low-fat menus and follow them. Now with your weight and added stress...well...I'm just concerned that you're the next in line for a heart attack."

Taking deep breath, Jaimee struggled to control her need to scream. Why, why did her mother have this effect on her? Jamiee loved her and yet sometimes the hate was palpable. "I've lost some. I've been going to the gym."

"Yes, I know, and I'm so proud of you. But you really need to start eating low fat too. We'll make out some menus together."

Rubbing at the tension in her neck, Jaimee clenched her teeth until her jaw hurt. Karen Bradley, now Covington, had a way of making her daughter want to bang her head against a brick wall. "Momma, I promise you I'm fine. I'm active. I even go out. As a matter of fact I have plans to go out weekend after next. I'm just really busy. You and I will get together later, okay?" Switching the phone to the other ear she grabbed her day planner off the dresser and walked down the hall to her office.

"Really? With someone from school?" Karen gasped. "On a date?"

Ha! She had totally skipped the dating stage and went straight to the foreplay. "No, Mother. With Maxine." The irritation in her voice didn't seem to faze her mother.

Karen sighed. "You know Dwayne is really interested in you. He's a good man and he loves the Lord. You should get to know him."

"I'm not interested in Dwayne," Jaimee said tersely. Dwayne Evans was a sweet guy. He was like Brent in a lot of ways: gracious, accommodating, respectful, her mother's choice for her. Nothing like Lucas, who was wild, mysterious, demanding and bold. Her mother would hate him. But Lucas wasn't interested in something so innocuous as dating. A shiver of excitement slithered up her spine. She squeezed her eyes shut and tried to force the memory of Lucas's mouth and hands and the rest of him from her overheated thoughts.

"Okay, okay, maybe it is a bit soon to start dating anyway."

So I guess getting finger fucked in a health club is totally out, huh? she thought cynically.

Karen's sigh of disgust warned Jaimee of what was to come next. "You know, Maxine is not a good friend for you, Jaimee."

"I don't agree." Feeling like she was fifteen again, she put a hand on her hip, scanning her office for her tote. She could have sworn she left it in the desk chair. She was almost positive she didn't take it to school.

"She drinks too much, she goes to bars and she's out with a

different man every week. You're not out drinking, going to bars are you? What could you two possibly have in common?"

We both think you're a self-righteous prude who enjoys judging others so you can feel better about yourself. "You don't know anything about Maxine, Mom," she said tightly, avoiding the question about the bar. Finally she found the tote under the desk leaning against the CPU cabinet. "Besides, it's really not up to you who I befriend."

"Hrumph. Well, where do you plan to go?"

Jaimee knew what her mother would say if she knew they were talking about going dancing or something like that. She would tell her that it was disgraceful for her to go to an establishment that sold liquor and what would her sainted grandfather have said if he were still alive, oh he'd be so disappointed. And on top of it all, what if Jesus came back and found her in a bar? Why, it would be like finding a sheep in a pig pen. Jaimee just didn't have the wherewithal to stand it tonight, so she lied. "To the movies, or shopping I guess."

"Well, good luck finding anything worth seeing. Most movies are just filth."

"Yeah, I know." Distracted now, she muttered. She could have sworn she set her case in the chair. "Look I have to go. I have work to get done for school tomorrow. I'll talk to you later, okay?"

"All right, Jaimee, be careful."

"I will, I love you."

"Okay, goodbye."

"Mondays suck." Jaimee grumbled as she filed through the paperwork in her tote looking for the essays she should have graded over the weekend. Finally giving up, she set the tote on the floor and sat down, scowling at it. They were there in the tote, she was sure of it. Now they were gone. She stared blankly at her desk, trying to mentally retrace her steps when the stack of papers she was looking for caught her eye. They were haphazardly tossed on her desk.

Confused, she snatched them up and arranged them neatly. It didn't make sense, she couldn't remember taking them out of the tote or moving the tote from the chair to the floor, but evidently she had. The doorbell rang, disrupting her train of thought.

Taking a deep breath, she shook the feeling of foreboding and headed down the stairs.

"Hey, Jaimee."

The last person she expected, or wanted to see, ever again was Ronald Marshall. Whether it was because she was caught off guard by his appearance or her bewilderment over her apparent memory loss she didn't know, but Ron brushed past her without an invitation or much effort at all on his part. She doubted very seriously she could physically stop him from coming in anyway. He was a broad, bulky man, about six feet tall, and not particularly attractive. The overpowering cloud of cologne he wore stung her nose. He kept his light brown hair cut short and wore a moustache that curled around his top lip.

"What do you need, Ron?" she asked as he walked into her home and scanned her small living room/dining room combination with humorous disdain.

"Just checkin' on ya, babe." He smirked. "Can't a guy check on a friend?"

She closed the door reluctantly but kept her distance, lingering at the staircase. The hairs on the back of her neck prickled in warning. Ronald wasn't a threat as much as he was a major irritant. Just get rid of him, she told herself, the sooner the better. "Well, I'm fine. Like I told you on the phone."

He let his gaze travel her body. The smile that curved his full lips didn't hide the disdain in his eyes. "You've lost weight, a bit more and you'll be lookin' pretty good."

No doubt he believed he'd complimented her, and any other time she would have rolled her eyes at him, but she was beginning to feel more and more nervous. She was dressed in the new pink tank top and satin lounge pants she'd bought Saturday on a whim. Now she wished she'd just stayed completely covered and secure in her baggy T-shirts and sweats.

"I look fine now. What do you want, Ronald?" She didn't bother to hide her irritation.

His faux smile faltered only slightly but the glitter of malice remained in his eyes. "Now, Jaimee. I'm really just seeing after you."

"Unnecessary." She shook her head. "I'm perfectly capable of seeing after myself."

He glared at her. "A single woman, living all by herself. It's not like you have many friends hanging around or checking in on you, Jaimee. A lot can happen and no one would be the wiser."

Why did she feel like he'd just threatened her? What reason would he have to want to be in her life anyway? He made it clear every chance he could that he found her quite unattractive. And just how did he know how many friends she had? Angry and puzzled, Jaimee was all the more anxious to get rid of him.

She scowled back at him. "I'll take that chance. What happens or doesn't happen to me is not your responsibility or concern." She went to show him out when his hand gripped her shoulder and turned her around to face him. Could she take him down if she needed to? She braced herself, praying to God she wouldn't have to find out.

"Don't be rude. It's not attractive." His hand slid up and down her naked arms.

Jaimee made an expression of disgust and jerked away from him. "When did I ever give you the impression I was attempting to attract you?"

He clenched and unclenched his fist at his side. She steeled herself, preparing for the blow. Instead he pretended to laugh it off.

"Don't take everything so seriously. You come across that day planner I was tellin' you about earlier?" He took a step toward her.

Refusing to retreat, Jaimee stood her ground. "I'd forgotten all about that." And she had. Alice never returned her call. That wasn't like her at all. Jaimee frowned. "Why are you interested in it?"

Ron's eyes narrowed. "There were some contacts Brent had that we need at the office."

Oh yeah, he was pissed. The smartest thing to do was to be agreeable and get him the hell out of her house, but she refused to be a wimp. He was lying and she wanted to know why. What was going on?

"Brent was in accounting. Why would he have contacts you didn't have?"

He took another step closer so that she had no choice but to step back. Ron scowled, all pretense gone. "Don't be a bitch, Jaimee," he spat.

Before he could complete his sentence or action, before she had time to shake off the initial shock and react, the doorbell rang. How ironic. Someone had come by for one reason or another, proof that he was wrong about her not having friends. Wasn't it? Jaimee glared up at him and stepped around him, sending a silent prayer that it was Max or Mrs. Stanley from next door and not a kid fundraising or a rep for *The Tennessean* wanting her to take the paper. It didn't matter really, anyone that would help her get rid of Ron would be a blessing.

Lucas leaned against the doorframe, filling her doorway. The look on his face sent a shudder through her body, more of those erotic memories racing through her mind. The muscle in his jaw flexed in warning as he looked past her. His warm brown eyes looked more like coffee-colored alabaster. They glittered hard and cold. Great, out of the frying pan into the fire.

He looked like a savage warrior come to devastate and destroy all who would try to impede his mission, a warrior in a tight green T-shirt and snug jeans riding low on his hips. His hair was down, flowing in waves over his shoulders to the middle of his back. Then he looked down at her and the rage in his expression was gone. His eyes warmed. She didn't have a chance to interpret it before he lightly touched her cheek, winked at her and chased every coherent thought from her brain.

"Hey, James," he said, intently searching her face. "I don't have my cable connected yet. Would you mind if I camped on your couch for a couple of hours?"

She blinked up at him. James? Did he call her James? When did they become best buds? At some point in the day she must have shifted into an alternate universe because everything was off kilter. "Huh?"

"Tennessee and Washington play tonight." His brows knit together at her blank expression.

Finally she got it. "Oh...Monday night football." He wasn't there for her. Duh. He'd probably already forgotten about the escapade at the gym. She hadn't; she didn't think she ever would. It didn't matter, she told herself, and whatever Ron had been about to do next had been thwarted. She made a mental note to look into self-defense lessons—karate, something, anything.

"I'll buy dinner. How about pizza?" He grinned and shrugged and looked so sexy she might start drooling. Good Lord, when had she become so shallow? Maybe she was coming down with something, wasn't PMS...maybe she had early onset menopause. That would explain why she was so damn horny for a guy she barely knew. Later, she'd figure it out later. Right now she was just glad he was here. As much as she hated to admit it, Ron was beginning to scare her.

"No, that's not necessary. Come on in." He seemed to take up all the space and she could swear she felt heat radiating from his big body.

"Yeah, I think pizza is a no-no for Jaimee these days." Ron chuckled.

Standing behind Lucas, she could see the tension in him. His big body was rigid, prepared to fight, almost territorial. Nah, that was ridiculous and she better get those kinds of ideas out of her head before she turned into a simpering fool.

She stepped around him. "Uh, this is Ronald Marshall. He and my late husband, Brent, were associates," she explained. Then, turning to

Lucas, she did a double take. There. That look was there in his eyes again. There was the promise of a painful death in that look.

Lucas's arm snaked around her waist faster than she could register the movement. His hand spanned her hip as he pulled her to his side. A thrill danced through her and though she should probably move away she was so thankful for the security of his presence, his protection, she couldn't make herself. Instead she bit her bottom lip and took a deep breath before continuing her introductions. "Ron, this is Lucas...ah..."

"Grayson," he said firmly.

"Lucas Grayson...he's my neighbor."

Chapter Eleven

The smug motherfucker standing there smirking at Jaimee had no idea how close he was to becoming a grease spot on her fine hardwood floor. Lucas had been listening in when Jaimee answered the door. He couldn't take a chance on the bastard being smart enough not to touch her.

"The T.V. is in the entertainment center, just open those doors. Make yourself at home," she said quietly, gesturing toward the living room. Though he suspected it had more to do with anger than fear, she was still shaking and he didn't want to let go. But he did, giving her hip a pat as he walked past Ron into the living room.

Jaimee's living room and dining room combo was warm and inviting. He really did envy her the oversized, overstuffed sofa that divided the rooms and the matching chair the sat against the left wall. Various houseplants sat and hung around. Nice, very nice. It was the sliding glass door to the right of him that opened onto a small bare patio that made him uneasy. It provided too easy an access.

Crossing the room to the large entertainment cabinet , he opened the doors that hid an impressive widescreen television. Picking up the remote, Lucas turned on the set and found the channel then sat and nearly sighed at the comfort of the sofa.

"Wow! Nice equipment, James!" They stood not twenty feet behind him but without turning around he shouted with excitement for effect. "Hot damn, surround sound and everything."

"Uh...thank you. It was a gift from my husband." Jaimee's soft laugh had him looking over his shoulder. "Actually it was more for my husband. The T.V. that is. The surround sound is great for music, that's my thing."

Music was her thing. She had music playing almost constantly. Rock mostly...all kinds of rock. He'd learned Jaimee was fond of a driving beat. Lucas caught her gaze and gave her a sexy wink. "I bet Berry White and Tina Turner would sound amazing on this system," he said, reminding her of their encounter at the spa. He waited, watching her eyes widen and her cheeks flush before turning back to the game he would be interested in if he weren't otherwise occupied.

"To answer your question, we had a computer system crash a couple of weeks ago and lost some contact information," Ron said sharply.

Bullshit. A company that size would back up nightly.

"I'm sorry, Ron, I haven't found the day planner."

"You need to understand how very important it is that we find it, Jaimee." *Yeah, Ronnie, and just how far would you go to get your hands on that day planner?*

"I understand perfectly," Jaimee pulled the door open. "Goodbye, Ronald."

There was a pause. "Listen, why don't you come to dinner some time? Sandy and I would love to have you over..."

"No." Lucas tensed at the pause and was about to get up when she continued. "Look, Ron, maybe you and Brent were friends. I just tagged along. We both know that. So you and Sandy are not obligated to try and be friendly to me."

"Fine. That's not how we feel about you but fine. Just let me know if you find the day planner."

"Goodbye, Ronald." She spoke with impatience, cutting off any further discussion, as if she were dealing with an insubordinate child.

When he heard the closing of the door he turned on the sofa and watched her standing just outside the room.

"You okay?"

"Sure." She shrugged without looking up. She looked so pretty, so innocent, her arms crossed over her stomach, frowning down at her sexy little bare toes.

"I overheard. Sorry to eavesdrop, it was kinda hard not to. Jaimee, is that guy giving you a hard time?"

Taking a deep breath, she smiled bleakly. "It's fine, I'm fine."

But it wasn't fine. Even without having the privilege of listening in on her life he knew her emotions were in turmoil by her troubled expression. She didn't hide her emotions well. She was open, sincere, wholesome and watching her stand there looking so lost and vulnerable made him feel fiercely protective and achingly hard. He wanted, needed, to be a part of her, desperate for a taste of her sweet innocence.

Whether it was that unnerving conversation with her mother, Marshall or memories of Turner that had her looking so fragile didn't seem to matter anymore. Lucas wanted to make it go away. Get her focused on him and the pleasure he could give her. He ached to touch her, hold her, make her forget, make her feel. A faint conscious thought in the back of his brain warned him to ignore his rampant libido. Now wasn't the time, she was too defenseless. Just watch the damn game, he told himself, go home and jack off. But it was too late, he'd made his choice when he'd sprinted across the road to her rescue. There was no way he'd leave her tonight.

"Jaimee," he said without smiling. Her head snapped up and she looked at him as though she forgot he was there. "Come here."

She hesitated and he knew she was warring with herself, her own desire. "No. I have work to do. But, you're welcome to watch the T.V. as long as you like."

"I said come here. If you don't, I'll come there."

She shook her head then paused, considering his threat. "Who's winning?" she asked weakly, foolishly thinking she could change his agenda.

"The game? Tennessee." He stood without taking his eyes off her. "This between us? I am."

"Lucas..." Again she shook her head. So nervous, he could see her trembling as he quickly walked toward her but she didn't back away. A gasp escaped her lips when he grabbed her around the waist and pulled her hard against him. Taking what he wanted, his hands moved down to cup her ass. Instantly he got lost in the feel of her, her softness. So incredibly soft, he loved the feel of her satiny skin under his fingers, his mouth. He wanted to touch every inch of her, the slope of her hip, and God help him, her breasts were so full, firm and responsive. But it was her moan of surrender, her sweet mouth opening to him, her tongue dipping shyly past his lips that sent him over the edge of reason.

It was wrong, but she just couldn't resist it anymore. To push him away now would hurt more than she could bear and what did she have to lose? She was no virgin, her husband was dead and she was so lonely she ached with it. God knew that. He had to understand that. Her desire for Lucas was so strong from the moment she'd met him. It was almost a relief to feel his hard body pressed against hers. She nearly sobbed. It seemed as though she'd been bound in a bleak world, void of touch, void of warmth and he was offering her fire. Nothing else seemed to matter. Nothing but the feel of Lucas, strong and solid, holding her, making her whole body pulse with pleasure at the artful way he was kissing her.

Somewhere in the back of her mind she knew if she had any sense or decency at all she should push him away, but she just didn't care about right or wrong anymore. She wasn't sure she could deny him now even if she wanted to. She made her decision and refused to allow herself to think about what she should do and go with what she wanted. Flooded with sensation, wonder and incredible need, she ignored her fear and let herself be swept away. She didn't care what giving in made her anymore.

Giving in, giving herself up to overwhelming need, she pressed closer. Her hands fisted in his hair as she tilted her head to give him better access and boldly tasted him, sweeping her tongue just past his lips to touch his. His groan rumbled through her and she didn't have time to analyze what it meant before he lifted her into his arms and mounted the steps. Her heart stuttered as she pulled her mouth away and stared at him. Regardless of how much weight she'd lost she was still a big woman and definitely not an easy burden to bear. Well, shouldn't have been, but Lucas carried her as if she weighed nothing.

"Lucas," she murmured. "I'm too ..."

What she saw in his eyes kept her from finishing her thought. The muscle in his jaw ticked and there was fire in his eyes. He looked savage, hungry, adamant. He wanted her as badly as she wanted him and suddenly it didn't matter. She forgot what she was going to argue about anyway as he sat her on her bed, once again his mouth taking possession of hers. He was giving her no time to consider what was going to happen. Only salacious, unrelenting sensation ruled her conscious thought.

Hot, his hands were so hot and urgent as they roughly ran up her sides, pulling her tank top over her head. His teeth grazed the sensitive skin below her earlobe, as he easily released the front clasp of her bra and slid it off her shoulders, tossing it aside. With a quick flick of his wrist he untied the drawstring of her lounge pants with one hand. The other cupped her breast. His thumb brushed over her nipple and she hissed at the sharp ache as her vagina contracted in response. His warm breath feathered over her throat, his lips nipped and sucked, making her wild with desire. She clutched at his shirt wanting to feel his skin, now.

He pulled away and she whimpered in protest. Grasping the material at her hips, he yanked them all the way down, along with her panties, and tossed them behind him. Suddenly flustered, she watched nervously as he stood, kicking off his shoes, his sultry gaze perusing her naked body. The light was still on. He could see everything. She could just imagine what he must be thinking with her round flabby tummy, wide hips...and oh God, the cellulite. Afraid of what she'd see in his eyes she didn't look up at him.

"Turn the light off," she whispered. "Please."

"Look at me." He waited until she obeyed his hoarse command then frowned down at her and shook his head. Embarrassed, she quickly crawled backward onto the bed and started to wrap her arms around her legs. Before she could succeed, his hand shot out, grasped her ankle and yanked her back down.

Lying there, breathless with shock, sprawled out and exposed, he bent over her until his very regal nose was mere inches from her own. "Don't do that again. Don't ever try and hide from me again." His eyes were incredibly dark, dilated, hungry, and he meant business. There was no playful glint, only intent and desire. Moisture gathered between her thighs in response. "I want to watch your beautiful face when you come."

Her heart thudded against her breastbone as she looked up at him, captivated by his words. She went to shake her head. "I..." Before she could finish her thought his mouth covered hers, his tongue swept over hers then gently sucked her bottom lip as he braced himself over her with one hand, the other splayed possessively over her stomach, his thumb drawing slow deliberate circles right above her mound. All coherent thought fled from her mind. Whatever it was she had been about to say didn't matter anymore.

She rose up to kiss him back, apprehensively meeting his tongue with her own. She had no clue if what she was doing was arousing Lucas or turning him off. She hadn't kissed this way since she'd married and the few times she had before had been clumsy and less than satisfactory. But her sexual insecurities were quickly being consumed in the heat of her passion. She didn't care if she was doing it right anymore or not. She just wanted to be connected, to taste more of him, to feel the weight of his body covering her, filling her.

A whimper of need bubbled up from deep inside her and she tore at his shirt. He caught her arms and held them down on either side of her head, his knee pushing her thighs apart as he gazed down at her.

"Hold still," he commanded hoarsely before he released her wrists and pulled his T-shirt over his head.

Fascinated with everything about his body, she reached out and touched him. She held her breath as she flattened her hand against his hard stomach. The muscles rippled under her touch as she explored higher until she reached his nipples. Her fingertips circled the warm gold hoops. The way his nipples puckered, his sharp intake of breath, the way he closed his eyes and clenched his teeth as she gently tugged at the hoops thrilled her. It made her feel powerful and sexy.

That intriguing muscle in his jaw pulsed. "Wait, dammit," he growled. Trapping her hands in his, he pressed them down on the bed on either side of her. To know her touch aroused him, that she caused that reaction in him, overwhelmed her and heightened her own arousal. Those strong hands were moving over her, branding her body, infusing her with his heat as his mouth covered hers. She threaded her fingers through his hair and kissed him back, taking whatever he had to offer her.

The rough denim rasping against her inner thighs made her breath catch in her throat. His thigh lay heavy against her mound. Suddenly aware of how perilously close she was to her climax, Jaimee froze. On fire and flooded with arousal her pussy throbbed in time with her heartbeat. Fiery pulses of sensations warned her that just a little pressure, a brush would send her careening over the edge. No, no, no, this wasn't gonna happen this way. She wouldn't allow it. Frustrated, she broke the kiss reluctantly and turned her head away, panting for breath. She wanted him inside her when she came, she needed him inside her.

"What is it, baby?" Lucas murmured against her neck. Pleasure radiated through her and she closed her eyes shut tight.

"Stop," she whimpered. "Please. Just, don't move."

His body went rigid, his hands left her body and he cautiously moved away from her a fraction. Instantly, she missed the sultry heat of his chest pressed against hers. He waited until she turned back and looked up at him.

"Did I hurt you?" he asked softly, his brows knit together in concern.

She shook her head and bit her kiss-swollen lip. Finally she got the nerve to meet his gaze. "I'm...um...I'm almost there and I don't want to yet."

His blank expression made her think he didn't understand what she was trying to tell him. She took a deep breath, winced and tried again. "If I climax now then it will be over and I wanted—"

"It won't be over." He grinned slowly. "Don't hold back, sweetness. I plan on making you come..." He leaned down and nipped at her nipple as he slipped his hand between their bodies. His fingers brushed over her wet, swollen pussy. "...And come... mmm... You're blazing hot, Jaimee," he whispered against the other nipple, flicking it with his tongue as he parted the sensitive folds.

One finger slid inside her spasming sheath as his thumb moved up, pressing, rubbing over her clit. She clutched the quilt in her fist and arched against his hand as her world shattered and her body was consumed in the fire of her orgasm. His lips captured hers, swallowing her helpless cries as he drove her on. His tongue swept the sensitive interior of her mouth as he stroked the slick muscled walls of her sheath. Although Lucas let up on the pressure he didn't stop caressing her even as the sensations subsided.

"Lucas." Jaimee shuddered and clutched Lucas's arm as the softening pleasure became a delicious ache that was very quickly sharpening under his continued stimulation. Disappointment was quickly clouding the delicious hum of satisfaction. It was too much, too sensitive and she hissed each time his fingers grazed over her inflamed clit. "Stop." She writhed, pleading with him.

"No," he murmured against the underside of her breast then continued his trek down her body. His hair skimmed over her, a cool contrast to the rest of him.

"But it hurts." She moaned, trying to wriggle away from his caressing fingers. It did hurt in a way, but in a sharp, intense blend of pleasure and pain that had her shying away. She would have clenched her thighs shut if his body wasn't firmly planted between them.

"It's a good pain." He grinned up at her from her stomach and nipped the top of her navel just as his fingers grazed her clit. Jaimee whimpered and rolled her lips inward as fire sizzled over her flesh, building her arousal.

"Relax, quit fighting it."

She tried to do as he said but the shards of sensation shooting relentlessly through her were making her crazy. It was happening. She could feel her body tightening, the incredible tension mounting. Panting with each assault that pushed her desire higher, she blinked down at him in shock. It was then she noticed that Lucas knelt at the end of her bed and had settled between her thighs, his fingers opening her to his view, sliding over her sodden flesh.

"You're so soft, here. So pretty, so incredibly hot and wet."

"Lucas," she whispered. If he got grossed out now she'd die. She was wet, too wet, and so swollen.

"I'm going to enjoy making you come, Jaimee. And when you think there's no way you can..." He paused, his lips curving into a mischievous smile. "I'll make you come again."

Jaimee's eyes widened as Lucas bent his head and flattened his hot tongue against her tender flesh and drew it up to flick over her clit. Then there was nothing at all but the bright starbursts of pleasure exploding behind her eyelids.

"Mmm, sweet," he whispered against her ultra-sensitive flesh, overwhelming her. Gritting her teeth, she tried to close her thighs but Lucas only lifted her hips, pressing them further apart, opening her even more to his feasting. His teeth nipped at the lips of her pussy, his tongue swirled in a figure eight around her clit, down, cross, around her entrance, up...

"Oh God, Lucas please," Jaimee cried, feeling her body tighten, the need for release growing stronger and stronger.

Vibrations built on her mounting arousal as Lucas groaned, his mouth, his tongue, his lips moved with skill, drawing out her pleasure. She sucked in air through her teeth at the delicious sensation as he eased two fingers inside her, stretching, stroking the clenching walls of her sheath.

"Incredible," he murmured against her pussy before his lips closed over her throbbing clit, drawing it between his lips and sucking on it gently.

He drew harder on her clit and curled his fingers upward, stroking firmly, rhythmically over what must be her G-spot. The raw pleasure of it was intense. The second orgasm started as a hard molten knot, growing, throbbing at the very core of her. The fury of it broke free and it expanded, gaining power as it went. It washed over her and every cell in her body seemed to respond, screaming in pleasure. As it began to subside and she could breathe again the sensitivity was even worse than before. Once again she tried to push Lucas away.

Without lifting his head from her, he caught her wrists and held her still as he continued to use his tongue, his lips, his teeth and even his nose. Jaimee moaned and fought, trying to move up the bed, away from the delicious torment she was sure she couldn't stand much more of. With a growl of warning that vibrated against her sensitive flesh, he ravaged her like a man starving. Her body trembled; bucked with such euphoric sensations she didn't think she could endure it anymore.

Chapter Twelve

When he finally released her, she lay there weak and sweaty. Her body was still on fire and quaking from the aftershocks. Lucas kissed her hip, her stomach, the valley between her breasts.

"I could get addicted to the taste of you."

Too stunned by her experience to say anything, she looked up into his mahogany eyes and tried to sort out the myriad of confusing and complicated emotions that assailed her. As his lips met hers she could taste herself on him. It shocked her even more that she found the scent, the taste of her own musky arousal incredibly erotic.

Once her mother told her that oral sex was one step over the line into perversion and that if she ever practiced such an act, God would "turn her over to a reprobate mind". She never really believed it but was never faced with the issue anyway. Now that she'd experienced it, for the first time in her thirty-two years, the idea was beyond ridiculous. It was, in fact, the most intimate thing she'd ever experienced. Ever.

Watching her, Lucas backed away and stood. At first she was sure he was going to leave her. She held her breath, clenched her hands to her sides to keep from pulling him back and prayed that he would stay. Even though she'd had her very first multiple orgasm, something she believed she was incapable of, her body still hummed for more. She was desperate to feel the hard, unyielding weight of him pressing down on her, covering her.

Relief flooded through her as he pushed his jeans down and stepped out of them. That relief was short-lived as her eyes dropped to his very substantial erection. She doubted he would be considered freakishly huge but she knew what her body was capable of taking. Watching his cock standing up long and thick and hard as steel she wasn't feeling confident about her abilities at all. Her reaction was probably not what he was expecting but she couldn't help it. Sure, she knew he was well endowed from the feel of him pressing against her through his jeans. But uninhibited, he looked much larger than she'd imagined.

"Jaimee?" His voice was husky with need, his brows furrowed in concern.

Excitement and apprehension were befuddling her. What if she couldn't take it all? What if she was too...short? What if she disappointed him? Maybe it would be best if they stopped now. No, she couldn't send him away in his present condition. That would have to be painful for him. Maybe he'd be somewhat satisfied even if she couldn't accommodate all of him. She chewed her bottom lip nervously and lifted her gaze to his.

He rose over her and once again captured her wrists, his thigh pressed against her pussy. She closed her eyes tight against the newly flourishing heat.

"Look at me," he said roughly.

She lifted her lids and looked into his eyes. Dark velvet heat. Her heart skipped a beat at the raw desire in them.

"Lucas, I've only been with one man." She rushed to explain before he had a chance to speak. "He wasn't...well, it was..." As full-on panic took hold of her she looked up at him, pleading for him to understand. It was so damn hard to form a rational thought when her body was screaming for more of his touch. "Look, I'm just not sure we can. I mean I'm not sure I was made to take all you have to give," she finished with frustration, feeling utterly idiotic.

He didn't smile or laugh at her; which was a relief, until he began to kiss her. Pulling her arms up over her head, his mouth left a heated trail across her jaw, down her throat. No, he didn't find her humorous. Maybe he was going to ignore her altogether.

"Lucas." She moaned and he continued to ignore her as he cuffed both wrists in one hand, freeing the other to lift and mold her breast. His shaft lay hot and hard against her thigh. She wanted to feel him slide inside. At the same time she was apprehensive he wouldn't fit comfortably. The truth was, Brent hadn't been large at all and he'd had trouble maintaining an erection so he was never very hard and still he'd had enough to satisfy her. Hadn't he?

"Jaimee, you were made for a lot more than this." His voice was quiet, deep and dark. It held authority that sent hot shivers blazing up her spine. "I intend to spend a long, long time proving it to you."

Derailing her train of thought completely, Lucas kissed along the inside slope of her breast as he released her wrists. Ever-increasing arousal expanded through her. His hands moved over her, his mouth closed over her nipples, sucking, laving the stiff peaks like a starving man. Her hands fisted in his hair, holding him closer as she arched against him.

"Lucas." She wrapped one leg around his thigh. Suddenly eager for him, she groaned. "Just do it, I need you now. I don't care if it hurts," she breathed. "I want—"

"Dammit, Jaimee, listen to me," he growled harshly. When she looked up at him she stilled at the savage lust in his expression. It thrilled her that she inspired so much want in him. The heat, the aggression in his eyes amplified all she was feeling. "I won't hurt you. I want your pleasure. I need it as much as I need my own. But we're going to do this my way. You're just going to have to trust me."

With crystal blue eyes, wide and bright with arousal, Jaimee gazed up at him and nodded. To lessen the sharpness of his tone he smoothed her hair back from her face and kissed her soft mouth. God, her skin, her mouth, her pretty pussy, everything about her was so soft, so inviting. She was such a sweet thing he was going to find it hard to ever leave her alone again.

There was no sense in denying that her reaction to the sight of his erection did amazing things for his masculine pride. It was one of those built-in male flaws, he guessed. Her amazement, mingled with her unmistakable lust, was incredibly provocative. Not that he needed his desire provoked. The taste and feel of her sweet body, the sound of her breathless cries of pleasure and her screams of ecstasy were enough to drive him mad. The way his cock ached to drive deep inside her had him gritting his teeth. She was much tighter than he'd expected her to be so he had no choice but to take it slow, allow her body to acclimate to him.

Jaimee's hands smoothed over his back, holding him closer. "You feel so good," she murmured against his lips as she shifted, arching her back. He tensed, his breath hissed through clenched teeth.

"Holy hell," he groaned. "Baby, be still. Don't move."

She wasn't listening. The little wildcat was nipping at his throat, his shoulder; her eager little hands were gripping his ass for all she was worth. As a desperate act to save his sanity he reached behind him, caught her wrists and pinned them down on either side of her head. He kissed her hard, thrust his tongue between her lips and swallowed her frustrated whimper. God she tasted so good.

"More," she groaned and lifted her hips, taking him inside.

He growled in warning as he pushed deeper inside her. Jaimee cried out and threw her head back as the tight walls of her channel convulsed, expanding to accommodate him. Her thighs tightened on his hips, her soft supple breasts pressed against his chest.

"Goddammit, Jaimee." His cock was throbbing, his body engulfed in pleasure and all he wanted to do was thrust hard and deep inside her. No, he shook his head; he had to give her body time to adjust, to accept him.

"Don't stop." She looked up at him, her eyes intense with pleasure and a depth of emotion he wasn't prepared for. Everything he'd ever wanted reflected back at him from Jaimee's beautiful cerulean eyes.

Fire coursed through her blood and her heart skipped several beats as she held Lucas's hot cinnamon gaze. It was a smoldering, intense gaze, his jaw set. Everything about him was so hard; it was amazing to her and incredibly arousing. Afraid to move, to break the spell, she stilled beneath him. Without looking away he withdrew, just a fraction and thrust deeper. She held her breath as the pleasure shuddered through her.

"Wrap your legs around me." It was a command, low and hoarse. She blinked up at him as she quickly did as he asked. Watching her, he released her wrists and brushed the damp hair from her face as he pushed deeper inside.

"Lucas," she whimpered, her breath coming in pants. The pleasure was so sharp, so close to shattering, she couldn't stand any more.

"Hold on to me." He lifted her hips and slid a pillow beneath them. Sweat beaded across his forehead and bathed his body in a slick sheen. Taking his face in her hands, she pulled him to her and kissed him with all the passion she could convey. She wanted him to know what he did to her, needed for him to feel it.

A strangled gasp escaped her throat as he gripped her hips and thrust into her fully. Her nails bit into his back and her legs tightened around his hips. Immersed in the erotic pulse of pleasure she cried out, her hips bucked to meet each soul-shattering thrust.

She clung to him, sinking her short nails into his back. He bared his teeth as he rammed against her, faster, harder. It was all so overwhelmingly incredible. She watched his face, trying to memorize his expression, the sound, the scent of this unbelievable moment. His eyes, so dark, unrelenting and intent locked with hers and she couldn't lower her lids if she wanted to.

His head fell back with a roar of pleasure just as an orgasm crested and took her breath away. All coherent thought spun away as she arched upward and cried out. Her body yielded to the overpowering euphoria of Lucas's cock pumping deep, filling her ultra-sensitive pussy with his hot seed.

As his own climax subsided, Lucas flipped onto his back, taking Jaimee with him. She collapsed on top of him. His shaft was still seated firmly inside her though it had relaxed some. Still, the sensation of being filled and so sensitive was absolutely wonderful. It took her a few moments to realize she was draped over him and how exposed she was. Lying down was one thing, gravity was in her favor then; her stomach seemed flatter, her breasts seemed perkier. It was obvious to her at this point that he was attracted to her but she didn't want to take chances. If there was any disapproval in his expression now it would hurt too much. And worse, what if he started instructing her on how she could improve herself? Well, if he did that she'd have to kill him.

Hoping to avoid the risk of any of that, she pushed herself up to roll off him. His cock flexed, thickened inside her once again. He grasped her hips and wouldn't let her move. "Fuck," he swore softly. "Be still."

She hissed at the aching ripples that radiated from the core of her but she was sure if she had another orgasm she'd die from it. Amazed she'd had more than one climax in the first place it further confounded her as to how easily Lucas had made her come.

"Lucas," she murmured against his throat. He smelled so good, so male, she couldn't help but nuzzle him, taste, just a little. She let her tongue stroke over his Adam's apple.

"Hmm?" His voice was hoarse, deep and sexy. It vibrated through her and her body erupted with little after tremors.

"If you make me come again, I think something in my mind will snap and you'll leave me a drooling idiot for the rest of my life."

Even his low chuckle was sensuous. He moved inside her and his hands slid down to cup her ass. Fresh desire welled from her core and radiated through her.

"I'm serious, Lucas," she breathed, shuddering against him as his fingers caressed the crease of her ass and lower to circle the taut flesh where they connected. "Mmm, no, no, I can't, you can't..."

"I love it when you challenge me." He groaned, pushing her up as he tilted his hips and pressed deeper inside her.

Fully erect and fully encased inside her he moved slowly, rotating his hips and he withdrew and drove her higher. Realizing her exposure she tried to cover herself and lean down against him. The sharp sting of Lucas's hand striking her ass had her jaw dropping. Pleasure spiked through her, searing her pussy, and tiny little vibrations feathered over her clit. Even her nipples tingled. She blinked down at him, gasping for breath amid the little earthquake the swat had caused.

"You hit me."

"I smacked your ass. I told you never to try and hide from me again." His tone was gruff. Frowning up at her, his hands smoothed over her hips and up her back. "I love to look at you. You're beautiful," he murmured as he began to move, his shaft slowly moving inside her again.

She would have been thoroughly pissed off if she wasn't so completely turned on. It was astonishing how powerfully erotic the act had been. Biting her lip, she lifted herself away from him. She wasn't like that, was she? The kind of girl who liked to have her ass smacked? She shuddered as his thumbs grazed over her nipples. But damn if she didn't want to disobey again. Spirals of sensation pushed the concern from her mind. Lucas cupped her breasts, molding and kneading them as he moved slow and steady inside her again.

She swore she could feel every pulsing vein in his shaft, the ridge of his thick round head as it grazed the over-sensitive walls of her vagina. Soft cries escaped the back of her throat with each slide of his shaft, each rotation of his hips as he ground his pelvis against hers.

Her fingers glided over his body until they found his nipple rings and tugged gently. His breath hissed through his teeth. His hips thrust hard against her as his fingers gripped her breasts tighter.

"Did I hurt you?" Jaimee's voice sounded breathy, weak. Frowning down at him, her palms flattened over his nipples. They were like hard beads against her palm and for some reason that was highly satisfying to her.

"Hell no," he croaked and she tugged again.

At the same time he pinched her nipples hard in return, rolling them between his fingers and thumbs. Pain wasn't always a bad thing she was learning. Not wanting to analyze what that meant, what she'd always believed about herself, she focused on the feel of Lucas's shaft stroking the walls of her sheath.

Lucas's hands left her breasts and slid down her stomach. For a moment she panicked as his hands lingered at her navel, her rounded belly.

"You feel so good," he groaned. "So soft, so perfect."

Her breath caught in her throat at his words. But before she could respond, his long fingers slid through the damp curls of her mound and delved inside the swollen folds of her pussy to glide over clit. She bucked against him, crying out at the pain/pleasure his touch caused her. He was driving her crazy with his slow withdraw, slide and rotating grind.

"Don't, Lucas. It's too much."

Ignoring her, his fingers circled the knot of over-stimulated nerves until she was nearly crying from the intense sensations.

"Jaimee, you have the most responsive little clit." He took her hand in his and made her touch herself. "See? Feel how tight and hard it is?"

"Lucas," she pleaded.

Brushing her hand away he took her clit between his finger and thumb as he licked her juices from her fingers. "I love the taste of you, the feel of your skin."

She struggled for breath as she grasped his wrist. She opened her mouth to tell him she wanted that little sting of pleasure that vibrated over her bottom. But the words got stuck in her throat and with a sigh that sounded more like a groan, she let her head fall back.

He rose until he met her gaze and held her in place. "What do you want, Jaimee?"

With a shudder, she squeezed her eyes closed and shook her head. "Nothing."

"Mmm. Not going to work. Tell me."

It was evident he wasn't going to let it go. Slowly his fingers moved over her hips, kneading and massaging. She whimpered as his finger lightly skimmed the crease of her bottom. It was shocking and interesting. It was hard to breathe, she wanted to let go, she really did but it didn't seem that easy. When his hands moved lower, pressing firmly, massaging the space between her vagina and her anus she thought she would cry. "Now, Jaimee. Tell me now."

Aw hell...he knew what she wanted without her asking. Dammit. But God she wanted it bad. Her heart was beating so hard. She gripped his back, squeezed her eyes closed and whispered harshly in his ear. "Smack my butt again."

Without hesitation, one wide palm connected sharply with her ass as he pressed a finger against her tight anus. She bucked in his arms, her eyes widening at the intense pleasure and shock that tore through her. His smile was wicked. Lying back against the pillows, he kept his hands in place, his hips rhythmically, slowly thrusting upward. Biting her lip, she concentrated on every tiny sensation.

"Fuck yes," he snarled and smacked her ass once more as his finger pushed just inside her anus. Jaimee stopped breathing. A low cry erupted from somewhere deep inside as the orgasm overtook her. So sharp, so intense, everything else faded and she was consumed in a vortex of pleasure. From somewhere far off it seemed Lucas groaned fiercely as he lost control, surging upward, his climax lengthening her own as his cock pulsed with each jet of hot come.

She fell against him, panting and sweaty, moaning with the aftershocks of the most incredible orgasm she'd ever experienced. He pulled her down beside him and kissed her possessively, his tongue staking claim and his heart pounding beneath her palm. She relaxed against him as his arms wrapped around her and held her tight, his fingers sifting through her hair as he rested her head on his shoulder.

Chapter Thirteen

There was so much about Jaimee that Lucas liked. Granted, right now he mostly liked the fact that her luscious body was snuggled close, her long curvaceous leg was draped over his, the warm silky curls covering her mound brushed softly against his hip. Making love to her had been better than he could have ever imagined. Lovely Jaimee. This lush beauty with her quiet strength and unimpeachable character had come alive in his arms, realizing her own eroticism with his every touch. It had been the most intoxicatingly sensual thing he'd ever experienced. She made him feel fiercely protective and possessive...which made the job he had to do increasingly uncomfortable for him.

Two fifteen glowed fire red at him from the alarm clock on Jaimee's bedside table. He couldn't put it off any longer. With a grimace of dread he kissed the top of her head and carefully untangled himself from her warmth without waking her. Standing at the end of her bed he watched her while he pulled on his jeans, leaving the button undone. Her cheeks were still pink and her lips were kiss swollen. Her thick mane of sable hair fanned her pillow. An enticing nymph, his enticing nymph. Without a doubt, she belonged to him now.

"Shit," he whispered to himself as he walked down the hall to her office.

Lucas sat at her perfunctory desk with all its little cubbies and drawers and booted up her computer. Searching though her desk drawers, it didn't take him long to ascertain that there were no hidden panels. He took the drawers out and looked beneath them. Nothing. Bank statements had been neatly filed and kept in the bottom drawer of the file cabinet that matched her desk. Wow, seven years of bank statements. No canceled checks. He inserted the flash drive on his key ring into the USB port on the front of her CPU and began uploading the person-to-person mirror program. After taking some time to scan the last three years of bank statements and finding nothing that triggered a red flag he turned his attention to the top drawer.

There was nothing in the first or second drawer but extremely organized files pertaining to her classes. Tests, assorted forms and project ideas. There was a phone log of the kids she had this year and whose parents she'd called. She'd made notes on each call. Evidently she was having problems with Braden Conner. A belligerent and disruptive young man whom she'd noted needed consistent discipline and guidance. The boy sounded like a pain-in-the-ass punk to Lucas. Shaking his head, he turned his attention to her disk file. All were in jewel cases and meticulously labeled with content lists. There didn't seem to be any floppies. Everything looked to be filed efficiently.

The sound of the shower had him abandoning his mission and heading back to the bedroom. If he had awakened her wouldn't she have come looking for him? Why didn't she come looking for him? And why was she taking a shower at ten after three in the morning? All those questions left his brain when he crossed her bedroom and stepped into the expansive, richly decorated bathroom.

For a long moment he stood mesmerized, watching her steamy silhouette standing under the shower. She moaned and let her head fall back as the hot spray beat against her. His already rigid shaft throbbed in response. He bit back a groan as he pushed his jeans past his hips and opened the shower door.

Jaimee screamed and backed into the corner of the stall, covering herself with one arm as she groped for the back scrubber to use as a weapon. Lucas caught her wrist before she could deliver the blow to his skull.

"Whoa, baby, it's me. It's okay," he rushed to assure her.

She slumped against him, panting as her fear dissipated. But her relief was evidently short lived if the quick jab to his stomach with her balled fist was any indication.

"You scared the hell out of me!" She glared up at him and he couldn't help but chuckle. She was adorable when she was mad. She punched him again and he grunted just to give her the satisfaction of feeling she had delivered at least one productive blow.

"Damn your ass. I thought you had left," she grumbled.

"No. I got up to use the bathroom, then I went downstairs to call my machine. I didn't want to wake you up. I'm supposed to be off tomorrow but they were going to call if they could use me. Just had to check and see if anyone had called me in." Lying came easy enough.

He'd done it for so long.

"Oh. So did they?" She paused and stepped closer, her breasts pressing lightly against his chest.

"Unfortunately." Then he sighed. "I have to be there in a couple of hours."

She nodded as she let her gaze take in his body, her hands cautiously reaching out to touch his chest.

"Jaimee, why are you taking a shower just after three in the morning?" He softened his voice and took her face in his hands.

"I woke up, you were gone and..." Smiling wryly, she wrinkled her nose. Damn she was pretty. "Well, I was kinda sticky...and cold."

"I'm sorry, sweetness." His mouth brushed hers soft, warm, wet. Then it hit him. He pulled back from her abruptly. "Fuck." How could he have been so irresponsible? Never. He'd never, ever forgotten a condom before. He was clean as far as disease went. He got tested regularly and he never had sex without a condom. Never until now.

"What?" Her brows furrowed.

He rested his forehead against hers. "We didn't use protection, sweetheart."

"Oh." She shrugged then quickly lifted her head. "Oh." Her eyes widened as she looked up at him. "Do you have...?"

"No, no, I'm clean. I'll get you the test results." For the second time she sagged against him in relief.

"I was tested a long time ago," she said quietly, her expression serious. "I can get tested again if you want but I've only been with Brent, and he and I..."

"Jaimee, it's not the possibility of you having an STD. I know you've only been with one man. I'm concerned that I'll get you pregnant." The image of Jaimee smiling contently at him, her tummy swollen with his baby flashed through his mind. The emotion that followed in its wake nearly staggered him. Taking a deep breath he shook himself mentally. Get a grip, he ordered himself. "Are you on the pill?"

She shook her head and looked up at him with a wistful smile. "But don't worry, I can't get pregnant. I was married for seven years and never used anything."

"Yeah, but that could have been your husband's problem, not yours."

The sadness that flashed in her eyes made him wish he'd never brought it up. "No, I wanted a baby. We tried and tried. Brent was tested and he was fine, better than fine. The doctor said scads of things could be the cause of my problem. Evidently, I don't ovulate. I can't...never have, never will..." She swallowed hard, looking away. "I should have gotten more tests but Brent seemed to not want to push it. He was content with just the two of us and since it wasn't a cancer threat, I just let it go."

Everything in him wanted to take that pain away. Make her forget again. He tilted her face up to him and kissed her gently, licking the warm water from her bottom lip. She was delicious.

"I'm turning into a prune," she murmured against his mouth.

He moaned, his hands smoothing over the round curve of her ass as he tasted her sweet mouth. His fingers found her hot and creamy for him again. "You don't feel pruney."

She laughed softly and pressed herself against him. Her arms circled his waist, ignoring the warm spray that cascaded over them. He slowly began washing her hair, loving the feel of the rich lather gliding over her supple curves as he washed the rest of her.

For that moment he wanted to push everything else aside: The Collective, Brent Turner, his assignment, the whole fucking FBI...and just be her lover. But, he couldn't forget The Collective and what they were willing to do to get what they wanted. He couldn't forget that asshole Brent Turner who left his wife aching while he went whoring after more money. And he couldn't forget his job, his oath, his assignment to keep this woman in the dark while he protected her, probed her for information, gave her the pleasure and attention she so desperately needed, making her realize she was desirable, all while betraying her.

They didn't speak as he led her from the shower, dried her hair and wrapped her up in a towel. There was more between them than he had the right to acknowledge. When The Collective was brought down, Brent Turner was listed as murdered and Jaimee was finally as safe and free as she believed herself to be all along...she would hate him. He pulled her into his arms and tilted her face up to kiss her gently on that sweet voluptuous mouth of hers then rested his forehead against hers.

"I hate that I have to go, baby," he murmured as he released her.

"It's okay." She smiled and nodded but there was a glimmer of uneasiness in her eyes that had tension twisting his gut.

"Today might be hectic but I'll see you tomorrow." He wasn't sure why he told her that, he was well aware of how it sounded but he wanted to reassure her. Now as she sat down on the bed, watching him dry himself and dress, she looked at him with a controlled expression that had him fighting the urge to toss her towel away, lay her down on the bed and hold her until dawn. Safe, warm and protected.

She met his gaze and smiled solemnly. "Lucas. I don't expect anything from you. You don't have to make promises or worry about me assuming things about..." she waved her hand, "...this."

He pulled his shirt over his head and didn't bother to tuck it in. "You don't expect anything from me?"

Anger laced through him, tightening every muscle in his body. This was a good thing, he kept telling himself. But what she was thinking was clear in her overly expressive pale blue eyes and it seriously pissed him off.

A shaky sigh escaping her lips. "I just meant that..."

He narrowed his eyes at her. "Lady, you better think before you finish that sentence."

She blinked, her guilt and confusion melted into indignation. "I was just letting you off the hook, okay?" she stammered, looking for the words.

"I know what you're doing." All the times he had loved 'em and left 'em hoping they wouldn't want more from him and here he stood irate that he was being *let off the hook*. Any other time he would have smiled, kissed her sweetly and left, thanking God he'd gotten so lucky. This time wasn't like any other time and her casual dismissal of any possible emotion he might have for her stung. Because this time he knew what was between them, even if he couldn't let the word form in his mind. From the moment she stood up to him at the gym, sweaty, red-faced, and poised for battle, he knew. "And it's bullshit."

"What is your problem?" she snapped. Fire flashed in her eyes, her jaw tightened. "It was nice..."

"Nice? It was *nice*?" he shouted and took a step toward her.

She lifted her chin. Her lips pressed together in determination as she held her ground, challenging him. "Yes! Well okay, yeah, it was more than nice. It was incredible. But look, we're both adults. No big deal. We both know I'm definitely not your type of female and you're not my type either so drop the righteous indignation." She paused, glaring at him. "You should just leave."

Did she think he'd done her a favor? That what had happened between them had been nothing more than a mercy fuck? The idea clawed at his stomach and made him furious. She'd like to take control of what had happened, label it, file it in one of her organized little cubbies and pretend she'd put it away. It was how she coped with everything. He'd be damned if he'd let her do that to him, or to herself.

Before she could say another word he closed the space between them and cupped her jaw with one hand, not caring that his fingers pressed uncomfortably into her soft cheek.

"This was not nice," he hissed through his teeth. "I am not nice. Do you understand me?" He couldn't help the growl that rumbled from deep in his chest even as he saw the bright fear in her eyes. He grasped her wrist and pressed her hand against the rigid length of his erection. "This is harsh reality, baby. You caused it. I didn't do you any favors. From the moment I laid eyes on you I've been hard and aching to fuck you. And now that I have, I only want more." He let go of her wrist, pulled her into his arms and held her tighter.

"Let go," she growled back and shoved at his shoulders. The tremor left her body as she looked up at him, her impossibly light blue eyes darkened and flashed not with fear but rage. Hot, instantaneous, electric fury and a smoldering hunger flooded through him.

"Hell no." The corner of his mouth tilted as he took in the beauty of her raw, real, and just emotion. Though he spoke more calmly his voice was still rough and edgy. Her jaw was tight, her body rigid, and her hands pressed against his chest. Her short little nails biting into his flesh through the cotton of his T-shirt had him fighting the urge to throw her back against the bed and surge into that hot velvet heat again. God, he was obsessed.

The kiss was hard. He'd meant for it to be. Hard and possessive. His thumb pressed gently against the corner of her jaw until she opened to him and he swept the delicate recesses of her warm sweet mouth. Staking his claim. His hands sifted through the damp strands of her hair, his fingers curled against her scalp as he held her there. Tilting his head, his lips moved against hers. His tongue hotly stroked the tender interior of her mouth until her whimper of protest melted into a moan of surrender.

He waited until her body relaxed in submission and her arms wrapped around his waist before he raised his head and looked down at her. He untangled his fingers from her hair as he watched the emotion play on her beautiful face. Patiently he waited for her to look up at him. Finally her breathing slowed and she swallowed hard. Her eyelids lifted slowly as she met his gaze. Hell no, he'd never let her go.

She frowned. Her painfully organized mind was working on what to say, how to process this situation. Without giving her a chance to regroup and execute her next attack he willed himself to take his hands off her and step away. Without saying a word he turned to walk out of the room.

"Lucas." Quietly she said his name, halting him. He looked over his shoulder at her, still angry with her, with himself. "If you plan on making this a more than one night thing..."

He turned to face her, tilted his head and studied her standing there, understanding sinking in to grip his heart in a tight vise. "Yes?"

"Know for sure. Don't play with me."

The vulnerability, the risk she believed she was taking was clear in her eyes even though her expression was inscrutable and resolved. He closed the short distance between them, knowing the choice he was making. He brushed her cool cheek with the back of his fingers, ran his thumb over her bottom lip. "This was never a game, Jaimee. I never do anything I'm unsure of."

He touched his lips to hers, lingering long enough to breathe in her scent, memorize the taste of her before he turned away once more and left her room.

Chapter Fourteen

It was his fault. He had brought Brent Turner in.

Frustrated, Ronald tugged at his tie as he stepped into his home office. He quietly shut the door behind him and tossed both his jacket and tie over the arm of the high back chair, offhandedly dropping his briefcase on his desk. He headed straight for his private bar, poured himself a double shot of Jack and tossed it back. The man had been a mathematical wizard, he reasoned, had good ideas and a healthy hunger for wealth, but he lacked common sense and Ronald should have recognized that. He sighed deeply as he refilled his glass. If he had, he wouldn't be in this fucked-up situation.

He sat, leaning back in his desk chair, breathing in the scent of leather and whiskey. The aroma of wealth, he mused, did little to soothe him tonight. His plans to flatter Turner's wife, flirt, lie out of his ass and bed her quickly should have been easy. That way he could have searched the house without much fuss, found the information he needed and given it to Zachary. Then it wouldn't have been necessary to get rid of Jaimee. His ass would be off the hook. No problem.

Yeah right, no problem. He swallowed the last of his drink and set the glass on the desk. Screwing the fat bitch had never been his idea of a good time. He preferred his women petite, slim, blonde and obedient. Jaimee wasn't any of those. Fucking her was the best way to find out where Turner had hidden the day planner and get the number for the Swiss account where he stashed the money he'd pilfered. Playing hide the salami with Jaimee would be better than taking the beating Zachary would deliver.

Good thing for Turner that he took a header over that ridge. Zachary's method of killing him would have been exceedingly more painful and would have taken a hell of a lot longer. A shudder passed through his body and he chewed on the inside of his cheek. Zachary was livid with him now though. He had to get that information or he'd get the full brunt of Edward Zachary's rage.

Leaning forward, he rubbed at his temples. It didn't make sense that Jaimee wasn't as easy to charm as he thought she'd be. That really chapped his ass. It wasn't like she had a lot of offers. Hell, she should have been grateful. He'd never had problems getting women a whole lot better-looking than that cow. Evidently Turner was right when he bitched about her being frigid. Shit, he shoulda just beaten it out of her. Better her than him He might have done just that if the neighbor hadn't shown up acting all protective.

His brow furrowed thinking about the look on the big man's face. What was that about anyway? Surely a guy like that wouldn't have the hots for a woman like Jaimee. Ronald shrugged off the feeling of foreboding that threatened to add to his already troubled mind. A guy that pretty and that pumped was more than likely a pansy-assed model on steroids. Probably gay, or maybe women like Jaimee were the best he could do. One of the main reasons Ronald never gave steroids a try was because he'd heard they'd shrink a man's dick. No way in hell was he gonna take that kind of chance. He wasn't willing to take on a guy that big by himself either. He picked up the phone and started to dial when his head snapped up at the sudden rap on the solid oak door.

"Ron?" Sandy said softly before peering around the door at him.

She looked like a damn rat when she did that. Her nose was too long, too pointy. He hung up and glared at her. "What?"

"You had some calls. I left the messages on your desk. I wanted to make sure you got them."

"I saw 'em."

She glared back. "Fine. Do you plan to come down for dinner?"

"No."

Her beady eyes narrowed and her lips pressed into a thin line. "Fine," she snapped as she turned to go.

"Sandy."

She halted and looked back at him over her shoulder.

"Don't ever come into my office again when I'm not here. You understand me? Ever!"

Without saying a word she walked out, slamming the door behind her. If only he'd had a prenup prepared before he'd married the hag. The private line trilled, punctuating his misery. He knew who it was before he answered and his heart skipped a beat.

"Hello."

"Tell me you have the day planner."

"Mr. Zachary. Not yet, but soon. I'll have it soon."

Silence.

"Things didn't go as planned."

"And what exactly were your fool plans, Marshall?"

"Well, I..."

"You're wasting time trying to manipulate Jaimee Turner with a sad seduction, aren't you?"

Anger roiled in Ronald's gut at the disparagement. He gripped the receiver tightly and gritted his teeth against the desire to tell Zachary to get fucked. "Rest assured the matter will be dealt with and you'll have the package in your hands soon," Ronald managed bitterly.

"Soon isn't acceptable, Marshall." Zachary's voice was calm, cold and eerie as the grave. It was that old slow southern accent, as smooth as Kentucky bourbon and just as destructive. "Your time is running out."

"Yes, I know, sir. I apologize."

"Only a weak man apologizes, Marshall. I don't trust weak men." Zachary sighed deeply. "I don't employ weak men."

"Yes, sir."

"Are you a weak man, Marshall?"

"No, sir," he answered tightly.

"No?"

"No."

"Are you retracting your apology then?"

"The issue will be resolved immediately."

Silence.

"You have my word, Mr. Zachary."

"Your word?" Edward Zachary's humorless chuckle was like cold claws on the back of Ronald's neck. "Get this cleaned up, Marshall, or I'll have your blood."

Zachary disconnected before Ronald could respond, which was probably a good thing. Anything he said would have been the wrong thing. Quickly, Ronald punched in the number he'd been intending to call before Sandy, then Zachary, interrupted.

Fury and fear melded into pulsating, violent emotion in the pit of his stomach. He let the vision of his hand tightening around Edward Zachary's throat swim in his mind. He fantasized the man's bulging eyes pleading for mercy; his face mottled from fear and lack of oxygen...

"Yeah." The harsh answer brought Ronald back to reality.

"I have a job for you."

Edward Zachary set the phone on the side table and took a long draw from his cigar. He sat back, propped his legs up on the leather ottoman and crossed his ankles. "He's gonna fuck it up."

"Mr. Zachary, you know Vannie and I can take care of it."

He opened his eyes and studied the man sitting across from him. Carl Cox was more than an associate. He was nearly a friend, not quite, but nearly. At any rate, Carl had earned his trust as much as anyone could. He could count on him. Otherwise he wouldn't be in his home, sitting on his Italian leather sofa smoking one of his fine, expensive Cubans.

Vannie Holt was another story. He was big and not as stupid as some, but he was still just a redneck from central Kentucky. The boy just couldn't rise above his raisings no matter how hard he tried. Still, he was useful and willing to do whatever he was asked. Ronald Marshall on the other hand had always been ambitious and willing to do the shit work as long as it meant he might achieve a higher status, but he lacked discretion and control, made bad choices and stupid mistakes. He was a colossal dumbass, and easily expendable...in time.

"Not yet. In due time. What have you discovered about the secretary?"

"Alice Sinclair has effectively disappeared."

"People don't just disappear, Carl."

"Yes, sir, that's true. But she hasn't been home since she quit. It's possible she went on vacation or something. I'm looking into it."

"Oh? I was under the impression you were sitting here with me smoking one of my best cigars."

Carl had the good sense to look abashed. "Yes, sir." Carefully he stood, seemingly unsure of what to do with the cigar.

"Take it with you," Edward said sharply, his voice tinged with disgust. "While you 'look into' Ms. Sinclair's whereabouts, see what you can find out about the grieving widow's new man, Lucas Grayson."

"Yes, sir," he said quietly and left the room quickly.

Jaimee Turner was a nice, well-bred, lovely lady. Much like his own baby girl. Probably didn't know a damn thing about her idiot dead husband or what he had gotten himself, and ultimately her, into. He'd take no pleasure in hurting her, marring that pretty peach skin, taking her blood, her life. It was a real shame. However, Ronald Marshall was another story.

Edward put out his cigar with a sigh, leaned back in his chair and closed his eyes once more. Time to put business out of his mind. Family was coming for dinner. At sixty-seven years old he wasn't as spry as he once was and he was going to need his rest to keep up with those grandbabies of his.

Chapter Fifteen

Eucalyptus-scented steam billowed thick and hot from the coals. Jaimee spread out her towel and sat on the top level of the tiered tiled benches, scooting all the way back to stretch out her legs and lean against the wall. She breathed in the humid air, closed her eyes and let go of the stress of the day, willing the tightness in her muscles to relax.

Three days had passed since Lucas made love to her. He called every night to ask her about her day, tell her about his and that he was thinking of her, missed her. Besides the short phone calls, she received a certificate in her mailbox proving he'd had a negative HIV test. It had made her feel a little weird and at the same time, in an odd way, she was touched that he didn't want her to worry. Maybe he understood how uncharacteristic it was of her to fall into bed with a man she hardly knew. She hoped so. Still, she wanted him, ached for him in a way that was all too unfamiliar. A wicked curiosity that she didn't even know existed inside her was let loose now.

Perhaps it really was a lapse in judgment that she gave in and had sex with Lucas, but she didn't care and she didn't regret it. However, she did reconcile herself to the possibility that he was easing away and she might never see him again. It was okay. Well, it would be okay eventually. No, it wasn't okay, but she refused to beat herself up over it.

Sighing again, she shifted, adjusted her bathing suit and tried to change her train of thought. No such luck. Images of Lucas above her invaded her mind, memories of his hands, his mouth, his rock-hard body. It was still disconcerting how much she liked it when he delved into the taboo area of her backside. Damn, she was going to have to figure out a way to tamp down her raging libido. Seriously. If her mother was right she was a full-fledged reprobate. Just what did that mean anyway? It was definitely making her wonder what it would feel like to have his cock enter her instead of just his finger. But it would hurt, wouldn't it? And that was the crux of her apprehension right there. She had to admit it to herself at least...she really liked the pain. Just a little anyway. And damn if she didn't want to push to find out how much was too much. Man, she really was a freak. She shifted and scowled. Why in the hell did God make it feel so amazingly good if it was forbidden?

The soft whoosh of the door opening jarred her sensual reflections. She cleared her throat to let whoever had come in know she was there. A metallic click that sounded a lot like a key in a lock had her tensing. Immediately she thought of Ron and her mind scrambled for the best plan of defense. Before she could act two very familiar hands circled her ankles and pulled her forward until she was sitting on the edge.

"I've been watching you work out." The husky, deep bass of his voice made her tremble.

"Sheesh, Lucas, you scared the hell outta me." Relief poured over her. Relief that he wasn't Ron or some other creep; relief that he was there with her, in the flesh, at least one more time. She scowled at him anyway. "I was ready to claw your eyes out."

"I watched you swim," he murmured, ignoring her threat as he kneeled on the lower bench, his lips a breath away from hers. His hands slowly slid up her damp thighs, easing them apart. Jaimee forgot to breathe. "Do you have any idea how fucking sexy you were gliding through the water?"

Every cell of her body seemed to come alive, alert to the onslaught of sensation. Oh man. Hard, muscled shoulders were hot and slick with steam and sweat under her palms. He pressed closer. Jaimee wanted to cry or sing or laugh with delight. The fact that this man wanted her, desired her the way he did was thrilling.

"Mmm, you smell so good," he groaned. His tongue rasped over her prickling skin as he rotated his hips and his thick shaft ground against her pussy. Fire ignited between them and she tried to stifle a moan.

Droplets of sweat trickled between her breasts like a tiny caress as Lucas freed them from the clinging bathing suit. "Lift," he urged. She complied, lifting her hips to allow him to rid her of the barrier.

"Oh my God. Someone could come in," she managed to say as his mouth closed over one aching nipple. His hand cupped the other breast, kneading it slowly, massaging her nipple with his palm. He was driving her insane.

"No one will come in," he whispered, blowing warm air across her wet skin. "I promise. The door's locked."

"How did you get a key?"

"Our buddy Blayne."

Somewhere through the sensual fog it occurred to her that she should complain about Blayne's willingness to help set her up. But, she couldn't form a logical argument. Being set up wasn't at all bad anymore. With a hoarse moan she let go, gave in to the wild desire clawing at her.

She clung to him, inhaled his scent. Her teeth closed on the tough, taut skin at the curve of his neck and tugged his shorts off his hips. Her tongue slowly soothed the bite, reveling in the taste of earthy male—salty, sexy. Exploring the planes and curves of his wet body was so erotic, so freeing; she wanted to feel him everywhere, all over, inside.

"You're so hard, everywhere."

"How well I know." The growl vibrated through her.

Her fingers found his cock, slowly trailed down and then up to the tip. That rounded plum-like head was dewy soft and hot. She imagined how it would feel against her lips, her tongue, filling her mouth. How would it taste? His mouth descended hungrily on hers. Her thumb caressed the delicate spot beneath the flair and smoothed upward to glide over the tiny slit. A pearl of moisture had gathered there, silky and slick. She was mesmerized by the sensation and wanted to make it go on and on.

Her wishes were thwarted when Lucas grasped her wrists. "You're killing me."

"I can't help it," she whispered against his mouth. "I love the way you feel." The heat, the arousal was intense and overwhelming. Her scalp prickled, her skin tingled, she trembled with need.

"Wrap your legs around me."

His tongue swept the sensitive interior of her mouth as his lips nipped at hers. God, Lucas's kisses were amazing; they curled her toes, made her wild. Never would she have guessed in a million years that just a kiss could make her wet and trembling. But that's exactly what he did to her. Lucas groaned, poised the fully engorged head of his incredible cock against the spasming entrance of her vagina and squeezed her knees to remind her of his command. Damn, she was sick, she loved his commands.

She did as he asked and leaned back. Her moan was lusty, desperate, as he guided his cock inside, a slow thrust, inch by inch, gradually filling her. The walls of her channel clenched at the invasion, drawing a hiss of pleasure from Lucas. His hands gripped her hips and she tightened her legs around him, tilting upward to bring him deeper. Droplets of sweat trickled down her body like tiny caressing fingers. Her heart thudded against her ribs as pure erotic fire seemed to course through her relentlessly with every withdraw and surge. She held on to his biceps as she met his rhythm. Pleasure built to a nearly unbearable crescendo.

"Lucas." She groaned as her hands slid up his arms to fist in his damp hair. The slick friction of his chest against her nipples only increased the intensity of the sensations firing through her.

He gently pressed her back, his hands gliding down her slick body between her breasts to her stomach and up again. Each achingly slow thrust of his cock pushed her closer to sensory overload. Her sheath tightened, convulsed with each withdraw, increasing the friction, the heat, the sensation. His palm pressed against her mound and moved down toward the hard knot of nerves. On the brink of explosion Jaimee shook her head as she gripped his wrist. "Don't. Please."

Lucas lifted her to him. Biting her neck, his hands moved down her back to her ass, gripping, his long fingers caressing deeper as he thrust hard into her. Her body quaked as finally the tension snapped and spun her into a bright vortex of ecstasy that took her breath away. She clenched her teeth against her need to cry out as the power of her orgasm washed over.

Her climax seemed to trigger his. Lucas held her tight against him as his own pleasure took control. His cock filled her, stretching the walls of her vagina to capacity. She could feel every ripple, every undulation of his shaft as he erupted. Still her channel contracted, wave after wave pulsing through her. As Lucas gained control he kissed her gently, brushing her wet hair back from her face. They were both panting for air.

"Are you all right?" Lucas asked hoarsely as he pulled away with a grimace, keeping his hands on her waist.

She could only nod.

His hands framed her face and made her meet his gaze. "I want you to leave first, okay, baby?"

She nodded again, mesmerized by his dark but gentle expression.

"I'll be right behind you. Take a cool shower. We're both too hot. I'll meet you outside."

"Okay," she whispered. Her knees were wobbly as she stood. Lucas steadied her as she stepped into her bathing suit and pulled it up her damp body. He unlocked the door and kissed her one last time.

The cool air that greeted her as she stepped out of the steam room was a shock and made her feel a little dizzy. The realization of what she had just done both astonished and thrilled her. It was so exciting to be so impulsive. It had been incredible sex. Unlike anything she'd ever dreamed of experiencing. Thankfully there was no one around to hear her mischievous giggle or notice her unsteady footing. They'd probably think she was drunk.

The tepid shower did little to diminish the hunger Lucas had awakened within her. The nerve endings all over her body seemed hypersensitive. Despite her very recent, very powerful orgasm her clit was throbbing and ached when the soft cloth she washed with brushed over it. More, she needed more of him.

Jaimee left the locker room and scanned the club as she walked toward the front. No sign of Lucas. The only people sitting at the café tables in the juice bar area were three women who were chatting in hushed tones. She considered the possibility that he planned on literally meeting her outside but went ahead and asked the small group before leaving.

"Excuse me." Three sets of eyes turned their attention on her and smiled. "I'm sorry to interrupt but by any chance have y'all seen a very tall, muscular guy with long dark hair come through here?"

The smallest of the three smiled warmly and offered her hand. "Hi, I'm Jasmine."

She returned her smile. "Jaimee."

"No, we haven't. Listen. Jaimee, we..." she gestured to two other women sitting there watching attentively, "...wanted to tell you that we think it's awesome that you've worked so hard. You look great."

"Thanks."

"I know it's none of our business. It's just that we really would hate to see you embarrassed. Lucas is the kind of guy who is all about appearances, you know? He's looking for an arm decoration, not someone like you. It's not that you're not pretty. But..." her brows furrowed, "...he's the type of guy who likes very thin, delicate, glamorous women."

"I see." How odd, she wasn't offended at all.

"You really seem to be a lovely, wonderful person. That's why I wanted to talk to you about it. You know?" Her hazel eyes were soft and held the same concern as her voice.

Jaimee nodded, searching for the right thing to say.

"Well, Lucas, isn't at all what you think he is. You've misjudged him, he's..." She should have known Lucas had walked up behind her when the ladies stared wide-eyed past her.

"Who's been misjudged?" He growled against her neck as his hands clasped her waist and pulled her back against him. Deliberately pressing his straining erection against her bottom. Jaimee's heartbeat quickened and she struggled not to give in to the rush of lust, close her eyes and lean back against him. "Uh...Prince. I was saying that I thought he was more masculine than he appeared. That he's been misjudged as being gay when I don't believe he is at all. As a matter of fact I think the man has some alpha tendencies."

"Ah." His hands slid down just fractions to the curve of her hips, his fingers tensed. "Let's go." It was a dark, raspy demand that left no room for refusal. At his touch, his mouth on her neck, the pleasant hum pulsing through her body accelerated.

"Nice to meet you." It was all she was able to say before Lucas took her hand and all but hauled her out of the building.

Moments later she found herself trapped between her car and Lucas's barely restrained, hard body. "Prince, my ass. I have excellent hearing." His mouth closed over hers, scorching her lips, drawing a tortured moan from her. When he stepped back she wanted to whimper in protest but resisted. His eyes held the promise of something powerful as he opened the car door. "Hurry home, I'm right behind you."

They'd picked a bad time to leave. Traffic was backing up with people getting off work. It was cool outside but she was still so hot and thinking about the last hour had her leaning over to turn the air conditioner on. With a sigh she searched her purse for her ringing cell phone and kept her eyes on the bumper in front of her at the same time.

"Hello?"

"You defended me." The deep bass of Lucas's voice rumbled through her.

"Well yeah I guess so. But I had to say something. You aren't shallow."

"Then you covered for them."

"What are you getting at?" She frowned at his silhouette in her rearview mirror.

"You're amazing."

The tone of his statement gave her goose bumps. It was silly, the pleasure his praise gave her. "You're pretty amazing yourself. And quite creative."

"You inspire me. Are you still wet?"

"How could I not be?" she answered. "You keep me in a constant state of arousal."

"Mmm. Damn traffic."

Jaimee chuckled. "It's rush hour."

"Yet no one is rushing anywhere."

"Good point."

"We should have just jumped in the back seat of my car. It's big enough. This is going to make me crazy. All I can think about is your soft pussy, dripping with all that sweet honey."

"I can't breathe when you say things like that. I can barely sit still."

"Fuck." He groaned. "Pull over."

"No." She laughed. "The anticipation will only make it feel better."

"If it feels any better I don't think I'll live through it."

"I'm willing to test that theory."

"Are your nipples hard?"

"Wait a minute, I'll check." She was being facetious. Of course they were; they were aching. But because she was feeling wild, racy and uncharacteristically uninhibited she grinned and bit her bottom lip as she unbuttoned her shirt and let her fingertips rasp over the stiff peaks through her bra. Her breath caught in her throat at the spiral of sensation that whipped through her. Had she ever been so salacious?

"I'll take that as a yes," he murmured. "Now touch your pussy."

"I can't do that..."

"Yes you can. Tell me how slick you are."

"But there are trucks." Someone could look over and see what she was doing.

"It doesn't matter. They won't know you're doing anything."

"What if the traffic starts moving?"

"Then you can stop. Do it."

It was wicked, and so exciting she couldn't resist. In all her adult life she'd never done anything as daring as she had today and damn if it didn't feel good. Jaimee took a deep breath and with shaky hands unbuttoned and unzipped her jeans. She slipped her hand beneath the elastic band of her panties and cupped her pussy.

"Tell me how wet are you?"

"My panties are soaked, I'm drenched," she breathed shakily.

"Touch your clit, Jaimee. Imagine it's my hand and with one finger circle it for me."

"Lucas, I can't, I'm too close."

"It's okay. You can. Do it now, our exit's coming up."

With a whimper she pushed on the brake, leaned back and pressed one finger between the swollen folds of her pussy to glide through the slick heat upward and over her hardened clit. A soft moan escaped her lips.

"That's it. Damn you're so beautiful. I can't wait to taste you, Jaimee..."

She watched the car in front of her, thankful that they were at a standstill at the moment, and traced her fingertip around the firm nub. "Oh God."

"...feel you around me, gripping my aching dick," he growled into the phone.

"Oh hell."

"I want you naked beneath me. I want to see your body flushed pink with arousal. I want to see your pretty pussy and your beautiful breasts with their juicy berries just begging to be sucked."

Her head fell back against the headrest, her body shuddering as sharp unrelenting pulses of her orgasm pounded through her.

"Mmm, yes. Good, that's so good. Jaimee, sweetheart."

"Hmm?"

"You need to drive now, baby."

She opened her eyes to see that the car in front had moved forward some distance. Keeping her eyes trained straight ahead, careful not to look at the people or person in the car beside her she drove forward. The heat crawled up her neck to burn her cheeks with embarrassment. "Um. I'm hanging up now. Bye."

Chapter Sixteen

Standing on the porch, Jaimee watched Lucas sprint across the street toward her. There was such grace in the fluid motion of his body, elegance and raw power. His hair was nearly dry now, lifted by the cool air. His eyes were focused on hers. Even at a distance he could command her attention, control her desire. As soon as he reached her he took her face between his wide palms and bent his head to kiss her, but she held up a hand, her fingertips lightly touched his lips.

"Oh no you don't. I'm mad at you."

"No, you're not."

The sensual curve of his lips had desire curling through her abdomen, urging her to give in. She resisted, barely. "Yes. I am. It's not fair that you get to torture me like that while you sit back all self-satisfied and arrogant."

His lids lowered slightly as he kissed her fingers, her palm, disarming her enough to take the keys from her without her even noticing. "Do you honestly think that wasn't torture for me? I had to stay in control or we may have caused a serious pile up."

"It was your fault though!" Somewhere in the back of her mind it occurred to her that the things they'd done, the things she still wanted to do, should probably mortify her. Instead she enjoyed being wild and mischievous. Free. A quick flush of heat infused her cheeks.

He reached around her, crowding her as he backed her into the house. His lips hovered above hers. "I'll gladly accept the blame. But arguing with you is not what I have in mind." With a kick he slammed the door closed. Jaimee was too mesmerized by the intensity in his eyes to move.

"Maybe I want to argue." Did that dark, husky voice really come from her?

Abruptly his hands fisted on the lapels of her blouse and her back met the wall, effectively silencing her and halting her retreat. His knee wedged between her shaky thighs and her lips parted on a gasp. "Too bad."

His kiss was rough, hungry, desperate. Fire ignited, raged uncontrollably, heating her blood, melting her bones. It was official— she'd become a kinky, perverted nympho and she didn't give a damn. As a matter of fact she was letting go, which only meant she would probably get a lot worse.

Provoking him turned her on. It had to be obvious to him that she was challenging him but she so loved it when he aggressively pursued, demanded, took and gave pleasure. It was addictive. She clutched at the material stretched across his back. She yanked and pulled until, with a chuckle, he let her get the shirt over his head and off. She tossed it to the floor and let her greedy hands indulge in the feel of him.

His hands slid down over her breasts, pausing long enough to massage them, rasp his thumbs over their aching crests before dropping to cup her ass. He lifted her hips against him and she gripped his biceps, her fingers flexing on the hard bulging muscles.

"You're turning me into a sex maniac," she murmured against his mouth.

"Hallelujah," he groaned.

Boldly she stroked his tongue with her own. "What if I asked you for sex everyday. Maybe two, three times a day?"

He caught her bottom lip between his strong white teeth, gently grazing her swollen lip as he pulled away, his eyes locking with hers. "Are you kidding me?"

The determined, sultry look in his eyes, the rapid pounding of his heartbeat against her palm, his heat, his erection, left no question as to whether or not he wanted her. To be wanted, truly wanted, was amazing and overwhelming. It affected her on every level and sent erotic shivers dancing through her. He moved so fast she could barely keep up.

Jaimee tried to make her expression serious but she couldn't help smiling. "No, I'm serious. What if I got addicted, became this raving sex fiend and hounded you for it constantly?"

"Hound me." His lips trailed a searing trail down her throat, licking the sensitive hollow between her collarbones. With one hand he deftly unbuttoned her shirt and unfastened the clasp, freeing her breasts. Before she had time to consider the slickness of the move he lifted her breast to his mouth, firm lips closing over the nipple. He

110

drew on it, laving the tip with his tongue. Jaimee couldn't think straight, she could only feel, only wanted to feel. Her fingers speared into his hair, clutching him in desperate need to hold his face to her chest.

Lucas groaned, cupping and kneading her breast as his warm breath fanned her damp nipples. The intensity of her arousal was fierce, like a beast clawing at her, tightening its grip on the core of her. "How?" she whimpered huskily. "How do you do this to me?"

"Hold on to me, baby." His voice was dark and rough.

Lucas moved away only fractions, just long enough to unbutton her jeans and push them down. Jaimee quickly wiggled to free herself from her pants as she tugged at his belt, her hands shaking. Lucas gently pushed them away and accomplished the task deftly.

His hand slid down her thigh, lifted it to wrap around his hip. There wasn't any time to consider the action or react with anything other than primal need. She rose on tiptoes and clung to him, holding her breath as he guided the thick head of his cock past her folds to the entrance of her sheath. With the very first savage thrust, she shattered. A scream tore from her as Lucas surged into her body.

"Good God," he groaned harshly through clenched teeth.

All she could do was hold on as the violent and unrelenting pleasure claimed her. The mind-numbing waves of sensation barely eased their grip before building again. The muscles of her legs tightened, her heel pressed into his hip as he pistoned into her harder, faster.

"Oh, please. Don't stop." Jaimee struggled for breath as a second orgasm ripped through her. Her cries blended with Lucas's harsh moan as his climax erupted in hard pulses, filling her with his liquid arousal.

Jaimee trembled, her breath shuddered from her lungs as Lucas pulled her into his arms. His hand sifted through her hair and held her head to his chest. The moment was earthshaking and tender. Lucas was breathing as heavily as she and his heart was pounding, strong and loud. She had failed to keep her head about her. Clearly her heart was leading and she didn't give a damn.

"Let's go upstairs," he murmured into her hair.

"Oh wait. I forgot the clothes." Jaimee's voice was soft and raspy. Lucas smiled into Jaimee's tousled hair and with his hands on her hips guided her up the next flight of stairs. He was sincerely surprised she'd made it to the landing before remembering their clothes strewn onto the hallway floor.

"Forget the clothes."

"But I really should pick 'em up."

"They'll still be there in the morning."

She grinned. "Okay. Fine. Whatever."

In her bedroom she turned in his arms, her fingers speared through his hair and pulled his head down to take his mouth. She was sexually aggressive, voracious, demanding and he loved it. Her soft sweet lips nibbled at his as her nails grazed his scalp. It sent electricity sparking a course through every nerve, firing his blood.

"Wait."

"For what?" He cupped her ample bottom and squeezed gently as he walked her back toward the bed. God, he loved her ass.

"Bathroom break. Just really quick." She kissed him hard and fast. "I'll be right back."

Letting her go, he sighed roughly and rubbed a hand over his face. "Okay. But hurry."

She giggled as he turned and fell back on the bed. He rose up on his elbows and shook his head as he watched her walk away. Soft waves of sable swung over her shoulders down to the gentle dip in her back which tapered perfectly at the waist then flared into the most incredibly sexy hips and ass God ever created. Her legs were long and shaped beautifully to fit around his waist, strong enough to hold on.

He sat up and glanced at her end table. As he expected it was all very orderly. There was only a lamp, a romance novel lying on top of a Bible and a phone. With one finger he hooked the handle and quietly opened the small drawer. It was empty except for an address book. Poor girl didn't even have a pocket rocket. He made a mental note to remedy that as soon as possible. The sound of the toilet flushing had him pausing. He listened for the faucet to be turned on before he picked up the address book and quickly scanned it. Nothing stuck out. He replaced it and shut the drawer. Jaimee was still washing up.

Again he shook his head as he picked up the romance novel, correction, erotic romance novel. *Shameless* by Lora Leigh. He leaned against her headboard and thumbed through the book. His brows slowly rose as he read the page she had bookmarked with her little beaded string thing.

"Khalid." His voice sounded torn from his throat as he continued to stare at Courtney.

"Yes, Ian." Khalid's darkly accented voice was harsh with arousal.

"I require a third."

"With pleasure, Ian."

Ms. Jaimee was reading some seriously risqué material. He doubted his prim little Jaimee would ever want two men at once. It wasn't all that surprising to him, however, that she would read about it. There was a wildfire inside her that had been banked way too damn long. If he had his way it would soon be blazing out of control, and he wanted to be caught right in the middle of it. Even if it meant he'd be burned alive.

This book was hot and he imagined what she looked like reading it. Did she nibble at that sweet bottom lip of hers? Did she squirm? Touch herself? God help him, he'd love to watch her read it. Watch her expression as she absorbed the fantasy of what was happening on the pages. Or better still, read it to her.

Finally the water stopped running and Jaimee came out of the bathroom. Unfortunately she'd wrapped herself up in her robe. Even wrapped in a bulky terrycloth robe she was sexy and so pretty. That curious ache that clutched at his heart was there again, making him want more than he could have, more than he deserved.

Pushing the troubling thoughts aside, Lucas inhaled deeply as he looked back at the words on the page. The urge to tease her was too strong to resist. He lifted his gaze without lifting his head.

"Sweetheart." Keeping his voice low, rough and seductive he continued. "Do you require a third?"

The corner of his mouth lifted as he watched her eyes widen, her cheeks go rosy pink. She recovered quickly, however, squared her shoulders and cleared her throat. Her lids lowered over eyes that sparkled in playful seduction.

"You know, I never thought about it," she teased, letting her robe fall open just slightly as she walked toward him. "Might not be a bad idea. Might lighten your load a little bit. It's something to consider."

Lucas chuckled as he dropped the book back on her nightstand and sat up. "Don't worry about me, baby. I believe I'll manage to keep up." He smiled mischievously, parted her robe, placed both hands on her bare waist and tugged her close to stand between his parted thighs. "Doesn't matter really, because I'm not willing to share." He nuzzled the soft flesh just below her breasts. Her fingers sifted through his hair. She smelled so good, warm, sweet...

"Lucas?"

There was a barely perceptible tremble in her voice that had him frowning slightly as he lifted his head to meet her gaze. "Jaimee?"

Her fingers flexed against his scalp nervously. "You know I was just teasing, right? I mean, I don't really want a threesome."

"Good." He grinned.

"Can I ask you a question?" Lucas had no idea what she was about to ask but judging from the tension in her body, the way she nibbled her bottom lip and furrowed her brow whatever the question was going to be, he'd better tread carefully with his answer.

He lay back on the bed and pulled her down beside him so they were facing each other. He gently tucked her hair behind her ear and kissed her before he answered. "You can ask me anything."

Chapter Seventeen

"Well, it's actually more of a suggestion." Oh God. Could he hear her heart thump against her ribs?

Lucas looked at her but said nothing.

"Um...I'm finding that the thing you've been doing..." She frowned; there was no delicate way to put this at all. Jaimee closed her eyes tight, took a deep breath and blew it out. "All right, well, I really like it when you do what you do to my...um...back door area." Well damn, that was stupid.

"Good. I'll keep doing it then," he murmured against her throat.

"Um, it would be okay with me if you wanted to...elaborate on it?" For a moment Lucas paused and met her gaze again. His eyes were so dark, so focused. The intensity in them was breathtaking. The heat that infused her cheeks was not from shame. Maybe she did feel a little sheepish but besides what she'd read in the very erotic romance novels she'd been reading, Maxine's occasional titillating accounts of her adventures in "boo fooin'" had her curious. However, the intense pleasure Lucas gave her when he did what he did made her bold.

"Anything you want, Jaimee." His kiss was powerful in its simplicity. His lips were so soft, so firm, warm, tender. "There is nothing I wouldn't do to please you, make you happy...well, almost nothing. I was serious about not sharing you." He smiled and gently stroking her back from shoulder to hip.

Jaimee let her gaze fall to his mouth again with a melodramatic sigh. "Fine, I guess I'll make do."

Putting a hand over his heart he affected an exaggerated expression of solemn indebtedness. "I promise to work night and day. I won't let you down, Ms. Turner."

She laughed and punched him lightly on the shoulder. "Goofy."

"You have no idea."

She smiled contently and cuddled closer. "I'm glad I didn't freak you out."

With one finger he lifted her face and took her mouth, his lips pressed possessively against hers, his tongue stroking her own. One kiss let her know his hunger, his need to be a part of her. When he finally pulled back, he held her face between his hands.

"Look at me." She lifted her eyes to his and held her breath. "Jaimee, baby, to me you are perfect. You aren't going to freak me out or push me away. Anytime, anywhere, anything, I'm yours. Understand?"

In that one statement, Lucas fulfilled a need in her that she didn't know she had. Silently Jaimee nodded and traced the strong line of his jaw with her fingertips as she struggled for control. His body tensed and he sat up, listening. A moment later the familiar sound of the slamming of a car door reached her ears. In record time she leapt off the bed and was across the room to peek out the window blinds.

"Damn! It's my mother."

Jaimee wanted to scream. It wasn't like she didn't know with the way things were going her mother would most likely meet Lucas eventually. Still, she wasn't looking forward to the occasion and she sure as hell didn't want it to happen unexpectedly. She gritted her teeth as she yanked open a dresser drawer and quickly pulled on a pair of loose-fitting black lounge pants and an oversized pale pink tee.

The doorbell was sounding by the time Jaimee got downstairs. As quietly as she could she gathered the clothes they'd hastily discarded earlier and started to run them back upstairs. Lucas met her on the first landing.

"Here, take these upstairs. I'll get rid of her."

He pulled on his pants and after a short pause, his shirt, then tossed the rest up the stairs. The doorbell rang again—three short impatient tones. She didn't have time to deal with whatever he was going to do.

"Seriously, Lucas, go back upstairs until I can get rid of her. Please."

"Wait," he said, grabbing her wrist as she turned to go.

"Lucas, you don't understand. My mother is a piranha. With all the grace of a born-again Southern belle, she will verbally shred you."

"I'm not worried."

Karen knocked, her muffled voice calling out. Panic rose, and with it, the beginnings of a tension headache started needling at her temple. Then Lucas kissed her palm.

"Jaimee, baby, this isn't you. You're an intelligent, incredibly strong and brave woman. Don't give her the power to change that. She can only do to you what you allow her to do."

Jaimee frowned up at him and pulled her hand away. "I'm not afraid of my mother, for cryin' out loud. I just don't want her to insult you."

He returned a frown of his own and crossed his arms. "I think I can handle myself."

"Fine then."

"Good. Answer the door," he snapped.

"I was going to," she snapped back. She was being snarky, but the whole pep talk thing he was laying on her just rankled. She made her way down the steps and to the door with her teeth and fists clenched. She wasn't afraid of anything, dammit. She pressed her lips together, unlocked the door and swung it open.

"What in the world took so long?" Karen gave Jaimee a head-to-toe glance. "Were you taking a nap?"

Before Jaimee could respond Karen stepped through the door, her sharp hazel eyes locking on Lucas. He casually leaned against the doorframe of the kitchen, his arms crossed over his chest, his dark mane of hair wild and free, falling over his shoulders. Karen froze, her expression of disapproval deepening to something closer to revulsion.

God, she hated that expression of disgust on her mother's face. It was when Karen turned her cold, scornful eyes on her that she realized Lucas was right. A lifetime of doing anything to avoid the look her mother was giving her now had produced nothing but disappointment for both of them. Resentment settled deep inside her and she tensed, straightened and threw all good sense to the wind. Taking a stiff step back, she glanced briefly at Lucas, not missing the slight smile that curved his lips, then met her mother's gaze with all the confidence she could muster.

"Momma, this Lucas Grayson. Lucas, this is my mother, Karen Covington."

Lucas stepped forward and offered his hand. Karen reluctantly shook it. "I didn't know you had company. I didn't see another car."

"I live around the corner," Lucas answered.

Karen cut her eyes to Jaimee, dismissing Lucas altogether. "I thought it would be nice to spend the evening together. I brought a movie."

Jaimee smiled even though she didn't feel like it. "I keep telling you, Momma, call first. Tonight won't work. I'm spending the evening with Lucas."

Karen didn't bother to smile. "I don't mind if Lucas stays and watches the movie with us."

"No, we'll have to watch it another night."

Karen frowned and looked from Jaimee to Lucas and back again. "It's not good for the two of you to be here together alone, Jaimee. Even if you are just friends. Do you know how that looks?"

"We aren't *just* friends and it doesn't matter to me how it looks." Jaimee struggled to keep her voice from hitching up an octave. She placed a hand on her mother's shoulder to encourage her to leave. "Go have dinner with Jason. I'll call you later."

Karen's tight expression shifted smoothly into that all too familiar scowl of disgust as she shrugged off Jaimee's touch. "Jaimee Elaine, have you been sleeping with this man?"

To hell with it. She was sick to death of this. Lucas was so right. "Yes. Yes, I have. I've had sex with him too. And, I want to have sex with him again. Which is why I'd like for you to go home. And call me next time."

"You know this is wrong. You know—"

"Momma," Jaimee interrupted. "Stop before you say something you can't take back."

Her mother's face was red, her eyes hard and cold. "I knew you'd turn out like your father," she whispered furiously. "I warned you, Jaimee, I did. You've given Satan an opening to destroy you and your calling." Karen sighed deeply. "You've always been hot-blooded, Jaimee. I thought if I prayed hard enough, if I kept you in church and raised you right you wouldn't turn out to be like your father. I did everything I could to raise you not to be like this."

Shoulders sagging in defeat, Jaimee watched her mother visibly shaking with righteous anger. "Like what, Momma? Go ahead and say it. I know you want to. Go on, spit it out so we can get this over with." The words were soft, resigned though they held so much pain. Years of pain.

"A whore, Jaimee, you've become no better than a common whore!"

There it was. Jaimee closed her eyes and exhaled. After taking a moment to steel herself, she lifted her eyes to meet her mother's hard, accusing gaze and straightened her spine as best as she could.

"It took me a while to finally realize that your opinion is wasted on me. In the big scheme of things it really doesn't matter what you think about me or anything or anyone anymore." It seemed to take insurmountable control to calmly open the door for Karen, but she didn't show it. She was careful not to show it. "Goodbye, Momma."

Karen walked out the door without another word, without looking back. Though everything she'd said was absolutely the truth, there was a sharp, sickening pain that pierced Jaimee's heart as she watched her mother get into the car. Still, she waited until Karen pulled out and drove away before closing the door.

She took one, two breaths, then turned to face Lucas. Before she could push past the numbness to form a coherent explanation, Lucas wrapped his arms around her. Without hesitation she returned his embrace, giving him a quick squeeze. She went to let him go, but he held her firm. Enveloped in the warm spicy scent of him, she nearly broke. Nearly. Jaimee bit her lip and tried to swallow the knot of emotion that formed in her throat. No one had ever held her before, really held her. The realization of that harsh fact made her sad. A deep, raw, vacant kind of sad that took her breath away.

But Lucas held her tightly against his solid warmth and rubbed her back, like he wanted to absorb her pain and offer her strength. In a way he was doing just that. If her "relationship" with Lucas was unconventional and improper, did that make her a whore? Did it even matter if it did? She was right where she wanted to be and that was all that mattered.

He'd been right, what he said on the stairs. With that one clear, very accurate statement he'd jerked her perspective. Changed her focus.

She really did believe he cared about her on some level. He had to care. Otherwise he probably would have bolted. Still, a soft warning in the back of her mind whispered to her not to read anything into it, and dammit, she really wanted to read more into it.

"You okay?" He kissed the top of her head.

"I will be." The sound of her voice, thick with unshed tears, made her wince.

"Want to talk about it?"

"Not really, no."

Gently he cupped her face between his warm palms and stroked a thumb over her cheek as he watched her, waiting for her to lift her eyes to his. The pounding of her heart, the fear of what she'd see in those rich, penetrating eyes of his. She bit her lip and laid a hand over his, maybe to steady herself, maybe just to make sure he didn't retreat, and looked up at him.

"Tell me you didn't buy into that bullshit." To her relief there was no annoyance, pity or disgust in his eyes but there was something. Some unnamed something she wasn't about to try and decipher.

"No." Jaimee paused and tried to look away but Lucas held her firmly. "I don't think I'm a whore. I haven't exactly been virtuous and I'm thinking God is probably less than pleased with me right now. I've known you for what, a week and a half?" She sighed. "Kinda easy maybe, but I'm not a whore."

The muscle in Lucas's jaw pulsed, his eyes darkened, hardened as he searched her face. For a moment Jaimee thought he was going to argue the point. If he did she'd just concede. The last thing she wanted to do was argue, and God, she'd die if he left her tonight.

Seconds ticked by while Jaimee held her breath, waiting, teetering on a kind of edge. Finally he tilted her face and kissed her so softly his lips barely brushed over hers and yet it made her toes curl. "No, you're not." His warm breath fanned her lips. "You're an angel."

The hard plane of his cheek beneath her palm was warm and rough with stubble. "You have so overestimated me." Her laugh was soft. "But thank you." And she meant it. She so meant it. Lifting herself up on her tiptoes, she kissed him hard and grasped the back of his head. Cool, thick hair sifted through her fingers as she tilted her head and aggressively nipped at his bottom lip while she clutched a fistful of his hair and tugged gently to bring him closer. With a groan, he took away her control of the situation as he grasped her waist and yanked her body against him, pulling her off her feet. Complaining was the furthest thing from her mind.

Chapter Eighteen

The small bar was packed to well over capacity. The hedonistic throng of sweaty, pheromone-laden bodies pressed together on the dance floor didn't seem to care much. Lucas sat stiffly in the back corner booth. His lukewarm bottle of beer was all but forgotten as he watched the people move to the music as though they were one undulating body.

The events of the night before played through his mind for what seemed like the millionth time. After Karen had ripped Jaimee's heart to shreds, he had spent the night trying to heal it to some extent. Waking up this morning with Jaimee's soft, naked body snuggled up to him, her head resting on his shoulder, her hand lying over his heart was soul shattering. She had been truly angelic. While she slept peacefully, his fingers had explored the silky softness of her relaxed brow, her pretty pink cheeks, her full, sexy-sweet lips. Kissing her awake had been achingly sweet. His chest tightened with raw emotion when she lifted her sleepy eyes to his, smiled and said "Thank you for staying."

That emotion stayed with him and made him feel restless all through the day. Now as he sat across from Michael Butler, all Lucas could think about was keeping Jaimee safe. He just wanted to get her through this entirely fucked-up ordeal as whole as possible.

"I want to bring her in." It was time. Besides, he had a better chance of keeping her safe if she was aware of Edward Zachary's intentions. They'd intercepted a call between Marshall and Zachary and knew they were getting restless and would move on Jaimee soon. With or without approval he would do whatever it took to protect her. Whatever it took.

"Not yet."

"Let me rephrase." His steady gaze met Michael Butler's across the table. "I'm going to bring her in."

Michael took a deep breath, his brows furrowed. "Grayson, you're no longer objective."

"It's not about objectivity. She's in some serious shit now. Marshall's got nothing to lose. He's going to do what he has to do to save his ass. I want her in protective custody."

"Your protective custody, right?"

The question didn't deserve an answer in Lucas's estimation. "She's not stupid, Butler. She can handle it. She'll be more helpful to us if she knows everything."

"Look, you've slept with her, made her believe you cared for her. Which means—"

"Fuck that." Lucas fought to rein in his anger.

Michael took a draw from his bottle, set it aside in disgust. "Which means, my friend, she's gonna be hurt, and pissed off, therefore...uncooperative at best."

"I told you she's a smart woman. Once she's briefed, she'll understand and she'll cooperate."

"I would have thought you of all people would know women better than that."

Butler's calm, confident debate was setting his teeth on edge. "I know this one. She'll be livid and she'll cooperate."

"Yeah but she doesn't know you. And when she does..." Michael lifted a brow. "Ah, I see. You more than care, you've fallen in love with her."

Lucas stilled, his scowl deepening. That's impossible, he told himself, all the while trying to analyze just what it was he was feeling for Jaimee. His protectiveness concerning her was a built-in drive he had for all women, although his need to keep Jaimee secure was fierce and all-consuming. She made him feel, made him think about the future. And family. Had he ever really thought of his life past the job before?

"Hey, man, this situation isn't at all unique. Hell, it happens on occasion, it's inevitable. But I'm gonna tell you right now, it never ends happily." Michael leaned forward. "Like I said, when she finds out the truth she'll hate you, especially in this situation. You'd best accept that and prepare yourself for it."

Michael was probably right but he had to take a chance, had to do everything in his power to make Jaimee believe in him. Whether it was love or not, he didn't want to think about being without her. And the longer he kept the truth from her the more damage would be done. The more probability he'd lose her forever. There was no way in hell he would give up the one glimmer of happiness that he'd had in ages. She was his now and if he had to move heaven and hell, he'd do what it took to keep it that way.

He met Michael's gaze. "As an agent. I'm telling you, the longer we keep her in the dark the more danger we're putting her in."

Michael sat back in the booth and sighed deeply. "Yeah I know, but we can't bring her in yet. Soon, but not yet, there's too much riding on this. And as a friend, I'm telling you to separate your heart and your dick from the situation and think this through. You'll see I'm right."

"You fucking bastard. You're using her as bait," Lucas growled through clenched teeth.

Michael scowled then and returned Lucas's heated glare. "You're wrong. Shit, Grayson. She's in it, she's fuckin' in it. Turner put her in it, I didn't. I know that sucks but that's the facts we have to deal with. This situation is riding a fragile fuckin' line."

Lucas narrowed his eyes and sat back, assessing Michael with cold fury. "I'll go so far as to say your argument has...some merit. That's all you're getting. She gets hurt, Butler, I'm coming after you."

The corner of Michael's mouth tilted. "Do your job, Grayson, and she won't get hurt."

"I want The Pope brought in on this."

Michael's brows rose "Now look..."

"Fuck you, Butler. Get The Pope on board."

Michael studied Lucas's gaze, his lips thinned as he finally nodded. "I'll see what I can do."

"Do it." Lucas controlled the urge to clench his fists as he slid out of the booth and stood over Michael. "Call me in the morning before twelve and tell me he's on his way or to hell with it. I'll pull Jaimee in whether you approve or not."

Lucas didn't give Michael a chance to respond as he walked away. Let the fucking Bureau pick up the bill. He made his way out of the crowded bar to the SUV. Was he on another plane than the rest of the agents working this fucking case? Or was Michael right? Had he let his feelings for Jaimee color his perceptions? If anything, the fact that he loved her—and yes goddammit he loved her—should only sharpen his resolve to wrap up this case with Jaimee as whole as possible. However, his focus had shifted from taking down The Collective. It had narrowed and sharpened to one very vibrant woman.

Slamming the car door behind him, he punched the dashboard, rattling the sensitive electronics as he punctuated the strike with a colorful string of profanity that would have had his mother scowling up at him in stern, tight-lipped disappointment. The violent growl of Metallica thundered from the sound system when Lucas started the engine. Leaning over he pressed the volume button up, filling the vehicle, enveloping himself in the rage of the music. It was a good fucking thing Turner was dead. If he were alive now he would kill the fucking bastard with his bare hands for putting Jaimee in this situation.

Anger and frustration made sleep elusive. At twelve a.m. Lucas still sat at his desk listening to Jaimee breathe deeply as she slept. He called her, talked to her, promised to see her soon but he couldn't go to her tonight. His thoughts and emotions were too volatile, too on edge. The realization that he loved her shook the foundation of everything he believed about himself. At the same time it gave him peace. It soothed something inside that he didn't even know was raw and aching.

Jaimee's soft whimper seemed to brush over his skin, igniting his senses. This damned constant throbbing erection was driving him mad. He stood and ripped the earphones from his head and threw them across the room with a roar. Somewhere along the way he'd become a sappy, love-crazed horn dog. What had happened to him? Finding himself so in need of her was disconcerting to say the least. Jaimee consumed him, his heart, his mind, his body and it was distracting him from his objective. Damn Butler. He was right.

He rubbed his hands over his face and took a deep breath. For the sake of them both he had to get a grip and focus on completing this assignment. When everything was said and done with Zachary and his minions either dead or behind bars, then he could focus on Jaimee and work on winning her trust back.

The recording indicator light told him Jaimee was on the phone. Hurriedly he retrieved the headset and pulled it on. The call Lucas had been expecting and halfway dreading was underway. Maxine was home from her business trip.

"...surprised?" Jaimee's voice held a hint of annoyance.

"No, girl, hell no. This is a good thing." Maxine, on the other hand, sounded ecstatic.

"I don't know, Max. Is it really a good thing? I mean, I don't know anything about him."

Lucas gritted his teeth. Her constant insistence that she didn't know him was seriously pissing him off. She knew her asshole husband for seven years and yet she didn't know a damn thing. But then he reminded himself that she was right, she didn't know the truth about him either. He pinched the bridge of his nose. God, this was going to hurt both of them so much.

"I'm thinkin' you know him pretty well..."

"I'm not talking about that. I mean, I don't know the important, serious stuff like where he was born. I don't know how he was raised, what he believes in, if his parents are even still alive..."

He furrowed his brow trying to remember the last time he'd seen his parents. His father understood why he had all but cut ties, his mother was another story. What would his parents think of Jaimee? What would she think of them? It mattered to him. He did what he had to do at the time and all but turned his back on his family years ago to keep them safe. He had to try and make a difference. Organized crime wasn't anything like the glitzy Italian godfathers they portrayed in film, nor was there anything respectable or redeemable about those connected to it. They were corrupt, sinister power gluttons who preyed on the innocent and the weak. They came in all shapes and sizes, all nationalities and stations of life.

During his few years as a cop he'd seen it all, the crack whores and the gang bangers. But it was the children, the forsaken defenseless ones. It was the broken and hopeless with hollow eyes. Their innocence had been stripped away and replaced with greed, fear, fury and even addiction. He rapidly grew tired of cleaning up the mess left in the wake of depraved criminals. He wanted to get at the source, bring the predatory, power-hungry bastards to their knees and make them pay.

Maybe it was selfish of him that he left his life, never looking back, never considering his family's feelings or how he would feel without them. He never believed he had the ability to care. Not until Jaimee.

"Yeah but—"

"Hell, I don't even know how old he is—"

"Wait, just shut up a minute and listen to me."

"Oh great, here comes the speech about me needing hot, nasty sex." She sighed.

"Hey, you know what I'm thinking? That's just fine with me, sweet thing. Why waste my breath? I'll just talk to you later when you got less attitude."

Jaimee sighed. "I didn't mean it that way, Max, don't hang up."

"I'm hanging up now. Good day."

"Don't you dare hang up. I'll just call you back."

"I said good day!"

Lucas couldn't help but smile.

"Grrrr! Maxine! Sheesh, okay I'm sorry. Tell me what you were gonna say, I'm listening."

There was a long pause and Lucas would have thought Maxine had actually hung up if he didn't know better. He was really starting to like her a lot.

"Max. Seriously, I need your help. I'm in way over my head here."

"Why do you think you're in over your head?"

"Because, he's... It's like he stepped out of a romance novel. He's gorgeous, painfully sexy, but sweet, considerate, protective, big..."

"Big? Hmmm—"

"Max-ine!"

Maxine snickered. "Okay, okay. So did he just get up and leave after or something?"

"No. He spent the night with me last night but he left before I woke up."

"And he didn't leave money on the nightstand?"

"No!" Jaimee laughed.

"Okay so did he say he wanted to see you again?"

"Yeah, he does." She said it with such incredulity and wonder it made him want to shake her.

"I'm waiting for the bad part." Lucas found himself grinning at Max's sarcastic snort.

"The bad part is nothing that good is real. And..." Lucas braced himself. "I don't know him..." He rolled his eyes and resisted the urge to growl "...and I didn't hesitate to have sex with him...many, many times." She did hesitate. He had played hardball and she had been vulnerable, but then she probably didn't see it that way. "Now, I feel guilty."

"Why?"

"Because, Max, you know how I believe. I don't love him."

Lucas tensed at the disappointment her denial caused in him. It didn't matter that it was irrational to expect her to love him. He'd had more time with her than she'd had with him. Still it didn't set well with him, not in the least. She may not love him but she cared or she wouldn't have had sex with him. She didn't do a damn thing she didn't want to do. They had a connection from the beginning even if it was chemical. Didn't matter.

"You sure about that?"

A long pause stretched out for what seemed like forever until finally on a deep sigh Jaimee nearly whispered. "I don't know..."

He fought the urge to storm her house and show her just how much she cared.

"I like him. He's intelligent, funny, like I said, considerate. But probably mostly just because it was the most incredible sex I've ever had."

"Feelings mutual, babe," he murmured to himself. It was pretty fan-fucking-tastic and it was only gonna get better.

"Yeah and you are *the* quintessential connoisseur of sex too, aren't you? You dirty slut."

Jaimee and Max laughed.

"I'm thinking this was pretty noteworthy sex, Max."

"He went downtown, didn't he?"

Oh yeah. His favorite part of the night. The memory of Jaimee's pretty pussy, all rosy and slick with her cream, had his erection thickening all the more. He'd thought of little else over the past week. He'd never get enough. She'd become an addiction.

"Yes," she said softly, as if she'd read his mind and responded to his need.

"And? No, wait, start from the beginning and tell me everything!"

Jaimee recounted the events of the past couple of days to Maxine with the kind of description only an English teacher would know how to use. Lucas listened with growing hunger. Then she told Maxine about the steam room escapade. God, it really had been incredible.

"Hot damn." Maxine nearly whispered the words.

"Yeah, I know. It was better than I expected. I never imagined sex in a steam room. I wasn't even sure that was healthy."

"Damn! And he spanked you!?"

"Well I'm not sure I'd say he spanked me. He smacked my butt and damn if it didn't feel amazing..."

"I told you!" Maxine laughed.

"But that's not the most shocking part, Max."

"Spill!"

"I sorta kinda asked him to... See... Okay let me back up. During sex he fondled my back door area."

"Your asshole?"

"Ugh! Yes!"

"And?"

"I really liked it. I mean...it feels really intense, sorta magnified everything." She drew out the "reallys" for emphasis. Lucas smiled and adjusted his pants.

"Okay so?"

"So, as I was saying, I asked him to, well more like encouraged..."

"Just spit it out, James," Maxine drawled.

"I want to try boo-fooin'." The words came out so fast they almost ran together.

"Cool. And you told him you wanted to?" Her smile was clear in her voice and a hint of pride that made him shake his head and chuckle.

"Yeah, in a roundabout way."

"Elaborate."

"Exactly! I told him he could elaborate on it if he wanted to."

Maxine sighed in exasperation. "And his response."

"He said anything I wanted, anytime I wanted it."

"Damn girl. He got a brother?"

"That's exactly what I'm telling you! I don't know! I'm ready to have butt sex with a man and I don't even know if he has siblings."

"Well hell, Jaimee, knowing a dude's family facts is not a prerequisite."

Lucas couldn't stop grinning.

"Don't sweat it, babe, I'll fill you in on everything you need to know. We're still on for Saturday, right?"

"You know what? Yeah! I think I'm really up for that."

"We gotta show you off after we get you made over."

Jaimee snorted. "Oh great."

"Be ready to head out early. You have an appointment with my stylist at eight thirty Saturday morning."

"Damn, Max, that's early for Saturday."

"We got a lot of work to do. Oh hey, I forgot to ask you one thing."

"What's that?"

"Did you go down on him?"

"No, I thought about it. I swear, Max, I didn't get the chance to try. He kept me so overwhelmed and over-stimulated my brain shorted out or something. I couldn't think straight." Lucas could hear the smile in her voice; it made him feel fiercely proud that he'd put it there. "I want to though. I really do. But I'm sort of afraid."

"Nothin' to be afraid of, just make sure you have a towel close you so you can spit it out without him even knowing."

Lucas froze and tried to remember if any woman had ever done that with him. Most of the time he didn't come in their mouths anyway and the few times he did, he really didn't pay attention. Damn, he really had been an ass. There hadn't been a special woman in his life since high school. He'd dated, but never seriously. He hadn't cared about any of the women he slept with. Well, except for Candice Snyder, his very first. She was a senior and he was a freshman. To him she had been a goddess. He'd learned a whole hell of a lot from Candi. After that, fucking wasn't much more than a hobby.

Some of the women he'd been with he'd treated pretty callously. Usually because the sex had been for an ulterior purpose, not pleasure. Still, a pang of remorse needled him . They were human beings after all and he'd used them. Jaimee's deep sigh brought his mind back to the phone conversation.

"No, it's not that. I don't think I'd mind swallowing. It's just that I've never done it. You know Lucas has had a ton of blow jobs, what if I screw up and don't do it right?" she asked softly.

Her voice had lowered to a sultry tone. Was she thinking about it? Was she aroused, hot, creamy? Lucas remembered her wet lips sliding down that damn popsicle a few days ago. The idea of those juicy lips of hers wrapped around his cock, stroking, sucking him had him hissing through his teeth.

"Hell, girl, don't worry about that. Men love BJs so much it won't matter how good you are at it. They're just grateful for it."

"Fuckin' A." Lucas shifted in his seat again.

"Just remember, if you're going to use your teeth, be very, very careful...and gentle."

"Mmm... If I get another chance, I might get up the nerve to try."

Damn her, she was going to get another chance, as soon as possible. And when he was done there would be no doubt as to what he was to her.

Chapter Nineteen

Thursdays were just a tease. Fridays were too long and tiring, this one especially. Since that sickening scene with her mom she hadn't heard from Lucas. Jaimee sighed as she stirred the melting caramel. Making caramel apples was supposed to distract her from worrying about it. She sighed again and squeezed her eyes shut, denying the thought that crawled through her mind that her mom was right. Even though she was half tempted to set the whole mess aside and take her horny self down the street and beg him to do his thing. Damn. She really was out of control.

Thankfully no work was looming over her this weekend and she was so looking forward to it. Hanging with Maxine would be good for her. She blew her hair out of her face and turned on the radio mounted above the cabinet before moving on to the apples. The DJ enthusiastically announced the next song was "Kiss You All Over" by Exile.

Jaimee snickered and shook her head. "How apropos," she murmured to herself as she pushed the wooden sticks into the top of the apples. "So show me, show me everything you do..." she sang along, swaying with the music as she lifted the double boiler to move it to the island to work on dipping the apples. "'Cause baby no one does it quite like you... Love you...need you...oh baby...I wanna kiss you all over..."

"Here I am, knock yourself out."

Startled, Jaimee jumped, nearly upending the double boiler filled with hot caramel and burning her thumb in the process.

"Ow shit! Damn it! You're a menace, do you know that?" she snapped and sucked on her thumb. A strange mixture of annoyance and delight washed over her at same time. Good Lord the man had her all messed up.

Lucas leaned casually against the doorframe, his hair tied back, arms crossed over his broad chest, watching her. The white shirt he wore open at the throat, sleeves rolled up, looked incredible against his dark skin and his black pants fit snug over his hips and thighs. All he needed was a sword at his hip to complete the look...and maybe an eye patch.

How long had he been there? She involuntarily took a step back as her gaze clashed with his. His eyes were dark, his mouth set and the muscle in his jaw twitched as his gaze traveled from her bare feet to her baggy, lime terry cloth shorts and lingered at her chest.

Damn, she wasn't wearing a bra, which meant her uninhibited breasts were swaying freely underneath her oversized yellow T-shirt with every breath, every move she made. On top of that, thanks to Mr. Sexy and her previous train of thought, her nipples were standing at full and eager attention. Too irritated to be embarrassed at how ridiculous she looked, she went to the sink to cool her burnt thumb under cold water.

"I could have been your worst nightmare," he said lazily. There was power in that voice. Dark, wicked power that captured her attention and sent heated shivers dancing over her already sensitive body.

Gathering her resolve, she gave him a snotty look. "Who says you aren't?"

Who the hell did he think he was anyway? Just barging in without knocking or alerting her of his presence. Did he think because she'd slept with him he had a right to come and go as he pleased? Well, dammit, he had another think coming.

That realization had heat crawling up her throat to burn her cheeks. Oh great, now she was red faced. He had a bad habit of just doing whatever he pleased, whenever. The man had no manners whatsoever. He tilted his head, stepping toward her. It was disconcerting and kind of rude. Okay, fine, it was seriously sexy, but it made her damned uncomfortable. It seemed as though he was analyzing her, seeing deep inside, much more than she wanted him to see.

"Would you rather it have been Ronald Marshall who just walked through your unlocked door?" He wasn't smiling; as a matter of fact he looked slightly pissed off. He walked purposefully toward her, ignoring the fact that, with every step, she retreated.

"No." She wrinkled her nose.

"Or worse?" He reached out to shut off the faucet with a quick twist of his wrist.

Did he just growl? She gasped as she found herself backed up against the counter. That sounded like a growl, the vibrations rumbled through her, awakening every cell of her body.

"Let me see."

"It's fine." She ignored the hand he held out to her.

If he touched her she'd go up in flames. Spontaneously combust from the restrained lust she kept trying to tamp down since he imposed himself into her sedate, boring life. With an exasperated sigh his fingers wrapped around her wrist, tugged her closer and lifted her hand to examine her burn. The burn he caused. Damn him. She concentrated on keeping her breathing even as his thumb brushed over her pulse point. His gaze held hers, his eyes smoldering with temper and maybe something more.

"Do you always have to be so damn bullheaded?" his voice rumbled, setting off little tremors in her tummy as he lowered his gaze to study the burn.

"Do you always have to be so...so..." She forgot what she was saying as he blew on her damp thumb. Holy crap.

He lifted his eyes from the small red welt rising on her thumb to watch her, his brow lifting slowly. "Right?"

"No." She wrinkled her nose at him again and tugged her hand, trying to free herself. "I was thinking overbearing, dogmatic, aggressive, arrogant...bossy."

He smelled so good she wanted to whimper. She wanted to wrap her arms around him, press her body against him, rest her head on his solid chest and absorb the feel of him, his scent, his security.

"Yes, I am. Isn't that what you want, James?"

Before she had a chance to respond he wound her ponytail around his hand and pulled her head back so she had no choice but to look up at him. The action was savage but she wasn't afraid. Instead, her body reacted with ferocity and instinctively she pressed her breasts against him, her lips parting on a shaky gasp. His lips brushed against hers as he spoke, just as his words seem to brush against her womb.

"A badass, tough, rugged...forceful?"

Her "yes" was somewhere between a groan and a whisper. It sounded animalistic and needy but God help her, this *was* what she wanted. It was what she'd been craving for years, someone stronger than her, someone with an all-consuming passion and need for her. A man who didn't wait on her to initiate every damn thing but took control and dominated.

He reached and dipped a finger in the cooling caramel and tasted it. "It's good. Sweet." A slow smile curved his lips as he dipped his finger in again and held it to her lips. Jaimee watched his eyes darken as she took his warm caramel-coated finger into her mouth. She let her desire lead her and wrapped her tongue around it, sucking gently.

Slowly he withdrew his finger and lowered his head. He let his tongue trace the ridge of her lower lip, sending fire sparking through every cell of her body. When his teeth grazed over the fuller part of her lip, need gripped her body like a living thing. Sparks of sensation rained over her body. A rush of heat infused her, spearing straight to her core. Her breasts ached for his touch.

"Mmm, the sweetest." His fingers flexed on her hip as he kissed her jaw. His teeth grazed over the sensitive skin of her throat. "I need this. I need you, Jaimee."

Her heart skipped several beats at his hoarse words. She was going up in flames, losing all control, all sense of reality. He was becoming an obsession. She had to get space before she lost more than she could afford. "Wait." She pushed against his chest but it was like trying to move a brick wall. "Lucas, I can't think."

"Good, you think too much," he whispered in her ear. "Except when you should be. Leaving the door unlocked was unacceptable."

"It's not that big a deal, really." Her voice was breathy and lacked the austerity she'd been going for. "It's a safe neighborhood. Why does it matter so much?"

He raised his head and glared at her as he tugged her ponytail again, making her look into his eyes. "It matters to me, Jaimee. It is a big deal to me. Don't fucking doubt that for one damn minute."

Excitement flared through her at his harsh words and the slight bite of pain. She wanted to push him. God help her, she wanted to be overpowered, forced. It was hard for her to recognize, to absorb and accept these new truths about herself. These were taboo desires, weren't they? Didn't this mean she was a reprobate?

His eyes were so rich and dark, glowing with anger and passion. "Wait." Her voice was weaker this time as his voracious mouth began trailing fiery kisses down her throat. She stiffened, struggled for reason, some logic to lay hold of and give her what she needed to step back. She had to step back or she'd drown.

"Stop analyzing it, Jaimee. Just feel."

"I don't want to." Even as the words slipped from her lips her fingers curled into his shirt.

"Yes, you do, you need to. I need you to." The hand at her hip worked its way under her shirt and slid up her side. Damn his hands were so warm against her skin. She shuddered as he cupped her breast, his thumb circling her nipple. A hungry groan rumbled from deep inside him, vibrating over every nerve in her body. "Don't leave the door unlocked again." The hard, thick length of his cock pressed against her lower stomach, leaving no doubt to what he wanted. "Promise me you won't forget to lock the door again."

Whether it made sense or not, his words and his touch unlocked something in her, awakening a passion she couldn't, wouldn't, deny anymore. If it meant she was perverted then God help her, it was truth. Her truth, right or wrong. Ignoring that need in her, pretending it didn't exist didn't make it go away. With acceptance came peace, and as corny as it may seem, joy.

She smiled up at him and the words were out of her mouth before she had time to think about them. "What are you gonna do if I don't? Spank me?" They sounded like they came from someone else, low, hoarse, dripping with lust, daring him.

One brow lifted. "There's a big difference between a spanking and having your ass smacked, sweetheart."

Her eyes widened. Damn if it didn't excite her to think of his big hand smacking her bottom—hard. Still, she wasn't sure she wanted that much.

"Do you want to spank me?" She looked up at him through lowered lashes and watched fire flare in his eyes as his lips slowly curved into a smile.

"You sure as hell deserve it."

His eyes dilated, darkened, as his mouth claimed hers. She kissed him back, boldly meeting his tongue with her own. She couldn't close her eyes; the heat in his mesmerized her.

He nipped her bottom lip as he released her hair and lifted her effortlessly onto the end of the island. Quickly, he moved the double boiler aside a bit before grasping her knees, parting her legs and stepping between them.

"God, I've missed you."

He missed her? It had only been a day and a half but he missed her. Had anyone ever told her that before, ever? No, no, no, she didn't want to think about anything or anyone but the pulsing need radiating through her and the way Lucas made her feel now, right this moment.

He pulled her shirt over her head and tossed it aside. With a mischievous tilt of his lips he dipped his fingers into the caramel. When she realized what he intended her eyes widened. Though it was cooling, the caramel was still very warm. Her eyes fluttered closed as he slowly spread the candy over her nipple. Heat spread from the tips of her breasts and radiated through her body. A flash fire of sensation washed over her as his tongue swirled over her caramel-coated nipple. He teased her, humming with pleasure as he drew her nipple into his mouth. Jaimee's gasp melted into a moan as he licked and sucked while spreading the caramel over her other nipple.

He licked, kissed and sucked her nipples as he drew a hot sticky swirl down the center of her body. His other hand slid up her thigh, his thumb making firm little circles as he went.

"Too much." Jaimee caught her breath as his thumb eased beneath the elastic leg of her comfortable cotton panties. Her entire body pulsed with need. He lifted his gaze. His eyes held hers, narrowing slightly as he touched her.

"Tell me." It was a demand, neither a request, nor a suggestion.

"I can't." Her voice was too high pitched. She couldn't think, could barely breathe. His touch was feather light as he stroked the swelling outer lips of her pussy.

"You can," he growled against the curve of her breast. Using his tongue, his lips, his teeth, he moved down, following the caramel trail he made. "God, Jaimee, you're so wet," he murmured against her navel.

All her excited bravado melted, all that joy and peace suddenly disintegrated into shame and she winced. "I know, I'm sorry." She stiffened. He hadn't said anything the other times. Did he just now notice? How could he not have noticed before? *Oh please*, she begged silently, *don't stop now*. If he left her like this it would hurt too much.

His head jerked up, his eyes searched hers and his hand grasped her thigh to keep her still. "Sorry? Why?"

She'd been thinking about him, talking to Max about him, she was already wet when he showed up. Then he had to go and play with her like this, growling into her neck, making her crazy with the caramel. Sheesh, what did he expect?

"Well, I know it's always been too much." Heat infused her face as she bit the inside of her cheek and looked away. If disgust had replaced that hot lust she'd seen on his face earlier her heart would break. She couldn't bear it. "It's sloppy and—"

"You think it's sloppy?" He interrupted her as his fingers continued to smooth over her intimate curves. "Doesn't it feel good? Hot and sleek, gliding over your soft little pussy?"

She hesitated, hope blooming. Resisting the urge to moan, she sort of shrugged. "I...I like it."

"I love it. I love the feel of all that sweet honey, like hot, liquid silk on my fingers. I love it on my tongue. The way it feels when my dick moves inside your tight pussy. Don't say you're sorry for that again."

She blinked at him, her mouth agape. The illicit words caressing her, making her sheath clench. "I didn't know. Brent was sometimes turned off when there was too much so...I didn't know." She shrugged and squeezed her eyes shut. No, damn it, she didn't want to think of him. She didn't want him in her mind, but there he was and she wanted Lucas to understand.

"Look at me."

She opened her eyes and looked down at his hands. He had the most amazing hands: big, strong, talented.

"I said look at me, dammit." He did it again, he growled at her again. When he did that it was like a trigger, setting her on fire, melting her insides. With a deep breath she raised her head and met his stormy gaze. "I'm not Brent."

She flinched. The savage look in his eyes made her instinctively pull back, and at the same time it made her crave him even more. He was fast becoming a raw, harsh reality. He'd invaded her life and occupied her mind, her body and was slowly overtaking her heart. When he looked her in the eye, he made her believe she mattered, that he could and wouldn't hesitate to protect her. He didn't ignore her, back down from her or patronize her.

"No, you're not. You're nothing like him."

Unsmiling, she framed his face in her hands. Even his face was hard, strong. The roughness of stubble against her palm added another layer of sensations to everything she was already feeling. She searched his eyes as if all the secrets of the world lay in those mysterious depths. Maybe they did. She leaned forward and kissed him, tasting the caramel on his tongue as she explored his mouth with slow, deliberate kisses. The way his work-roughened palms moved slowly over her body, kneaded her breasts, drew soft moans from her. For a while he let her have her way and that simple freedom to explore was arousing. It was wonderful just being able to slowly touch and be touched, to experiment with all of her senses.

Her tongue caressed his boldly, slowly stroking over his lips as her hands fumbled with his shirt buttons, until she got it open. Her palms smoothed over the muscles of his chest, feeling them bunch under her touch. The hoops in his nipples were too enticing to ignore. He inhaled sharply and took control of the kiss when she toyed with them, her thumb circling the hard nipples. Her legs wrapped around his hips and pulled him closer.

"You make me crazy. I'm so fucking hard, I hurt," he groaned against her mouth. His hands gripped the sides of her shorts. "Raise up."

Leaning back, her palms flat behind her, she lifted her hips with his help as he made short work of freeing her of her shorts and panties.

"Beautiful, perfect..." He tossed the shorts aside, his gaze burning her. Splaying one hand over her naked stomach, he dipped his fingers in the caramel again. He smoothed it over her tight clit, blending it with her own cream. He massaged around and over it until she wanted to cry. The heat from the caramel, the gentle, firm friction of his thumb was overwhelming but she fought against her climax.

His eyes devoured her as he slowly worked outward from her clit to the delicate and sensitive folds of her pussy. He raised his eyes to hers without lifting his head.

"Mine, Jaimee."

Captivated by the intensity of his gaze she could have sworn her heart fluttered in her chest and for a moment she forgot to breathe. His? "Yes." In one word that claimed and bound her she'd been set free.

Lucas kissed her stomach as his fingers dipped inside her. Her head fell back on a frustrated moan as his thumb continued to play over her, delving lightly between the delicate folds of her flaming flesh while his fingers massaged in and out of her convulsing vagina. She gasped, tilting her hips. She liked the sweet torture, loved the way the heated sensations were building, thrumming through her. "Tell me what you want, Jaimee."

"I don't know," she said huskily, her frustration growing. Her muscles ached, her body shook with her need to climax. "I want you."

"You do know. Let go for me, baby. Just feel. What do you want?"

"I want..." She bit her bottom lip on a moan.

"Yes, come on, baby, tell me." A hard shudder wracked her body as his warm breath fanned her heated flesh.

"Oh please, Lucas, you're killing me."

Frustrated, her breath ragged, she was too close to the edge of her climax to think clearly. She didn't want it to softly peak and fade in long wispy waves of pleasure. That would only frustrate her more. She wanted an orgasm that was unrelenting and violent. One like those he'd given her before.

"Please Lucas what?"

"I want you inside me. I want your mouth on me." Her breath caught in her throat as her orgasm began to unravel. "Oh God, Lucas, now, please, suck my clit."

Lucas lifted her legs, supporting them on his shoulders as his tongue laved her, licking, sucking the caramel from her. When his hungry lips finally closed over her clit and sucked hard, his tongue flicking the pulsing tip, she screamed his name. She couldn't help it, couldn't contain it. Her orgasm tore through her in a hot, devastating surge she was powerless against. Clutching his hair, she held on to him as the release gripped her, claimed her.

Jaimee arched her back as Lucas thrust his finger inside her. She tightened her muscles, struggling to keep him inside as he withdrew and thrust in again. Adding another finger, he curled them upward to press firmly against her G-spot. One orgasm faded only to crescendo into another peak stronger than the one before. The pleasure was nearly overwhelming, gushing from her in a torrent. It took her breath, stripping away everything but the feel of Lucas's tongue stroking her, his fingers massaging the contracting walls of her vagina, drawing more from her, driving her further than she believed possible.

Chapter Twenty

"Don't think I've forgotten that you left the door unlocked, Jaimee," Lucas warned, setting Jaimee on her wobbly legs.

She looked up at him in speculation. "Okay, okay. I'll be more careful." Deep, husky, and sensual, her voice sounded like it came from someone else. She gazed at the double boiler of caramel. "We've ruined the caramel. I can't use that batch on the apples." She grinned up at him, comfortable being naked in front of him now. "Wow, I don't think I'll be able to look at caramel the same again."

"Mmm, we'll get more caramel, sweetness. I've developed a new appreciation for it." As he shrugged out of his shirt his expression turned serious. "Jaimee, I mean what I say. You're easy prey. You're a young, single woman, living alone."

With lowered lashes she watched him free his hair and toss the leather clasp that had held it onto the counter and then began to unbuckle his belt. With his long black mane of hair loose and flowing over his muscular shoulders he looked wildly sensual and primitive. The last time he'd "spanked" her had been eye opening. It hadn't repulsed her as she'd always thought it would when she'd read those scenes in her sexy novels. The act had evoked quite the opposite reaction in fact. She smoothed a hand over her quivering stomach. But something more along the lines of punishment wasn't as appealing to her as she imagined it might be. She was all for play. Full-on BDSM was a whole other thing entirely.

"You're not going to use that belt on me, are you?"

"I should." The wickedly rough tone of his voice reached out and touched her womb. "Would it help you remember to be a good girl and keep the door locked?"

His gaze was smoldering as he took a step toward her, eyes narrowed, nostrils flared. She took a step back, unsure of whether she was excited or afraid. Slowly he advanced on her as he whipped his belt out of its loops with a flourish and wrapped it around his palm.

Oh hell. She nearly stumbled in her retreat. Maybe she pushed him too far. Her smile faded as her eyes widened in alarm.

"Come on now, Lucas. You wouldn't spank me with a belt, would you?"

The corner of his mouth twitched. "Of course not. I may like it rough, but I'm not a sadist." She sighed in relief. "However—" before she could respond, he arched a brow and lowered his head without releasing her from a hungry gaze that told her he wouldn't be denied, "—I'm not above showing you who's in charge."

"Who's in...?" She stood ramrod straight, hands on her hips, her brows lifting in defiance. No way in hell was she gonna be tied up. However, his hungry expression, the way he was advancing toward her all went to stoke the flames of her arousal. Still she wasn't about to just go all weak and submissive. Not that easily she wasn't. "Ha, yeah right, not in this lifetime. You're dreaming, Mr. Man."

"Then my dream is about to come true. Come here, Jaimee." He wasn't smiling.

"Hell no. You think you're tough enough to be my master, come get me." Good Lord she just challenged him. She couldn't help it. It excited her and made her all tingly and exhilarated. From the look in his eyes and the way his lips curled into a wicked smile she had no doubt he was going to take on that challenge. What did she have in her damn mind?

Lucas flashed a quick, toothy grin as he stepped out of his pants and stalked toward her. Jaimee's mouth watered at the sight of his erect cock. He used her moment of wonder and admiration to pounce. She squealed, jumped away and bolted for the living room. He laughed as he doggedly stayed after her. Damn, what a stupid move. She'd gotten herself cornered.

"No fair." She stuck out her bottom lip in a pretend pout. "You're stronger and faster than me."

"Did you bite off more than you can chew, baby?"

There was no way she was going to escape the situation but she hated to surrender. Even if the idea of being taken, really taken, made her seriously hot and wet, it took her a bit off guard to realize how kinky she really was.

She turned her attention back to Lucas and his predatory intentions. Seconds before he could jump for her again, she did the only thing she knew to do. She went on the offensive. In two swift strides she was standing in front of him, her hand wrapped firmly around his cock. God, it was hard, hot and it actually throbbed against her palm.

"Not yet," she purred, kinda like Eartha Kitt as Catwoman, and licked her lips for effect.

In that instant she felt invincible. After all, she did have the power in her hand at that moment. The fingers of her free hand speared into his hair and cupped the back of his head, pulling him down as she lifted up on her tip toes. She kissed him as passionately as she knew how while she began slowly stroking his rigid erection. His tongue invaded her mouth, rubbing against hers with a hunger that rivaled her own.

"You feel so fucking good," he groaned against her mouth as he gripped her hips and pulled her hard against him, trapping her hand in place against her stomach. The warm leather of his belt pressed against her hip.

She released his cock and let her hands roam over the warm, unyielding muscle of his wide shoulders. "So do you." With her senses on overload a whisper was the best she could muster.

She nipped at his throat then licked, amazed at how erotic it was to taste him, feel his skin against her tongue. Moving down, her lips closed over his right nipple. She teased the little ring, letting the tiny metal ball glide over her tongue as she sucked. His sharp intake of breath encouraged her.

Straightening, she looked up into his smoldering eyes and pushed him back until his calves came in contact with the leather chair draped with her thick chenille throw.

Perfect. This was the chance she'd been waiting for. She flattened her palms against his chest and shoved him hard. He barely swayed. The corner of his mouth quirked as he stood, unmoving.

"If you wanted me to sit, sweetness, you could have just said so."

"Okay then, sit. Please." She laughed, smiling mischievously as he obliged her. Inside she wanted to shout with joy. She couldn't remember the last time she was this happy. All her nervous trepidation about blow jobs paled in comparison to her newly discovered liberation. She was just going to take Maxine's words to heart and hope he would like whatever she did because she wasn't passing up this chance. At that moment his body was hers and she wanted to drive him wild.

Keeping her gaze locked with his, she knelt in front of him. The muscles of his thighs bunched under her hands as she urged his legs further apart and moved between them. She sat back and pressed her lips against his inner thigh. The hair there was a fine dusting, feathery, and an odd question occurred to her. She looked up, reveling in his dark, heated expression.

"Lucas?"

"Hmm?"

"Do you have Native American blood?"

Tilting his head, his brows furrowed slightly as he gazed down at her. "Yeah. Mostly Apache. Why?"

How wild. She'd guessed as much. He didn't only look like an Apache warrior. Everything about him exuded power. "Not much body hair," she murmured, nuzzling his warm inner thigh, loving the feel, the scent of him.

He smelled musky, spicy, aroused. His hand smoothed her hair away from her face; his knuckles caressed her cheek before he cupped her neck. His thumb made slow tantalizing circles beneath her ear. "Is that a bad thing or a good thing?"

She sat up straighter and scooted closer. "It's a Lucas thing." When he frowned down at her she added, "It's wonderful." Sudden shyness kept her from meeting his gaze. Instead she focused her attention on his impressive erection.

Lucas's fingers tenderly grasped her chin, tilting her face up. "Jaimee." His voice was like a caress. "You don't have to do anything you don't want to do."

"I know." She wanted to explore his body, to feel every inch of him against her tongue, taste him. Most of all she wanted to please him and that's what had her hesitant and nervous. "I want to." She had to warn him, he had a right to know what to expect, or not to expect. "I'm just not sure how..."

Leaning forward, he took her face between his hands and kissed her. His lips were gentle, his tongue caressing. "You can't do it wrong, baby."

"But I want you to enjoy it."

Lucas gave a short laugh. "You make me crazy, Jaimee. Just the way you're looking up at me like that makes me want to fuck you senseless. There's no way I won't enjoy it." He paused. "Unless you bite me. No biting." He growled that. God she loved it when he growled.

"You'll let me know if I'm doing it wrong?"

"Relax." He sat back with a grimace. "But please, do something. You're driving me insane."

His eyes dilated, darkened, his lips parted as he sucked in a breath. Her hands slid up his thighs and her tongue glided over the tip. She wasn't sure if it was his reaction, the soft velvety heat against her tongue or the salty, earthy taste of him that sent warm shivers snaking down her spine.

With kisses and firm, stroking licks she explored his cock. She loved the textures, the slight variations of taste. Trailing her fingers up and down his shaft she took the head into her mouth, her tongue stroking up from the little fissure on the underside to the tiny opening at the tip.

"That's good, baby. Yes," he moaned.

She took him deeper then withdrew to lick her lips, then took him in again. She didn't realize how erotic this act would be for her. Everything around her seemed to fade as she focused all her energies on caressing him with her mouth. She cupped his balls gently and was rewarded with a groan. His fingers tightened against her scalp as his hips began to move in rhythm. Jaimee closed her eyes and breathed through her nose, swallowing as she worked him as deeply as she could.

"...Jaimee." Her name got her attention but she didn't hear what he'd said. She was caught up in the sensations. Every sound seemed muffled by the whoosh of her heartbeat pounding in her ears. Looking up at him, she released him with a kiss to the tip. "Suck me, Jaimee," he said again through clenched teeth.

Oh, why didn't she think of that? Again her lips closed over the head and she sucked on it as though it were a popsicle—a very large, hot popsicle. "Mmm," she moaned as she took him deeper, sucking him hard as she massaged him with her tongue. His hands held her head as he fucked her mouth.

"Yes, baby." He grasped her face between his palms and seemed to encourage her to pull away. But she didn't want to stop. She watched his expression grow hungry and fierce. She picked up the pace and sucked him as if her life depended on his pleasure. She loved this, the steely hardness, silky smoothness, salty sweetness and the way she was driving him over the edge. That she could make him lose control made her feel incredible. She pressed her thighs together and ripples of pleasure danced through her. It amazed her how close she was to climaxing as well. His head fell back with a deep guttural groan as the orgasm gripped him. She swallowed with each pulse, ridiculously satisfied with herself.

Chapter Twenty-One

Looking up at him like a naughty kitten that had just devoured the last of the milk, Jaimee licked her lips. Because it was her first time, he hadn't meant to let it go that far, he didn't want to freak her out. Like a fool he'd underestimated her. She had her own ideas, was just discovering her own desires, and she was strong enough to pursue them. Her eyes glittered with triumphant satisfaction. Fuck yeah, he loved her and he needed her.

Still, he wanted more, and he loved pushing her limits. There was also the spanking she had due. He leaned forward and rubbed his thumb over her mouth. "Feeling proud of yourself, sweetness?"

Her lips curved into a self-satisfied grin. "Mmm hmm."

"You should feel proud. You have a talented mouth." He lowered himself to the floor beside her, careful to keep his belt close but out of sight. He cupped the back of her head, pulling her to him as he kissed her. It was savage, demanding. and she responded eagerly, her hands gripping his shoulders as she pressed closer. Grasping each wrist, he pulled away abruptly. "But don't get cocky, baby." He wanted to smile at her wide-eyed surprise but restrained himself.

A myriad of emotions passed over her lovely face and darkened those incredibly light eyes of hers as he crossed her wrists one over the other and wrapped the belt around them. It was tight enough to hold her but loose enough that it wouldn't bite into her skin. If she really wanted to get free, she could. This time.

"What do you think you're doing?" she finally asked, hesitantly.

"I think I'm doing exactly what I want to do." He met her heated gaze without smiling.

Her brows furrowed and her sweet little pink tongue darted between her swollen lips again. Nervous and aroused, yes, but curiosity was just as clear in her expression. Her cheeks were flushed, her eyes glowing. God, she was incredibly beautiful.

Brushing the back of his hand over her stiff nipples, he lowered his voice. "Trust me?"

For a moment he expected her to say stop then and there. Lucas cupped her breast without taking his eyes from hers and circled her areola with his thumb. Her eyelids fluttered, lowering just a bit, as her lip parted. She leaned toward him, pressing her breast more firmly against his hand and nodded.

"Good girl." Smiling, he kissed her brow, her nose, the corner of her mouth but pulled away when she moved to kiss him more fully. "Not yet. Lay on your tummy with your arms over your head."

She was hesitant but did as he asked. "Lucas, wait." Trepidation softened her voice.

"Jaimee?" He smoothed a hand over her hip, her ass, caressing her lightly.

"Are you gonna do that thing I asked you about?"

"What thing?" He frowned for a moment then remembered. Sweet, innocent Jaimee asking for anal sex, it was incredibly erotic. It still made him crazy to think about it. "Oh! You want to know if I'm gonna fuck your sexy ass?"

Her body jerked and he pressed his hand firmly to the middle of her back. "Lucas?" Her whispered question was threaded with a tinge of uneasiness.

"No, sweetness. Soon, but not yet." A smile curved his lips as his hand moved up her back to smooth away the goose bumps. "You're trembling. Are you cold?"

"No." The way her soft voice wavered gave him pause.

It was a small step, only the beginning, but like nothing else he wanted this from her. What's more, she wanted, needed to submit. Even though she didn't fully realize that was what she was hungry for quite yet. Watching her awaken to her own sexuality was going to be the most erotic experience of his life. It was going to be a slow, satisfying process. He just needed to be sure not to push too hard or too fast.

"If you're afraid, I'll untie you."

"I'm not afraid," she snapped then took a deep breath and continued a bit steadier. "I'm just...apprehensive."

"Don't think. Just surrender to the feel of what I'm doing to you." He touched the dip in her lower back right above the crevice of her curvy backside. "You have such a beautiful ass, Jaimee." Lightly, he traced wide circles on each round cheek with the palm of his hand. He waited until she exhaled and her tightened muscles began to relax.

Quickly he lifted his palm and brought it down with a sharp slap against her smooth ass cheek before continuing the soothing caress. Lucas smiled at her surprised yelp, followed by a heated gasp, her hands clenched into fists.

"Lucas." Her voice was thick with anger and arousal.

"James, baby, keep quiet or this will take all night long."

"Excuse me?" Her voice raised an octave.

A smile tugged at the corner of his mouth as he smacked her pretty ass again. She was breathing hard now. "I can go on and on, sweetness, as long as it takes. I suggest you give way to the sensations. Don't fight them...or me." His fingertips trailed over her heated, reddening curves as her body quivered. She didn't make a sound.

"Good girl. Open for me, Jaimee, spread your legs." Her skin was like velvet against his fingertips as he explored up her spine, back down. So slowly and feather light he followed the soft crease of her backside to honey-slicked curves between her thighs. "Holy shit, you're on fire."

She whimpered, tilting her hips to rub against his fingers as he gently probed the sodden folds. Blood pounded hot and hard downward, thickening his already rigid cock. He drew his finger up, spreading her cream further back toward her backside. He massaged the delicate space between her vagina and anus. "Do you know what I want to do to you?"

"I think so," she murmured.

He chuckled softly. "Right now my dick is so hard it aches. I want to feel that sweet pussy gripping me." His fingers circled her opening, drawing more dew from her. "I want to make you so fucking hot. I want to hear you scream my name as you come apart around me." His voice was harsh, betraying his need.

Her breath caught on a soft cry.

"Raise up on your knees." Lucas helped her lift her hips and get her knees under her. Kneeling behind her, he urged her legs farther apart. "Brace yourself with your forearms, baby. Tilt that pretty ass up for me. Yes, that's it." She was so completely open to him. It took everything in him to keep from moving between those honey-dripping thighs, grabbing her hips and thrusting home. But that wouldn't be nearly as satisfying as watching Jaimee lose herself in the pleasure he could give her.

As soon as he was sure she wouldn't fall forward on her face he spanked her in rhythmic succession. He alternated between striking her tender pussy and her ass. It was just hard enough to heat, just enough sting to drive her need higher, but not hard enough to hurt. Her breath caught in little gasps and moans with each carefully applied slap and had his control faltering.

"So beautiful." The groan was ripped from deep inside him as he soothed her burning flesh with kisses and soft caresses. His lips traveled up her body to nuzzle her neck. "Raise up a little," he whispered as he helped her raise her body from her elbows to her hands. His shaft nestled against the cushion of silky pussy.

He quickly brushed her ponytail to the side to tease her with gentle little nips and soothing licks along her neck. She was so sensitive there, so responsive. Slowly he began to move against her, his cock glided through her creamy folds, rasping lightly over her swollen clit. Cupping her breast, her diamond-hard nipple pressed eagerly against his palm as he kneaded her, his teeth scraped sharply over the curve of her neck.

"Please, Lucas." It was a cry of desperation, husky, needy.

"Tell me."

"Dammit, don't make me beg."

"Do you want me to kiss it and make it better?" he whispered hoarsely as he moved back to rub his stiff shaft up and down the soft folds.

Her body was quaking as she shook her head. "I want you inside me."

With a harsh groan he guided the throbbing head of his cock through her sweet silky slit, her liquid heat coating him, luring him in, making his balls tighten and ache for release. "Fuck. You're so hot, so wet." Too close, he was too close. "Tell me what you want." It was a demand, nearly a shout, raw, savage.

She groaned and arched her back. "I want you to fuck me," she growled at him.

The fury in her demand would have made him smile if he wasn't so close to losing his tenuous hold on his sanity. Sinking inside her tight sheath, he clenched his teeth and resisted the urge to go too fast. He caressed her reddened ass cheeks as his thumbs made firm little circles in the thick cream, moving closer and closer to her tight entrance.

He focused on restraint as he pressed a thumb against her anus, circling firmly, working her carefully, gently. With a desperate moan she rocked back, contracting drawing him deeper. Finally he thrust hard and was immersed to his balls inside her tight heat. He paused, breathing deeply, trying to get a grip on his control. Her muscled walls undulated in tiny teasing ripples, stroking his cock, and escalating his need to erupt.

"You feel so good, baby." It was a harsh groan that exposed the burning pleasure radiating through him as he continued to massage the little ring with his thumb.

"If you don't stop teasing me, Lucas, I swear to God I'm going to kill you with my bare hands." Her voice was thick, hoarse with a raw passion that matched his. Gritting his teeth, he withdrew slowly, until only the throbbing head of his straining cock remained inside before driving hard and fast into her. At the same time his thumb entered her and gently massaged just inside the incredibly tight ring of her anus. Her low throaty cry spurred him on as he withdrew and slammed against her again. He slid his free hand around her hip to span low on her belly and press firmly so that his shaft would rasp over that ultra sensitive spot inside her snug channel with each primal thrust.

She screamed his name as her orgasm tore through her. She brought him deeper still as she pushed back against him. He supported her quaking body and continued to torture them both with each thrust and slow withdraw. He clenched his teeth against his need to climax and sat back, taking her with him. Her head fell back against his shoulder. They both struggled for breath.

"Turn around," he whispered against her cheek.

With his hands at her waist, he held her steady as she turned to face him. He groaned and she whimpered softly as his ridged cock eased from her still-undulating sheath. The way her arms were bound plumped her swollen breasts, making them rise higher, lifting to him, begging for attention. They were flushed peachy pink, her nipples so firm and erect he had to have a taste. Fucking hell, would he ever get enough of her?

One hand pressed low at the base of her spine, holding her steady as he cupped one breast, teasing the tightly drawn peak with his thumb. Bending closer, his tongue swirled, firmly, slowly around the other before sucking the reddened berry into his mouth. With a hard shudder, her head fell back on a high breathy cry, her fingers extending, reaching for his cock. He easily kept her from achieving her goal. One touch of her eager little fingers and he'd lose control. When finally he left her breast and found her mouth he lingered there, tasting her hungry, little kisses, sharing the same breath. Just kissing Jaimee was an incredibly erotic experience.

Slowly he unwound the belt without saying a word, brushed his lips over each reddened wrist and pulled her close to kiss the soft silky skin of her throat, that sensitive area just below and behind her ear lobe.

"I don't think I can get enough of you." Lucas held her tighter against him, relishing the feel of her plump breasts, her nipples straining against his chest. His hot aching cock rested against the soft cushion of her stomach as his hands explored her body and kneaded her luscious ass. Lifting her, he positioned her over his shaft, moaning low as her hot sheath clutched at his turgid cock, drawing it deeper.

He tilted her away just enough to press his palm to her lower stomach. "So soft, sexy."

Jaimee whimpered as she began to move over him, her eyes closed. Lucas gripped her hips to slow her down. "Easy."

Stormy blue pleasure swirled in the depths of her eyes as she met his gaze. "Lucas..."

"It's okay, just let go, give me your pleasure, baby."

They began to move in rhythm, every silken glide of his hands over her sweat-dampened body corresponded with each deliberate, achingly slow thrust. Every little moan and shuddered sigh as her channel rippled around him pushed him higher. He eased Jaimee back further to take one rosy nipple into his mouth. He watched her as the pleasure took control and washed over her. He wanted to memorize it all, lock it inside him.

It could have been moments or hours before they finally untangled from each other. He wasn't sure. The moment had been raw, submerged in the surging pleasure of his own orgasm he was aware of nothing but Jaimee. After a few moments he stood and lifted her to her feet. Immediately her arms wrapped around him as she looked up at him. Those gorgeous, luminous eyes were so full of emotion and vulnerability it made him hurt.

"Lucas, don't leave me tonight."

"I'm not going anywhere." Hell no, he wasn't going anywhere. There was nothing he wanted more than to take her to bed and hold her, love her, never let her go. The emotion clawed at his heart. He couldn't leave her, not tonight, not ever. With a low groan he kissed her and she opened to him on a sigh. That sweet little timid tongue of hers made him want to do even more scandalous things to her.

"But, if you keep kissing me like that we'll never make it upstairs," he murmured against her mouth. Her sheepish grin had him chuckling as he took her hand and led her toward the stairs.

"Oh man, I have to finish the apples," she sighed, looking at the work she'd left unfinished on the counter.

"Leave 'em." Tugging gently, he urged her to follow him. "They aren't going anywhere."

She shook her head. "No, but I can't just leave that stuff sitting out all night." She pulled away and he watched ,appreciating the alluring way her voluptuous ass swayed as she walked into the kitchen. It was still rosy from her spanking. She was such a lush beauty.

Pulling her shirt over her head, she gave him a quick smile. "It won't take me long to just put the stuff away." The ridiculously oversized shirt covered her to mid thigh.

"What did you have to go and do that for?" He didn't bother to hide his disappointment. She stuck her tongue out at him as she busily covered the pot of cooled caramel. "Don't stick it out unless you plan to use it."

She lifted her brows at that and stuck her tongue out again, quickly glancing down at his burgeoning cock. "Amazing." She grinned mischievously at him. Damn she was adorable. With a surprised yelp, her playful seduction turned to befuddlement as she stared down at his pants rumpled on the floor by her feet. "Lucas. Your pants are vibrating."

Giving her a crooked smile, he bent to pick them up. "My cell."

"Ah. I figured." She laughed.

"Grayson," he said without taking his gaze from hers.

"Where's your fucking phone been, Grayson?"

In my fucking pants, Butler, he wanted to say. *Which were lying on Jaimee's kitchen floor.* But because Jaimee was close by, instead he just said, "You found me."

"You got The Pope." Michael's voice was edged with irritation.

Chapter Twenty-Two

There wasn't a whole lot she could glean from his phone conversation but she did note the muscle ticking in his jaw and his eyes narrowing slightly before he turned his back to her. And what a fine back it was. Her fingers itched to trace the sinewy muscles that bunched with every movement, grip that tight ass. With a sigh she brushed past him as she crossed to the laundry nook and dropped her shorts and panties into the washer. She turned to find him watching her. Ruthless determination had displaced the wicked playfulness that had his eyes sparkling earlier. Now they were cold, angry.

She frowned and mouthed, "*What's wrong?*"

Without answering, he reached out to her, his eyes warming just a bit as his fingertips skimmed over her cheek. Finally he shook his head and gave her a crooked smile, but the change in his mood was disconcerting. Who was he talking to anyway? Unsure whether she had a right to ask she chose not to, not right now. But a heavy feeling of foreboding had formed a lump in her throat. Later. She would have to ask later. For now, she shook it off, tilted her head against his caressing hand and whispered as quietly as she could, "I'm gonna go upstairs and take a quick shower. Will you be up?"

"Hold," he grumbled into the phone before putting his thumb over the receiver. "Apparently," he said, his gaze flicking downward to indicate his meaning. It was unbelievable but he was still rock hard and ready.

"Amazing." She shook her head slightly. To her relief he smiled down at her and his dark mahogany eyes glowed with passion.

"Your fault." He winked, then kissed her gently. "I'm right behind you."

She shook her head again as she walked away. This incredibly potent man with god-like good looks was her lover and he made her

Veronica Chadwick

feel wanted. Any minute she would wake up. Damn it, she couldn't fall for him, could she? He'd said she was his. Did he mean that? Did she want him to mean that? And could she possibly hold a man like Lucas, forever? Good God she was way out of her league.

She knew so little about him, and his changing expression during this phone conversation made her wonder. Maybe he had secrets; possibly those secrets could end up hurting her. That he wanted her was no secret, she was sure of that. Her hand on the banister, she paused, blinking as she sorted her thoughts. This altogether new emotion was exhilarating and uplifting. There was hope, there was anticipation and a desire to reach for more. There was a distinct need to let go of her past and transcend the present. Sheesh. She sounded like one of those motivational speakers. How many times did she deny it when her mother told her she wasn't happy, had never been happy, ever? Wow, had she been right the whole time? Had she never been happy, until now?

A scraping noise coming from the living room interrupted her introspection, distracting her from this fresh revelation. She took a step back from the stairs and narrowed her eyes to see better into the darkened living room. The shadow of a silhouette stood at her sliding glass doors working on the lock. Anger flared to life within her and she reacted without hesitation. In the hall closet beside the stairs she found her Louisville Slugger. Hefting it over her shoulder, she cautiously peered around the corner. The asshole was still there, still working on the lock. Idiot.

Adrenaline took over as she sprinted across the narrow hall back into the kitchen. Lucas said something as she ran past him but she didn't have the time or the inclination to stop.

"Shhh. Call 911. Someone's trying to break in," she said in a harsh whisper as she went through the swinging door into the dining room.

As best she could she pressed herself into the angle made by the china cabinet and the far wall to wait. When the bastard came through the door, she'd clobber him. She had just inched forward a couple of steps before Lucas's arm circled her waist and pulled her against him. His chest was like a rock wall and she could feel his heartbeat strong and rapid. He'd pulled his pants on, but his cock was still fully erect and unyielding pressed against her backside.

"Go back through the kitchen and upstairs," Lucas whispered, his lips brushing her ear. "Keep the bat. Lock the bedroom door."

She stiffened. "Hell no. This is my damn house," she whispered

152

back harshly.

His hand gripped her upper arm and jerked her roughly, pulling her behind him as he went back through the darkened kitchen, then across the hall, giving her no choice but to follow. At the stairs he spun her around and she gasped at his expression. The shadows across the hard planes of his face made him look brutal and menacing. There was deadly violence in his eyes, nearly black as onyx. "Just go. Do what I told you." He growled through his teeth and she scowled back at him defiantly. "Jaimee, don't fucking piss me off."

Too shocked to speak for a moment, she stared up at him, her heart in her throat. However, it didn't take long for her anger to override her surprise. Piss *him* off? Ha! He had no clue. She didn't care how he made her feel, she'd be damned if she'd allow him to boss her around. He towered over her, glaring at her as if he expected her to dutifully cower and obey. Did he think her a too-stupid-to-live little twit, some pitifully weak damsel in distress? Oh hell no. She'd always taken care of herself and she wasn't going to be a coward now that he'd barged into her life.

"If you think—" She had begun to tell him just that when his mouth descended on hers. His lips were hot, hard, his tongue swept over hers. Unlike any kiss she'd ever experienced from Brent or any other man it conveyed his dominance, fierce and unrelenting.

"Go. Now," he commanded her as he released her and left her swaying for a moment while he slipped quietly out the front door.

It took her breath away. She shuddered under the onslaught of conflicting emotions that bombarded her mind at once. For a moment there she forgot all about the danger and wanted him to throw her against the wall and fuck her mindless. At the same time she wanted to scratch his arrogant, Neanderthal eyes out! He didn't know what pissed off was.

Fuming she ran back through the kitchen to where she had been when Lucas got all "Mr. Big Man" on her. Damn him. She hoped she got a swipe at the idiot trying to break in. She seriously needed to hit something. When she heard something crashing into her grill the possibility of Lucas getting hurt entered her mind. To hell with waiting. She ran for the sliding glass doors and fumbled with the steel rod she'd laid in the track after she found the files in her office messed with. She watched the two figures struggling on her patio. *God what if the burglar had a knife, or a gun...* she silently prayed. She found the door was already open when she went to unlock it.

It was so dark, all she could see as she stepped out into the cool night air was Lucas's bare back as he grappled a man, dressed in black from head to toe. She squinted and hefted her bat, ready to swing when she got a clear shot. He was probably about three or four inches shorter than Lucas and not as big. The intruder's fist glanced off Lucas's hard jaw, hardly even making contact before he reeled back as Lucas clocked him.

The intruder recovered pretty quickly and came back for more, shoving Lucas against the concrete wall. One, two blows to the gut in rapid succession had the intruder doubling over in pain and backpedaling, trying to escape Lucas's fists. As Lucas advanced on the man again, Jaimee saw the glint of a blade in the intruder's fist. Taking the split second chance she had to bash the asshole in the head, she gritted her teeth and leapt forward without hesitation.

"Fuck!" Lucas pivoted when he saw her, effectively throwing himself between her and the intruder.

The intruder's head snapped up, startled, then he immediately bolted. The breath whooshed from Jaimee's lungs with a relief that was short lived. Lucas cursed viciously as he took off after him.

"Lucas!" she yelled. Oh hell, he should have just let him go. Jaimee ran back into the kitchen to the laundry alcove. With shaking hands she fished her shorts out of the washer and pulled them on. The intruder had on a ski mask so identifying facial features was out. He'd spun away and ran too quickly for her to even see what color his eyes were. But she could tell the police about his height and build. Maybe it would help a little. The police should arrive any second. Should already be there. Surely Lucas called them. Why weren't they there yet?

She was heading back to the patio when Lucas stalked through the open sliding glass doors, the ski mask clenched in his fist. His expression was frightening, his eyes blazing with rage. His jaw was tight and fury had color blooming high on his cheekbones. A dark red rivulet of blood slid down his arm from a gash in his shoulder. Jaimee shuddered then, grappling with her sudden fear. She stiffened her spine.

"You're bleeding. He cut you," she stammered, fear slithering through her. "You should sit. I'll get some clean towels...I think I have some peroxide..."

"It's not deep. Just get dressed." His voice was hoarse, as hard and as cold as marble. She stopped in her tracks and turned to face him again.

"If you had just waited I could have hit him in the head and he wouldn't have gotten away and you wouldn't be hurt. Really, this is your fault." Her voice was a bit too soft, too weak. She scowled to make up for it.

His eyes narrowed on hers as he advanced on her, stopping himself a few feet away. "Men are coming. Go get dressed."

She shuddered again. He looked as though he wanted to kill her with his bare hands. He wouldn't, she knew he wouldn't hurt her. But if he was going to be this mad just because she chose to defend her own home, and him, rather than run and hide then it was time she learned about it now. Swallowing, she braced herself. "I am dressed. Lucas, you need to understand something..."

"Jaimee." His voice was a low rolling thunder and it shook her to her core. "Go upstairs. Dress in something that won't have every male in sight drooling over you. I won't be able to deal with it tonight."

All she could do was blink, her mouth open. The muscles of his upper body bulged with tension. It seemed as though he was struggling to keep a tidal wave of emotion at bay, to breathe evenly.

"Lucas..." she whispered.

"Goddammit!" he roared, then closed his eyes, gritting his teeth. "Just fucking do it now or I'll carry you up there and dress you myself."

Anger she had expected, but this was more than anger. When his eyes met hers again she hesitated, torn between wanting to tell him where he could shove his attitude and wanting to do whatever she could to drive the cold dark hatred and pain from his eyes. It gripped her heart and squeezed so hard she gasped. It was true that his strength and dominance drew her to him and made her feel secure and free. But she didn't think she could abide this. She would be no man's puppet. Finally she turned, paused, and then swallowed hard as she walked away. She guessed it had all been a dream after all and now it was time to wake up.

Rage boiled inside him, so much rage he trembled with it. God, he'd hurt her. He hadn't meant to hurt her. The way the clear blue light dimmed in her eyes and turned stormy silver-gray had ripped at his heart. Crystal tears had welled up in them, shimmered there, but refused to fall. Even now he wanted to go to her, his arms ached to hold her, make it all go away. But there was nothing he could do, he couldn't explain right now. Looking down at the knit ski mask in his hand, he cursed viciously. He'd lost him. Jaimee was right. It was his fault. The fucking waste of carbon had jabbed at him, nicking his shoulder, slipped out of his grip and pulled a fucking pistol. He'd gotten away, but not before Lucas saw his face. In that split second everything he'd hoped for, his world, had shattered into oblivion.

With a roar, he punched the wall, leaving a crater in the drywall but it didn't make him feel any better. There was only one solution. This shit had to end. The only thing left to do now was protect Jaimee. Make it as easy on her as possible. Until then it was going to be pure hell. He'd fix it for her if he could. Jaimee had shown him his heart. In her sweet, innocent way she had staked her claim. Everything he was belonged to her even if she would never be his.

He swung open the front door after the first sharp rap. Michael stood, flanked by two uniformed police officers. Behind them stood Malaki Zareb Papalu, a six-foot-eight mountain of a man. Known as "The Pope" because of his unshakeable faith, indisputable wisdom and exacting justice. They said the man was psychic to boot. Nevertheless, he was the best. When it came to Jaimee's security he wouldn't accept less. Very seldom did Lucas have to look up to anyone and it was unnerving to have to do so in this case. The Pope's expression was closed, his obsidian eyes sharp and assessing as Lucas narrowed his eyes and motioned them back, stepped outside into the cool autumn night.

Butler opened his mouth to speak but Lucas cut him off. Thrusting the mask into Butler's hands, he whispered low and harsh, "Brent Turner is still alive. If you want to keep him that way, you'd best find him before I do."

Chapter Twenty-Three

Every light in the house was on downstairs, the glass doors were open, and her small patio was crowded with men. Jaimee had taken the time to shower before dressing. She'd needed the extra fifteen minutes to gather her chaotic emotions and get them under control. She looked at the uniformed men surveying her home. Any control she'd managed to reclaim hold on was tenuous at best.

Lucas stood outside with his back to her. He still hadn't put his shirt on and the muscles of his back were tense. There was a small bandage on his arm now. It stood out brilliant white against his tanned skin. Almost instinctively she wanted to smooth her hands over the rigid muscles, to soothe him. He stood just a little taller than the other man, his hands on his hips, his feet braced apart, aggressive. The other man had his arms crossed over his chest, his body tense and unmoving, and his expression formidable, angry. Odd. Her perceptions must be off.

Everything was off kilter. She stood there in her flannel lounge pants and baggy T-shirt, her hair still damp and unbound. Overwhelmed by her own inadequacy, she shifted from one foot to the other. She wasn't used to being so unnecessary. The bewilderment and confusion wasn't something she dealt with easily. She scrambled to sort the maelstrom of emotions from her tangled thoughts and make sense of them. She just couldn't seem to reason past the dull pain gripping her heart. Biting her lip, she took a deep breath and fought to still the tremors that had begun to rattle her once again.

Manage, dammit, she admonished herself. *Let your mind rule your heart.* More than a philosophy her mother had instilled in her, it had been her creed, her failsafe. It gave her strength. *Emotions come and go. Logic is steadfast and will not fail you. Feelings will lead you astray. Let wisdom, knowledge and reason guide you.* She steeled herself, determined to face whatever came next. Determined to remain calm, confident and levelheaded, even if she had to fake it, she lifted her chin and walked toward Lucas. She combed her fingers through her unruly mop of hair, pushing it away from her face and swallowing hard.

The man standing with Lucas nodded, indicating her presence almost imperceptibly as she stepped through the glass doors. Lucas abruptly turned his head and caught her gaze, watching her as she neared them. Resisting the urge to turn and run she forced herself forward. His eyes were dark and angry. He didn't touch her. Almost since the moment they'd met he'd reached out for her as if he needed the contact. She hadn't even realized he did that or that she'd come expect it until this moment. For the first time he went so far as to cross his arms to avoid touching her. The slight rejection had pain ripping at her heart. For what had to be the zillionth time she reminded herself, *You never really knew him.*

"Jaimee Turner." He watched her closely as he stepped back. "This is Michael Butler. He's the detective on this case."

Detective Butler was tall, just an inch or two shy of Lucas. His head was shaved and his skin was smooth, dark chocolate brown. His eyes were the most amazing gold green she'd ever seen and seemed to glow with what she could only describe as cool sympathy. Hesitantly, she took the hand he offered and found it strong and warm. "Detective."

"Mrs. Turner. We're nearly done here. We'll need your statement and then we'll be out of your way."

She just nodded, trying not to look back at Lucas even though she could feel his gaze on her. "That's okay." What was she supposed to say?

Movement along the ominously dark tree line caught her attention and she forgot to breathe. The biggest man she'd ever seen in her life seemed to materialize from the edge of the woods and walk toward them. As he crossed the patio, Jaimee instinctively stepped back a couple of paces and was relieved to feel Lucas's hands rest on her shoulders. The man was dressed in a black tank top, camo fatigue pants and black combat boots. Around his hips was strapped a thick black leather gun belt that held a sinister-looking hand cannon. You couldn't call a weapon like that a gun. The tattoo that circled his right biceps was a black intricate tribal design that oddly tempered his otherwise primitive and barbaric appearance.

She had to crane her neck to look up at him. His black hair was cropped short in a military cut. A short well-groomed goatee framed his mouth. Onyx eyes met hers, the erratic pounding of her heart quieted a bit and she shuddered at the peace that seemed to descend over her like a veil. This man knew God. She didn't know how she knew, but she had no doubt. Her gaze fell on the small and simple gold cross that hung from the black leather cord tied around his neck.

"It's okay, Jaimee, he's one of the good guys..." Lucas spoke softly from behind her, his hands moving up and down her upper arms.

"Mrs. Turner, this is 'The Pope'..." Detective Butler began.

"Malaki." His eyes never left hers. His incredibly deep bass voice was matter of fact and surprisingly gentle. "My name is Malaki, ma'am."

Torn between exhaustion and intrigue Jaimee took a deep breath and accepted the hand he offered. It easily enveloped hers. "Nice to meet you."

He gave her hand a squeeze before he released it and stepped back. Malaki was a walking contradiction. Her brows furrowed as she studied him. She was being rude, but she couldn't look away. What she saw in his eyes just didn't match the rest of him.

"Let's go in and talk." Detective Butler caught her attention and distracted her.

With her senses reeling, she allowed herself to be led into her living room. Lucas took her hand as he sat down on the sofa beside her, weaving his fingers with hers. It was ridiculous that the gesture had relief flooded through her. At the same time it irritated her. On top of everything that was happening, the mixed signals Lucas was giving her set her teeth on edge. Detective Butler took the chair and Malaki stood, watching.

She forced herself to push her confused feelings about her relationship with Lucas aside. The fact that someone had tried to invade her home had her uneasy and emotional enough. If Lucas hadn't been there she would have been in bed asleep. She had no way of knowing whether the intruder's intentions had been merely mercenary or something altogether more sinister. Summoning every ounce of determination she had, she reminded herself that *ifs* didn't matter now. She had to focus on what was.

"Mrs. Turner. Are you all right?" Detective Butler asked, interrupting her thoughts a second time.

Malaki walked around the couch and into the hall without saying a word. She chose to ignore him. "Yes." She just wanted to get on with this and get everyone out. There were too many people in her house. Too many men and all were looking at her like she was some sort of odd specimen of toenail fungus.

"Do you need anything?"

"What?" She didn't mean to snap but she couldn't help it. The whole situation was damn unnerving.

"Can I get you something? A drink of water?"

"No, I'm fine." Lucas's thumb caressed her wrist, making her remember. She squeezed her eyes closed for a second, tugging gently to try and free her hand but he wouldn't let her go.

"You're shaking, baby." Though Lucas spoke softly his voice held an edge of violence.

"I am?"

Jaimee didn't realize Malaki was standing beside her until he handed Lucas the crocheted afghan her grandmother had given her when she went away to college. It held so many sweet memories. Even though she'd carefully laundered it over the years it still held the faint scent of her grandmother's delicate perfume. Lucas wrapped it around her shoulders and somehow the familiar weight, the warmth of the afghan calmed her. Lucas murmured something in her hair. Her mind didn't register the words but she didn't try and resist when he pulled her closer to him. Grandma would have loved Lucas. *She* loved Lucas.

"We've been looking for this man for a while now. We brought The Pope in on this case because of his exceptional ability in tracking. As far as security goes, there's no one better. Mrs. Turner, he's here to help, there's no need to fear him."

"I'm not afraid of him." At least the attention of the men shifted to Malaki and away from her, all but Lucas's anyway. She turned to Malaki, making sure she looked him in the eye. "Why do they call you 'The Pope'?"

"You'll have to ask them." The deep bass of his voice was commanding and strong.

"Are you Catholic?"

"No."

"Oh." She glanced at the cross at his throat. "You're Protestant then?"

"No."

"Well then what—"

"I am Malaki Papalu, Mrs. Turner," he interrupted her.

"I'm sorry, I didn't mean to offend you," she said quickly. Must be the residual adrenaline that had her mouth running faster than her brain.

Malaki's expression remained impassive though his eyes seemed to smile. "I am not offended, ma'am."

"Okay good." She yawned and slumped against Lucas. His solid body was warm and strong, his powerful arms held her close; it would be so nice just to curl into him and go to sleep.

"Mrs. Turner, I'm truly sorry, I know it's late. But I need your statement."

Jaimee nodded and sat up. Her eyelids and her heart were heavy and her body ached as if she'd run after the asshole herself.

"Just recount for us what happened with as many details you can remember."

Jaimee left out everything that transpired before Butler called to tell him The Pope was in. She walked them through the events following like a pro. Step by step, she was careful not to leave out so much as one tiny detail. Her voice was stronger now and she seemed steadier. At least she wasn't trembling anymore.

She was snuggled against him, warm and soft. Just to hold her like this gave him a sense of peace, of blessed contentment. *She isn't free*, he reminded himself, and when she found out she was still married the guilt would be crushing. His jaw tightened as rage coursed through him. So much pain awaited Jaimee and it was killing him to know that he'd be the one to deliver it. He couldn't let her take it on alone.

Nothing would please him more at that moment than beating Brent Turner to a bloody pulp with his bare hands. It took a special kind of reprehensible to do what Turner had done to the one person he had committed to love and protect. Jaimee, with all her bravado and tenacity, needed to be cherished. She was a woman worthy of devotion, respect and adoration. Instead Turner had slandered her, ignored her, used her and then deserted her. For that alone Lucas wanted the idiot to feel pain...lots of pain.

God, how in the hell was he going to be able to let her go? Pain seared his chest and it was only going to get worse. It was just supposed to be another job but one taste of her and he was hooked. Then somewhere along the way she'd shown him he had a heart after all, only to leave it decimated. Fucking irony. It was best to get it over with now. Tonight he'd tell her and watch her turn away from him forever, cold and distant. Until then he was going to absorb as much of her warmth as he could. He pressed a kiss to the top of her head, inhaling her warm vanilla scent, branding it into his memory.

Butler stood and offered his hand. "Thank you, Mrs. Turner. You've been very helpful."

Jaimee took the hand he offered. "I hope so." She unfolded her legs from under her to stand.

"You have."

Lucas stood to lead them out. "I'll see them out, Jaimee, stay comfortable. I'll be right back."

Once they were outside, Lucas shut the door behind him and turned to The Pope. "Where did you find the blanket?"

"On a shelf in her bedroom closet."

Lucas narrowed his eyes. "She had blankets in the hall closet."

"Not that one. Women keep their most treasured comfort items in their bedroom." The Pope turned to go then stopped abruptly and turned, meeting Lucas's gaze. "It was not sex that nurtured the bond. It was the bond that encouraged sex." He walked away without looking back.

"Anyway." Butler glanced over his shoulder, watching The Pope walk toward the house in which Lucas had been staying. "I figured you'd be staying with Mrs. Turner."

Still processing what The Pope had said, Lucas said nothing. Butler eyed him for a moment before continuing. "The Pope can bunk at the house and..." he paused, shook his head wearily and shrugged, "...do what he does best."

"It's time. Now. She needs to be told." Butler shook his head but Lucas gave him no time to speak. "Fuck you, Butler, I'm not going to keep stringing her along like this. She has a right to know the piece of shit isn't dead."

"You don't know for certain that this guy was Turner."

Lucas took a step forward and stared menacingly into Butler's eyes. "There was enough hair in the cap. Run your goddamn tests. It was Turner."

"Back up, pretty boy, before I put my size twelve up your ass."

Lucas didn't move, wasn't about to back down. "Take your best shot," he growled.

"Lucas?" He tensed further and took a short step back at Jaimee's soft voice. Butler's scowl faded but he held eye contact.

"It's okay, Jaimee. I just had some questions, I'll be right in."

He didn't have to look back at her to know she was frowning at him. She didn't like being treated like a fragile flower. But damn it to hell that's exactly what she was to him. She'd been hurt too fucking much already and the worst was coming. The door closed behind him a little harder than it should have, just short of a slam and he turned his ire back on Butler.

"She's in trouble, Grayson. Even I know she's not the swooning female type. You tell her now and she will react. Probably try and hunt the asshole down herself."

Lucas clenched his teeth. Butler was right, damn him, he was right. He pushed his wild hair back from his face. "Understand, as soon as Turner is found, I'm bringing Jaimee in."

Butler scowled but nodded. "All right."

"Ready a safe house. And Michael—" Lucas wanted him to know that he was asking him as a friend rather than his case agent. "I want her as comfortable as possible. I'll finance it myself."

Butler nodded again, taking a deep breath. "It'll be taken care of."

Still clutching her grandmother's afghan around her shoulders, she paced the small space in front of her sofa. She was brooding, her brows knit together, reasoning, speculating, contemplating all the events of the evening as she nibbled on her bottom lip. He could all but see her mind working like well-oiled cogs.

"Jaimee," he said softly.

She turned to him. "Before you say anything there's something you need to understand." Her hair was nearly dry now. Glossy sable ringlets curled around her face, caressing her pretty pink cheeks. Though her eyelids were heavy with fatigue her eyes were sharp. There was anger in those fathomless clear blue depths but it wasn't the anger that had his heart clenching. It was the pain.

"I was raised by strong women. I come from a long line of ball busters. That's just the way I was raised—"

"Jaimee—"

"I don't take orders, nor do I bow down to any man. I will not sit around like Rapunzel waiting for some prince to come save me. I am more than capable of defending and protecting myself and mine—"

She was pushing him now. "Jaimee." It was a warning, one he knew with growing anger that she wouldn't heed.

"—even you. I've never expected a man to save me and I've never needed a knight in shining armor, Lucas. I don't need one now."

"The hell you don't." The hoarse growl through clenched teeth sounded as though it came from somewhere else as he closed the distance between them. He buried his hand in her thick hair and caught it in a fist then pulled her hard against him and tugged her head back. His mouth covered hers, silencing her attempt at a snide retort. Her lips were so full, so sweet.

"Open, goddammit." He groaned against her mouth, slightly

tightening his grip on her hair as his tongue stroked her bottom lip. With his other hand he cupped her ass, kneading her lush fullness as he held her against him.

Her moan of protest quickly became one of pleasure, her fingers curled against his chest as her lips parted on a sigh. Spontaneous combustion. If he didn't gain control of his libido, and quickly, he'd take her against the wall. He couldn't do that, not now. *She's still fucking married*, he roared at himself even as his tongue stroked over hers, his rock-hard shaft eagerly pressed against her soft belly. Forcing himself to release her, he tore his mouth from hers and stepped back breathlessly.

With his hands clenched at his sides to keep from reaching for her, he waited for her to lift her eyes to his. When she did he winced at the confusion, the pain, and his heart thundered in his chest, threatening to explode. "Let's go to bed. You're exhausted." It was a feeble, clumsy attempt at an excuse. With wide eyes she stared up at him, dumbfounded and dejected. This would kill them both.

Chapter Twenty-Four

Glancing up at the clock on the wall, Jaimee covered her mouth and tried to stifle yet another yawn. This day had to be longest day of her life. Lucas had tried to get her to call for a sub but she honestly didn't want to spend the day with him and his confusing mixed signals. All day she'd tried to figure it out. It wasn't like he could hide the fact that he was aroused but he went out of his way to keep his distance. Even went so far as to sleep in his pants, on top of the comforter, at the same time he held her close all through what was left of the night. At the time the only explanation she could think of was that maybe he believed he was obligated to spend the night in case the burglar came back. In any case the rejection hurt, even if he did kiss her like his life depended on it. It was odd, but she was tired of trying to make sense of it. Her thoughts and emotions were too befuddled from lack of sleep. Maybe he really did just want her to get a few hours of sleep.

"Mrs. Turner?"

Jaimee looked up and scanned the class. Twenty-five pairs of eyes were watching her curiously. Taking a deep breath, she straightened in her chair and answered the student wearily. "Yes, Molly?"

"Someone's knocking on the door."

"Oh." Jaimee gave her a half smile and rolled her eyes. "Sheesh. See what happens when you stay up late watching T.V." It was a reasonable enough fictitious excuse.

There was a spattering of chuckles from the students as Jaimee stood and walked to the door. The interruption had them whispering amongst themselves.

"Shhh, no talking, people. You're taking a test," she admonished them as she opened the door.

Another English teacher, Janice Benningfield, stood waiting. "Hey,

Jaimee, sorry to interrupt."

"No problem."

Janice flashed her famous mischievous pixie grin. "I was blessed with a new transfer student and wondered if you had an extra text book."

"Yeah." Jaimee smiled. "I think I have a couple in the cabinet." She motioned for Janice to follow and she went to her desk to retrieve the key from her tote. "I know it's in here somewhere," she said half to herself before remembering she'd put it in her top desk drawer. "Sheesh, I'm brain-dead today, I swear."

"It's Friday, dear, we're all brain-dead."

"True, very true." Jaimee laughed as she unlocked the metal cabinet. "You just need one?"

"Yep. For now. You never know, the powers that be may deem me worthy of even more blessings."

"Well I have more if they do." Grinning, Jaimee took a book from the top of the pile. Her smile faded and she did a double take. Behind the pile, against the back wall of the cabinet was wedged what looked like a black leather day planner.

"Something wrong?" Janice asked.

"Huh?" Jaimee forced herself to turn her attention away. "Oh no, I just remembered something I had forgotten to do," she covered with a smile.

"Ah." Janice eyed her suspiciously.

Janice was very intuitive, and combined with her natural curiosity and downright nosiness, it made it hard to pull anything over on her. Her students as well as her own children detested that quality in her. Jaimee didn't mind usually. But she did envy her keen intuition. Especially now, when she was so unsure of what was happening around her. Her life had always been so ordered, serene, boring even. Now she had a sinking feeling it was about to be turned upside down. Surprisingly Janice didn't push but thanked Jaimee for the book, apologized for the interruption and told her pointedly she'd see her later. Jaimee continued to smile, nodded and closed the door quietly behind her.

Scanning the heads bowed over their work, she sat down behind her desk with a sigh. Two more class periods to go. Thank God they all had tests today. She wasn't sure she could have stood at the board or led them through a lesson with any clarity at all. All she could think about now was the day planner. Brent must have put it there to hide it, but why and from whom? Those were the questions making her nervous.

Absently she rubbed her arms as she reviewed the facts. Ronald wanted the day planner, badly. Brent hid the day planner. Brent was dead. Someone tried to break into her home, possibly twice. Was all this connected? Brent must have found out something on Ronald. Something incriminating.

By the time sixth period was over and the students had all scrambled out to their various modes of transport home, Jaimee was afraid to find out what was in that day planner that Ronald wanted so badly. She quickly shut the door as the last tone sounded and went to the cabinet. She stood on tiptoes, reached behind the stack of books, and retrieved Brent's day planner. Her hands were shaking as she opened it while walking back to her desk. More than likely it was whatever was on the small flash drive that was tucked into the inside pocket. Maybe he wasn't hiding it, she tried to convince herself. Maybe there was another explanation. But there wasn't much else that made sense. No, there had to be. She was just being paranoid, letting her imagination run away with her. For crying out loud she was exhausted, she couldn't think straight anyway.

Hadn't Ronald said that there were addresses and information the company needed? Okay so that did seem a little—a lot—odd. No, that Brent had *hid* the day planner made the whole situation suspicious. That Ronald was so antsy to get a hold of it meant that it had something to do with Ronald. She was sure of it. But Detective Butler said they'd been looking for the burglar for a while. So, more than likely the break-in had nothing to do with the day planner. Unless, they knew she usually kept the key to the cabinet in her tote. But how would they know that? Jaimee straightened and tried to think past her budding headache. The day she found her files moved, could someone have been after the key then?

Besides the flash drive there was a list of names and numbers that appeared to be scratched down hurriedly in Brent's handwriting. Addresses and contact information, dates neatly recorded on the calendar: meetings, office events, work deadlines, her birthday. He'd gotten her a very nice leather-trimmed desk set complete with desk blotter, pencil and letter holder. Brent never was the intimate, romantic type. She'd always just accepted that about him. But now as she sat there thumbing through his personal day planner, her mind and emotions whirling around like mad, she could only think about Brent. What had their seven years of marriage meant? Had she ever really connected with him?

With a sigh she closed the book, snapped it shut and frowned down at it, rubbing her thumb over the fine leather. Their life together was so very uneventful. Brent was supposed to be uncomplicated and predictable, kind of dull even. She shrugged. Now she wasn't sure that was true. Did he not tell her about this because he was trying to protect her? Did he ever talk to her about much of anything? Her frown deepened as the pain in her head bloomed brighter.

She hated to wonder, to call their relationship into question. He was gone from her now. When she lost him she'd hurt, she'd been devastated. She'd lost her best friend. But did she lose her heart? She loved him, but she was never passionate about him, he was never passionate about her, never her champion.

Lucas was her champion. He treated her like a goddess. He was passionate for her. He made her feel beautiful, sexy, even admired, and she had fallen for it completely. But with Lucas it was lust. Right? What was the difference between love and lust anyway? The truth was, she wanted more than just sex with Lucas. But he was always trying to take over, take charge of her. It was arrogant and infuriating and at the same time a part of her didn't want him to back down from it. And it turned her on in a major way. She took a deep breath and cleared her throat as she recalled just how aroused his dominance could make her. *Focus, Jaimee,* she admonished herself.

"I can't think about this now." Her head was pounding now and she was desperate for sleep—deep, dreamless sleep.

"Mrs. Turner."

The strong bass of Malaki's voice had Jaimee jumping, nearly falling off her chair. "Yes?" she squeaked.

"I'm sorry, I didn't mean to frighten you," he said, much quieter this time. "I'm here to escort you home."

Jaimee's surprise turned quickly to annoyance. "I don't need an escort."

Malaki's expression didn't change. "Doesn't matter. You have one."

She gave him her sternest look, even narrowed her eyes. He just crossed his arms and waited. He filled the classroom doorway, dressed for battle. His black T-shirt fit him like a second skin, stretching over his broad chest and massive biceps. The black jeans he wore seemed molded to his hips and thighs, no gun belt. Jaimee wasn't fooled, the man had a weapon tucked somewhere. A man like Malaki was always armed.

"I don't *want* an escort."

Not a word, his body remained solidly planted. Not so much as a twitch marred his mask of indifference. Damn, was he a robot? His expression remained stoic as she glared at him.

"Grrr. Fine!" She dropped the day planner in her file drawer, locked it and slid the key into the side pocket of her tote. After gathering her things she sent him another icy gaze that would have had her most unruly student cringing in fear. Nothing.

He stepped back as she passed, took her heavy tote from her, gripping the straps in his big fist as though he were hauling out the trash and motioned for her to lead the way. With an exasperated sigh she flipped the lights off and moved past him. He closed the door behind her and followed her down the hall. It amazed her that the huge combat boots Malaki wore made no sound on the tiled floor when even her soft-soled slides made a soft pitter pat that echoed through the hall. The man was like a ghost, a very large, very intimidating, very good-looking ghost.

Wait. Homes got broken into every day. Did all burglary victims get escorted home from work after? Do they all get huge Polynesian bodyguards? She halted and spun around. "*Why* do I need an escort?"

"Not for me to answer," he said simply, gazing down at her.

"Which means?"

"Not for me to answer," he repeated.

"You know, you just won't tell me."

He said nothing. Just continued to unflinchingly meet her gaze.

"I have a right to know what's going on, especially if my life is on the line."

"Yes."

"So?"

"Not for me to answer. Walk, or I'll carry you out."

"Hey, Jai...Whoa!" Janice came around the corner and froze, her eyes wide, her mouth hanging open. "Are you being kidnapped? 'Cause if you are, I don't know whether to call for help or ask if I can come along."

Jaimee could have sworn she saw the corner of Malaki's mouth twitch when she looked back at him. "This is Janice Benningfield, she also teaches eighth-grade English. Janice, this is Malaki Papalu. He's...uh..."

Malaki offered her his hand and Janice gave him hers, still in awe. "Hello, Janice, I'm Jaimee's cousin."

Jaimee nearly snorted at the hilarity of Malaki's lie, but managed, she hoped, to keep a straight face.

"Oh wow, no family resemblance at all." Janice smiled brightly up at him.

It appeared there was one person on the planet who was impervious to those infectious smiles of hers. There wasn't so much as a slight curve of his lips but there was a silvery glint that lit his dark eyes. It occurred to Jaimee at that moment that one sharp look from those eyes could shake a person to their soul. One way or another.

"I was adopted," he answered blandly.

"Ah...well, that explains it," Janice said softly, her eyes focused on his mouth. Jaimee resisted the urge to roll her eyes.

"Yes." Malaki looked down at the hand Janice now held between both of hers.

"Oh sorry." She laughed, her cheeks flushing pink as she released his hand. "It was *very* nice meeting you, Malaki." Just because she had two children at home and a very attentive husband didn't make Janice immune to the sheer maleness of Malaki's presence.

"And you, Janice." He actually bowed slightly.

"See ya Monday, Jaimee." There was that wicked grin again which meant she'd be having a chat with Ms. Janice over planning period Monday. Thank God she wouldn't be asking her to fix them up. It was best they got out of there before they ran into a fellow teacher who was actually available.

"Oh hey, Jaimee. Your class is going to read *The Count of Monte Cristo* next quarter, aren't they?"

"Yep. Planning on it."

"Good. I have a whole unit planned. We'll take both classes to the library and work on it together."

This was the part of Janice's personality Jaimee had so much trouble with. She had a tendency to be controlling to a fault.

"Well, no. I've already made my own plans. But thank you for the offer." Jaimee's smile was forced.

"This unit is better. I've already discussed it with Mr. Harmon, he's all for it."

Jaimee blinked at her. "You discussed this with the principal before you even talked to me about it?"

Janice grinned and waved her hand as though it were not a big deal. "Oh you're so easy-going, Jaimee. I didn't think you'd care one way or another."

Jaimee just shook her head. "I do care. I've already planned out that unit myself so you'll have to do yours on your own."

The bright smile on Janice's face fell a fraction and she shrugged. "Okay then. I was just trying to be helpful."

"I know. I appreciate it. Gotta run now, you have a good weekend."

"You too," Janice called back to them as she walked away, wiggling her fingers in goodbye over her shoulder.

Malaki walked a pace behind her as she made her way to the car. He held out his hand, waiting for the keys. Too tired to fight about it, she slapped them into his palm and scowled up at him. If there was one thing she'd learned long ago it was to pick your battles wisely and don't sweat the small stuff.

After setting her tote on the passenger seat, he held the car door open and motioned for her to get in. "Mrs. Turner. Are you awake enough to drive?"

"Yes." The word came out in a snotty tone, making her sound like a spoiled teenager. She wrinkled her nose. "And quit calling me Mrs. Turner. Jaimee is fine."

Malaki merely nodded, shut the door and headed to his own vehicle.

All the way home his truck stayed in her rearview mirror. It was irritating but it would have been a waste of time to try and shake him. Besides, Malaki was a nice guy even if he did look like he could rip somebody apart with his bare hands. She shuddered and willed the scary pictures in her mind to dissipate. Blaming her wild imagination on fatigue, she turned the radio up and rolled the window down. Had she ever been this sleepy?

Amazingly she managed to get herself home without an altercation. Her lame attempt to lose Malaki by speeding though the bottom of a yellow light was thwarted when Malaki ran the red light that followed. She sighed with relief as she turned onto her street. She spotted Lucas walking across the road toward her house as she pulled into her driveway. Jaimee didn't even bother to stifle her appreciative moan. Her body heat rose a few degrees instantly at the sight of him, his arrogant swagger and intense expression. Damn, he looked so good. He wore a beige shirt and jeans that rode low on his hips, hugging his body in all the right places.

Malaki barely slowed to wave back at Lucas before driving away. Lucas opened the car door and offered his hand. For a moment she just looked at it: wide, lightly calloused, capable. An unfamiliar need bloomed deep within her, making her feel empty. It just served to bring home that raw, aching loneliness she'd tried to ignore for so long as she laid her hand in his. "Why did you have The Incredible Hulk follow me home?"

One brow lifted slightly as he helped her out of the car and took her tote bag from her. "The Pope?"

"He doesn't like that. It's Malaki, why did you have Malaki *escort* me home?"

Firmly pressing his hand to her lower back, Lucas walked close beside her as he led her into the house without answering her question. In spite of the irritation of being ignored or at the very least put off, the warmth radiating from his body made her feel cared for and protected. She was really getting used to that. Then she reminded herself that she really shouldn't get used to that.

She shivered involuntarily as he moved away from her to close the door and lock it. Jaimee crossed her arms over her chest, resisting the urge to cling to him, snuggle against him and give in to her need for oblivion. His dark eyes softened, warmed when he turned to face her.

"I asked The Pope to make sure you got home all right because I couldn't get away from work to do it myself."

Jaimee narrowed her eyes. "That's a little over the top, don't you think?"

"I don't. Not if what happened last night was personal. I'm not completely convinced the break-in was a random thing. Especially after that guy threatened you."

"What guy?" She frowned and tugged at the tote bag in his hand until he released it.

"Ronald Marshall."

So Lucas suspected the same thing she did. For a moment she debated on telling him about the day planner she'd found.

"It's plain that the guy wants something from you, Jaimee, and whatever that something is, I mean to see that he doesn't get it." His expression darkened, his eyes glinted with malice, a promise of retribution. Jaimee didn't even try to hide her shudder.

Her frown had edged over into scowl. "Uh huh." Why it irritated her, she didn't know for sure. Maybe it was because he was treating her like a helpless female again. Or maybe it was the uncertainty of their relationship. Either way her head was beginning to ache with all the speculation. "Whatever you say, big guy." Wanting to shut down, escape into a deep dreamless sleep and just forget it all for a while, she turned away from him and moved to the stairs, intent on taking herself to bed.

Lucas took hold of her arm, delaying her retreat and turned her around to face him. "Don't do that."

"What?" she snapped, jerking away. "Don't do what, Lucas? Can your massive ego not handle my rejection of your arrogant, overbearing attitude or do you just have to believe I'm some helpless twit desperate for a man to love me and save me and protect me from the big ole mean world?"

"I don't think you're helpless, I certainly don't believe you're a twit and, Jaimee, everyone wants to be loved." With one finger he traced the lower curve of her bottom lip and she gritted her teeth against the rush of emotion, the surge of arousal.

"Stop it."

Without a word he pulled her into his arms. She wanted to resist, really she did, but he smelled so good and his body was so steady and strong. He cradled her head in that perfect spot between his shoulder and his neck. Holding her like that had her resistance melting. The truth was she wanted to surrender, but she couldn't, wouldn't, stand there and be patronized. Not even for the moment of peaceful harbor his embrace offered her.

"Ugh. You're patronizing me." She pushed away. Her voice was hoarse with frustration, anger and a tangle of complex emotions she didn't feel up to analyzing. Not tonight anyway. Heat curled low in her belly causing her womb to tighten, her vagina to clench achingly. "Do you have problems comprehending me?"

He didn't move and his scowl deepened, the muscle in his jaw jumped. Was it her imagination or was that vein in his neck throbbing? If she weren't so tired she'd probably be nervous, possibly a little bit afraid. Lack of sleep gave her courage it seemed, no matter how foolhardy.

He took a step toward her and she retreated. "Now you look here, Maxine has a very busy day scheduled tomorrow that she wouldn't let me out of if both my legs were broken. On top of that she'll be here way too damn early in the morning and if I'm going to endure all she's planned in that devious mind of hers I'm going to need rest. So you need to get over yourself and run along." She poked him in the chest, not for a minute missing the hard, tense muscles beneath his soft shirt. "You need to get it through that thick, testosterone-laden skull of yours what I've told you too many times already: I can take care of myself. Always have. Always will. Now, go away, go on." She dismissed him with a flick of her hand.

He moved so fast she didn't have time to register what he intended. Her strangled yelp was cut short as her breath left her lungs in a whoosh and her world tipped, turning upside down as Lucas tossed her over his shoulder and mounted the steps.

His strong arms held her legs tightly against him so she couldn't give him a good swift kick. All she got for her thrashing about was a hard, sharp swat to her backside.

"Ow! That hurt!" she yelled breathlessly.

In retaliation she dug her fingernails into his back and sunk her teeth into the taut muscled flesh. The satisfaction she got from his grunt of pain was short lived when he delivered yet another blow to her posterior, this time harder. It really stung!

"Damn you, Lucas!"

When finally he dumped her on the bed she lost her breath for a moment. As he slid up her body, synapses fired, logic clouded with a sudden flash fire of desire. She panted, torn between fury and lust. His eyes, so dilated they were nearly black, glittered ominously. A hot shiver wracked her body beneath him as he rotated his hips, firmly seated at the apex of her shaky thighs. His significant erection pressed urgently against her mound.

"Things have changed, Jaimee," he growled through his teeth. "Adjust."

She watched in shock as he rose from the bed, his penetrating glare searing her before he turned and stalked away. The windows and possibly her teeth rattled at the slamming of her door as he left the room.

Lucas snatched the receiver from its cradle before the first ring had finished. His answer was sharper than it should have been but he was still pissed off at Jaimee and at the same time he was so hard, he ached to just touch her. "Turner residence."

"Well hello. Lucas, right?" That sultry alto voice could belong to none other than Ms. Maxine.

"Yes."

"Well, Lucas, this is Maxine, Jaimee's best friend. May I speak to James please?" she asked a little too sweetly.

"No. She's asleep. May I take a message?"

"Already? It's only eight o'clock. Is she okay?"

"Yes. She was up late last night and worked all day today so she went to bed early."

"Ooooh! So that's why you sound pissed off. She went to sleep and didn't give you any." She went on before Lucas could interject a denial. "Give her time to recharge, babe. She's just not used to your kinda fuckin'."

"My kind of..."

"Yeah you know: hard, fast, mind-blowing, all night long sex."

Lucas was grinning now. If it had been anyone else he would have seen red. "Tell me, lovely Maxine, what makes you think you know how I fuck?"

"Come on, Lucas, don't tell me you didn't know that girlfriends talk."

Lucas laughed. "Oh I'm completely aware of that fact. Unfortunately it wasn't me that kept Jaimee up all night. I wish it had been. Someone tried to break in to her house late last night."

"Oh God! Is she hurt? Why didn't she call me?"

"Calm down. She wasn't hurt and she hasn't had time to call you yet. She's planning on going shopping with you in the morning. I'm sure she'll tell you all about it then."

"Hmph. Damn straight she will. Now you listen, Lucas, Jaimee is not only my best friend, she's more my sister than my own blood sisters and I love her. If you hurt her I'll separate you from your favorite body parts. Got that?"

With a deep sigh Lucas closed his eyes tight and pinched the bridge of his nose. He wanted to tell her he would never hurt Jaimee. With everything inside him he wanted to but it was a lie. He was going to hurt Jaimee worse than she could imagine and the knowledge of that was killing him.

"Got it, Maxine."

Chapter Twenty-Five

Rob Thomas woke her up, his sultry voice serenading her from the clock radio on her nightstand...no, it was across the room on her dresser. How did it get over there? Lucas. It wasn't too loud, she could ignore it and go back to sleep. Red numbers glowed "seven thirty" at her insistently and she remembered her appointment with Maxine and her stylist.

With a sigh Jaimee slowly pushed the covers aside, sat up and scooted to the edge of her bed. She was naked. Lucas. She groaned. His name whispered through her mind and brought back softer remnants of a hunger that had her in its grip the evening before. *"Things have changed, Jaimee..."* Groaning again at the memory, she rubbed her eyes and stumbled into the bathroom to turn the shower on. She adjusted the water temperature to as hot as she could stand it, stepped in, and let the heat flow over her body. The steam enveloped her as she tried to organize her emotions.

Maybe it would be best to ignore all the emotions involved. There was nothing solid or lasting about emotion anyway. Maybe it was a good thing Lucas didn't touch her last night. They needed to take a step back and evaluate this relationship anyway. What was going on between them was too volatile. It was downright explosive. They needed to find out if there was anything solid to build upon.

Half an hour later Jaimee emerged physically refreshed and ready to take on the day and whatever Maxine intended to throw her way. Still, Lucas pervaded her mind. She couldn't seem to will away the image of his face hovering so close above her own, flushed with anger, dark eyes narrowed, teeth bared, nostrils flared. A whisper of heat curled through her involuntarily. How sick was that? Lucas was livid with her, and it turned her on. She was losing her mind. There was no other explanation.

Maxine was due any moment so she tried shifting her focus from Lucas to the things she had planned for the day. It was going to be a fun day if it killed her. She needed to have fun, to laugh and not worry about the break-in and that stupid day planner...oh yeah...she'd almost forgotten about that thing. And she was really beginning to worry about Alice. What if all of it was connected? No, she was letting her imagination get the best of her. And she wasn't going to worry about what was or wasn't happening with Lucas. Before she went out tonight she'd make sure and call Detective Butler and tell him about Ron, the day planner and Alice. Just go ahead and put her concerns to rest. But this afternoon she was going to enjoy herself.

She skipped down the stairs and as she grabbed her tennis shoes from where she'd left them in the hallway she noticed a long, naked foot propped up on the arm of her sofa and did a double take. Lucas was stretched out on her sofa, one arm behind his head for a pillow, asleep. The soft smile that curved her lips was spontaneous, a reaction to genuine happiness. He didn't leave after all, which made her feel ridiculously relieved and pleased. Hell, who was she kidding? It made her giddy.

Not wanting to wake him, she moved around the sofa slowly and sat in the chair to watch him while she put on her tennis shoes. Even in sleep he didn't look peaceful. So still and quiet, yet he looked like a warrior tensed for attack. Jaimee finished tying her shoelaces then slid to her knees and crawled as silently as she could to his side. His deep breathing let her know that he was still asleep. Tentatively, she traced his brow with her fingertips then smoothed the tense lines of his forehead. He didn't move, not so much as a twitch as she let her hands explore the planes of his chiseled face, the bridge of his regal nose, his firm lips.

God, he was beautiful, like a dream. He was the best-looking man she'd ever known and the most arrogant, bullheaded and dogmatic as well. At the same time he'd been so kind, even gentle, but never soft, and he'd made her laugh. Lucas was good, in every sense of the word. And didn't that make him all the more extraordinary? Every indication was that he wanted her, had staked his claim on her. That fact had shaken her very soul. The all-consuming passion was an incredible experience and she couldn't ignore her need for that. But she had to admit to herself that it was that strength and dominance she'd craved so badly, for so long.

She laid a hand on the bicep of his left arm where he'd been cut. It wasn't hot so infection wasn't likely, thank God. Her heart had tripped over itself when she'd seen the blood, registered that he'd been hurt. Maybe it was her fault. Maybe she should have let him deal with the jerk, but she just couldn't make herself run upstairs and lock herself in her room like a scared little idiot waif.

She tried to make him understand that she'd never depended on anyone to take care of her before and she never intended to. Now he was mad at her—no, furious was more like it, but he hadn't left her. Even so, as much as she wanted Lucas, she wasn't sure she could go through trying to be "softer" anymore. It wasn't in her to be meek and passive.

It dawned on her that for all her efforts to be what she believed Brent needed, to allow him to take the lead, he never did. Brent wasn't the soft place to fall. He was just soft. She couldn't change Brent so she had to try and change herself and in doing so she'd become uncomfortable in her own skin. Finally learning to be herself again was incredibly liberating and there was no going back to a life of emotional and mental bondage. Not even for Lucas. She shook her head, no, a man like Lucas wouldn't want a spineless woman. And that's exactly what she'd become with Brent.

A soft place to fall wasn't what she needed at all. What she needed was someone strong enough to catch her if she stumbled. So far Lucas had been the strength she wanted and his apparent desire seemed to validate her. Maybe he wasn't real at all, maybe he was an angel and this was all a dream from which she would soon abruptly awaken. Her hand trailed over his shoulder, moved down his chest to his stomach. The warm smooth skin covering steely muscles intrigued her. It would have been wonderful to take her time drinking in the feel of him, just touching him. With a shaky sigh of resignation she stood up and pressed her lips to his temple. This man had unlocked and released something inside her that had kept her shackled and cold. No matter what happened between them, she would always love him for that.

Holding still while she touched him nearly drove him crazy but he didn't want to shatter whatever it was that was happening between them at the moment. It would have been worth anything to know what was going on in that analytical, methodically motivated head of hers. He could still feel the pressure of her warm lips against his skin, her soft hand caressing his body. It had been a test of endurance not to pull her against him and taste her. God, he loved the taste of her. Instead he'd held still, trying to brand the feel of her touch into his memory, his heart, never to forget how precious that gesture had been.

Sitting up as he heard the car door close and Maxine's little Jeep back out of the drive, he rubbed his hands over his face. The hell they were about to face would rip them both to shreds. Somehow he had to find a way to hold on to her and he was willing to do whatever that took. Life without Jaimee would be dull and miserable. When she smiled everything in his life seemed to slide into place. She gave him something to look forward to, something to work for. She was his world, his heart, his love. He couldn't lose her now.

"I know you told her to do it, Max, don't even play." Jaimee scowled out the car window, her arms crossed over her chest.

Maxine was struggling to keep the car on the road and laugh hysterically at the same time. "I swear...I didn't! Are you sure she didn't leave you a landing strip?"

Jaimee turned to glare at Maxine, still smarting in her nether regions thanks to Maxine's stylist and her overzealous waxing methods. "I...have...nothing! I'm completely naked down there! Completely! And you know what else she wanted to do? Do you?!"

Maxine wiped tears from her eyes. "I'm not sure, should I pull over first?"

"Anal bleaching!"

Maxine howled with laughter and nearly ran off the road. Thankfully she pulled into the mall and into the nearest parking space she could find. "Oh my God. Stop, I'm gonna pee myself."

"Good! Have you ever heard of that? Why would anyone need a bleached anus, huh? Do you have a bleached anus?" Jaimee's voice was sharp and shrill but she didn't care. She'd been traumatized not to mention robbed of not only her pubic hair but of every ounce of pride she might have once had.

Maxine was laughing so hard she couldn't answer.

"I'm glad you think this is so funny. My tootie still stings." Not so much sting as tingle. But she didn't want to tell Maxine that.

"Come on, James, it's not that bad."

"Well maybe you have a tough twat but mine is sensitive and ripping all my hair out by the roots was damn painful." Not to mention embarrassing to have this woman she didn't know touching her most private area.

"You're crazy too. My kitty is as soft and smooth as a baby's butt." Maxine scowled with feigned offense. "Rub some oil on it tonight when you get home. Or better still have Lucas rub some oil on it for ya." An intriguing suggestion that made Jaimee quiver and at the same time it filled her with a sense of dread. She'd told Maxine all about the break-in. Well, that wasn't quite accurate. Maxine told her about her conversation with Lucas and demanded to know every detail of what had occurred.

"I have a feeling Lucas might have had all of me he wants."

"Maybe, you did piss him off. But, I seriously doubt it. As a matter of fact when I talked to him last night he sounded frustrated as hell. Sounded to me like he was in a bad way for some more of what you've been giving him."

Jaimee waited until they'd stepped into the mall before she answered. "He was irritated because I wouldn't let him treat me like an idiot, like I couldn't take care of myself. I can't be like that, Maxine, not anymore. You know that better than anyone."

Maxine just nodded.

"So we sort of had an argument and I basically told him I didn't need him to coddle me and to go away then he went all Neanderthal on me and carried me up stairs and I bit him."

"Hot damn, sounds good to me."

Jaimee nibbled the inside of her cheek and took a deep breath. "Yeah, but he stormed out of the room seriously pissed off." The whole ordeal had been very exciting and provocative but her pride would not allow her to call him back, nor go to him. Somehow in spite of it she fell asleep even though she was hot, wet and throbbing all over. Besides the pride thing there was the very real chance of rejection. She wasn't sure she could have handled a cold dismissal from him. The fact that she'd just dealt him that very thing didn't escape her consideration. Had she made him feel unwanted? Rejected?

Maxine interrupted her troubled musings with a snort and a sardonic sideways glance. "You don't know much about men do you, hon?"

By lunchtime Jaimee and Maxine had visited most of the stores Opry Mills Mall had to offer. And that was no small feat. The Rainforest Café for lunch was infinitely more appealing than grabbing something in the food court. It had been a long wait to be seated but it didn't matter when their very young, very hunky waiter with thick, curly blond hair strolled up to the table, knelt right beside Jaimee, flashed the most vivid green eyes she'd ever seen and announced with a sexy southern drawl, "Name's Isaac. I'm all yours, ladies. What's your pleasure?"

Maxine didn't miss a beat. "Isaac, honey, it would be illegal to serve that here."

Isaac's grin was quick, utterly sexy and perfectly polished to garner the biggest tips possible from the ladies. "Now that's a shame." He paused for effect. "How about I get you a drink instead?"

"I believe I'm gonna need something cold." Maxine winked seductively. Jaimee bit her lip trying to keep from laughing. "I'll have a raspberry tea...with extra ice."

Nodding, he quickly jotted Max's order down before turning his full attention and thousand-watt smile on Jaimee. "And for you, love?"

Jaimee cut Maxine a glance. She was pretending to take in the atmosphere. "I'll have the same, thank you."

He gave her a wink and a sharp nod before walking away. Both Jaimee and Maxine enjoyed watching him walk away. When they looked back at each other across the table they burst into laughter.

"Isaac was interested in more than your order, James," Maxine teased.

Jaimee snorted. "Oh yeah, I know, he was interested in a big tip."

"Now see." Maxine slouched back in her seat and sighed with exasperation. "Why do you do that? Why you gotta be like that?" Her big dark eyes widened and she crossed her arms, waiting for an answer.

"Like what?"

"Pessimistic. You are so fucking pessimistic. Emphasis on 'so'."

"I am not." Jaimee straightened in her chair, frowning a little. "I'm a realist."

Ugh, there was the famous Maxine "oh please" eye roll. Leaning forward, she braced her crossed arms on the table. "Jaimee, guys look at you all the time."

"Pshaw, no they don't."

"Yes, they do." She held up one finely manicured finger, effectively cutting off Jaimee's continuing protest. "And what makes you think they don't like what they see? Huh? For the last several months you've been coming out of that weird...I don't know...numbness you've been in for the past five years and you're finally starting to carry yourself like the goddess you are. Why wouldn't any man want some of that? Lucas certainly does. And with the way you look today: hair slammin', perfect makeup... Girl, Isaac ain't immune."

Jaimee couldn't help but snicker. Though what Maxine said did boost her self-esteem a few thousand notches. And she really did love the way her hair turned out. It was all shiny and soft. Sasha, Maxine's stylist, had left her length. She'd layered and highlighted, low-lighted, washed, conditioned, spritzed and blow-dried her hair into a mane of fat, golden brown curls that hung just past her shoulders. She felt pretty and confident...maybe even a little goddess-like. A slow smile curved her lips and she wiggled in her seat. "You think he's lookin' for some attention from a woman at least six or seven years older huh?"

"I'm just sayin'." Maxine pursed her glossy lips and lifted a brow.

Jaimee matched Maxine's expression and nodded with determination. "Okay, fine. Let's test this theory. Here he comes with the drinks."

Isaac strode to the table and immediately made eye contact with Jaimee. She held his gaze and smiled as he set the drinks in front of them. "Are you ladies ready to order?"

Isaac finished jotting down their orders, flashed a smile and started to go when Jaimee, deciding to try her hand at bold, lightly touched his arm. "Hey, Isaac, do you mind if I ask you how old you are?"

He turned his whole body toward her and met her gaze. "I'm twenty-three."

Yep, got that one right. He was either in college or an aspiring country music hopeful. His baritone voice was smooth and pleasant. "You sing, don't you?"

"Yes, I do." His eyes lit up at that. "That obvious?"

"Well, it was a lucky guess. You're a young, sexy guy, with a nice voice, waiting tables in Nashville, Tennessee. I figure I had a fifty-fifty chance of guessing right."

He cleared his throat. "Sexy huh?"

She gave him a look that said "come on, don't play coy". "So, do you play or just sing?"

"Guitar and keyboards."

"That will give you better odds. Still, tough business."

"Yes. It is." Did his voice drop a little lower? "What about you?"

"What about me?"

"Do you sing?"

"Nah."

Maxine, who was sitting back enjoying the show, piped in. "She *can* sing, but she doesn't."

Isaac looked from Maxine back to Jaimee. "Aw now that's a shame. You have a nice speaking voice, I bet you sing real nice."

She smiled down at her tea and ran her fingertip over the rim of the glass. "Not a shame at all. I'm a middle school English teacher, it's what I do best and I love it." She let her gaze travel up his body before meeting his too-green eyes again. "Maybe I should get your autograph, you might be famous someday soon."

"Maybe you should." He winked and walked away.

"Oh he's good," Maxine said with exaggerated awe. They both laughed.

"Did you see those eyes?" Jaimee asked.

"Contacts."

"Has to be." She took a long sip from her straw and curled her lip at Maxine. "That was downright creepy I'm tellin' you."

"Why's that?"

"That guy isn't much older than my students." Jaimee shuddered. "I'm just not the cradle robber type."

Maxine snickered. "Maybe, but it was fun wasn't it?"

"Okay, yeah it was." Had she ever even had this much fun hangin' out and cuttin' up with Maxine before? She definitely had never engaged in careless, meaningless flirtation with a complete stranger like that before. Flirting with Lucas had been anything but careless and meaningless. Was that pull between them even in the same category as flirtation? It was nothing like flirting with the sexy waiter. There was no sensual attraction whatsoever. It was exhilarating and fun, even if she was a little clumsy.

Sure, when she was younger she was flirty with the guys they hung around with. She'd even been flirty with Brent, although he'd always just blushed and laughed her off. Her attempts at seductive flirtation had never been productive. Thinking back, he'd shrugged her off, made her feel silly, not stupid. After they started dating she stopped it altogether. Brent never looked at other women, not ever. He never flirted with anyone.

A misty, melancholy thought bloomed in her mind—she didn't miss him. Did she ever really miss him, or was it herself she missed? Unwilling to analyze what that meant she pushed it away and turned her attention to Maxine.

They had finished their lunch and Jaimee was anxious to do some more shopping. Impulsively she gave in on that sexy dress Maxine had tried to get her to buy. So what if the dress was ridiculously extravagant and seriously daring, especially for a woman of her size? To hell with that, she wanted to make a statement. Let her outside match her inside and be bold, be Jaimee.

"Let's flag down Isaac, I'm ready to go. I'm gonna go get that dress."

"You mean the blue one? Seriously?"

"Yeah, and I'm not gonna wear panty hose. Thanks to Sasha my legs have never been this smooth. Oh! I'm gonna need new shoes. Hey! There's a little lingerie boutique in Green Hills that caters to larger ladies. Let's go. I wanna see if I can carry off a pair of thongs."

"Oh God help me, I've created a monster." Maxine chuckled as she scanned the room for their waiter.

Isaac made his way to their table. "Leaving already, ladies?"

"Looks like," Maxine grinned. "Miss Thang here needs a new pair of shoes and possibly a matching thong."

That did it. Embarrassment burned Jaimee's cheeks and she refused to look up from fishing through her purse for her wallet even though she could feel Isaac's interested gaze on her.

"Mmm, sounds hot." He paused before quickly adding, "Hey listen, I'll be playing tonight...here..." He wrote quickly and slid her check across the table to her. There in bold green ink was his name, an address and two, count 'em, two phone numbers. "Come see me, let me buy you dinner, show you a good time."

Jaimee would have laughed if she weren't afraid she'd offend him. It wouldn't have been directed at him anyway. It was just that the whole situation was completely foreign to her, just unreal. She glanced at Maxine's check, careful to avoid the humor sparkling in her friend's eyes.

"Isaac, I'm sorry." Ignoring Maxine's fervent protest, she handed him cash for both their meals, including a healthy tip. "There's a man I'm sorta, kinda seeing."

Unaffected by her announcement he simply flashed her another winning smile. "You got a ring and a date?"

That took her off guard. "Well, no."

Isaac smiled as he separated the tip from the amount for the bill, tucked the latter into his black order pad, dropped it into the apron slung around his waist and took her hand in his. "Then you don't have a man. That means you're a free agent." He placed her generous tip in her hand. "Think about it. I'll be broken-hearted if I never get to see those...shoes." With a wink that was quickly becoming annoying, he turned and walked away.

"He then gave her his number and returned the tip she gave him."

"Amateur," Lucas growled into the cell phone. On edge already, his body tensed further and he clenched his teeth. Slamming his car door didn't help relieve that tension either. No, the only thing that was going to give him peace at this point was putting this case to bed and then, taking Jaimee to bed and keeping her there until he could chase away all the pain that was inevitably to come.

Thankfully he trusted the men sent to keep an eye on Jaimee. Jason Whitman was tailing them now. Saturday night Jaimee and Maxine hit the town and Lucas had been on edge since then. They'd been safe. Adrian Robertson had fit nicely into the role of bouncer, which allowed him to keep a close eye on Jaimee and Maxine.

Whitman taunted with an exaggerated gasp. "Holy shit, Grayson's jealous. The devil's gonna be ice skatin' tonight."

"I don't get jealous."

"Right, what was I thinking?"

"Evidently they're going out again tonight. The Pope will tail them there. Don't let them out of your sight." Lucas took the steps to the motel's second level two at a time.

"Duh."

There was no one on the balcony walkway as Lucas strode quickly, glancing into each room as he went. Malaki stepped outside the room Brent had occupied just hours before and motioned to him. Lucas nodded and picked up his pace. Damn asshole got away again. The slippery fuck was beginning to seriously piss him off.

"He left quickly, didn't cover his tracks well. Not too bright," Malaki reported as Lucas entered the motel room.

"Bright enough to evade capture. Any idea who tipped him?" Lucas glanced at the officer sifting through the small trashcan for notes or anything else that might be a lead.

"Wasn't tipped, just bolted. The clerk said he was pretty shook up when he checked in early this morning, about one a.m., had a fat lip and what appeared to be a broken nose. Didn't bother checking out." Malaki nodded toward the back of the room. "Left his hair in the bathroom sink."

"His hair?"

Malaki shrugged. "Guess he thought shaving his head would change his looks enough to give him an advantage."

Lucas didn't even bother rolling his eyes. "The Collective knows he's still alive."

"If they don't know for sure, they suspect."

Lucas nodded as he finished up his search. "Then they're looking for him too." If they hoped to retrieve any information at all, obviously, Turner had to be found before The Collective caught up with him.

Malaki nodded. "I have a few things to check out. Will you be available?"

"I'm meeting Butler downtown then back to the house. You have my cell."

"Jaimee's?"

"No. She and Maxine Pruitt are going to the bar again tonight."

Malaki didn't respond, just turned and left the room. After speaking with the men searching the room, Lucas left as well. He was anxious to get things done, to have everything in place when the shit hit the fan. And when the shit hit the fan it wouldn't be evenly distributed. Lucas just wanted to make clean up as quick and easy as possible for Jaimee. Until then, he was going to have to maintain some distance. For all intents and purposes she was still married and therefore, off limits. At least when all was said and done she wouldn't hate him for knowingly adding to the mangled wreckage that was her marriage.

Nothing was happening fast enough and it was making him crazy. As if trying to stay away from Jaimee wasn't bad enough, listening to her tell Max she believed he'd had enough of her frustrated the hell out of him. But there was no way at this point he could reassure her. Even though she said she understood when he told her he was slammed at work, he knew she thought he was trying to get rid of her. Funny thing, it was the honest to God truth. He was slammed at work. Trying to protect her from The Collective, trying to find Brent's idiot ass and trying not to think of her soft supple body beneath his hands was going to drive him out of his mind.

Chapter Twenty-Six

Big Phil's Little Bit of Texas Bar and Grill was more bar than grill. Jaimee played with the amethyst heart that dangled from the black velvet choker circling her throat as they stepped into the same bar she and Maxine visited the weekend before. There were a few things she was really starting to get used to. One was Max's stylist. Her hair had never been this full, softly curling, no, cascading down her back. Even the Brazilian wax job had its positives once she got used to the sensitivity.

Jaimee was finally letting go of all of her stodgy inhibitions and it was incredibly liberating. The snug, deep purple lace corset Maxine talked her into buying wasn't exactly comfortable but it wasn't uncomfortable either. Her breasts did feel like they were extraordinarily lifted and were all but spilling out the top. She was doing a great job not giving in to the desire to tug it up. Even though she had insisted on the little black jacket, much to Maxine's irritation.

Nevertheless, her wild and wicked side was given free rein in her new swingy black shirt and "fuck me" boots, not to mention the barely there purple lace thong. The whole outfit had cost a fortune but it was worth it. She was actually glad that she broke out of her usual strict budget and went nuts. Hell, this outfit was a statement that she had let go of more than just her strict budget.

"Good evening, ladies." Adrian, the same tall handsome bouncer who greeted them last week, rested his hip on the stool and smiled.

His dark eyes were trained provocatively on Maxine. And she was a sight to behold. Not a modest bone in that woman's body and yet she was oozing with class. She looked fabulous in her cream and bronze, figure-hugging dress. Runway fabulous.

"That remains to be seen now, doesn't it?" Max teased.

"I'll get a short break in an hour or so. Save me a dance and it's a guarantee." His voice deepened.

Max lifted a brow. "We'll see."

Adrian chuckled. "Sweetness, I'm freaky, chocolate-covered and habit-forming. And yes, ma'am, you *will* see."

Jaimee was grinning. She couldn't help it. The sparks leaping between the two fascinated her and it was obvious Max was a bit flustered; that was a new one. She and Max held out their five-dollar cover charge but he waved them away.

"I've got it. Go enjoy yourselves, I'll have some drinks sent over." He didn't take his eyes off Maxine. He was nice-looking. The vest he wore exposed his well-muscled shoulders and arms and smooth skin the color of dark espresso. Jaimee guessed he stood a few inches above six feet. A thick fall of long braids fell just past his shoulders. A nicely trimmed goatee framed lips made for kissing. She couldn't blame Max in the least. He made her feel a little lightheaded as well.

Max's eyes narrowed but she said nothing, just watched him closely. Finally Jaimee cleared her throat and looked from Max to Adrian. "Okay, but not an amaretto sour. Tried that last week and it didn't set well."

"Not a problem, sugar." He winked.

"Thanks." She smiled as she took Max by the arm and led her away. "What has gotten into you?" Jaimee chuckled.

"Nothing. I'm just trying to figure out what that man is up to."

"Sheesh, Max, even I know that. He wants some Maxine booty."

Maxine snorted. "Well he ain't gonna get any. There's something about him that makes me nervous."

Jaimee just shook her head. It took a special kinda man to unnerve Maxine. Maybe, just maybe, Miss Maxine had finally met her match.

The DJ was doing a pretty good job. There were already a few couples dancing as Jaimee and Maxine found a table and sat down. Jaimee watched them swaying together, close, in sync, and she thought of Lucas. She should probably let go, but her heart wasn't listening. The two times they talked since the break-in had been rushed and awkward. She believed he was swamped at work, but she just had a feeling that wasn't all there was to it. She would let go. She would not call him or seek him out, but the very thought of not having him in her life made her heart physically hurt.

The waitress, looking barely twenty-one herself, brought their drinks and interrupted her morose train of thought. "Okay I have a Bushwacker, light on the rum, for Jaimee, and a French Kiss for

Maxine." She sat the drinks down with a wink at Max. "Y'all need anything else? Maybe a basket of wings or something?"

"Maybe later," Max said, staring at the frothy pink drink. "What's in this?"

"Um...let's see...raspberry schnapps, vodka, white crème de cocoa, cream—"

"Okay, thanks." She waved her away.

"All righty then. I'm Sonya, if y'all need anything else just holler. I'll check on ya later. Enjoy!" Sonya said cheerfully as she turned and sashayed away, her long red hair swinging as she walked. Maxine turned and scowled at Adrian, who blew her a kiss.

Jaimee snickered. "Go ahead and try it. It sounds really good."

Maxine was a Crown Royal and Coke kind of woman; she wasn't all about the froo froo "girly drinks" as she called them. That didn't mean she would be a bitch about it. She took a hesitant sip. "Not bad. It's really sweet though. How's yours?"

"Really good." Jaimee took another sip. That's when the nausea hit her. "On second thought..." Biting her lip she pushed the drink back and drew in a slow deep breath. Nope, wasn't going to work. "Be back in a minute," she murmured and headed for the bathroom as quickly as she could.

A half an hour later Jaimee brushed her teeth with the little travel-sized toothbrush and toothpaste she always carried in her purse and patted her face with a cool damp paper towel. She stared at herself in the mirror as she touched up her makeup. There wasn't much to touch up, another sore spot with Maxine. But too much makeup made her feel clownish. Just some light foundation, a little blush, a little mascara, the very popular smoky eye sans the eyeliner. A touch of light plum lip gloss and that was it. With a sigh she tucked everything away and studied her image for another moment.

She didn't look sick and she didn't feel sick anymore. If she didn't know better she'd think she was pregnant, but she did know better. More than likely, she just couldn't handle liquor. Weird. It wasn't like this was the first time she'd ever had a drink. She'd had a few glasses of wine in her lifetime and there was that time in college when she drank a wine cooler. It had made her queasy too. Oh well, the nausea had passed. She'd just go order a soda instead. No biggie.

With another, more wistful sigh she looked away from her reflection, tugged gently at the top of her corset and smoothed her hands down her skirt. It really was a good thing she couldn't conceive.

Lucas hadn't made the kind of commitment that making a baby together required and she certainly didn't want him to make one out of obligation. The last thing she wanted to do was subject a child to a life like she'd had, one that lacked a physically as well as emotionally present father. It hurt too badly. Even so, a profound wave of melancholy drifted over her and settled heavily in her heart.

"Don't be stupid, James," she chided herself softly as she put on her jacket.

Maxine was still waiting at the table, frowning. She'd already ordered her a soda and what appeared to be spinach dip and chips.

"I'm okay," Jaimee assured her as she sat down. "I guess I just don't mix well with drinking."

"Not buyin' it." Maxine lifted a brow.

"Can't explain it then." She shrugged and nibbled at a chip. It was obvious where Maxine was going with it and she'd be lying to herself if she didn't acknowledge the fact that the thought had zipped quite quickly through her mind. Still, she had it straight from the doctor's mouth, not possible.

Maxine gave her a pointed look but said nothing. Just waited. Damn it was annoying the way Max could speak volumes with the subtle lift of her brow.

"C'mon, Max, I can't be pregnant. You know that." Jaimee tried to smile, tried to ignore the empty feeling expanding in her heart.

"Still think you should get a test. Just to be sure."

"Unnecessary. Waste of time and money." She shook her head. "Trust me I know. I've wasted plenty of money and time on them." Odd how not being pregnant was a good thing after all those years of trying, praying hoping. But it was a good thing. Especially after assuring Lucas pregnancy wasn't possible. Turning up "with child" now would be very suspicious. Lucas would totally feel trapped if that happened. But, she reminded herself yet again, it wouldn't happen. There was no child, would never be any child, therefore no reason to worry. Taking a sip of her soda to help swallow the lump that had formed in her throat she tried to hurriedly change the subject. "Is that drink as good as it looks?"

Max downed the last of her French Kiss. "Nice, but now I need something with teeth."

"That bouncer guy has you all discombobulated." Jaimee was happy for the chance to turn the conversation to another direction. "He's pretty hot, Max."

190

"Yeah, but he's cocky."

Jaimee snorted. "Since when did you not like cocky?"

The corner of Maxine's mouth lifted as she glanced back at Adrian. Their eyes met and Jaimee couldn't help but grin at what she saw in the exchanged glances. Adrian was obviously enamored with the lovely Ms. Maxine and Max wasn't immune to Adrian's smooth sexiness. She was resisting. That meant something. Max always embraced a chance to flirt. With a hrumph, Max turned back to Jaimee, blinked, then shook her head. "Whoa...evidently that drink had teeth it wasn't showing."

Jaimee grinned. "Probably should slow down then huh?"

"Maybe." Max snickered as she munched on a chip. "That dog. Probably tryin' to get me drunk so he can take advantage."

"Do you think so?"

Max sighed. "God, I hope so."

Jaimee laughed and swayed in her seat to the slow song that began to play. She watched as a few couples walked onto the dance floor, moving together as one. Once again, her thoughts turned to Lucas. The way his warmth, his strength, his scent, enveloped her when she was in his arms. She craved it. She craved him. Dammit she never played games well so she refused to play at all. She was too old to start now.

"Um, James, either you've packed something interesting in that purse or you're getting a call."

Lucas rubbed a hand over his face and watched the nightclub entrance as he dialed Jaimee's cell phone for the third time. He hadn't expected her and Maxine to hit the town until tomorrow. He was mistaken. It was still early Thursday night and here they were. When her voicemail picked up for the third time, he disconnected with a curse. He was about to call his contact inside the club when his cell vibrated. At the same time Adrian Robertson, his contact, opened the door for Jaimee. She walked out onto the sidewalk in an outfit that put the blue dress she wore last weekend to shame. Her cell was pressed to her ear and she was shivering in the unseasonably cool night air.

"Grayson," he growled into the phone.

"Lucas? I missed your call." Her voice was soft and breathy. He watched her standing at the club entrance in black boots with at least four-inch heels. Holy shit. She was sex walking. From where he sat, he could clearly see the full, creamy mounds of her breasts rounding out the top of the corset thing she was wearing.

He clenched his teeth. "Calls, plural. You okay? You sound cold."

"I am cold. I'm sorry I missed your calls." Her temper was evident in the snarky way she emphasized the "s". "I didn't hear the phone ring, it's loud inside."

"Where are you and Maxine partying tonight?"

"Big Phil's."

"Ah." He searched for something to say that would close the distance growing between them.

"Been here before?" she asked, her voice a little softer, a little sadder.

"Nope, heard of it though. You having a good time?"

"Yeah. Some of Maxine's friends are supposed to meet us here too. I'm thinking it's gonna be hopping here in a half hour or so."

He loved that soft laugh. God help him, he needed to hold her, touch her, just a little bit. "I miss you, Jaimee."

There was a long pause before she cleared her throat and said, "You're welcome to join us."

"Very tempting. Unfortunately I'm still at work. Could we meet for lunch or something tomorrow?"

"I would love to but I can't. I have to attend a seminar for school. I'd cancel but I've already canceled two. I just can't. You could come over after work though. I could make dinner."

A note of hopefulness was clear in her sweet voice but there was no way in hell he'd be able to be there, in her home alone with her, without taking her to bed.

"Can't. It'll be too late when I'm done. I'll only have about an hour for lunch tomorrow."

"Lucas. Look, is there a problem? If there's a problem just tell me. I'm a big girl, I can handle it."

Her voice shook from the cold or from insecurity, maybe both. Dammit. Lucas grit his teeth then took a deep breath. "Baby." He paused, pinched the bridge of his nose. God how he wanted to wipe away the frown he knew was pulling at those lush sensual lips. "There's no problem. How about Sunday?"

"I have church Sunday."

Church. Perfect. He'd be safe in church. He'd have to keep his hands to himself in church and he'd still be able to see her, at least hold her hand.

"I'll pick you up and we'll go together."

"Well okay. If you're absolutely sure?" She sounded stunned that he would consider going to church.

"Well yeah. My God too, you know."

"Actually, I didn't." Her answer was warm, he could hear her smile. "Oh, excuse me."

His smile fell as he watched two men standing too close to Jaimee. They had stepped up to the entrance and were seemingly nonchalant, smoking and talking. However, they had subtly forced her to step aside, away from the entrance. She was unmindful of the fact that she had been effectively moved away from the light, into the shadows.

"Okay well, church starts at ten thirty. Pick me up at ten fifteen?"

"I'll be there. You sound cold. Go back inside, Jaimee." He was aware that his voice took on an edge. He just hoped Jaimee did what he said for once.

"I can talk to you for a little while longer. I think the bouncer guy likes Maxine. He asked her to dance."

"Really? Well you'd better keep an eye on the poor guy then. Jaimee, baby, I wish I could talk more but I have to go back to work. Get inside before you catch cold."

"Okay." Jaimee hid no emotion. He could hear the disappointment in her voice.

"I'll call you when I get off work. Goodnight, sweetheart."

"Goodnight." Disappointment melted into longing.

The men blocking her way to the entrance didn't make it easy for her to get back inside. Lucas had his hand on the car door handle when Robertson swung open the door and said something to Jaimee, then to the men. They flicked their cigarette butts into the street and followed her in.

Lucas dialed Robertson's number.

"Spotted you out there," he answered. "I got her, Grayson. She's okay."

"Where did they go?" God, he hated not being able to see her.

"They're sitting across the dance floor from the ladies. They're watching her. I'm watching them."

"I hear you're drooling over Ms. Pruitt. Do you need back up?" Distractions were not good. Lucas knew this all too well. And the sumptuous Maxine was definitely a distraction.

Adrian snorted. "Grayson, man, that's an insult. I'm no rookie.

You know that. We got this. The owner has his own men lookin' out at the east side of the building and Saunders is covering the only other exit on the west side. It's cool for now. I'll ping you if it becomes otherwise."

Lucas wasn't at all concerned about offending him, even if he did trust Adrian Robertson with his life. This was Jaimee's life and Lucas was a hands-on kinda guy, especially when it came to what he considered his own. The constant surveillance and lack of action was hard enough to take. Not having Jaimee within arm's length only made the tense inactivity more stressful.

"Keep in touch."

"No doubt."

Chapter Twenty-Seven

Max was having a blast. Everyone knew her and she knew everyone. Jaimee smiled as she watched Max and Lora, one of Max's very lovely, very lively friends, laughing and dancing with three very nice-looking guys. Max had introduced her to the four of them as well as about ten other friends of hers. Everyone loved Max. What was not to love? Maxine: vivacious, fun loving, clever and wonderful friend with a wall around her that would rival the Berlin Wall. Before they tore it down, that is. Any who dare try and cross the barrier she'd constructed she'd gun down. There'd be nothing left but hamburger meat. In so many ways Max was happy but there was still one small empty space that you could see if you looked very closely. If Max allowed you to get close enough to see.

Jaimee's dancing skills were mediocre at best but moving to the music helped keep her mind off Lucas. It would be wise to distance herself. It was all about self-preservation. Nevertheless, that dim and struggling glimmer of hope that he would become a permanent part of her life was just too precious to let go of yet. Even if letting her emotions get in the way of good sense would be foolish and ultimately end in an agonizingly painful broken heart. Because, she loved him like she'd loved no one else.

That sad realization brought with it the revelation that she never truly loved Brent. Not like she should have. The love she had for Brent was comfortable and in so many ways co-dependant. They'd been great friends. Amazing friends, but they never should have married.

Her dance partner moved a little too far into her personal space and shook her out of her introspection. Why in the hell did she agree to accompany him to the dance floor? His name was Tim and he wasn't unattractive. Thin and lanky, he stood an inch or two taller than Jaimee. However, as he got closer it was obvious he wasn't exactly clear-headed. His breath reeked of whiskey and beer. And God did he ever stop talking?

To her immense relief the music changed to a slow dance. Jaimee politely thanked Tim and turned to walk away when he snagged her wrist and pulled her into his arms. "Hey, pretty lady, where ya goin'?"

Shoving at his chest did her no good at first. Although his frame seemed slight he was strong and sinewy. She wasn't afraid, strangely enough. He was stupid drunk, but then, she was stupid for agreeing to dance with him in the first place and she couldn't blame it on the booze. "I'm going to join my friend over there. So you need to let me go."

He tightened his embrace. "No, you ain't. Just give me one more dance."

"Yes. I am." Jaimee tried pushing away.

"Come on, sugar, don't be a tease."

Nausea was returning, combined with her rising anger. Jaimee took a shaky breath in an effort to keep from panicking. If he didn't let go she was gonna be sick. Again. And she hated throwing up. In situations such as this it was best to get right to the point, quickly. She had no other choice and niceties would never work with this creep.

"Tim, if you don't back off me now, I'm going shove your balls into your throat." Jaimee kept her voice low and deceptively pleasant.

Tim's sneering chuckle made her stomach lurch. "Oh yeah, I knew you was a fire cat when I seen ya."

With one hand he grabbed her ass, held her tight against his body with the other arm as he tried to shove a knee between her thighs. Revulsion traveled through her. She should have worn pants, shouldn't have worn that damn thong.

Without giving herself time to allow the ripple of fear free rein, Jaimee tensed and clenched her teeth as she gripped his shoulders and drove her knee upward as hard as she could. His eyes bulged. Stale, stinky breath wheezed from his lungs as he bent in half.

"Fff-uckin' bitch!" Tim spat at her, holding his wounded balls. "You fuckin' fat bitch."

The look in his eyes should have made Jaimee take a step back. Instead, the wall holding back the molten rage that simmered inside her crumbled. Fury erupted and washed over her. All sense of decorum left her. Her hands were tight fists at her sides, aching to collide with his jaw as she took a step toward him. The desire to hurt him some more was overwhelming and she didn't even care that everyone had stopped dancing, stopped talking, stopped doing whatever they were doing. She didn't care that all eyes were trained on the two of them.

She didn't give a good goddamn.

"That's the best you can come up with? Fat bitch? That's all the creativity your tiny, alcohol-soaked, pea brain can formulate? You pathetic piece of..." She would have launched herself at him, claws and teeth bared, if she hadn't found herself held back by a giant of a man. His big hands grasped her shoulders lightly but somehow that light grip was enough to hold her in place. At the same time, scowling intensely, growling something she couldn't discern, Adrian seized Tim by the collar and jerked him back.

"That's it, Tim. You just wore out your welcome." The giant spoke, his husky voice solemn and hard. "Better not see you 'round here again."

Before Tim could form a coherent sentence Adrian dragged him from the bar spitting and screaming. She hoped Adrian pummeled him. The patrons of the bar clapped and cheered but Jaimee ignored them. Her heart was thudding hard against her chest as reality descended. She struggled to breathe normally.

"You all right, ma'am?" the giant asked, slowly releasing her. His deep bass voice softened marginally but the Texan drawl wasn't compromised in the least.

"Yeah, fine," Jaimee snapped. She closed her eyes, breathed in deeply through her nose and held an arm across her middle. It was hard to be still. Her skin still crawled from Tim's grope and she still wanted to hurt him for it. "Sorry, I just lost my cool." She craned her neck to look up at the giant and exhaled slowly. He had to be all of six and a half feet tall, dressed in a button-down white oxford shirt, well-worn jeans complete with a huge brass buckle and cowboy boots.

A slow crooked grin curved his lips. "I'm Big Phil. Nothin' to apologize for. I'm impressed. You handled yourself real well. And I don't blame you one bit. He deserved what he got and more. I, however, do need to apologize. I'm real sorry you were accosted here in my house. Least I can do is get y'all's bill and if there's anything else I can do, you be sure and let me know."

Still pissed off, Jaimee couldn't seem to muster even a weak smile. "That's not necessary. It wasn't your fault."

"Yeah it was. I shoulda banned his sorry ass some time back. I'll be glad to call the police if you'd like to press charges."

Jaimee considered that for a moment, then quickly decided against it. The last thing she wanted to do now was deal with a bunch of cops, again. She'd had enough of that lately. "Thank you, it won't be necessary."

"Well, all right. Let me know if you change your mind. And listen, you and your friend come back anytime y'all want. Consider yourselves Big Phil's VIPs from now on. Enjoy the rest of the evening, ladies, it's on me."

Thankfully everyone in the bar seemed to resume what he or she was doing before the ruckus. Most of them did anyway. Jaimee tried not to let those who continued to watch her stress her out further. With a reassuring smile and a nod, Big Phil turned and sauntered over to Adrian just as the bouncer stomped back into the building. Phil placed one hand on Adrian's shoulder and bent to say something to him. Adrian nodded once. And then the long, tall Texan sauntered through the back door labeled *Employees Only.*

"Now he's one tall drink of water. S'cuse the cliché," Maxine said from behind her. Not so subtly trying to break the tension. Thank God for Maxine.

"Oh heck yeah. Did you see that big honkin' gold wedding band though?" Still a little shaky, Jaimee managed a smile, grateful for the levity. Maxine was wonderful at turning a bad situation around. "Just screams *taken, paws off.*"

"Mm hmm." Maxine hummed then took a deep breath and caught Jaimee's gaze. "You okay, James? You want to go home?"

"No, I'm fine." She took another deep breath. "He didn't hurt me. Just made me so mad."

"Yeah he did!" Lora spoke breathlessly. "You were awesome, I was fuckin' impressed!"

"Me too." Maxine grinned. "And I was damn proud of how you gave him a taste of his own balls."

"Me too. I bet he won't pee straight for a week." Lora laughed. Lora had a lusty laugh that was contagious. Jaimee grinned, she had to admit she was impressed with herself. The wave of dizziness however, kept her from basking in the glory and instead prodded her to find a seat.

At the table she sat and took a sip of her watered-down soda. The nausea was passing but she swayed a bit as another wave of dizziness hit her. She was trembling, probably from unspent adrenaline.

Maxine had her eyes trained on Adrian the bouncer as he answered his cell phone...again. "Mr. Sexy Bouncer guy gets a lot of calls."

"Yeah," Jaimee agreed, grateful for the distraction. "I've noticed that. He never looks happy about it either."

"No, he doesn't," Lora added.

"You know, he owes you a dance. I'm going to sit here for a while and calm down. You should go call in that dance."

Maxine frowned. "You sure you're okay?"

"Absolutely. Now go." Jaimee waved her away.

"She's okay. Don't hover over her. Go on. I'll keep her company." Lora shooed her away.

Exhaling slowly, Jaimee smiled and took another sip of her soda. Being a badass was definitely a good thing, even if it did leave her a little shaky. Freedom was what she'd gained the last several months, and that freedom gave her hope of so much more. She expected more from herself now. Just to get out there, make friends and have fun again was going to be great for her.

She sat back, sharing the remaining chips with Lora as they laughed, joked and watched Maxine flirt shamelessly with Adrian. Jaimee found herself surveying the room. Most everyone was dancing now, save a few groups here and there. Briefly she paused as she noticed a man across the dance floor looking her way. He was watching her intently and he didn't bother looking away or smiling as their eyes met. Finally he looked away and spoke to the man in the booth across from him. A chill, like an icy finger, slid down her back. Trying to feign indifference she let her gaze move away.

It wasn't that he appeared threatening in any way. He and his friend were dressed casually in jeans and nondescript button-down shirts. Maybe it was that the two men didn't seem to fit in. They were the rude men who bumped her aside as they stood outside smoking.

Shaking her head, she told herself it was the adrenaline. Her imagination was on overload because of it, that's all.

"Who are they?" she asked Lora and nodded toward them.

"Got no clue." Her brows furrowed as she studied them.

Jaimee shrugged off the uneasy feeling and smiled up at Sonya as she sat a fresh soda in front of her and an amaretto sour in front of Lora.

"That was great how you took care of Tim," Sonya said.

Jaimee searched for the right words in response but coming up with nothing profound she went with: "Oh. Well. My pleasure."

Sonya nodded and smiled brightly. "He's not so bad when he's sober, just talks too much. But he's been more of a problem lately. Big P said this was his last chance. So, anyway, you did good. The other girls and I want to thank you for letting him have it. He's been getting on our collective last nerve lately. Can I get you anything else? We got pie."

"No, I'm good, thanks." As she nodded and started to move away Jaimee stopped her. "Hey, do you know those guys across from us?"

Sonya looked across the room at the men for a long minute then shook her head. "No, I haven't seen them here before. I could ask the girls."

"No that's okay. Thanks anyway."

"You want me to take 'em a drink for y'all?"

Lora snorted and Jaimee chuckled.

"Oh no, no, I just thought they looked familiar is all. No biggie."

"Okie doke. Holler if y'all need anything else."

Jaimee smiled. "Thanks, Sonya."

As Sonya walked away, another new friend, Nick, approached the table with a gleam in his eye. "Wanna dance, Lora?"

"Hell yeah." She stood and smoothed her hands down her skirt. "Oh wait. You okay, babe? I can dance later."

"Don't hover, Lora." She laughed. "Go dance! I'm fine."

Lora bent and gave her a quick, tight hug, then winked and sashayed onto the dance floor. Nick followed behind her, watching her hips sway all the way. He turned back and waggled his brows at her before taking Lora in his arms. Laughing, Jaimee shook her head at him, amazed and happy with the certainty that she'd found a lifetime friend in Lora.

Fatigue washed over her as the adrenaline high faded and in all truth Jaimee did feel like heading home. Then again, going home to her dark, silent and empty town house didn't sound so inviting. On top of that, Maxine was having a good time and she so didn't want to spoil it by bailing on her.

Looking up from her soda, she glanced over to see another man join the two in the booth. Maxine was walking back toward her at the same time.

"Brushed me off." Her voice was cool and deceptively nonchalant. "Told me he had to take a raincheck on the dance and asked for my number but wouldn't give me his."

"That's not a brush off, is it, Maxine? You don't know. He might call."

"Phsaw, yeah. I'm not holding my breath. Anyway, I told him that we're taking you home..."

"No, you're not," Jaimee interrupted. "But, I do think I'm gonna head on home...and I can get there all by myself," she added with a smile.

"You're a little pale and you've been sick. I'm not sure you need to be driving. We can leave your car and come pick it up later. I'm sure they'll be fine with it here."

"Max, I love you. You're my best friend in the world, and if I really needed you to, I'd let you take me home. I'm fine."

Maxine's brows lifted and she took her determined, hand-on-her-hip stance. "I'll get Nick, we'll follow you then."

Jaimee leaned back in her chair and crossed her arms. "Okay, fine, I'll just stay then."

"Why do you have to be so damned stubborn?"

"I don't know, same reason you do I suppose," Jaimee shot back with a grin.

"Okay, dammit. But you better call me on my cell as soon as you get home so I know you're okay." She lifted a hand as Jaimee opened her mouth to speak. "And before you ask, as I mentioned before, Nick will make sure we all get home safe and sound. He's the designated driver tonight."

"I like Nick. Nick is cute."

"Nick is gay," Maxine said with a smirk.

"No way! He is not." Nick was tall, muscular, very sexy and he smelled wonderful.

"Yes way."

Jaimee shook her head as she stood and laid a hand over her uneasy stomach. "My gaydar is totally busted."

"Sadly, this is true." Maxine nodded.

Jaimee hugged her tightly and thanked her for being there for her, again, as always. After making her way around to everyone she'd met that night with promises to get together again, Jaimee headed out. Adrian's smile seemed stilted as he held the door open for her and wished her a good night.

As creepy as it was walking through a deserted parking lot in the middle of the night she already had her keys in her clenched fist, poking out between her fingers, just in case. That way she could jab an attacker in the eyes. It made her feel somewhat safe anyway. She was tough, strong, and she was pretty sure she could hold her own. Wrong. Her attacker was quick, came from behind. She wasn't nearly as prepared as she thought.

The gloved hand that covered her mouth and the arm that banded across her arms and her ribs were too quick, too strong. Jaimee found herself jerked back hard against someone solid, effectively immobilized. Though she kicked, jerked against her attacker and tried to grasp at

Veronica Chadwick

something, anything to get loose. The arm binding her was like iron, crushing, forcing the air from her lungs. The gloved hand moved away from her mouth but it didn't matter, she couldn't draw in enough air to scream. The cold steel of the gun against her temple stilled her.

"I'm gonna let you breathe but you even act like you're gonna scream and I'll kill you." The raspy, malevolent whisper turned Jaimee's blood to ice. "Don't doubt me."

She nodded, simply reacting. Her brain had gone on emergency mode the minute he touched her. Fight or flight. Neither were options at this point. The realization settled over her that she was probably going to die and the only thought formulating in her mind was "*Why?*"

As she slowly drew air into her lungs, through the thundering sound of her heart pounding in her ears she heard another low male voice, and another. The sound of a vehicle closing in.

"...here they come..."

"...into the van..."

Oh God, they were going to take her away. She couldn't let them take her from the parking lot or she was dead for sure. Her mind raced, trying to compose some sort of plan. The way she saw it, her only option was to fight. Even though the cold steel pressed hard against her temple she stiffened, resisting him. Being shot would be better than what she would face if they got her into the van.

"Drop the gun and let her go."

Jaimee lifted her eyes to see Lucas standing slightly to her right. He didn't so much as glance at her. His eyes and gun were trained on the man holding her. His expression held dark, unyielding fury. Lucas was here. Lucas had a gun. Her mind couldn't seem to sort out the facts and come up with anything coherent.

Her attacker laughed as his buddies drew their guns. "Stupid bastard," the attacker spat out. "You're outnumbered."

The streetlights afforded them little light but Jaimee registered movement to her left. Three guys other than the guy holding her and one sitting in the driver's seat of the van. That was four guns against Lucas's one and a big black van to haul the bodies away in.

"Think again, asshole," Lucas growled.

"FBI. Drop your weapons. Hands in the air."

Men with weapons surrounded them. Was that Detective Butler? FBI? The question barely had time to flit through her mind when the van headlights flashed on. Lucas only narrowed his eyes as one of the bad guys jumped into the passenger seat just as the van sped away. Her attacker pushed the gun harder against her temple. He was

202

breathing hard and his grip on her tightened to the point of pain.

"I'll kill her!"

Jaimee closed her eyes and tried to breathe.

"And I'll drop you where you stand if you so much as twitch," Lucas said calmly. Too calmly.

Everything seemed to erupt from there, although for Jaimee, it happened in slow motion. The man shoved her hard. Lucas caught her, his grip tightening around her for a split second before pushing her behind him.

Shots exploded around her and then just shouts of the men from the FBI ordering those remaining to stay down. Jaimee stayed close behind Lucas, absorbing his warmth, watching the ordered chaos. The man who had held her captive lay on the pavement, blood pooling around his head.

"We're on their tail," crackled over several walkie talkie thingys hanging from the belts of the men surrounding them, from Lucas's belt.

"Fuck. Grayson. Your cover is blown, man," one of the agents snapped.

Cover? Nausea returned full force as numbness settled in everywhere else. Lucas was undercover? FBI. "Lucas?" Her voice wasn't much more than a whisper as reality burned into her heart. It was a denial, a plea that all this was wrong, a misunderstanding, a mistake. Lucas couldn't be FBI. He was in construction. He was at work. Working late.

Lucas lowered the gun and turned to her, his gaze hard, distant and detached. Detective Butler stepped up to her. No, not Detective... "Go with Agent Whitman, Ms. Turner. He'll take you to the station. We'll explain everything there."

"I don't understand." Bewildered, she laid a hand on Lucas's arm "Lucas." Though she spoke with more volume this time, her voice shook.

Then she saw it, very clear in the depths of his sober and savage gaze. Regret and remorse. Somehow through his impossibly clenched jaw he spoke—no growled. "Go. I'll be there soon. Wait for me."

Chapter Twenty-Eight

The ride to the police station in the black sedan was a quiet one that seemed to take forever. Agent Whitman was nice enough. He only spoke once to ask if she was okay. Jaimee couldn't make her throat work so she just nodded. It was a lie. She was far from okay, but she refused to assume anything until she talked to Lucas. She wished she could just stop shaking. Sickness coiled in her stomach, icy and cloying. Countless emotions engulfed her, each one threatening to destroy her, heart and soul.

The pieces were beginning to fall into place but with big segments missing. Apparently Lucas was FBI. She was afraid to allow her deductions follow that cognitive path.

Absently she stepped out of the cruiser and thanked Agent Whitman for holding the door for her. She followed behind him as he led her down one hall then another until he finally opened a door that led into a lounge room of sorts. A coffee bar sat along the wall right inside the entrance. A few steps through a short hallway to the left the room opened up. Two beat-up leather sofas sat perpendicular to each other, a coffee table in the corner between them.

"Have a seat, Ms. Turner." Agent Whitman spoke softly, concern etched in his face. He seemed to be a kind man, in his late forties maybe. He probably had a sweet little family too. "Can I get you some coffee, or tea, or something?"

"Something warm would be good. Thank you." The damn cold had seeped into her bones.

He walked away with a nod. Seconds later he reappeared from around the corner with a steaming cup of coffee. "I put cream and sugar in it. I hope that's okay."

"Perfect. Thank you." Jaimee wrapped her hands around the chunky blue ceramic mug and slowly sipped.

"Good?"

She managed to nod and give him a weak smile.

He grinned. "We pride ourselves on our coffee. Hate that cliché about station house coffee in Styrofoam cups."

She tried not to stare at him like he'd lost his mind. But she couldn't help it. So what? Excellent coffee, in a mug, in a law enforcement establishment wasn't thrilling enough to distract her from the foremost concern in her mind at the moment. She didn't give a damn about the stupid coffee.

"I need some answers. I need to talk to Lucas. Or someone. Now." Clenching her teeth, she gripped the mug tighter to keep from hurling it at the man. "Do you have answers?"

Agent Whitman cleared his throat. "I'm sorry, ma'am. I don't. I have to go. Someone will be with you soon." With that he turned on his heel and walked out.

Jaimee took another sip of coffee, laid her head back and closed her eyes. Questions were swirling around in her head like a hurricane. She was trying hard not to come to any solid conclusions until she talked to Lucas. Until then, she was going to focus on what she did know: Brent had really fucked up her life with whatever it was in that day planner he'd hid in her classroom. Before she could expound on that stunning revelation someone entered the room and stopped at the coffee bar.

"...from what I've heard." The voice belonged to a man.

"Well duh." Another male voice answered.

Neither knew she sat just around the corner. She started to stand and ask if they had any information when the second man continued.

"Grayson never has a problem seducing a female. This one was no different. Women think he's a sex god."

"Yeah but evidently this one wasn't like the others. This one was an innocent. From what I hear, she's a plump and very cute little schoolteacher. She never knew what hit her."

"Fell hard, huh?"

He sighed. "What I heard."

"Damn. That's sad. You know Grayson is heartless when it comes to a mission. He fucks 'em then fries 'em and that's that. It's all about the job to him."

Jaimee's breath froze in her lungs and her heart splintered, threatening to shatter. *...all about the job...* She had been his job. He had just *fucked* her for his *mission*? No, that couldn't be true. God. No. She wanted to scream at them. Tell them to shut up but the words lodged, hot and spiked, in her throat. She couldn't move. Her throat ached, her chest burned and all she could do was listen to them.

"Why'd they put him on her case anyway if she wasn't up to her neck in the mess? Looks like we should have dealt with this one with some more subtlety." The man sounded disgusted.

"I believe the jury was still out on whether she was guilt free or not at first. Seems her husband put her name on the Swiss account and tied her to it all nice and tight."

What Swiss account? God. What had Brent done?

"Damn. That's some fucked-up shit."

"Yeah. It is that."

"They should have pulled him off the case as soon as they realized she wasn't the real target."

"I asked Whitman the same thing. He said they tried but Grayson wouldn't have it. Said she was in the line of fire. Butler was convinced that she still needed surveillance. Convinced enough to install sleeper transmitters. He wanted to make sure she came out of this in one piece, I guess. So Grayson was determined to stay in place in order to protect her from fallout from The Collective."

Sleeper transmitters? The Collective? Anger flashed through her and warred for first place with her pain. It was just too much. Her head was buzzing and she wanted to throw up.

"It makes no damn sense though. I mean, granted, Grayson is a cold son-of-a-bitch but he isn't a sadist and he isn't that hard up for pussy."

"I'm tellin' ya, it's a mind fuck."

"So now that his cover is blown, he's off the case I suppose. Any idea where they're sending Don Juan next?"

"That's just it, he ain't off the case. Way I heard it he won't back down. Even fighting Butler on it as we speak. He's stickin' with this one until the end."

"Should be interesting to say the least. Still, hate it for the poor lady. She just got caught in the middle of a cluster-fuck."

"Yeah, she did. All I can say is..." He paused, sighing again, pity resounding in every word. It made her lip curl involuntarily. "I just hope she's strong enough to deal with..." The man's voice trailed off as he moved out of the room and down the hall.

Jaimee just sat staring at nothing as the weeks past played through her mind. He'd been watching her. But he wasn't the only one. Everyone had been watching her. Pain seemed to sink deep inside her with every flash of memory, weighing her down. They would be arriving soon to manipulate her further. She had actually bought it, believed Lucas cared for her, truly cared. But no, he'd been handling her, manipulating and humiliating her. Was he laughing now? Her throat burned and her head hurt but she'd be damned if she gave them the satisfaction of seeing her cry. God. She'd been so stupid. Everything in her wanted to walk out, take her control back. To hell with them. But that would be stupid too.

She was going to find someone who would be straight with her if she had to interrogate every damn person in the building.

Just as she stood up, *Agent* Michael Butler walked in.

"Ms. Turner. If you'd follow me to my office we'll get this over with as quickly as possible and get you home." She didn't move. Only rage motivated her now. Before she could say anything Lucas stormed into the room.

"Jaimee."

Jaimee stiffened, slowly raising her eyes to meet Lucas's gaze. He ducked. The heavy mug missed his head by centimeters and dented the wall with a loud thunk before falling to the floor. The station's "excellent" coffee splashed everywhere. Lucas straightened and glared at her.

"Do you feel better now?" He lifted one brow.

Jaimee's eyes narrowed. "Hell no. I missed."

"Ms. Turner." Agent Butler attempted to calm her, reached for her. "Please, let's discuss this..."

"Don't. Touch. Me." Her voice was low and calm, totally opposite from what was happening inside her. "*Now* you want to discuss things, now that you've manipulated me and made a fool of me. Hell, the boys at the station all know and don't mind discussing my wretched, pathetic humiliation on break over non-clichéd coffee but you didn't bother *discussing* anything with me before you sent Grayson here poking around in my life." The pain took her breath away. Just for a moment. She had to pause to catch it again. "So now it's too late to discuss anything with me, *Agent* Butler."

"Someone was talking about the case here in front of you?" Lucas seemed to vibrate with rage as he spoke.

Jaimee slowly turned her head and looked up at him. She didn't even try to hide the pain she knew had to be clear in her eyes. "That's what bothers you? They were discussing your secret case. That's all you're worried about?" A soft derisive laugh escaped her throat. "No, not in front of me. They didn't know I was here." She lifted a shaky hand. "And before you ask, I couldn't tell you who they were or what they look like. But they knew me, the plump, and apparently desperate, little schoolteacher. They knew all about *the case*...and you. Evidently, Agent Grayson, you're legendary and they feel sorry for me." The last came out almost a whisper. She turned back to Butler. It was better to focus on Butler. "What are sleeper transmitters?"

Butler chewed on the inside of his cheek for a moment then with a deep sigh, shifted his gaze from Lucas back to Jaimee. "They're hidden listening devices that..."

"Bugs."

"Yes."

"You bugged my house."

"Yes."

"My phone?"

"Yes."

"Get them out. Now. Send someone to my house and clean them out right now." She said it through clenched teeth as she struggled not to scream and cry and throw up. Her heartbeat seemed so loud, pounding in her ears, every other sound was muffled, even the sound of her own voice.

Butler had the good sense to look ashamed. She couldn't look at Lucas again. Not without falling completely apart.

"We can't yet, Ms. Turner. You're still in danger and it's our job to keep you safe."

"Safe." The laugh that bubbled up from inside her sounded a little hysterical now. She swallowed and squeezed her eyes shut for a moment. Willing herself to pull it together, to fight against the intense desire to sink into herself, the need to mentally shrink away from the pain expanding inside her.

"Could we please go discuss this somewhere private?" Butler asked quietly. "We'll tell you everything and explain what happens next."

She opened her eyes and pinned him with a look she could only hope made him understand the fury that swirled within her at that moment. "What happens next is I'm leaving. You go ahead and watch all you want, follow me, do whatever you have to do but stay the hell away from me."

Lucas stepped between her and the door. His hands fisted at his sides, his expression stern and resolved. "You're not going anywhere, Jaimee."

She met his gaze boldly and marveled at the fire raging in his eyes. What right did he have to be angry?

"Why do you care?" she snarled and went for the jugular. "You're just their hired whore. You did your job. Oh, sorry I wasn't the bad bitch I was supposed to be so that you could get your rocks off busting me now that you've won my trust and love." It was almost undetectable, the small twitch of a grimace in Lucas's expression. Other than that he didn't respond. He just stood there. Watching her. "Move on to the next *fuck and fry.*"

He moved too quickly. Her upper arm was clasped in his steely grip and he was moving her from the room and down the hall before she had time to process his actions and evade him. In the interest of her own self-preservation she bit her lip to keep from screaming at him and calling more attention to the scene. She didn't resist, didn't acknowledge the people watching him manhandle her. Although she didn't know why, what was a little more humiliation added to everything else. Butler strode behind them, grumbling under his breath at Lucas about having some tact and compassion. Ha! Too late for that shit.

Finally they ended up in an office at the end of a long hallway. Lucas pushed her into one of the leather chairs facing a wide cherry desk. Butler closed the door behind him and locked it, then sat in the high back leather office chair behind the desk and turned sideways away from her. Lucas stood in front of her, leaning back against the desk, and glared down at her.

"The Collective is a criminal organization that has its tentacles in several illegal activities, Sheppard & Zachary being one of the largest firm fronts. As an associate CPA for the firm, Brent Turner was a pivotal member of the organization. Mr. Turner was a dumbass and embezzled eighty-eight point four million dollars of the organization's money and put it in a Swiss bank account in your name. But, of course, Zachary caught on to him. So..." He paused and looked away from her. A muscle pulsed in his clenched jaw. Suddenly numb, Jaimee watched him, waiting for him to finish.

"So..." Michael Butler swiveled toward her. His voice was soft but his expression savage. "Turner took the information he had, addresses, names, incriminating company files that were supposed to have been destroyed, the access codes for the Swiss account and God knows what else and tucked it away on a flash drive in a black day planner and hid it somewhere. Then he offered an unsuspecting homeless man a hot meal and a ride. He killed the man...suffocated him, we believe...and used his body to fake his own death. Now he's after that day planner and possibly you. He's not stable."

Jaimee stared at him, trying to process what he was telling her.

"Brent is alive?" Her voice sounded far away, muffled.

"Yes, ma'am. He is," Butler answered gently.

"Oh God, he killed someone."

"Yes."

Her mind was racing. Months. Brent had been gone for months, nearly a year. Let her believe he was dead. Let her grieve and...oh God...move on. She was an adulteress now. And he took a life. Actually killed someone. If things could get worse she didn't want to know. She'd been married to a man she never knew. A murderer. She wanted to go somewhere warm and curl up and disappear. Her heart hurt so badly.

"But he never contacted me." Her voice trembled and she swallowed.

"Actually he was the one who tried to break into your house that night." Butler leaned back in his chair.

Memories of the things Lucas had done, had made her feel, flooded her body. Heat crawled up her neck and she crossed her arms over her chest in a lame attempt to hide her body's reaction. She resisted the urge to glance at Lucas.

"And you didn't tell me in order to keep me safe, I suppose."

"Correct."

Jaimee shook her head, struggled to process the information, the shock. She steeled herself and finally looked up at Lucas. "The night, after the break-in...you wouldn't touch me after that." Her voice was hoarse, full of pain. "You avoided me. Because I was still married?"

"Yes," he bit out then met her gaze.

His expression wasn't smug as she had expected. It was surprisingly gentle, softening as he knelt in front of her and wiped a tear she didn't know had fallen from her cheek. Oh God help her, she wanted to buy in to his kindness, his tenderness.

"We'll find him. I won't let him or anyone else hurt you."

It was all a lie, she reminded herself. That fact was inescapable.

"Yeah?" She looked into his eyes, trying to decide whether to speak her heart or shield it. Hell, it was in a gazillion pieces now, what was the point of trying to protect it? "That's going to be difficult for you, Lucas. You hurt me more than anyone else could have."

"Jaimee," he whispered hoarsely. When he raised his eyes to hers again they were sharp, dark and clear. "I will try to explain everything...in time. Right now I just need you to do what we ask you to. The Collective thinks you know more than you do. They want you. If they get a hold of you they will torture you until they're satisfied. Baby, that would take an excruciatingly long time. Finally, they'll let your body die long after they've destroyed your mind and soul. I won't let that happen. I'll do whatever I have to do to keep you safe whether you like it or not. Do you understand me?"

The weight of reality was crushing her. It was so hard just to inhale. It hurt so badly. Basically, she had no free will at this point. He and Brent had taken even that from her.

"Yes, I understand."

"Good." He brushed away another tear, his fingers lingered on her cheek before he stood.

"I have the day planner. I found it hidden in the back of my metal cabinet at school. I hardly ever go into it and I keep it locked." Without actually meeting Lucas's gaze she lifted her head. "Weeks ago I noticed some papers and things that had been in my tote were lying on the desk in my office instead. Now it makes sense. I normally keep the keys to my desk and cabinet in my tote. Brent would have known that. But I had moved them to the top drawer of my desk so he didn't find them."

"Where is the day planner now?" Agent Butler had leaned forward in his chair.

"I moved it to a desk drawer. I meant to turn it over to you but my mind has been so cluttered lately. I'm sorry."

"Not a problem, Ms. Turner. Someone will go with you and pick it up."

Jaimee nodded and faced Lucas. "Lucas, when this is all over...?"

"Yes?"

She swallowed and looked down at her hands clasped together. She couldn't look into those fathomless dark eyes anymore. She was afraid she might drown in them. Losing herself in this jumble of hurt and questions and confusion was not an option. No matter how much she wanted to just give in to all of it. It would be so easy, but it would destroy her.

"...I never want to see your face again." The words sounded as tattered as her heart and she couldn't look up at him, she wouldn't sacrifice herself to some imitation of love again. Never again.

Edward Zachary set his granddaughter off his lap as he stood and wiped pumpkin innards from his hands with a nearby dishtowel.

"Allen, help your baby sister with her pumpkin. I'll be right back."

"Okay, Grandpa," the boy answered.

Zachary smiled and ruffled his hair as he passed him. Good kid. He met his wife in the kitchen doorway and kissed her cheek. "Thank you, dear, it shouldn't take long."

"It's all right. I'll help the children finish up their pumpkins."

He patted her cheek before walking away. His smile faded as he made his way through the house to his study where his men were waiting. He didn't say anything until he'd crossed the room and sat comfortably in his chair. Neither did they. They knew better.

"What was so goddamn important that you felt the need to interrupt my family time? I was carving Halloween pumpkins with my grandbabies, for Christ's sake."

"We're sorry, Mr. Zachary, but we thought you'd better be made aware of what happened tonight."

Idiots. He could tell by looking at them that they'd screwed up the whole mission. How hard was it to kidnap one little girl anyway?

"Go on. I'm waiting."

"The Feds showed up. Crenshaw is dead. They have the girl. The man we thought was her boyfriend is an undercover agent. Lucas Grayson. We're getting intel on him now."

Why did they need him to tell them step-by-step what they needed to do as though they were mentally challenged children? Did they think he cared if Crenshaw was dead? If Crenshaw was dead he deserved to be dead.

"This is why Ms. Turner's lover should already be dead. Now that his cover is blown he'll either go deep or he'll retire, either way it's just going to take more time and more expense. I don't like paying for nothing." He stood with a heavy sigh of disgust. "Get the girl. Keep her alive. Kill the agent if need be." He crossed to the study door and held it open for the men then followed them to the front door. "Do not come to my home again without an invitation. I hired you to do a job, gentlemen. Get it done without a handholding. I don't believe I need to remind you of the consequences of disappointing me further."

"No, sir," they said. Stepping outside into the cool October air, they turned just in time to see the door slam in their faces.

Chapter Twenty-Nine

"*...never want to see your face again.*"

Jaimee's words were burned into his brain. All along he knew this would happen, prepared for it, steeled himself for it. What he wasn't prepared for was how violently her pain would affect him. It was agony for her. Jaimee didn't hide her emotions, no matter how hard she tried. Every one of them was there in her crystal gaze, in the devastated expression on her beautiful face.

At the traffic light Lucas glanced at her briefly before turning his eyes back to the road ahead of them. The night was giving way to a stormy morning. Her face was shadowed and stark in the dusky light as she sat motionless, staring blankly straight ahead. Every breath she took was too controlled, as if she was concentrating on each inhale and exhale. Her hands were tight fists resting on the little purse in her lap.

It was just beginning to drizzle. Rain, like little tears, slid down the windshield. Fitting, considering Jaimee hadn't cried. Not really. A few errant tears had escaped but she was holding it all in. Trapping it behind the anger. Inevitably a flood was coming. He wanted to hold her through that storm, soothe the pain, touch her and make her forget all about it. Not possible. He'd caused it. He nearly punched Whitman for putting her in there and leaving her in the first place. He'd threatened to hunt the two fuckers gossiping like a couple of old women and feed them their own testicles, if they had any. This was his own damn fault. He never should have touched her. And yet, he wasn't sorry.

He wished now he'd let the mug hit him. God knows he deserved it; he deserved that and much worse. But she didn't. And the last thing he wanted was for her to feel bad because he was bleeding. And she would. Open-hearted and generous to a fault, she was just good. She was too good for him. But she was his, even if she didn't accept that right now. He could give her time. He couldn't give her up.

"There are other men watching the house," Lucas said quietly as he pulled into her driveway. "I'll be downstairs. You'll be safe, Jaimee."

"I know," she murmured without looking at him.

If she would just talk to him, give him a chance... There was so much he wanted to say to her, to explain, but it would be a waste of words. Right now anyway. She didn't wait for him to open the door for her or to protect her from the icy drizzle. She got out and walked toward her home, keys in hand. He fell into step behind her and she stiffened as if she was afraid he might touch her. Even though every fiber of his being wanted to, he wouldn't. He'd give her space if it killed him. And it just might. Which was why he kept his hands balled into fists at his sides.

She hesitated at the door and met his gaze, pulling her jacket together over her chest like a shield. The cacophony of emotion in her eyes was like a punch in the gut. He found it hard to breathe. For a moment he thought she might say something. Anything.

He stared down at her, at war with himself over whether to say something to her at this point. Before he could make up his mind she turned away from him and pressed her lips together, her brows furrowed. Quickly, she unlocked the door and moved to step inside.

"Wait," he said more harshly than he'd meant to. She stopped but didn't look at him. "Stand right here. Don't move," he commanded.

Lucas moved into the house ahead of her. The security guy was just putting his things away in the living room as another tech was bounding down the stairs. Lucas turned and motioned for Jaimee to come in. With an irritated scowl and sigh she stepped in and closed the door behind her.

"Mornin', Agent Grayson," the tech said much too cheerily, and then nodded at Jaimee. "Ma'am."

He was probably in his late twenties, chewing gum and sort of bouncing on the balls of his feet. Too hyper.

"Done?" Lucas resisted the urge to snarl.

"Yep. Master bedroom. Master bath. Swept clean," he answered as he gathered his equipment.

Lucas just nodded.

"The P2P has been removed from the PC too. Deleted without a trace. Like we'd never been there."

Peripherally, he could see Jaimee's head snap up to glare at him with unmistakable disdain and he gritted his teeth.

The tech gave Jaimee a tight smile, cleared his throat and continued. "Uh...I noticed you were in desperate need of a defrag so I went ahead and ran one. Also, did a virus update and scan. Should be good to go."

"My computer too?"

Lucas clenched his jaw tighter, ignoring the aching protest of his molars. "Yes."

"Okay, you're set." The security guy came into the hallway from the living room carrying his things. He was an older man and wasn't interested in staying any longer than he had to. Good. "Windows are secure. Sliding glass door too. Just don't open any of them. I had to do a rush job. No time to install a code panel. A window opens...the cavalry arrive en force. Got it?" The question was asked of Jaimee with one of the man's bushy eyebrows raised.

"I got it." Her shoulders sagged a little.

"Good." He glanced from Lucas to Jaimee and back again. "If you're done with us we're out," he said uncomfortably as he moved toward the door.

Lucas just nodded, let them out and locked the door behind them.

Jaimee stood on the second step, her body so stiff she had to ache. Her hair was damp from the rain. Tendrils curled, clinging to her cheeks. Her lips were full and pink, her eyes red rimmed from refusing to cry. She was achingly beautiful. But it was painfully obvious by the way she narrowed her eyes as she stared down at him that she didn't want to talk. "What did he do to my bedroom and bathroom?"

"He removed the transmitters. The rest of the house is still wired for sound. The phone too."

"But my bedroom and bathroom aren't?"

"Not anymore." He looked up at her, trying with all his heart not to take her right there on the stairs, show her exactly how much he wanted her. That would be a colossal mistake. Maybe she did need to be held, but more than that she needed to feel safe now. Debugging her sanctuary was something. He was trying to at least give her something.

"You can go too. I don't want you here." The bleak expression in her eyes and the tone of her voice were in direct contradiction with her words. If she kept looking at him with all that hurt and need in her eyes he was going to lose his waning control.

"Go to bed, Jaimee. If you need anything I'll be here. Or pick up the phone and start talking. Or, you could always just open the window." The last he said derisively as he turned away. His irritation and frustration with the whole situation was clear as was his own pain but he didn't have the inclination to mask them anymore.

Jaimee locked her bedroom door behind her, stripped off her jacket and tossed it on her bed as she headed for the bathroom. Holding back the tears made her head hurt. Right now, she just wanted to take a hot shower, then fall into bed and find oblivion. Actually she wanted to soak for hours in her very roomy garden tub until her skin was all pruney and her bones dissolved like Jello. But that would take too long and she didn't want to give herself that much time to think. The goal was unconsciousness as soon as humanly possible.

She didn't want to think or feel anymore. Routine helped. Clothes went into the hamper, towels selected from the closet and set on the counter. Somehow, she managed to brush her hair, her teeth and wash her face all without really looking too closely at herself in the mirror. She wasn't sure what she'd see in her eyes but whatever it was she didn't know if she could handle it. One more thing, just one more blow would completely obliterate what was left of her at this point.

The water temperature was set to just below boiling. Jaimee stepped into the shower and closed her eyes. Lucas. His face was all she saw as she stood there letting the driving spray pour over her. In her mind she could see his eyes dark, intense with desire. Fool that she was she had begun thinking that maybe he cared for her, possibly even loved her. He'd listened to her talk about her students, her beliefs, all the things she dreamed of doing, hoped to achieve. He'd listened like he cared, like they all mattered. Many times he told her how much he wanted her and that she belonged to him. Dammit, he made her feel cherished. Lies, all of it was just an act. He was just doing his job. Why did she let herself believe she could be loved like that?

Maybe it was the heat of the unrelenting water melting away the numbness. Maybe she just couldn't ignore the pain any longer. The force of it was just too strong. It was torrential and rushed in so fast and hard that she couldn't stop it. With something between a hiccup and a gasp the tears started. She let herself slide down the shower wall to the tile floor and gave in to the wracking sobs choking her. The burning pain in her shattered heart was so intense she had to struggle to catch her breath.

God only knew how long she sat there, holding her knees, crying, shaking, but she finally pulled herself up and weakly went through the motions of washing her body then her hair. Her skin was red from the heat of the water but she was still chilled to the bone as she dried off and pulled on her terry cloth robe. Without bothering to brush out her hair or put on underwear or pajamas, Jaimee crawled into bed. Sleep came quickly. But peace did not. The tormenting dreams wouldn't allow it.

The afternoon brought with it driving rain, lightning and thunder so loud it rattled the windows. Jaimee woke with a start, breathing heavy, her heart in her throat. She sat up and scooted to the edge of her bed, waiting for her heart to regain a more normal rhythm. The door to her bedroom swung open with a whoosh and Lucas rushed in. Still in a sleepy fog she squealed in shock and jumped up.

He stood there, bare-chested, jeans riding low on his hips, his hair flowing over his shoulders. His smoldering gaze was exacting and dark as it traveled over her body, staring at her like a newly discovered oddity. "You screamed." His voice, when it was all low and husky like that, made her shiver.

"I did?" she breathed, fighting to control the need suddenly whipping through her body. It was as if it had a mind all its own and Lucas could summon the most potent reactions. Those intense eyes focusing on her lower body didn't help.

"You did."

Pushing the wild hair from her face, she frowned. It wasn't lust in his eyes, she reminded herself. He never wanted her. It was all just part of his job. "Bad dream I guess." Her voice dropped an octave and took on a hard, cold tone.

His eyes narrowed. "So you're okay."

Her frown deepened, bordering on a scowl. "Peachy." If he'd stop looking at her like that... "What?" She didn't care that she snapped either. "What do you want?"

He was torturing her now, probably enjoying it. Just watching to see if she would shatter and fall apart because Lucas, god of sex, didn't want her, didn't love her. But she would not fall apart. Not on his watch. Not while the rage was keeping her intact.

Lightning flashed again and fire flared in those familiar eyes as they slowly lifted to meet hers. A searing gaze filled with the promise of unrestrained pleasure. A promise made to be broken. Resounding thunder made her shudder involuntarily. Just like all the other unspoken promises that mounted up in her heart over the past weeks. It was just another lie.

Absently, she lifted a hand to rub at the ache in her chest. Yet another gasp escaped her dry lips, her rope had fallen open. There she stood, for all intents and purposes, completely naked even down to her recent wax job. Clenching her teeth, she pulled the robe closed tight around her. "You—"

"Get dressed. There's food downstairs." He interrupted her intended accusation, turned and walked out, slamming the door behind him.

A part of her wanted to go back to bed and hide under the covers, however, mortification and anger did not mix well nor was it conducive to sleep. Besides, there were too many things that required attention, too many questions that needed answers. And no way in hell was Lucas going to get away with bullying her in her own home.

It wasn't like he hadn't seen her naked before. For a few moments there, she could have sworn desire burned in his eyes. Probably, she was just seeing what she wanted to see. Maybe all along that look in his eyes was more close to disgust. It infuriated her and God, how it hurt, but she would be okay. Eventually.

What shamed her more was the fact that Brent was alive and the only emotion she could summon about that was rage. Odd how she wasn't even that surprised to find out what a weasel he was. Love was never really there for either of them. She tried and failed. Not only Brent, but she'd failed herself as well by trying to be right for him. It just wasn't in her to be sad or to spend the time being mad about her "late" husband anymore. All that was left to do now was to sever all ties, stand up straight and move on. Again. Dammit.

She grumbled to herself as she hooked her bra. If Lucas would just go the hell away and leave her alone then she wouldn't have to worry about her clothes or lack thereof. But then that wasn't exactly true now, was it? Someone else was probably watching, most definitely listening. If the foggy threat of a headache wasn't throbbing in her skull, she'd scream.

On top of all this, people wanted to kill her, or at least kidnap her and torture her until she handed over the day planner. She'd throw Agent Lucas Grayson out of her house and Monday she'd hand over the stupid day planner. Still, probably wouldn't get her out of hot water with The Collective. Either way the Feds were gonna have to put someone else on her case. She wanted Lucas gone.

She dressed in a pretty, baby blue tank top and a new pair of snug-fitting mid-rise jeans. Then she made sure the whole curvy sexy look was covered by enshrouding herself in a shapeless, oversized, black sweater. "Good God, Jaimee," she mumbled to the morose, puffy, red-eyed mess staring blankly back at her from the bathroom mirror as she pushed the sleeves up. "You gotta snap the hell out of this." She couldn't let him see her all pitiful and broody. Besides, as soon as this mess was all over, the divorce was underway and Brent was in jail, she'd be just fine. In time her heart would be whole again. In the meantime she'd be damned if she'd let this make her fearful and weak.

Although she brushed her unruly hair into some semblance of submission she didn't have the inclination or the patience to coax it into any sort of style. Instead she smoothed it back and secured it into a ponytail. It was a poofy ponytail, but a ponytail nonetheless. Concealer did little to hide the puffiness but it did lighten the dark circles under her eyes. Some powder, light blush, just a brush of mascara and some lip balm and she didn't look as wretched. For another moment or two she stared at herself in the mirror, ignoring the doubt in her eyes, and willed herself strength.

The spicy scent of whatever Lucas was cooking met her as she descended the stairs and her stomach growled. Funny how the mind and body didn't agree on what they wanted most of the time.

Lucas briefly glanced up from the pot he was stirring on the stove as she walked into the kitchen. He had put on his T-shirt and tied his hair back. His movements were sharp, jerky and stiff. Probably wanted to get as far away from her as he could. Well she sure as hell wasn't holding him here.

She stood there stiffly and crossed her arms over her chest. "Why are you still here? You don't have to be. I told you already, your job here is done, you can go now."

"Sit down, you need to eat." He kept his voice level but she could see the hostile tension in his eyes, the way his lips pressed into a line.

Jaimee didn't budge. "If you're waiting around because you're hoping I'll break down, bawl and beg you to stay, you're in for disappointment."

The muscle in his jaw pulsed as he wiped a small splatter from the stove with a little more aggression than was necessary. "You've been crying most of the night, Jaimee." He flung the towel onto the counter and lifted his eyes, just his eyes, to hers. "Do I look pleased?"

No, he looked pissed off. The fierceness of his gaze caused the exact opposite reaction than it should have. Heat flared through her, settling low in her stomach, pulsing outward. She wanted to squeeze her thighs together to quell the arousal building there, dampening her panties. She didn't, she forced herself to stay still inhaling slowly, deeply in an effort to calm the riot between pain and lust brewing inside her. It took amazing effort to make sure her expression didn't falter. And thank God she wore the bulky sweater over her tank top or she would have had to keep her arms over her stiffening nipples for who knew how long.

The last thing she wanted was one more humiliating blow that would result from Lucas seeing just how much she still wanted him. Fury shook her hard, making her body tremble with the force of it. That she couldn't hide. The millions of little shards piercing her heart were another story.

"You didn't answer my question."

He moved around her kitchen like it was his own. Taking a bowl down from the cabinet he began filling it with chili. "There are powerful people looking to hurt you. I'm making sure that doesn't happen."

Watching him add cheese and sour cream to the top of her bowl made her stomach growl again. "And there's no one else in the whole Federal Bureau of Investigation and beyond that could do that?" she asked in her well-honed teacherly tone.

"No, there isn't." He shoved a spoon into the bowl.

She took the bowl he offered and walked toward the dining room, snatching the chips from the counter as she went. "Hmm, sucks to be you, I guess." Sarcasm made her feel a little better. Oddly enough it relieved a little of the tightness gathering between her shoulders.

Chapter Thirty

Watching the storm of emotions ripping Jaimee apart from the inside was twisting him in knots and making him edgy. He'd listened to her sob in the shower and the way she cried softly, off and on, all the while she was supposed to be asleep. It had just about brought Lucas to his knees. From the moment he looked into her eyes and saw clearly the pure beauty of her soul, leaving her alone was never an option. She was his and he broke her heart. All the foreknowing couldn't have and didn't prepare him for the deluge of pain and anger that poured from her once she learned the truth. It was best just to keep cool, take whatever blows she needed to land and wait. Right now, however, he wanted to put his fist through a wall.

She was so damn stubborn and it annoyed the hell out of him when she turned that schoolmarm, prissy-proper attitude on him. It sucked to admit, but she had a point. Being around each other was making both of them crazy. The snarky comments coming from that lush mouth of hers were pushing him too far. All he wanted to do was back her against the wall and make her forget. That would be a bad idea, really bad. He kept telling himself that but his rock-hard dick wasn't listening. He couldn't let his guard down while protecting her, he couldn't allow himself to be distracted. Not even for a second. Not now. Add to it that he wasn't exactly out of the line of fire.

A year ago a contract on his life wouldn't have fazed him or slowed him down. Dying wasn't an acceptable risk now. That was an unexpected and jarring revelation. There was too much life he wanted to experience. Too much Jaimee he had yet to discover.

He flipped open his phone and dialed The Pope. It didn't take long to set things up. This way he could take a step back and still keep an eye on her. At least maybe Jaimee could relax a little.

Jaimee was sitting at the table with her back to him, still picking at her food when he came into the dining room.

"Why aren't you eating? Do you want something else?" The question came out a little harsher than he'd intended.

She sighed and sat back. "No. It's fine. I'm just not feeling well again."

"What do you mean again?" He walked around the table to get a better look at her. He reached out to touch her forehead when she batted his hand away.

"Stop it," she grumbled but didn't look up at him. She just sat there, scowling down at her chili. "I'm okay, I might just be coming down with a virus or something. Just leave me alone."

She didn't look pale, if anything she was flushed and she didn't seem to have a temperature. However, that fact didn't give him any comfort. Last night had been hellish.

"Look, I'm going to give you some space. I'm going to check in with Butler and see if there's any news. Do you remember Samson?"

Jaimee frowned and shook her head. All these people involved in her life and she never noticed. It had to be overwhelming for her.

"He was here the night of the break-in. He's part of the team, one of The Pope's men. He'll be present in the house until I get back. Maxine will be here at five." He glanced at his watch. "About an hour from now. You still okay with that?"

Still not looking up, she nodded and swallowed hard.

"Shit. Jaimee, look at me."

Tears shimmered in her ice blue eyes as she lifted her chin and met his gaze without flinching. Those tears wouldn't fall. By sheer defiance she wouldn't let them. Somehow that pissed him off even more. He clenched his teeth, tensed his body against the need to touch her. Show her everything that was in his heart. He craved her trust again. Losing that one seemingly small element between them clawed at him. He wanted to shake her, or better yet, pull her into his arms, tell her how sorry he was, how much he loved her and wanted her. Not yet. God help him, not yet.

Bracing his hands on the table instead he leaned in close, ignoring her darkening expression, and inhaled her warm clean scent. It made his mouth water, his blood pound its way to his groin. He was edgy, tired of grappling for control.

"Don't think for one second you can hide from me, Jaimee. You and I have unfinished business. I'm leaving now, but you better damn well believe I will be back. Now get up and lock the damn door behind me."

222

With stalwart effort Lucas straightened and walked away, slamming the door on his way out. He stood on the porch watching the rain fall and pelt the ground with fat heavy drops. Satisfaction filled him at the metallic sound of the bolt turning as Jaimee did as he told her. Samson pulled into the drive minutes later and nodded sharply as he jogged across the yard. Up on the porch he shook water from his mane of shoulder-length hair like an oversized cocker spaniel.

"I'll be at the house. After she's in bed tonight I'll come back and you can leave."

Samson studied Lucas for a moment before he nodded and entered Jaimee's number into his cell.

"You touch her, I'll fuck you up." Lucas knew and trusted The Pope without hesitation. He knew Samson much less but The Pope vouched for him. That was enough. Still the possessiveness was instinctual and strong in spite of the fact that the chances of Samson touching her at all were slim to none. It just made him feel better, making it clear.

Samson snorted, his expression derisive as he cut his eyes to the door and spoke into the phone. "Afternoon, ma'am. Eli Samson here. I'm on the porch."

Lucas waited and watched. Jaimee looked through the peep hole before unlocking and opening the door for Samson. Surprise widened her eyes as she caught sight of Lucas. "Good girl," he said firmly.

He caught the slight tilt of Samson's lips before Jaimee snarled at him, her eyes narrowing as she slammed the door in his face.

Maxine arrived at five sharp. She couldn't blame Max for gawking. It was hard not to look at Samson. He was about six feet tall, dark, lean, muscular. Big fathomless black eyes and glossy black curls fell to his shoulders, and a goatee made him look positively wicked. When Jaimee finally managed to snag her attention away from Samson, she dragged her drooling friend upstairs to her room.

She sat on her bed and crossed her legs Indian-style. Maxine did the same. "Okay, girl. Spill."

With a sigh Jaimee did just that. She told Maxine all about what she'd learned about Brent. Everything she knew about The Collective and Sheppard & Zachary Inc. And she did a great job holding it together through the whole sordid tale. It was when she told her the truth about Lucas that the tears came. Maxine scooted next to her, put her arm around Jaimee and let her cry. When the worst of the torrent had passed, Jaimee got up and padded into the bathroom to blow her nose and wash her face.

"I just wish I could stay furious and quit crying."

"No chance of that, sugar. These things take quite some time."

"On top of that I think I'm coming down with a cold or the flu or something."

Maxine frowned before she leaned over the side of the bed and picked up her purse from the floor. She withdrew a paper bag and handed it to Jaimee without a word.

"What's this?" She had a pretty good idea what the answer would be.

Maxine just lifted one brow. Jaimee took a shaky breath, opened the bag and looked in at not just one but three home pregnancy tests.

"You wouldn't be convinced with just one test result and you know it. Just take 'em, James. You got nothin' to lose one way or the other."

Jaimee shrugged. Max had a point. She opened one of the boxes and read the instructions. "So, I just pee on it. Do I pee on all of them?"

"Pretty much." Maxine smiled.

"Not sure I have to pee that much."

"So use a paper cup and dip instead." Maxine shrugged.

Jaimee rolled her lips inward as she took the box into the bathroom and shut the door. She followed the short instructions then laid the little stick on a towel and, without looking at it, opened the next box. Finishing the last one she laid it beside the other two in a neat little row, then washed her hands and went back into the bedroom. "Gotta wait three minutes."

Maxine nodded, smiling at her. "How late are you anyway?"

Jaimee shrugged. "Maybe a week or two or three. I'm never regular so I'm never really sure."

"You know that's crazy, right?" Maxine didn't wait for an answer. "So what does your gyno say about that? Can't you go on the Pill or something?"

She had enough sense to look ashamed. It was stupid of her not to go to the doctor yearly but she hated it. She was never comfortable with her gynecologist. The only reason she'd gone to him in the first place was because he was in the company's health group and she didn't have much choice. She'd always been busy and just conveniently forgot to make an appointment. "Um, well. I haven't seen my doctor since..." Jaimee stiffened. She hadn't been to a check up since the one before Brent died...left. Since then she just hadn't thought of trying to find another. He told her there was no way. Ever. What if the doctor had been wrong?

"Since?" Maxine prompted.

"It was several months before Brent died...left." She shrugged "Has it been three minutes?" Her heart thundered in her chest.

Maxine glanced at her watch. "Almost."

But Jaimee was already in the bathroom. She picked up the first stick and held her breath as she looked down at it. Oh God. Quickly setting it down she picked up the little square. Oh no. Then the next stick. "Max." It was more of a whimper.

"It should say in the window, and the square one will have a dot if it's positive and nothing if it isn't." Maxine stood at the door watching Jaimee with wide eyes.

"Oh God," Jaimee sobbed. "Max. There's a dot, this one says pregnant, and this one has two lines."

Oh God, oh God, oh God.

Maxine moved closer and looked from Jaimee to the stick and back again. "Jaimee. You're pregnant."

"This can't be right. It can't be. The doctor told me I definitely could not have a baby. He said I didn't ovulate. He said it was probably a genetic defect. Since I'm an only child I thought he was right." Jaimee walked back into the bedroom, staring down at the tests in her hands.

"He must have been wrong."

"He said they could do more tests but they'd be long, drawn out and painful. Brent wasn't interested in pursuing it." Stunned numb, Jaimee sat down onto the bed. Memories, things Brent had said started floating through her mind. There was something not quite right there. Didn't matter now though. Now she was pregnant by a man who was about to walk out of her life forever. "What am I gonna do, Max?"

"Well, first you gotta make an appointment with my gyno. She's cool. Then you gotta tell Lucas."

As the weight of reality descended over her, she turned to look at Maxine in horror.

"No! I can't. I swore to him that I couldn't get pregnant. He'll think I've tried to trap him. He never wanted me, don't you see?" Panic clawed at her throat. "I was an assignment. Lucas only pretended to want me. He won't care about the baby."

Oh God. The baby. She was having Lucas's baby. An odd mixture of fear and dread filled her mind. Then came the guilt. Guilt because in spite of the fact that being pregnant was the last thing she expected and the worst possible thing that could happen right now, joy flooded her heart. Something she'd wanted more than anything and never allowed herself to hope for had been gifted to her. A child. Lucas's child. And she would be subjecting that sweet innocent child to a fatherless life, just like her own.

"I don't believe that, James. I know that's what they told you but I just don't buy it. He's done too many things that show he cares about you. Like taking all the bugs out of your room."

It was incredibly human of him to make sure she had some place where she felt safe to some extent. He fixed her lunch then got mad at her because she wouldn't eat. When he made love to her, she saw more than just lust in the intensity of his gaze. Wasn't there a reverence of sorts in the way he touched her? She clenched her teeth and shook the hope off.

"Probably did it out of guilt. Evidently I was the first assignment that didn't have it coming."

Maxine scowled. "Men are such shits. What has he said about all of this?"

Jaimee looked down at her hands clasped around one of the test sticks. "He hasn't said anything."

Maxine took the stick from her and laid it on the nightstand then took Jaimee's hands in hers. "Look, James. Lucas doesn't matter. You're not alone in this. I'm here for you no matter what you want to do."

"I'll have the baby." The pain gently, slowly sunk into her.

"I know." Maxine's voice was warm and soothing. "I won't say anything to Lucas. But you have to tell him. Just for the legality of it all. He needs to cough up child support at the very least. You know that, right?"

"After." Jaimee shook her head and took a deep breath. "After the danger is passed. Right before he walks away for good. I'll tell him then." She paused then met Maxine's concerned gaze. "I'm scared, Max."

"I know, hon. It's not gonna be easy." Maxine sighed and hugged her tightly. "But it's gonna be okay."

"Promise?" Jaimee managed a smile.

"Promise. Now, come on downstairs, I'll fix us hot chocolate and popcorn and we can ogle your sexy bodyguard...I mean a movie."

Laughing softly, Jaimee dropped the tests into her end table drawer. Maxine could always make her laugh even when her brain was fuzzy and her heart was broken.

"Good idea."

Brain candy was the perfect remedy for the maelstrom of thoughts and emotions swirling through her. Even if only for a few minutes, she could sit with Max and escape into the romantic comedy playing on the television. Although they watched Samson watch the movie more than they actually watched the movie. His lips barely moved and yet his smile made his impossibly dark eyes sparkle with humor. When his cell quietly chirped his expression went stoic automatically as he rose from the chair and left the room.

Jaimee yawned as the closing music played and the credits began to roll. "I think I'm gonna go to bed. You wanna stay?"

Max yawned in response but didn't have time to say anything before Samson interrupted as he flipped his phone closed. "According to the powers that be, she's staying."

"'Scuse me?" Maxine lifted one brow as she stood, placing a hand on her hip.

Samson's expression never changed. "It really isn't safe for you to head home alone this late."

"I'll have you know I can take care of my own damn self," Max informed him with attitude.

"Of that I have no doubt, Ms. Pruitt. Nevertheless, you aren't going anywhere tonight. I'll make sure you get home safe tomorrow," Samson informed her without giving her a chance to retort.

Maxine studied his stony expression, clearly weighing her chances in a debate with him. Finally she blinked twice and then turned to Jaimee. "Well...hell. I guess I'm staying. Damn."

Jaimee chuckled and rose with a stretch. "Good, this way I won't worry. Um...y'all gonna fight over the guest room or what?"

"Ms. Pruitt is welcome to use the guest room. I won't be sleeping anyway."

"Oh for cryin' out loud. You can call me Maxine. Sheesh." Maxine rolled her eyes.

Samson chuckled as he walked away from them, disappearing into the kitchen.

"That guy is so weird," Maxine murmured.

"The whole FBI crew is weird. The guest room has fresh sheets and stuff, I'll get you another blanket for those icebergs you call feet."

"Thanks." Maxine laughed as Jaimee mounted the stairs. "You care if I stay up a little longer?"

"Nope." Jaimee shook her head. "I'm just wiped. I'll lay the quilt on the bed. See ya in the morning."

"Ms. Turner," Samson called out, halting her ascension.

"Just call me Jaimee, please."

"Jaimee. You still going to church in the morning?"

Lucas must have told him. The church family atmosphere might be just what she needed. It might help her regain some inner balance. Balance was good. She really needed some balance. "Yes."

"You got it then. Jaimee," he said with a wink.

It was a friendly wink...like a big brother. It would be so nice to have a big brother right now. Really sucked being an only child sometimes. "'Night, Samson. Thanks."

"My pleasure."

It was ten forty-five when Samson opened the door for Lucas. Unnecessarily, Samson filled him in on the events of the evening before he left the house and faded into the darkness. Lucas had listened to them watching the movie, whispering about Samson whenever he left the room. Maxine being there was calming to Jaimee. They were careful not to say anything about him within audio range. Maxine kept her spirits up as best she could. Jaimee's few soft laughs were a relief. He was so thankful for that.

Meeting Maxine's hard accusing gaze was jolting, if not surprising. The woman was a badass if there ever was one. He really liked Maxine.

"I made you a promise. Do you remember?" Maxine's voice was low, her sharp eyes hooded.

"Yes. You think you can wait to castrate me until after Jaimee is out of danger?"

"I don't know. You, asshole, are the one that hurt her first. I'd say that makes *you* danger."

Lucas stared at her a moment before nodding as he sat down in the overstuffed chair that he had grown to love, for the most part, for the memories it held.

Maxine stayed draped elegantly on the couch, watching him, her foot shaking off the edge with agitation as she chewed on the inside of her cheek. "I told her I think you care. Did I lie?"

"I care." Finally he looked up and met her gaze unflinchingly. "Let it go, Maxine. Just for a little while longer. Let it go."

"Fuck all that." Maxine sat up and squared off with him. "When

James is *out of danger*, are you out? As in, *out of the picture*. Gone?"

"No."

"No?" Maxine's voice shook with anger as she narrowed her eyes. "Why? Why the hell not?"

Lifting his eyes, just his eyes, to meet hers. It was an aggressive clashing, like ebony slamming into mahogany. "Stop trying to manipulate me, Maxine. Now drop it."

The smile that curved her lips made Lucas want to snarl. "All right. For now." He had the sneaking suspicion that she had just managed to manipulate him very smoothly.

With an irritated grunt he reached around and tugged at the band holding his hair back. His scalp was sore from the thing. Leaving it down was even more of a pain in the ass so he put it back. "Shit. I hate this fucking hair. First chance I get to have the shit hacked off, I'm taking it. Gives me a fucking headache."

"Wow, you kiss your momma with that mouth?" Maxine sniped.

Lucas speared her with an annoyed look and grunted again as she rose and left the room. When she took the stairs, he figured she'd gone to bed and left him in peace. A few minutes later his hopes were dashed when she returned with what looked to be her purse.

"Jaimee is sound asleep. She was even snoring," she said, searching through her purse.

Lucas eyed Maxine warily. "Good. She didn't sleep well today." The image of her standing by her bed, her all but naked body illuminated by the staccato flashes of lightning, materialized in his mind and stole his breath all over again.

Lifting a brow Maxine frowned as she withdrew a brush and a red pouch. "And we both know why that is, don't we, Agent Grayson?"

Lucas tensed as he watched her open the pouch, expecting just about anything from Maxine. When she withdrew the scissors he wondered just how far she meant to take the *I'll separate you from your favorite body parts* threat. Damn, he really didn't feel like fighting off a crazed, overprotective woman tonight.

"Nervous, Lucas?" Maxine laughed. She had a nice laugh. Didn't sound the least bit deranged. "Relax, big boy. Come to the dining room and I'll cut your hair for you."

Dubious at best, Lucas just stared at her. "Yeah right. I'm not stupid enough to let you anywhere near my throat with a sharp implement right now."

Maxine grinned. "My mom was once the best beautician in all of Nashville and she taught me everything I know." She motioned him to her. "Come on. I'm not going to hurt you...yet. You afraid?"

"Pshhh, terrified." He narrowed his eyes and weighed his chances. He was reasonably certain he could unarm her pretty quickly if need be with little damage and he couldn't wait to lose the hair.

"How short you want it?" she asked as he sat down in a dining room chair.

"I don't really care as long as it's not hanging in my face and doesn't look stupid."

Maxine ran her fingers through the length of it. "Wow, it's long. Hey, this is way past ten inches long. You care if I put it in a braid and cut it off to send to Locks of Love? My stylist sends them donations all the time. I can drop it off with her Monday."

"That's cool. Go for it."

"Great, when did you wash it last?"

"Couple of hours ago. I was at the surveillance house, took a shower there."

"Perfect. Let me go see if James has a plastic bag."

At least something good could come of it. To him it was a glaring reminder of what he'd done over the years. It was all a part of the romance novel fantasy women loved, wanted and bought into. It was another time, another part of him he really wanted to let die. Never once had he wanted to be anything other than the job. He'd been willing to do whatever it took. No matter how wrong the wrong that made the right was, no matter how obscene, how vulgar and cheap, he did it without a second thought. Never considering what he was giving away. Unquestionably, he'd done it without remorse. Until Jaimee.

Now, looking back with a sick heaviness pulling at his insides, he realized he'd done too much. He'd given, no, thrown away too much. There was nothing good or wholesome left in him for Jaimee. God knows she deserved better. Because that's what she was. She made him forget the filth inside him with a simple smile, the genuine kindness in her eyes, the timid touch of her lips. Didn't she deserve the same? Didn't she deserve so much better than what he had to offer? He just wasn't sure at this point how, or even if, he could muster up the courage to let her go. No matter how honorable and redemptive that sacrifice might be.

Chapter Thirty-One

The morning started off with a jolt. Jaimee hadn't expected Lucas to be there when she came down the stairs. There he stood watching her descend, his hands in the pants pockets of his expensive jet-black suit. The top two buttons of his crisp white banded-collar dress shirt were left undone. At some point during the evening he'd had his hair cut short. It looked so much thicker. It was glossy and somewhat spiky on the top but still looked so soft she wanted to run her fingers through it.

It was enough to make her want to punch him. She had been all ready, mentally and physically, to attend Sunday morning services and he disrupted her whole mindset. How was she supposed to keep her mind on higher things when he was always there? Always watching her, tempting her. It didn't help that he'd been touching her nearly constantly ever since they left her house either. His firm hand pressed against her lower back as he led her from the house to the car. At church he very gentlemanly offered his hand as she exited his SUV then pulled her to him, his hand resting possessively on her hip as he led her from the car into the church building. But that was probably because of the menacing look of the dark green sedan with the tinted windows that sat idling on the perimeter of the parking lot. The sedan was also very likely one reason for the gun-shaped bulge she noticed resting under his jacket, just at his side.

Her church wasn't the typical somber house of prayer so she was interested to see his response to the service. No one would be running up and down the aisles speaking in tongues but still, the praise and worship was enthusiastic to say the least. There was a large stage that housed the band complete with drums, keyboards, as well as electric, steel and bass guitars. Then there was the choir and the podium.

Instead of the traditional hard wooden pews there were rows of interlocking padded chairs. The sound system was state of the art and the décor was contemporary in soothing earth tones, sage and deep wine. The congregation prided themselves on their friendly openness and welcoming spirit. It was a church of which Jaimee was proud to be a member—even if her mother did attend there.

She had to forgo singing in the choir at Lucas's suggestion, which made it easier for her to avoid her mother. Besides, she didn't feel much like singing anyway. A couple of the ladies had mentioned offhandedly that she should call her mom and talk to her. Evidently, her mother had put her on the ladies' prayer list again for being such a disappointment. Probably told them all what a raging slut she was too. Good. God knew she needed all the prayer she could get right now. Ha, and here she'd gone to all the trouble of introducing Lucas as a friend. Even if her mom hadn't been running her mouth about her, she was sure that everyone would suspect more by the way Lucas kept watching her and touching her.

It was surreal sitting with him like this, his arm around her, resting on the back of her chair as though it was the most natural thing to do. His thumb absently caressing the curve of her shoulder sent warm tingles showering over her. The masculine scent of soap and Lucas filled her senses. The way he possessed and protected her made her want to wrap her arms around him and bury her face in his neck. He made it so damn hard for her to pay attention. Who knew Lucas with short hair would look fiercer and even more incredibly sexy. Damn him. She resisted the urge to sigh in frustration as she glanced at him from the corner of her eye.

Every time she did that, his gaze was focused straight ahead, seemingly engrossed in the sermon. At the same time the tension in his jaw let her know he was far from relaxed. He probably didn't even realize how irritated and resentful she was toward him. Then again, he probably didn't care. Still, just playing his role. Doing his job. *Keep reminding yourself, Jaimee.*

Maybe she should have skipped church this morning. Especially since she wasn't able to focus anyway. What if whoever or whatever was in the sedan on the corner caused trouble or, worse, hurt someone? That would be more than she could handle. She couldn't let anything happen if she could at all help it. Leaning close to Lucas she whispered, "Maybe we should sneak out and leave now."

Lucas inclined his head. "Everything is fine. Relax," he murmured.

"Yeah right," she scoffed under her breath. Damn him.

Time went by way too slowly. Finally the pastor gave the invitation and asked them to stand. Jaimee couldn't resist nudging Lucas in the ribs and giving him a sardonic smirk.

"It took the first time, Jaimee, when I was fifteen." His words were without emotion or inflection.

Well hell, she didn't expect that at all, which meant she'd become a cynical and judgmental snot just like her mother. That sucked.

"Sorry, that was...I'm sorry," she mumbled to him.

His chuckle was nearly silent. "You're apologizing to me?"

Confused, she just looked up into his eyes, frowning still.

"Don't. You have nothing to be sorry for, I haven't exactly been walking the walk for some years now." Sadness tinged his voice as he snagged her hand, entwining his fingers with hers, palm to palm. Confusion disintegrated into ash as anger burned through her. The jig was up dammit. It was just plain cruel to keep up the act knowing she was never acting. "Hug somebody's neck and tell them to have a blessed week," the pastor admonished the congregation before he stepped down and began making his way to the back of the sanctuary.

Several came by and hugged Jaimee and she tried to appear jovial, hugging them back, smiling, chatting pleasantly. But Lucas never released her hand. A few of the ladies hugged him as well. Men introduced themselves and shook his hand. Still, he never let go of her. She tried subtly tugging at her hand, wanting to escape, but he wasn't letting her go. If she was more assertive about it she'd probably make a scene and she wasn't sure she wanted to go there. For some reason his touch, his gentleness, made her want to scream, cry, possibly throw things. God, why was he doing this to her?

"We missed your lovely voice today, Jaimee." Rebekah, the choir director, said as she hugged her tightly. "Everything all right?"

"Yeah, my throat is a little scratchy this morning." Rebekah gave Lucas a quick hug, telling him she was glad he'd attended and hoped he'd visit often.

"Nice meeting you, Lucas."

"Nice to meet you too, Rebekah." Lucas gave her a pleasant smile.

"Make sure and bring him back with you, Jaimee." Rebekah indicated Lucas with a tilt of her head.

"Definitely, she can't get rid of me now. She's stuck." Lucas answered before Jaimee had a chance to respond. That was just over the line. Jaimee let him know it as she dug her nails into his hand.

Rebekah laughed. "That's good to hear. Y'all have a blessed week now." She turned to walk away, then spun around, walking backward as she pointed at Jaimee. "Practice, Wednesday night after bible study,

I expect you there. We're starting the Christmas music. Bring your man. We'll see if he can sing too."

Your man. Feeling utterly defeated, Jaimee just smiled, withdrew her claws and nodded. Her man. Ha! When she and Lucas turned away she hissed quietly through her teeth. "Please, stop." He said nothing as he frowned down at her then slowly led her to the side exit.

The sedan was nowhere to be seen when they got to the SUV. Lucas flipped open his phone and pressed a button before opening the door for her. He said nothing, just listened then closed his phone and opened the door. Finally letting go of her hand to usher her into the vehicle.

His charming demeanor evaporated into a savage expression that made Jaimee shiver with something between fear and lust. Thankfully she was completely inside when he slammed her door shut. Still, he made her jump which only heightened the already seething anger brewing in her.

Moments later he swung up into the SUV beside her and slammed his own door. "What exactly do you want me to stop, Jaimee?"

Jaimee's eyes widened with incredulity. "I'm not *even* gonna answer that."

"The hell you aren't. I didn't do a damn thing to piss you off. I was polite and courteous. I was a goddamn gentleman."

"Just perfect," Jaimee snipped. "Except that I don't enjoy the game. I'm not good at playing pretend, Lucas. On top of that I don't like deceiving the people in my life."

"What?" he snapped.

Jaimee turned to him then and noticed the half-moon shapes in the back of his left hand. They weren't bleeding but they were red and angry. Shrugging off the guilt, she gave fury free rein and lifted her chin defiantly. "I'll do whatever it is you people need me to do because I have to, but I'm not in this willingly. I'm not your friend, *Agent* Grayson, nor your lover. So from now could we just drop the act and would you please keep your fucking hands off me."

The rage, hurt, and even the guilt resonated in her hoarse request. And dammit he made her drop the F-bomb. She hated dropping the F-bomb.

Lucas moved with speed and efficiency, giving her no time to react or resist. She gasped, his right hand fisting in her hair. He tilted her head back, as he captured her with his left arm circling around her back and pulling her tight against him. His eyes were dark, fathomless, hot and violent as he took advantage of her shocked gasp and kissed her. It was more like a punishment, a demand for her submission, than a kiss. Jaimee wasn't planning on surrendering. She ineffectively shoved at his chest as his lips moved against hers with expertise, his tongue sweeping over her own. But she fought, she fought him and her own body's desire to become pliant, to arch against him.

With a groan that had her trembling, nearly losing her fight, he released her. Jaimee struggled to regulate her breathing as she watched him twist the key in the ignition. The muscle in his jaw pulsed, his knuckles going white as his hands gripped the steering wheel. Not sure if she wanted to rage at him or beg him to have his way with her right there in the church parking lot, she turned away.

Her lips felt bruised, ultra sensitive. She bit her bottom lip, wishing it would stop tingling, wishing her whole body would stop tingling. The tears were there again, threatening, clogging her throat. Vibrating with need, she clenched her teeth and inhaled slowly as she stared out the window, thankful they were tinted.

If a man could go insane from the need to fuck then he'd just crossed the line. Jaimee had no idea the restraint he was using; the sheer will it took to keep his "fucking hands" off her. Who knew hearing such a carnal word uttered from those sweet Kewpie doll lips would make his cock thicken in demand. If Jaimee knew how badly he wanted her, if she knew how badly he wanted to make her go mindless and wild beneath him she wouldn't tempt him with dirty word challenges.

"Don't fucking challenge me right now, Jaimee. Just... Don't." Shit, he couldn't even speak right now. His brain wouldn't even form a decent reasoning. Instead of trying again he pulled out of the parking lot, into the traffic and headed for her home.

"I wasn't aware that me telling you to keep your hands off me was a challenge," she said sharply, then turned her too-bright blue eyes on him. "So if I tell you again to leave me alone what are you gonna do? Huh? Rape me?"

He jerked around to look at her as though she'd slapped him. "Rape you?"

He'd seen way too much rape in his lifetime. To be accused of it, or to even suggest that he would ever do such a thing, made his blood boil. As irrational as it seemed, it made his heart hammer relentlessly against his ribs. "That's fucking bullshit, Jaimee. Do you really believe I'm capable of rape? Do you?"

She had enough sense not to look up at him. Instead she just shook her head. "No, Lucas. I'm just—"

He didn't let her finish, couldn't. "Do you think I didn't notice you arching against me, your fingers curling into my shirt? You think I didn't feel your nipples grow diamond hard? Even through our clothes I could feel them press against my chest. I bet your pretty little *bare* pussy is coated in your juices as we speak. Your panties are probably soaked through. That sweet little pink bud throbbing for attention." He watched the heat crawl up her neck, watched her tense and resist the urge to squirm. His laugh was humorless, scornful.

At the traffic light he turned to her, met her gaze and hoped to God she saw the promise in his eyes. "If you honestly believe you are in danger with me, you pick up that phone when I get you home. You pick it the fuck up and you tell the agent on the other end that you've been assaulted and that you're afraid I'm going to rape you. But you better damn well mean it because trust me, baby, they won't take it lightly."

Her whole body trembled as she fought the tears and slowly shook her head. "I shouldn't have said that. I'm just...Lucas...I just need you to stop." There was a soft quiver in her voice that clawed at his heart and at his soul. "I can't take you constantly touching me."

"I can't promise you I won't touch you."

She met his gaze with her own, blazing hot with pain and fury. "But it's torture. Can't you understand that?" she asked through her teeth, one lone tear sliding slowly down her flushed cheek. "Why? Why do you want to keep on hurting me?"

God, he just wanted to make her stop hurting. He wanted to take her in his arms and make her forget everything but his love for her. Lucas brushed the tear away with his thumb. Her skin was like fresh picked peaches: warm, incredibly soft.

"I don't want you to hurt, Jaimee. In spite of what you believe, I've never wanted that. I'll do whatever I have to do to make sure no one else hurts you."

The sound of car horns shattered the moment between them. Lucas cursed in frustration as he hit the gas.

"You confuse me," Jaimee murmured softly.

"Yeah I know, baby. I confuse me too." That was an understatement. Since this whole assignment started he'd been confused. Jaimee brought out a part of him that he hadn't known existed and now he had to deal with it and didn't have a clue how.

They rode in silence to Jaimee's home. When they pulled into her driveway and he cut the engine, she turned to him. Her expression was stoic even though emotion swirled in her eyes.

"Lucas, you've got to leave me alone. I need to sort this all out."

He studied her, his eyes narrowing. "You spend too much energy and effort sorting thing out. You catalog every emotion, every word that's said and file them away in neat order."

With a deep breath she nodded. "Maybe. But that's what I have to do."

Frustrated, Lucas took the keys from the ignition and opened his door. "Okay. I'll give you space. But I'm not leaving you alone. You'll just have to deal with that."

Chapter Thirty-Two

Monday came and went without incident. Same routine, nothing of any interest or threat happened. Jaimee passed off the day planner to Lucas. That was a relief. He had been true to his word. He'd spent most of the day at the house around the corner, busy working with the team on decoding the information they got from the day planner. Which wasn't much of a relief because he was there at night, shirtless, stretched out on her couch, making her want to forget everything and hope.

It had been suggested that she take a week or two off from school until everyone was rounded up and Brent was brought in but there were always agents close by. She was just as safe there as she would at home and she really needed to keep busy. Besides, there was little chance she'd be able to relax at home with Lucas hovering about.

She checked her appearance once more in the mirror and grabbed her tote. Lucas was waiting for her, leaning against the kitchen counter sipping coffee in nothing but his jeans and nipple rings. His hair was messed up, spiky from sleeping. He was downright gorgeous. He even had sexy feet.

"Good morning." Damn his husky morning voice was sexy. "Sure I can't talk you into staying home today?"

"No, thank you."

"I could insist." He watched her over the rim of his mug.

"You could. But I told you guys already, today is a mandatory planning day. I have to be there."

She was completely aware that the mandatory thing was easily wriggled out of with one phone call. Lucas didn't play that card however. Thank God. She needed the space, needed to immerse herself into the tediousness of a planning day. His slow crooked smile made her groan inwardly. She forced a smile as she rejected the mug he offered her. It smelled so good but the caffeine wasn't good for the baby.

Wow, the thought of a baby growing inside her was so hard to get used to.

"No coffee? You feeling okay?" His brows furrowed as he reached out and touched her forehead with the back of his fingers.

Actually no. Queasiness was a dull threat but she knew exactly why. "I'm fine." She smiled at him. "Tell me something. And be honest."

Lucas nodded.

"Are the phones at school bugged?" She so needed to set up an OB/GYN appointment with Maxine's doctor. Like soon.

One brow lifted as he tilted his head and studied her. Damn that was disconcerting. For a moment she was worried he'd ask more questions. She'd never been good at lying and she didn't want to have to now.

"No." There was a question in that "no". Jaimee chose to ignore it and just nodded. "Has anyone contacted you at school, Jaimee?"

"No." She shrugged and snagged a water from the fridge. "I just wanted to be aware is all."

He wasn't buying it but to her relief, he didn't push. After he grabbed his shirt from the back of the couch he pulled it over his head as he walked back to her. "I'll take you to school. Samson will be posted outside the building all day. I'll be there when you leave."

Not even attempting to get out of the constant chaperone, she nodded. She'd learned such efforts would be an exercise in futility anyway. "I'll be ready to leave early. I'll call you when I'm done."

"Got your cell?" He stood too close. His coffee-scented breath, his body heat were so enticing she had to struggle to keep from leaning in to him, tasting his mouth.

Instead she turned away and opened the door. "Yep, let's go. I'm gonna be late."

Normally she'd leave around lunchtime, along with everyone else, after all the meetings were over. But this time she'd stay. It would give her some quiet time. Time to call and get an appointment with Maxine's OB/GYN.

By one o'clock most, if not all, of the other teachers were gone. Jaimee was pleased with her progress. She'd managed to get lesson plans for the rest of November and December done, November's assignment schedule printed and posted on the freshly decorated bulletin board and grades entered into the computer grading program. Gathering the last thirty copies of the exam she'd planned to give next week, she flipped open her cell and dialed Lucas as she headed back to her room.

He answered on the first ring. "Ready to go?"

"Just about. I'll be ready to walk out in about twenty minutes."

"I'll be there in five."

So easily she could buy in to this false sense of rightness between them. She frowned as she dropped her phone into her pocket. But it wasn't real. It was all just a means to an end. And that was the crux of it all. There would definitely be an end. Reminding herself of that caused her heart to ache. She sighed and shrugged off the sudden feeling of foreboding. *Grow up, Jaimee,* she admonished herself silently. *Grow up and deal.*

Shock didn't have time to register. As she stepped into her classroom a question concerning the janitor, clearly not Mr. Fitz, barely had time to formulate in her mind before something dark and musty descended over her head. Gasping, she fought against the hands gripping her arms, yanking them back, then the sharp blow to her head before everything went black.

When Jaimee came to she was lying on her side, her hands bound tightly behind her. Her feet were bound as well. She was moving, in a vehicle of some sort. The soft rumble of an engine made that evident. Nausea uncoiled and threatened to overcome her restraint. The back of her head throbbed from where she was struck, hard. Breathing through her mouth to keep from throwing up, she struggled to push aside the pain. She had to think. It was hard to breathe in the musty bag and her heart was pounding in her ears.

"Damn that bitch was heavy," one of her captors panted. "We won't have that big garbage can to toss her in when we get there so you're haulin' her fat ass."

The other man laughed. "Like hell, that's why you're getting paid the big bucks, son." She knew that laugh, that voice. Ronald. Oh God. Fear was not an option and she refused to let herself give in to it. "Be glad she lost weight."

Oh no, she hoped they hadn't hurt Mr. Fitz. The maintenance man who was supposed to be rolling around the big garbage can was such a sweet old man. No time to worry. Facts. Focus on the facts, she told herself. Lucas had been minutes away so he would be looking for her soon. She had her cell! She tugged at the ropes binding her hands. Clenching her teeth against the pain she pulled hard against the ropes as quietly as she could. She didn't want to give the goons a heads up that she was awake.

The ropes were just tied too tightly, but she kept tugging, twisting. She couldn't just give up, lie there and wait for them to do what they wanted to with her. Anger and adrenaline pumped through her body, making her hot and sweaty, dizzy and sick.

As quietly as possible she shifted and the cell phone slid against her leg in her loose pants. Biting her lip she lifted her hips, wiggled and squirmed until the cell fell out of her pocket with a soft thud onto the carpeted van floor.

Frantically she shifted again, patting the ground until her fingers found it. Relief flooded through her as she flipped open her cell phone and ran her thumb over the buttons, picturing them in her mind as she fought to focus, to breath through the nausea, fear, and the pain. The soft tone that redialed Lucas went undetected.

"*Jaimee!*" She closed her eyes and nearly sobbed at the sound of Lucas's voice. She twisted again and pushed the phone against the side panel of the vehicle beside what felt like the wheel well and prayed they didn't hear him. Prayed that somehow he could track her with just being connected. Prayed that the call wouldn't drop.

The bag over her face, though it was some sort of cloth, completely blinded her to any light whatsoever. In addition, she had trouble breathing. She concentrated on taking shallow breaths as she continued to work on getting her wrists free of the rope and fought against the pull into unconsciousness.

Jaimee had no concept of how long she lay there trying to work her hands from the ropes. It seemed like forever but the dizziness and disorientation was making it difficult. The nausea had faded but the headache was relentless. She tried not to think about what was about to happen. It was frustrating, infuriating. Maybe most of her life had been dull and insignificant but it was still worth more than this. The life of her unborn child, her own personal miracle, was priceless. She'd do whatever she had to do to protect that precious life.

When the car stopped and the engine died she had to swallow the rise of panic that threatened to swamp her senses. Stay calm, stay alert, stay alive, she chanted in her brain. Once again she found herself turning to prayer for her baby, Lucas's baby. This was crazy. What could they possibly hope to gain from her anyway? Other than that day planner, she had nothing. And she didn't even have that anymore.

A yelp escaped her dry throat when the back hatch door finally popped open and rough hands grabbed her bound ankles and quickly dragged her downward. They released her legs only to grab the neckline of her blouse and yank her to standing before they pulled the stuffy bag from her head. Gasping the fresh, oxygen-rich air, she shook her head to get the hair out of her face. Trying to ignore the pain throbbing at her temple she glared up at Ronald and his oafish accomplice.

"Awake, Jaimee?" Ronald taunted as he jerked her up against him. She swayed on her still-bound feet, trying to find balance. She gritted her teeth against the rage, the humiliation and the fear. She wouldn't give him the satisfaction of seeing her fear.

She scowled at him in disgust. "What do you hope to accomplish by kidnapping me?"

"Even tied up and helpless you're a condescending bitch."

"I'm not condescending, Ron, you're just stupid."

Ronald's mocking smile faltered seconds before he delivered the blow to her abdomen.

Jaimee doubled over, heaved and struggled to breathe through her nose as the tears stung her eyes and fear dug its jagged claws into her heart.

"Clever girl." Lucas pressed mute on his cell and listened to Jaimee's labored breathing. She was frightened but strong and smart. He was so fucking proud of her.

Making the necessary calls was easy enough. The Hostage Rescue Team was mobilized. The HRT was made up of the sniper, react and assault team. The Pope, part of the react team, had quickly informed him that he had her on that psychic radar of his. They were headed east into a very rural part of Wilson County. Lucas listened.

Lucas frowned when the sounds changed, the engine died. Muffled voices, he couldn't make out words but he heard Jaimee's voice followed by her cry of pain, her moan. He clenched his teeth to near cracking, his body tensing further as he drove faster, moving ever closer to her. Fucking Ronald would pay dearly for that.

The team was assembled to extract the hostage safe and sound, neutralize Marshall and his men, if at all possible, and bring them in for interrogation. For Lucas, the objective was rescue Jaimee, protect Jaimee at all costs. He had sense enough to know that kind of single mindedness could jeopardize more than the mission. It could ultimately mean Jaimee's life. How ironic.

No, Edward Zachary was the objective. Ronald Marshall and all of the lesser minions were a means to the objective. So Lucas would harness the rage and thirst for vengeance until the job was done and Jaimee was safe again.

Yeah, that speech sounded really nice, crisp and logical. But if Jaimee was hurt all bets were off. He loved her madly even if a man without a heart or soul wasn't supposed to possess that particular capability.

All the things he'd done, believing the ends justified the means whatever those means might entail, weighed on him now. Without Jaimee the weight of it all would crush him, grind him to dust. Ah, but Jaimee was light and home and goodness. Her smile made him believe nothing was impossible. He could feel her inside him, in every cell of his being and it made him better. She was his heart.

"Easy, Grayson." The Pope's quiet voice coming through his earpiece didn't have the intended calming effect. *Fuck that.* Easy was not how this was going to go down.

"We have a visual. Looks to be a farmhouse. Old barn in back. Blue Suburban parked in front of the barn," Samson reported.

Lucas saw the farm as he crested the rise. He pulled off the road and parked out of sight in a wooded area over the rise. He hoofed it from there, making his way through trees until he was past the farmhouse and finally sprinted to the rundown barn.

"Zachary in there?" He spoke quietly as he pulled the pistol from the waistband of his jeans.

"Don't have a visual yet...," Robinson answered. "We're still..."

"Negative." The Pope interrupted.

"You got a visual, MP?"

"Negative." The Pope answered matter-of-fact.

Just another instance of The Pope *knowing* things. Sometimes. Sometimes he didn't know anything more than they did, but in those cases he would say nothing. If he had something to say, however, they all knew his word was golden and they'd learned questioning what he called his "spiritual gift" was pointless.

"Got three inside including one hostage. Hostage is in bad shape," an agent whispered.

Lucas went cold as he drew up against the west side of the barn. "Define bad shape."

"Beat up, bloody. The dude looks unconscious from here. Tied to a post. Looks like they worked him over good."

"Dude?" Relief flooded his body.

"It's Brent Turner, Grayson," Samson answered.

"Don't see Ms. Turner," replied another agent.

"There are two men bringing Ms. Turner through the front now." The Pope spoke low and confident. "Snipers in place." There were two snipers who had no compunction about pulling the trigger. One shot, one kill.

Lucas was agent-in-charge. The Pope and Robinson were react. The react team would make sure none of the bad guys got away. Robinson was also known for excellent negotiating skills if there became a need for them. Then again, The Pope was known to be on an assault from time to time if needed. The man was huge. Samson and the two men Lucas didn't know were assault, basically the bulldozers. Once everyone was in place, it would go down fast.

Lucas moved slowly to the front of the barn and watched through a crack between two ancient wood planks as Ronald and another goon tied Jaimee to the thick center post beside Brent, away from Lucas's view. Brent didn't lift his head but Lucas could see his lips moving. He had a strong urge just to blow the fucker away for putting Jaimee in this situation. Then again, in a sick, twisted way the piece of shit was the reason he found Jaimee in the first place. Too fucking ironic.

"Grayson. Sounds like they're trying to get Zachary out here."

"Good. Be ready to move but let's wait it out and see if he shows. Keep an eye on the two at the post," Lucas instructed as he watched Brent talk, Jaimee react.

"We won't let them hurt Jaimee, Grayson."

She could feel Brent watching her from hooded eyes as they roughly brought her arms in front of her to retie them tighter. She rubbed at her stomach, concentrating on the soreness there, wishing somehow that she could tell if baby was okay after the blow Ronald dealt her. Maybe it was okay, probably it was okay. God, please let it be okay.

Her breath left her lungs in a rush as another man shoved her hard against the thick post beside Brent and began tying her to it.

"I shouldn't have come back for you. It's all your fault, Jaimee," Brent whispered to her without lifting his head.

"This was a mess of your own making, Brent. I had nothing to do with this," she hissed through her teeth.

"You didn't know. You're just a whore." It wasn't as though he hadn't implied that he thought that of her before. To Brent any woman who was interested in sex was a whore. She'd never realized before how whiney Brent's voice was. Couldn't he just shut up? Jaimee grimaced against the frustration.

"Are you pregnant?" Pain was clear in his hoarse murmur.

"What?" She breathed after a pause and shifted to hear him better.

"You keep rubbing your stomach. You could be, you know. You've been screwin' around. I saw you with him."

The headache pounding at her temples rose in tempo as she tried to assimilate the meaning of his nonsensical babbling. "What are you talking about?"

"You wouldn't let up. I had to do something. I didn't want kids. I never wanted kids. They're a liability. They cost too much. But you wouldn't stop."

Jaimee scanned the men standing several feet away discussing what would become of her and Brent. She swallowed hard then asked, even though she was pretty sure she knew. "What did you do?'

"I had a vasectomy. Soon after we were married. Then I paid your doctor to lie. That's what I did. There was no other way to get you to stop. All you could think about was having sex. Having babies. I wanted more than that, Jaimee. I could have been somebody. We, we could have been powerful and respected..."

She quit listening to his self-important tirade. He would have never been anything but the slimy weasel he'd become. So she was never unable to conceive. The whole time, the pain and sadness she went through, it was all because of his greed. "Why did you marry me?"

Brent sighed. "Because I loved you, Jaimee."

Jaimee shook her head. "You don't know anything about love, Brent. You only love yourself."

Brent's reply was cut off when Ronald cursed viciously and hurled his cell phone. "Son of a bitch!" he roared. His face was livid red. "He's not coming."

Jaimee held her breath as he snatched a pistol from one of the other men. Everything seemed to move in slow motion as he lifted the gun, cocked it and pointed it at Brent's forehead. "Then we don't fuckin' need him anymore."

The gunshot exploded and shook Jaimee to her core. Brent's blood splattered over the side of her face. The whimper that escaped her throat didn't seem as though it came from her. Trembling, she closed her eyes. Waiting for her turn. Thinking of Lucas.

"I'm not gonna kill you yet, Jaimee. Open your eyes," Ronald snarled. Slowly, Jaimee did as she was told. Ronald stood before her and pushed the gun into her chest, between her breasts. "It seems my boss isn't interested in hostages. He just wants one thing. You have that one thing." Slowly he drew an icy line around her left breast to stop at the pulsing artery at her throat. "Where is the fuckin' day planner?"

Jaimee didn't even try to hide her fear. Would it really do any good to try and buy time? She swallowed hard before answering. "I don't have it."

Ronald's face went red, his nostrils flared, his lips peeled back in a vicious snarl before he backhanded her so hard she would have fallen if she weren't tied to the post. "Stupid lying bitch!" he screamed, just centimeters from her face.

The metallic taste of blood was making her seriously nauseous and surprisingly furious. "If I did have it, why would I give the thing to you?"

"Because I have the power to let you live."

"No, you don't. You're too desperate. Someone's got you by the balls, Ron. Looks like you're the stupid bitch." The way her voice shook belied the bravado of her words. Still she couldn't seem to hold her tongue. What was the point?

This time when he backhanded her it didn't seem to hurt as bad. Maybe her cheek was numb. Maybe it was the anger pumping through her veins. He was gonna do what he was gonna do but she wasn't gonna make it easy for him. She wouldn't give him the pleasure of seeing her pain or fear either. However, it might not have been her smartest move, goading him like that, being that he was insane and all. Her head swam as meaty fingers clamped over her chin. Ronald leaned in and sneered, she could feel his breath on her and nearly heaved. "It's gonna be a long time before I let you die, honey."

A flurry of movement behind Ronald caught Jaimee's attention seconds before it caught Ronald's. He had her untied, flipped around and yanked up against him before she could register what was happening. When she lifted her eyes her heart leapt. Lucas was standing before them. His feet spread apart in combat stance, body tense, pistol raised pointing at them, at Ronald. His eyes were hard, his expression deadly.

There were men behind him standing over Ronald's goons, who were now somehow hand cuffed and lying face down.

The man from the bar, the bouncer, Adrian Robinson, he had Ronald's phone. "Damning evidence here, Ron, my man." His lips quirked, but his eyes were as hard and cold as Lucas's. "Let her go, we'll negotiate."

Ronald's arm banded across Jaimee's ribs tightened. Jaimee gasped, trying to breathe. "No. No." He panicked. "There's nothing to negotiate."

"Look, Ron, Zachary left you high and dry, man. Didn't you do everything in your power to make everything right after Turner screwed y'all? Did he give you any credit whatsoever for that? Hell no, he didn't."

"Stop it!" he screamed. "You can't play me!"

With his weapon still in his hand Adrian put his hands on his hips and sighed as he looked down and shook his head. "Man, I am so not trying to play you right now. Do you see this man standing next to me?" He lifted just his eyes and nodded toward Lucas. "That dude wants nothing more than to watch you bleed. Now you and I can prevent that with one simple agreement." He paused, lifting his head, waiting.

Ronald didn't say anything, he shifted from one foot to the other. His eyes darted back and forth between Adrian and Lucas. He stank of sweat and fear. Jaimee swallowed her need to heave and glanced at Lucas. His whole body was pulled tight, ready to react, but not rigid. She wanted to hold him more than anything at that moment. Tell him she loved him and that she loved the baby he'd given her and beg him not to walk away from her. The barrel of Ronald's pistol jabbed her in the head again and she winced. That is, if she lived through this. "What happens if I give up?"

"Well one, you get to live. Two, we'll take you in for questioning and you'll tell us everything you know about The Collective and Edward Zachary. And three, we'll make you a sweet deal."

Ronald was shaking. Or was that her? "How sweet?"

Adrian shrugged, his expression unconcerned. Jaimee knew by the intense glow of his green eyes that wasn't true. "You'll do time, I can't get you out of that. But, you won't get gassed. We'll keep you safe from Zachary, and there's a good chance we can get you a lenient sentence with a parole option."

Ronald shook his head vigorously. His body odor, coupled with the smell of blood and death, was quickly becoming overwhelming. "Not good enough. I want to walk and I want Witness Protection."

Adrian sucked in air through his teeth and affected an expression of skepticism. "I don't know, dude. You killed a guy and that's just the one we witnessed." Adrian motioned to Jaimee with his pistol. "On top of that, you kidnapped and hurt this lady pretty badly. That's his woman." He tilted his head toward Lucas. "He ain't happy about that and he wants you to pay."

"*No!*" He screamed in her ear. Jaimee took a deep breath through her mouth and tasted salt. It was then she realized tears were streaming down her face. His woman. She shook her head slightly. "Witness Protection or I blow her away. I have nothing more to lose. Do you understand me?"

Lucas leaned over and whispered something to Adrian; he straightened and cleared his throat. "Witness Protection is a long shot, man. I can't make it happen whether you kill her or not. We can negotiate. You turn on Zachary and you'll probably end up doing very little time if any. But come on, Ron, you gotta help us out here."

Ronald shifted from one foot to another again. "How do I know you'll keep your word?"

Adrian narrowed his eyes and took a step closer. Ronald tightened his grip on Jaimee and pressed the gun harder against her temple. A whimper escaped her lips. She didn't mean to. She wanted to be tough, but she was losing the battle quickly.

"Do not piss me the fuck off, asshole. I'm tired of playing around with you. There are two snipers with their sites on your forehead right this fucking minute. And Grayson here is getting antsy. We don't want to kill you, because frankly, you're just eat up with information we really need. However, I'm done playing nice. Now let her go and we'll make sure you're safe from any fallout from Zachary. Hell, I'll even check into the goddamn Witness Protection Program for you. Otherwise we're gonna blow you the fuck away before your finger ever gets the message from your pea brain to pull that trigger."

Ronald hesitated, but only briefly before he released Jaimee and lifted his hands into the air, dropping his weapon as he did. "Okay, I'll take the deal."

Jaimee took two steps forward and found herself floating. No, lifted. Lucas had her in his arms, carrying her out of the barn and into the waning sunlight. She moaned and turned her face away from the brightness of the daylight and inhaled the warm masculine scent of Lucas. He was murmuring to her, dropping sweet, gentle kisses on her forehead. The sound of vehicles pulling up, car doors opening and closing couldn't distract her from where she was right now.

The nausea began to subside though she was riddled with various aches and pains. Not to mention the fact that she had to pee like crazy. But being in Lucas's arms was like heaven and she didn't want it to end. "Thanks, Butler," Lucas said hoarsely as he sat her in the warm plush passenger seat of someone's car and knelt down beside her. He didn't seem to notice her sigh of disappointment.

"Not a problem. EMTs on their way," Butler answered.

Lucas nodded, stood, then knelt again and handed her a bottle of water. "How you doing, James?" His voice was soft, husky, as he wiped at the smeared blood on her face.

"Oh peachy." She tried to smile.

He lifted her hand and pressed his lips to her palm. "You scared the shit outta me."

"Sorry." The cold water was soothing to her lips and throat. "Thank you for carrying me. I know I'm not exactly petite but my legs are really wobbly."

"Sweetness, having you in my arms is a pleasure. You're not heavy."

"Hey, Grayson!" Adrian Robinson called out. Lucas straightened. All Jaimee could see was his torso as he stood to answer Adrian. "They're takin' them in now. You wanna call Ms. Sinclair or should I?"

Jaimee sucked in her breath as her heart flipped in her chest. Alice. Alice was okay? She grabbed Lucas by his belt loop and tugged. "Alice Sinclair?" The question came out a whisper. She loved, and had all but mourned, Alice since this whole thing began unfolding.

Lucas grinned and nodded. "Yes. She's fine. And as soon as we have Edward Zachary in custody she'll be able to go back to her life. She's getting pretty antsy. Giving poor Robinson here a hard time."

Taking a deep breath she relaxed back against the cushion of the leather seat and asked the question she didn't really want to know the answer to. "Lucas. Is it over now?"

"Yeah, baby. It's over."

Chapter Thirty-Three

This was it. The end had come and Jaimee wasn't prepared, she wasn't ready to let go yet. She kept her eyes trained on the road in front of them as they turned onto her street. At least the baby was fine. It had taken a feat of great strength and determination to get Lucas to leave the room while she talked to the emergency room doctor. Thank God for the female doctor and her willingness to lie by omission to Lucas about the ultrasound machine being rolled into her room. Nothing was wrong that wouldn't heal. The baby was safe and sound and healthy. She'd heard the strong heartbeat and she knew that it was all worth it. Even though he was leaving her now.

Lucas had consumed her—heart, body and soul—and now he was going to leave her wanting. He had given her the love and passion she'd always craved but never believed she could have. The love, the passion, had been real and tangible to her, even if he'd been acting. Funny thing was it never seemed like an act. Whatever, it was part of her now and he was on the brink of ripping it away from her. Forever.

As soon as the car stopped she got out and headed for the door. Her emotions were so raw she just might shatter, fragment, fly apart into nothing. She didn't want him to watch that. Maybe he would just leave without saying a word and she could go into her home, back into her cocoon and hopefully the need would dull and muffle as it had been before Lucas. Maybe the love would fade and die. Maybe she could go back to the mechanical day-to-day reality she'd lived in just fine before he showed up and ripped it all to hell.

Fumbling with her key, she tried to steady her shaking hands long enough to get the door unlocked. Lucas seemed to materialize behind her and laid a hand gently but firmly on her hip. The heat from his body so close infused her, made her hot, her mind and thoughts gave way to the searing lust he inspired in her. She swallowed the pain that bubbled up and closed her eyes as he took the key from her. He opened the door and guided her through it.

As soon as the door was closed behind them Jaimee turned and gazed up at him. "Thank you, Lucas." Unshed tears burned her throat, making her hoarse. *Don't let him go!* Her heart entreated. *Just hold him one last time,* her mind cried. One more taste, one more firestorm of sensation, emotion and need.

"Jaimee." He said her name softly, and it sounded like a promise. Reaching for him, she wrapped her arms around his neck and nearly sobbed as he pulled her close. *Just one more memory.* The words whispered through her mind. *A good memory to hold on to.* Her fingers speared into his hair and fisted as she pulled him to her. Her lips, tongue, teeth devoured his mouth. Desperation gave way to impetuous determination. She would have him, one more time she would love him.

Her body pressed eagerly against him and knew he wasn't immune. His hands gripped her hips, his fingers flexed in response to her voracious kisses. Her mouth moved down his jaw, nipping, licking. She wanted to taste all of him. She released his hair and gripped his shirt. With a hungry growl that even surprised her she ripped it open. A few buttons pinged as they hit the hardwood floor. She pushed his hands from her hips and freed his arms from the torn shirt.

Without trying to hold it back this time she whimpered in frustration as her fingers found the cotton T-shirt, keeping her from his flesh. She wanted his skin against hers. She needed him naked. Lucas tried to hold her arms but she fought him off. It was otherworldly the way she craved him. It seemed her body was on fire, ready to combust. She tugged at the shirt, pulling it from his pants. She sighed as she ran her hands over his smooth hard stomach, up to his pierced nipples, ignoring the gentle grip he had on her wrists.

"Jaimee," he whispered roughly. "Slow down."

She shook her head as she tasted him, running her tongue up, over the contours of his chest. Her tongue swirled around one flat disk before her teeth closed over the ringed nipple and tugged just hard enough to make him groan, hissing in pleasure or pain, she wasn't sure.

"I need..." Her voice sounded animalistic, like it came from someone, something, else. She was losing herself in the hunger, the lust and she didn't care.

"Okay," he breathed, "okay." He pulled his shirt over his head. "Take what you need, baby. Anything you need."

Panting, she lifted her eyes and met his. Her fingers rubbed over his nipples, played with the rings. Her entire body felt like it was pulsing, glowing. Her fingers trailed downward as she watched him watch her. She unbuckled his belt and yanked it from his pants with a snarl. Somewhere in her mind she was shocked at her own aggressiveness but she ignored it. She was running on pure animal desire, she let it reign and savored the incredible pleasure such freedom gave her. The corner of Lucas's mouth lifted sensually. "My wildcat." He reached for her.

She slapped his hands away. It wasn't that she didn't want his hands all over her, she did, just not yet. It would go too fast if he touched her. She watched his eyes darken, his lips part, as she pushed his pants past his hips and then took his rock-hard cock in her hands.

Every pulsing vein, every ridge and curve was so hard, so soft. Her head tilted as she watched him clench his teeth, the muscle in his jaw tighten and release. Hot arousal flowed from her body, making her slick and ultra sensitive. With one hand she cupped his balls as she circled the velvety head of his cock with the thumb of her other hand. He was so beautiful, generous, she loved him violently and for these last moments she was going to pretend he loved her too.

The power of her arousal was devastating. Her body trembled, screamed for his touch. He took her mouth with a hunger of his own, his hands fisting at his sides. His tongue undulated against hers.

Lucas watched her as she released him and stepped back. His breathing was labored, biceps bulging with an effort to give her the control she wanted. His cock jerked in rhythm with his pumping heart, cream pearling at the tip. Jaimee pulled her top off over her head. He was looking at her breasts now and she could feel her nipples tighten further against the rough white lace.

His eyes narrowed, his jaw clenched as she unzipped her slacks and let them fall to the floor. Her lace panties emphasized her wide hips but she didn't care. She smoothed a hand over her tummy as she stepped out of her low heels and away from her discarded clothes.

She bit her lip as she watched Lucas watch her with a hungry gaze. It was obvious that he wanted her and she relished in that fact, soaked it in. The way he watched her emboldened her. Her hand moved down, over the damp lace, as she braced her legs apart. Her fingers rubbed over the smooth, lace-covered lips of her sex, careful not to touch her clit. She was so wet, her fingers came away glossy. Lucas grasped her wrist and brought her fingers to his lips. His mouth closed over them with a groan. She blinked and fought to breathe as she pulled them free. Her thighs quivered with need.

She kissed his mouth hard, slapping his hands away again as she moved down his throat. His body, damp with sweat, tasted salty, musky, erotic. She nipped at his clavicle, the tough skin at his chest, his nipples. He trembled as her tongue trailed down his stomach. She kissed and nibbled at his body, trying to devour him, trying to memorize his taste. When finally she took his thick cock in her mouth she sucked hard, drawing a hoarse moan from him.

Her tongue massaged the head, swirling over it as she took him deeper, sucking him in. She couldn't hear anything but his rough breaths and her blood pumping hard and fast in her ears as she swallowed him, relishing the textures against her tongue, her hands caressing his thighs, his balls.

"Ah, Jaimee." He groaned tightly, his hands gripping her head.

She released him and lifted her head to meet his gaze. Before she could make her next move, she was lifted from the floor, the sound of ripping lace amping up her arousal. Lucas grasped her hips and walked her backward into the living room as he took control. He bent and flicked his tongue over her throbbing nipple then gently sucked.

Jaimee cried out, she couldn't help it. She wanted to fight him, take back control but she'd lost it.

Lucas spun her around and bent her over the back of the couch before she could think to resist. Not that she would have resisted. She gasped as Lucas spread her open with both hands. His hot breath caressed her swollen pussy and her body shuddered as, incredibly, even more liquid heat eased from her.

Then he tasted her, groaned against her sensitive wet flesh, his tongue stroking the inner folds of her body. Any minute she was going to combust into a fireball. If his talented tongue so much as grazed her clit she'd be lost. There'd be nothing left of her other than a quivering puddle of liquid and she didn't give a damn. The way he teased her pussy was making her insane, building the need but denying her release. Consumed in the heat, the hunger, she needed to move. She tried to wiggle away.

Lucas slapped her ass. That one firm fiery strike sent her over the edge and she cried out. Lucas was there. His lips closed over her clit and sucked, his tongue raking it painfully, giving her orgasm a brutal edge. Jaimee's breath left her body as she screamed, her knees gave way but Lucas supported her. Waves of savage pleasure crashed over her. Just as they began to subside Lucas rose and drove into her. Her vagina contracted hard around his rigid cock. He groaned as he pulled from her and thrust hard, unrelentingly, into her again, and again.

Jaimee sobbed as another climax raged through her, claiming her body and mind. Lucas's roar of release, his hot semen filling her in pulses matched her softening undulating aftershocks.

Still inside her, Lucas lifted her against him, his arms enfolding her as he kissed her neck and nuzzled her ear. Jaimee melted like hot butter. She lacked the strength to move, to speak. There was so much she wanted to say. Sadness threatened to descend over her but she pushed it back. Later, when he'd walked out and was gone forever then she'd give herself over to it. Now she was going to soak up every second of warmth, every tender gesture.

Involuntarily, she shuddered as he left her body. Silently he turned her in his arms and kissed her softly. His hand smoothed over her cheek. She didn't look up at him, she couldn't stand to see the pity there in his eyes. Instead she lay her head against his chest. Without a word he lifted her effortlessly into his arms, carried her up the steps and into the bathroom. He sat her on the bench beside her wide garden tub and began running a bath.

It was too much. He was being too gentle. "Lucas, I can bathe myself."

She gasped as he lifted her again and set her carefully into the steamy water. "Too hot?" he asked, ignoring her declaration, his voice hard but anything but cold.

Jaimee shook her head and closed her eyes as he began washing her hair. No one had ever done this for her, taken care of her like this. Her sigh was ragged. "You don't have to—"

"Jaimee." He waited until she lifted her eyes to his. "I don't do anything I don't want to do. Relax."

She bit her lip against the tears that his words induced. That statement was such a double-edged sword but she was confident he meant it.

After he finished washing and rinsing her hair, he handed her a towel and added bubbles to the bath. She wrapped the towel around her head and turned around so that her back wasn't to the faucet. Once again Lucas surprised her by sliding into the tub behind her and eased her back against him. He lathered the washcloth and began at her neck, massaging while he washed.

Moving down he gently washed her breasts, letting the washcloth softly rasp over her distended nipples. He took his time making each stroke an erotic caress. Nuzzling her neck, he bit and licked, awaking every cell to the sensual assault. Her eyes fluttered closed as she laid her head back on his shoulder. "Jaimee," he whispered near her ear.

"Mmmm," was all she could manage.

"Are you still interested in that little adventure?"

The thought of him taking her ass made her arousal peak. Her whole body quivered with anticipation. But her ever sensible and logical mind reminded her that this was the end. He'd said so himself. She couldn't take this any further. She'd already taken it too far. Leaning forward she pulled herself up and stepped out of the tub. She wrapped herself up in her robe as he got out and snatched a towel from the rack. He didn't bother hiding his arousal. She didn't bother averting her eyes. They stood there assessing each other for moments before she finally opened her mouth to explain.

"I want to." She paused, trying to formulate a way to express herself without sounding like a crazy woman. "But since it's over now, I'm not sure it's a good idea. I'm sorry that I..." She lifted her eyes to his fathomless gaze. The first of what she was sure would be thousands of tears slid down her cheeks. His frown deepened and he looked confused. With a deep breath she struggled to continue, to explain. "I know it's over, I just needed you one more time before you go away."

Lucas dropped the towel and closed the distance between them. "I don't want it to be over, Jaimee. We could start over and go slow if you—"

"But you said it was over, in Agent Butler's car you said—"

"Oh God. No, baby, I meant the job. The job is over. Not us. Never us." He cupped her face and kissed her.

Jaimee's breath caught on a sob as she tried to push him away. "But that's just it, I am the job."

Lucas wouldn't budge. "No, listen to me." He held her face in his hands. "I had to lie to you about who I was and what I was doing in your life. I had no choice. But I swear to you the way I felt was never a lie. I fell in love with you at the very beginning." He gazed down at her, a plea in his expression. "There were times I could have drowned in your wide expressive eyes. Your every emotion is always clear and honest. You're so real, so good. I wanted to be a part of you. You may have been part of the job when this all began but that changed very quickly. Now you're my heart."

Jaimee stared up at him, her heart thumping hard. "You love me?"

Lucas lowered his head, his lips a breath from hers. "I'm so in love with you." He kissed her twice. "Marry me, James."

A yelp escaped her throat and her eyes went wide. "Marry you..."

Lucas chuckled softly at her expression. "Mmhmm. Please, baby. If you say no you'll break my heart." His voice was a groan as he touched his forehead to hers. "And that would suck, because you are the one who made me realize I had one."

"Um...okay," Jaimee said softly. "I won't say no."

"You'll marry me?" He kissed her mouth.

"Yes."

He pushed her robe over her shoulders, his hands moving down her arms until the robe fell to the floor, and led her to the bed.

From the top of her head to her feet she tingled, her nerves alive, begging to be stroked. Lucas rose over her, turning her onto her tummy, and ran his hands down her back, the slope of her butt. "Have I told you how much I adore this beautiful ass?"

"I think you've been more than demonstrative of your feelings about that particular body part."

"Well let me reiterate." Warm liquid drizzled over her rear.

"What's that?"

"Baby oil. I dropped it in the tub with you so it would be warm." Damn, he was good. She didn't even notice that he'd snagged it from the side of the tub. While he stroked, kneaded and massaged her ass she held on to the pillow. His hand glided down her inner thighs, moving them apart to give him better access. Flames seemed to lick at her inside as his fingers brushed over her smooth damp flesh.

"Mmm." He moaned. "I like it waxed. It's so soft, moist, like a sweet, juicy peach." Jaimee yelped at the long firm stroke of his tongue over her bare flesh. "Sweet."

Jaimee couldn't form words, and she couldn't help moving against his exploring fingers and mouth. He stoked those flames as he stroked the slippery inner flesh. A hiss escaped between her clenched teeth as his finger slipped inside her, moved in and out so achingly slowly, building the sensation until she thought she might cry from the need. She went still as he parted her cheeks and drizzled the warm oil all over the crevice of her backside, smoothing it over and around in hot firm circles.

His fingers found her tight entrance and pressed firmer. Jaimee bit her lip and tried not to move away. The sensation was unlike anything she'd ever experienced. It burned and pulsed, sending waves of pleasure radiating outward. She could feel her channel flooding with arousal. "Lucas," she whimpered.

He lay on his side, taking her with him. "Easy, baby. If you say stop, I'll stop," he breathed.

Jaimee just nodded as Lucas pulled her close to him. His cock was so thick, so hard as it eased between her closed thighs, stroking over her impossibly slick pussy. Jaimee moaned and pushed back against him; it was all she could do. She was scared but excited. She wanted to stop but knew if she did, she'd regret it. No, she was going to follow through. She wanted to feel, to experience every sensation Lucas could give her. He wanted to give her that. For so long she'd denied herself the right to pleasure, now she would indulge in all the hedonistic pleasures of the flesh. Pleasures she'd come to believe God created her body to experience and that the man she loved with her entire being could give her.

Lucas spread kisses over her shoulder, her neck as his fingers massaged her opening relentlessly. "I love you, Jaimee." His voice was like a living thing rasping over her skin.

"I love you, Lucas." She moaned softly as the head of his cock pressed against the opening.

"Easy, bear down a little." He gripped her hips as he eased inside.

The burning sensation increased and she cried out, tried to relax around him. Her head lay on the arm he had curled around her, caressing her breast, her stomach. Just as her ass relaxed he eased in a little more. She was on sensory overload, panting, wanting him to take it out, wanting him to give her more. "Oh God." She clenched, pushing back, bearing down like he said.

Lucas hissed as he moved out a fraction and then sank in deeper. The mixture of pain and pleasure was unbearable. When he was finally seated fully inside her the fullness made her want to scream. Her body seemed to pulse with the need to climax.

"Relax now, baby." He took the hand she had the pillow fisted in and gently unclenched it, splaying it on her stomach. "Touch yourself, Jaimee." His voice was raspy as he covered her hand with his own and moved it down to her pussy. She cupped her pussy and moaned at the sharpness of the pleasure.

"I can't stand it." She struggled to breathe through the savage sensations pounding outward.

"Yes you can," he panted, moving her fingers over the heated soaked folds of her flesh, pushing her fingers inside as he began to move inside her. Panting she inserted two of her fingers inside her snug sheath and moved opposite of Lucas's smooth strokes inside her ass. She couldn't help bucking against him. There was only the violently intense pleasure of her building orgasm making her feel crazed and overheated.

"Lucas." She screamed, hovering on a threshold of ecstasy she wasn't sure she could endure.

"Let go, Jaimee. Just let it have you." His breathless words whispered over her with each even and steady thrust. His teeth clamping on the tender flesh behind her ear somehow sent her over the edge and she screamed through her release, crying for mercy, for more. She rode wave after wave of pleasure so intense she never thought it would end. Lucas was right there, holding on. His primal groans vibrating through her as his own orgasm claimed him.

Minutes...maybe hours later, she wasn't sure, they lay there panting, a mass of sweaty limbs. Lucas pulled from her and turned her in his arms. His kisses were slow and gentle.

"I think I might need a shower," Jaimee murmured without opening her eyes.

"Bath. Quick bath but you should take a bath. You hungry?"

Jaimee shook her head.

"Me neither."

Jaimee cuddled closer to Lucas. "Okay gonna go take a shower now."

"Mmhmm. Bath. I'll run your water."

In no hurry, Jaimee sighed, nuzzling his neck. "M'kay."

Chapter Thirty-Four

It was three in the morning when they woke up. After they took that bath at Lucas's insistence, Jaimee pulled on a warm pair of sleep pants and matching tee and followed Lucas downstairs to find food. He'd pulled on his jeans and left them unbuttoned. It seemed the man had no unsexy moments. And he was hers. It boggled her mind.

"You know I might get used to the whole being bathed thing." Jaimee flipped the eggs.

"And you expect me to what? Complain?" he teased as he dropped the bread into the toaster.

"You know, I've been bigger than I am now. I hope I never get that big again but I can't guarantee that I won't gain weight. What if—"

Lucas grinned, waggled his brows and smacked her ass as he walked past her. "I'd hit it."

Jaimee snorted but it did worry her. Working out at the gym was something she would never want to give up. She had no idea what pregnancy would do to her body or what would happen in the future.

When they sat at the table with their egg sandwiches and glasses of milk, Jaimee stared down at her plate and sighed.

"James, listen to me. I will always want you. I love you, all that you are, no matter what size you are. As long as you're happy, I'm happy. Do you understand?"

"I'm trying to."

Lucas nodded. "I know I haven't given you reason to, but you'll see eventually that you can trust me."

"I do trust you. Even though I really don't know anything about you."

"You know more than you think." He took a bite of his sandwich.

Jaimee shrugged. "I don't know if you have family. Have you ever been married? Do you have kids? Do you want kids? What will your

Veronica Chadwick

job be with FBI now?" She lifted her gaze to his and narrowed her eyes, but softened the expression with a crooked smile. "Because you are no longer allowed to 'fuck 'em and fry 'em'."

Lucas cringed and he took a drink of his milk. Jaimee watched his throat work and found it arousing. He wiped his mouth, then met her gaze again.

"I have three brothers, one older, two younger. My older brother is married and they just had a baby girl, who I have yet to meet." He sighed and shook his head before continuing. "We have an obnoxious teenybopper sister. She makes us all nuts, but we're crazy about her. My parents are great; loving, supportive...everyone is going to adore you. I have never been married. I do not have any kids. My job with the FBI will change to something a bit more grounded." He paused then raised his gaze to hers. "I've never had with anyone what I have with you. Sex never meant anything to me before. It means something with you. From the very first time I touched you, and each time since, it has meant something. It was never a means to an end with you. I love you, only you. I've never loved anyone but you and I want no one else. I will never be unfaithful to you, Jaimee."

Jaimee's smile came straight from her heart. "I know." And she did. He had a big family and he didn't already have kids but he didn't mention whether he wanted kids or not. What if he didn't want any? What if that was one of the positives, her supposed inability to conceive? What if he was unhappy when he found out? "Wow. You have a big family." She stood and gathered the empty plates, biting her lip as she turned to take them to the kitchen.

Lucas put his arms around her middle as she stood at the sink and it struck her how old-fashioned and romantic the gesture was. Through the years that simple affectionate act had melted many a woman's heart. She was no different. "What is it, James?"

"Huh?" She turned in his arms and kissed his mouth. She loved his mouth.

He frowned down at her. "Don't give me 'huh'. What's bugging you? Spill it."

Damn "expressive eyes". She just came out and asked. "Do you want kids?"

Lucas studied her face for a moment. "I want you, Jaimee. Whatever that means. I know you want children." He touched the bruise on her cheek, his brows furrowing. "We can look into fertility treatments if you like. Or we can adopt. Or we can just be you and me. I want you to be happy. Whatever it takes."

"I want a baby," she said bluntly. Staring up at him. Waiting.

His mouth curved into a warm smile. "Then we'll look into it first thing tomorrow morning. Let's go back upstairs. I want to keep you in bed today."

Jaimee shook her head. "I'm fine, Lucas. Just a few bruises…"

"You misunderstand," Lucas said, lifting a brow. "I wasn't being all noble, sweetness. I want to hold you all day, touch you, make love to you. Assure myself you're real and you're mine."

"Oh, okay I'm all for that." He took her hand as he headed for the stairs. "Wait." She tugged on his hand. He turned and tilted his head, watching her. "Lucas, I have to tell you something."

"Okay. Listening."

She took a deep breath. "Brent lied to me. I mean, he tricked me. He paid the doctor to lie." She chewed on her bottom lip as she searched for the right words.

"Jaimee, there's nothing you can say that will change how I feel. Just say it."

"I'm pregnant."

He didn't move. Just stood there like he was frozen. Jaimee looked up at him, still nibbling on her bottom lip. Waiting for some kind of response. Finally he blinked.

"You're pregnant?" He blinked again.

Jaimee nodded, a frown lining her forehead as Lucas's face swam before her through the unshed tears.

"I was wrong," he said, stunned.

"Lucas?" She whispered his name like a plea as her heart stuttered.

"I was wrong." He pulled her into his arms and kissed her like his life depended on it. "Life just gets better and better."

"So you're okay with—" she began breathlessly, tears of relief, of elation welling in her eyes.

"Okay?" Lucas chuckled. "I'm so much better than okay." Sweeping her into his arms, he kissed her again. "I intend to take you to bed and keep you there until there's no doubt in your mind just how much better than 'okay' I am."

Lucas growled and bit her shoulder as she pulled away and answered the phone against his demand that she "let it ring". All the pampering was spoiling her. True to his word Lucas had kept her in bed, for the most part for two days. She scowled at him with all the teacherly rebuke she could muster. From the way his mouth curved into a lascivious grin she knew she'd, once again, failed in her attempt.

"Hello." She answered the phone as she smiled and shook her head at him. His wicked grin widening, he turned his attention to her thigh.

"Hello, Ms. Turner. I wouldn't bother you but it's quite important. May I speak to Agent Grayson, please?" The slight accent of Malaki's voice was unmistakable, so was the solemnity.

"Sure, hold on just a minute." She covered the mouthpiece as his fingers slid higher up her inner thigh. "Lucas. It's Malaki."

Lucas lifted his head, his brows knitting together as he took the phone.

"What's up?"

Jaimee watched Lucas's face as he listened to Malaki. His expression darkened as his thumb continued to brush against the whisker-reddened flesh of her inner thigh. She reached out to touch his rough unshaven cheek. She liked the stubble and also wore the red whisker burns on her breasts and stomach to prove it. Even after three days of uninhibited hedonistic sex he could arouse her. It was amazing. His brows pulled low over his intense, heated gaze.

"And Zachary?" His voice was hard.

Jaimee sat up straighter and waited impatiently for Lucas to finish his conversation. She nibbled at her lip and watched him closely.

"Thank you, for everything. What? Yes," Lucas chuckled. "We'll think about it. Thanks again, man. Bye." Lucas shook his head as he raised up and reached across Jaimee to hang up the phone, forcing her to lay back.

"I'm safe, right?" Jaimee's brows furrowed as she looked up into Lucas's dark eyes and considered the possibility that the danger wasn't completely eliminated. Mr. Zachary, along with many of his associates, was supposed to be safely behind bars. Ronald was supposed to have given his statement and was off to some far away place where he would be out of the way and safe from Mr. Zachary's vengeance. She was no longer a pawn for anyone at this point. There was nothing to be worried about. Right?

Lucas watched her for several moments, his hand cupping her cheek. "You're safe." His mouth covered hers in a kiss that nearly made her forget what she was worried about, but not entirely.

She pushed at his chest. "Lucas."

He smiled and rolled onto his back, taking her with him. "It seems old Ron didn't like the arrangements we worked out for him and tried to make a break for it. The Pope took him out early this morning around three a.m."

Jaimee frowned down at him as he searched her face, his hand trailing up and down her back, causing warm shivers to dance over her body. "Ronald is dead."

"Very. The Pope don't play." His voice was husky as he cupped her ass and squeezed. "He asked me if I knew we were having a baby."

Jaimee's eyes widened, then it occurred to her. "Maybe Maxine told him."

"I wouldn't be surprised if nobody told him. The man just knows things. It's spooky," he murmured against her throat as he pulled her thigh upward, his cock sliding inside her ready sheath.

"But everything's okay? We're safe?" She was breathless, again.

"We're safe." His words whispered against her mouth.

Any worry over Malaki's call was dispatched as Lucas skillfully took command of her mind and body.

Epilogue

Crystal Lake, Illinois

The welcome Jaimee received when they arrived at the Grayson family home left her overwhelmed and speechless. There had only been his parents and siblings at the whirlwind wedding the week before. Here there were aunts and uncles, cousins, babies, teenagers, brothers and sisters...it was amazing and devastatingly wonderful. Jaimee never had this. Her mother and her siblings had been estranged so she'd never gotten to know them. The few family events she'd been to were cold and unpleasant.

The Graysons' home was grand in size and yet not extravagant in the least. It was open and spacious but warm. Understatedly beautiful and elegant, it felt like...home. The atmosphere was filled with a love that was tangible.

Jaimee stood just inside the doorway that led from the welcoming entranceway and hall into the great room, watching the family watch the video of the wedding. Jaimee had wanted the wedding for Lucas. She and Brent had a very formal wedding with all the expected by-the-book etiquette. She didn't need all that. Nor did she want it. But even though Lucas made it clear that all he wasn't into the pomp and circumstance of it all, she wanted the ceremony to be beautiful, for him.

Thankfully his mom, Rachel and his sister, Annmarie, had come to the rescue. They'd proven invaluable and handled the whole affair. The wedding had been breathtakingly lovely. The two weeks they had to throw the wedding together flew by but the two ladies rose to the occasion with efficient grace. Annmarie had definite leadership qualities. The way she directed the florist and caterer was simply amazing for a girl of fifteen years old. Rachel had been so welcoming, accepting, genuinely happy to have Jaimee join the family.

Surprisingly, her mother had attended the wedding. She'd been gracious and conceded that she had misjudged Lucas. That was the closest she'd come to an apology and that was good enough for Jaimee. Maxine was, of course, her maid of honor. Lora and Lucas's sister were bridesmaids. Maxine picked out the midnight blue gowns and made certain they were all fabulous in their own right.

Her eyes misted, her heart overwhelmed as she watched herself turn to Lucas. Rachel had found the most perfect dress for her. Blue satin flowed over her like it was made for her. The palest icy blue she'd ever seen. And there had been crystals sewed into the fitted bodice. Despite Jaimee's insistence that she just rent a dress, Rachel and Jaimee's mother had gone in together to buy it. Rachel was adamant that Jaimee marry her son in a new dress and refused to divulge the price, but Jaimee wasn't so much out of the fashion loop that she didn't know it was expensive.

Dressed in his black tux Lucas looked powerful, sexy and formidable. But it was his expression that captivated Jaimee. He looked at her with such intensity and love. No one but Lucas had ever looked at her that way. And he was hers. All hers. Forever. The magnitude of her love for him was staggering at times. There was no doubt in her heart or mind that he loved her. That in itself was incredible to her.

For the second time her heart skipped a beat when he said in that deep, husky voice, "I do." It probably would any and every time she watched this video. It was like a dream she never knew she had. Lucas had given her love in all its many aspects.

The room watched in awe as they exchanged rings. His brothers occasionally made teasing comments. Annmarie attempted to shush them and rolled her eyes at them in between her own commentary. "Oh! Watch this! This is the most romantic kiss ever!"

And it was.

"Hey, you," Lucas said as he came into the room behind her and wrapped his arms around her middle. She jumped and shivered as he nuzzled her neck with his cold nose. "Mmm, you're warm."

Jaimee laughed softly. "You're freezing!"

"Warm me up then. Our stuff is put in my old room. Let's go fulfill an old fantasy of mine."

She laughed again and elbowed him. "Perv."

"You like that about me." He nipped her earlobe.

Everyone had abandoned the video to watch them. Heat crawled up her neck as Lucas's brothers snatched up the chance at another

Veronica Chadwick

round of ribald taunts. Lucas's father, Joseph, just shook his head and smiled. "Son, you opened yourself up for this, you know that, right?"

Lucas just grinned.

Joseph looked a lot like Lucas. They were the same height, though Joseph was leaner. Joseph's cheekbones were more prominent than Lucas's and his hair was silver, but his eyes were exactly the same. He held his son Aaron's new baby girl, his very first grandbaby, in his arms. She quickly recaptured his full attention. Those dark mahogany eyes that so matched Jaimee's husband's were now filled with adoration as he gazed into the eyes of his granddaughter. Her little fist rested against his cheek. Jaimee's heart melted.

A grumbling Rachel came from the kitchen, waving a wooden spoon at three giggling little boys then. Her hair was pulled back into a loose bun. The silver that shot through it only added to her elegance. She was small and not very tall at around five feet two or three. She smiled a lot and her chocolate brown eyes were warm and kind. She wore a black apron that said "*Will cook for shoes*" over a soft pink sweater and black trousers. She was simply lovely and Jaimee loved her already.

Rachel scanned the room until she spotted her husband, Joseph, standing by the fireplace. She looked back at Rachel. Her heart melted at the tender sight just as Jaimee's had.

"To the table everyone! Before these little scamps sneak any more rolls." She laughed. "Annmarie, Jacob..." She motioned toward the kitchen with her head. "Come help me get the food on the table."

Jaimee took Lucas's hand and pulled him along as she followed Rachel into the kitchen to help. The kitchen was huge and gleamed with stainless steel appliances and Italian marble. Jaimee didn't bother hiding her "oh" as she stopped and took it all in. Rachel was passing platters of food to Annmarie from a warming drawer. Jaimee was in awe.

"How can I help, Mrs. Grayson?"

Rachel straightened and wrinkled her nose. "You can call me Mom or Rachel, dear. And you can help me by going into the dining room and finding a seat," she said with a very familiar lift of a brow and tilt to her lips.

"Hey! I don't see why the *love* birds don't have to help out," Jacob teased.

Jaimee speared Jacob a sardonic look that had him chuckling.

"Are you sure? I would love to help," Jaimee nearly pleaded. No one had let her lift a finger for anything since they'd arrived.

"Absolutely. Next year I'll put you to work cooking. This year, you just relax." Rachel winked.

"She makes some amazing caramel...apples," Lucas said as he pulled her close. "Very decadent." Jaimee struggled to keep from blushing but the heat in her cheeks told her she'd failed.

"Wonderful," Rachel said cheerfully. "I'll expect you to make them for us next year then."

Jacob's wide grin told her he'd noticed her reaction. "Oh there's a story there."

Jaimee glared at Lucas, hoping her eyes told him he was in big trouble. Lucas just chuckled and dropped a quick kiss on her lips before punching his brother in the arm. "Grab the turkey, runt."

Lucas led her through the double swinging doors into the expansive dining room. The atmosphere was festive and elegant with lovely table settings and lit candles. The family was seated around the large dining table, laughing and chatting. It was just incredible. Joseph sat at the head of the table, as he should. Baby Lauren had been fed and put down for a nap in a pretty bassinet set up in the great room. Aaron had his arm around his wife, Beth. She looked tired but happy as she rested against her husband.

Aaron was the oldest, an architect. He was very gregarious and fun-loving. His eyes were warm and kind like his mother's. Just the way he looked at Beth told Jaimee how much he cherished her. And he doted adoringly on his baby girl, Lauren. Even so, he was just as much a scamp as his younger siblings and was just as bad as the rest of them when they got to ribbing each other.

Micah, the lawyer, was a bit different from his brothers. His reserved and quiet demeanor was at odds with the mischievous glint in his golden brown eyes. With his shaved head and goatee and usual dark clothing he seemed mysterious and aloof, maybe a little dangerous if given a cursory glance. He was in fact shrewdly watching, taking everything in...always. But he was, as were his brothers, a charming gentleman.

Jacob, the veterinarian, was the youngest of the boys and the most energetic and outgoing of the bunch as well as an irrepressible flirt with a wicked sense of humor. He'd broken a few hearts in his time, Jaimee was sure of it. He probably wasn't even aware of it himself, she was sure of that too.

At the wedding Maxine had summed it up quite well when she plopped down in a chair and sighed heavily in exhausted appreciation after she'd danced with every single one of the Grayson men more than once. She'd said dreamily, "Those Grayson men are a hot mess. Emphasis on hot. Especially the bald one with the goatee."

Then there was the ever-precocious Annmarie. Her dark wavy hair was much like Lucas's had been. Long, thick and beautiful. Her eyes were dark and clear and wise beyond her years. Her quick wit was invaluable when verbal sparring with her brothers came in to play. She could hold her own. They cherished her like the precious treasure she was and protected her as such as well. Which was why she hadn't mentioned the boy she had a crush on to anyone but her mom, and recently Jaimee. It meant so much to Jaimee that Annmarie had trusted her with her precious secret. It meant she was accepted.

After everyone gathered around the table and settled into their seats Joseph slowly stood and smiled at his lovely wife with such adoration Jaimee wanted to sigh. "Thank you, sweetheart, for once again making everything wonderful for us." His smile widened as his gaze swept over the faces of his family nodding in agreement. "Before we bow our heads to pray for this enormous Thanksgiving feast, I have something I'd like to say."

He paused and cleared his throat, placing his hands on the table in front of him. "We've much to be thankful for this year. Annmarie has excelled in her classes at school and won first place in the art show. Micah made junior partner. Jacob and his friend opened their own clinic. And our sweet baby, Lauren, was born healthy and beautiful just like her mother." He winked at Beth and she blushed and shyly returned his smile. Aaron grinned and pulled her closer.

"And another new addition." He turned to Jaimee. "Lucas's bride, Jaimee." Lucas squeezed her hand under the table. Jaimee turned her eyes from Lucas to Joseph and blinked as she saw those sharp eyes of his go misty. "My family is all together now. Thank you, Jaimee girl, for loving our son, showing him his own heart. You brought him back to us. He is blessed to have found such a perfect match, such a powerful love."

Lucas leaned over and kissed her temple. "I am," he whispered, his voice rough with emotion. Tears welled in her own eyes as Jaimee looked up at her father-in-law in stunned silence. The emotion was contagious it seemed, if the whispered agreements from around the table were any indication. Jaimee shook her head. "No," she croaked then closed her eyes for a second and swallowed the lump of emotion forming in her throat. She took a deep breath and began again. "I'm the one who is blessed. I've never had this. Ever. This kind of family. This kind of love. You're a remarkable family. I'm still trying to take it all in and let myself believe it's real. I'm not going to wake up and you're not all going to go poof."

Everyone laughed softly. Rachel blotted her tears with her napkin and said softly, "You're definitely awake, dear. We're so happy Lucas found you. Not just because Lucas has come home to us, but because we love you. You're welcome here now. This is your home. You're part of us."

"Thank you." Jaimee didn't think she'd quit smiling, even when a slight wave of nausea swept over her. She laid a hand on her tummy and waited for it to pass. It had been a while since they stopped to eat. It seemed if she didn't eat on time she got a little nauseous.

Lucas smoothed a tear away with his thumb and whispered softly, "You okay, James?"

Jaimee lifted her eyes to his. "Yes, I think I'm just hungry. You know. It's just a little..." She smiled up at the family watching her and laughed nervously. "I'm just fine."

Rachel's eyes went wide and bright. Her hopeful question was breathless with excitement. "Could it be morning sickness?"

Her sheepish grin gave her away, but Lucas answered anyway. "Yes, we're having a baby."

"I knew it!" she shouted with delight.

Excited chatter rose around the table. Questions and congratulations. Beth grinned at her and said softly, "How far into your first trimester?"

Fresh tears spilled down Jaimee's cheeks. "Six weeks."

Joseph loudly cleared his throat and the voices went quiet. "Personally, I think the child is hungry and tired of all this sappy love talk. Let's pray so we can get my grandbaby fed."

About the Author

To learn more about Veronica Chadwick, please visit www.veronicachadwick.com. Send an email to Veronica at veronicachadwick@comcast.net or join her Yahoo! group to join in the fun with other readers as well as Veronica! http://groups.yahoo.com/group/RonisRetreat

LaVergne, TN USA
23 March 2010
176864LV00005B/2/P